NEVER

LET

YOU

GO

NOVELS BY ERIN HEALY
COAUTHORED WITH TED DEKKER

Burn
Kiss

NEVER
LET
YOU
GO

ERIN HEALY

THOMAS NELSON
Since 1798

NASHVILLE   DALLAS   MEXICO CITY   RIO DE JANEIRO

Published in Nashville, Tennessee, by Thomas Nelson. Thomas Nelson is a registered trademark of Thomas Nelson, Inc.

Published in association with Thomas Nelson and Creative Trust, Inc., 5141 Virginia Way, Suite 320, Brentwood, TN 37027.

Thomas Nelson, Inc., titles may be purchased in bulk for educational, business, fund-raising, or sales promotional use. For information, please e-mail SpecialMarkets@ThomasNelson.com.

Scriptures are taken from the Holy Bible: New International Version®. © 1973, 1978, 1984 by International Bible Society. Used by permission of Zondervan Publishing House. All rights reserved.

Publisher's note: This novel is a work of fiction. Names, characters, places, and incidents are either products of the author's imagination or used fictitiously. All characters are fictional, and any similarity to people, living or dead, is purely coincidental.

ISBN 978-1-61664-695-0

Printed in the United States of America

For Amber,
who keeps forgiving me

{ chapter 1 }

For seven years, Lexi Solomon had been as cold as the wind that raced down the mountain above her home. She was not ice-in-her-veins cold, or I'll-freeze-you-with-a-glance cold, but numb with the chill that came from being uncovered and abandoned.

Only the love of her daughter, a warm and innocent love that was so easy to return, had prevented her from dying of exposure.

At the back of the Red Rocks Bar and Grill, Lexi checked to make sure the rear stoop wasn't icy, then exited and pulled the kitchen door closed. The blustery elements had spent decades huffing and puffing on the backside of the local haunt with nothing to show for the effort but a tattered awning and a battered screen door. The stalwart cinder block, painted to match the russet clay dirt that coated Crag's Nest, was as stubborn as the snow that refused to melt before midsummer at this altitude. And it was only March.

At her throat Lexi clutched her ratty down jacket, the same one she had worn since high school, while she fumbled with the restaurant keys in her other gloveless hand. She'd forced her only pair of gloves into her daughter's coat pockets that morning because Molly had lost hers coming home from school.

Which could only mean she hadn't been wearing them. Chances were, Molly hadn't worn the gloves today either. Well, she was only nine. Lexi smiled at that and thought she might get them back. If only she could be a kid again, oblivious to weather and wet.

Lexi shoved the key into the cheap lock and turned it easily. That hamburger grease coated everything. Above her head a yellow bug light shone over a cracked concrete slab. Her tired breath formed a cloud in the night air and then a fog on the wire-threaded glass of the door.

It was 2:13 a.m. Thirteen minutes later than Lexi usually locked up, thanks to the frozen computer that she had to reboot twice before she could close out the cash drawer and lock the day's receipts in the safe. Thirteen minutes gone from the precious few she got to spend with Molly, curled up next to her in their one flimsy bed. Between Lexi's two jobs and Molly's school days, she figured they had an average of ninety-four minutes together, awake, per day. It wasn't enough.

Lexi closed the restaurant every Monday, Thursday, and Friday night. *Restaurant* was too generous a word for the greasy spoon a half mile off the main tourist drag, too far off to draw many out-of-towners. But the staff was familylike enough, and the locals were loyal and tipped fair, and the extra fifty dollars she got for being the last to leave three times a week didn't hurt. Every little bit put her and Molly that much closer to a better situation. A better home in a better part of town. A more reliable car. Warmer clothes.

Molly needed new shoes, and once Lexi got caught up on that past-due utility bill, she thought she'd have enough to buy the pair with sequins stitched onto the sides. Maybe for Molly's birthday. She'd seen her daughter bent over a picture of the shoes in the Sunday circulars left out by their roommate, Gina.

After jiggling the locked kitchen door for good measure, Lexi turned her back on the glare of the naked bulb and headed toward her Volvo. The sturdy old thing was parked on the far side of the sprawling blacktop, fender nosing a swaying field of tall grasses, because that was where the only operating lamppost stood, and Lexi was no idiot when it came to vacant lots and late-night lockups.

The wind cut through her thin khaki pants, numbing her thighs.

She fingered the can of pepper spray on her key chain as she passed the shadowy Dumpster behind the kitchen. A large man could squeeze between it and the trash can's cinder block cove easily enough. The dishwasher Jacob did this on his breaks to catch a smoke, because the manager wouldn't tolerate cigarettes, not even outside.

A dark form darted out, leaping over the long shadow of her body cast by the gold light behind. She flinched, then scolded.

"Scat, Felix." The resident alley cat carried something in his mouth. Lexi guessed a chicken bone, but it might have been a mouse. He jumped the wobbly wood-slat fence between the restaurant and the dry cleaner next door.

The grasses in the field, as tall as her shoulders, whispered secrets.

She stepped from the slab onto the asphalt lot. The spotlight over her dull silver Volvo, which tilted to the left due to a weak strut, went out for a second, then hiccupped back to life. It was only a matter of time before the lamp finally died, then weeks or months would probably pass before the property manager got around to resurrecting it. Each time she locked up, she found herself hoping the light would last one more night. She weighed whether she ought to start parking closer to the kitchen. Just in case.

Just in case what? Tara had been murdered in a bright shopping mall, in a bustling crowd. Maybe where a woman parked in the darkness of night didn't matter as much as she hoped.

Lexi's soft-soled shoes made an audible, squishy noise on the cold blacktop as she quickened her step, eyes sweeping the lot like some state-of-the-art scanner. Her keys sang a metallic song as they swung against the can of pepper spray. There was an extra can in the book bag slung over her shoulder. Another one in her glove box. A fourth buried in the planter outside her kitchen window at home, right by the front door. Lexi wondered for the millionth time how old Molly should be before starting to carry some in her backpack.

Glimpsing the dark glass of the car's rear doors, she wished again that she had one of those key fobs that could turn on the interior lights from a cautious distance.

The parking lot light gasped again and this time faded to black. The steady yellow light behind her also flickered once and died, stranding Lexi in black air exactly halfway between the restaurant and car. She stopped. A second later, two at most, the light over the Volvo staggered back to relative brilliance.

She gasped. The thin air knifed her throat. The grasses had fallen silent, and the winds were as still as if God had stepped between them and the earth.

All four doors of her car were flung wide. Two seconds earlier they had been sealed shut, but now they gaped open like Lexi's disbelieving mouth, popped open with the speed of a switchblade, with the flip of an invisible lever, the flick of an illusionist's light.

A heavy hand came down on her shoulder from behind. Lexi yelped and whirled out from under the palm.

"Sexy Lexi."

Her hand was at her throat, her pulse pounding through the layers of the thin jacket, her breathing too shallow for her to speak.

A slim white envelope fluttered between the restless fingers of the man's left hand. A tattoo peeked out from under his T-shirt sleeve on the left, filling most of his upper arm. It was a set of keys, skeleton keys, hanging from a wide round ring.

He was middle-aged, sallow skinned, and his dark hair needed a trim. Oily strands flipped up in little curls that stuck out the bottom of a knit cap. The scrappy T-shirt looked thin across his narrow chest and sinewy arms, but he did not shiver in the low temperatures.

He said, "I half expected you'd be out of town after all these years."

Lexi's fright came off its startled high and settled into unease. She took a step back, glancing involuntarily at her car. Years ago, Warden Pavo had taken adolescent delight in pranks. She wondered how many people would have to be involved to pull off one like this.

"Why would I leave Crag's Nest if I thought you'd never set foot here again, Ward?"

"Warden."

"Yeah. I forgot."

He smirked. "How's the family?"

"Fine."

"Your mom's still globe-trotting?"

Lexi stared at him, finding his interest in her family new and strange, and perhaps offensive.

"Any improvement in dear old dad?" he asked.

"What do you want, Ward?"

"Warden."

Lexi crossed her arms to hide their quivering.

"What?" he said. "I heard that your old man fell off the deep end, and I've been worried about you."

"You've never worried about anyone but yourself. Besides, that happened years ago."

"After that whole thing with your sister. What a tragedy. Man, I'm really sorry about that, you know."

Ward removed a nylon lanyard from the pocket of his jeans. A small key chain weighted the end of it. Twirling the cord like a propeller blade, he wound it around his wrist, wrapping and unwrapping it.

Lexi looked away. "It's behind us now," she said.

"Is it? Von Ruden's up for parole. I assume you heard."

She hadn't. A shiver shook her shoulders though the wind had not picked up again. Up for parole after only seven years.

Norman Von Ruden had killed Tara, Lexi's older sister. He knifed her in a food court at lunchtime during the Christmas rush, when there were so many people that no one noticed she'd been attacked until someone accidentally whacked her crumpled form with a shopping bag. After Tara's funeral, Lexi's father raised the drawbridge of his mind and left her with her mother on the wrong side of the moat.

"Why is it that whenever you show up, I can expect bad news?"

"Aw, that's not fair, Lexi. I'm only here to help you, as always."

"One finger is too many to count the ways you've helped me."

"Be nice."

"I am. You could have helped me years ago by refusing to sell to Norm."

"C'mon now. You know that's not what happened."

Lexi turned away and moved quickly toward her gaping Volvo.

Ward's voice chased her. "Norm was Grant's client, not mine."

Lexi kept walking. Ward followed.

"If you blame anyone, gotta blame Grant." Ward's keys clanked together as they hit the inside of his wrist. "You can blame Grant for a whole lotta your problems."

"I'd appreciate you not bringing Grant up," she said.

It was true that Lexi's husband had not paved the streets of her life with gold. The same year Tara was killed, Grant drove their only car out of town and never came back. Lexi, having no money to pay for a divorce, never received divorce papers from Grant either and sometimes wondered whether abandonment laws alone made their separation official.

Beyond that, she'd managed to prevent her thoughts from chasing Grant too often. Only Molly was worth Lexi's wholehearted concentration. For Molly's sake, Lexi had made a vow to be more clearheaded than Grant ever was.

Lexi reached out and slammed the door behind the driver's seat. The metal frame was warm to the touch, sun-baked without the sun. The unexpected sensation caused her to hesitate before she walked around the back to the other side and slammed the other rear door. It, too, was unnaturally heated. She wiped her palm on the seat of her pants.

"If that's all you came to tell me, good night."

"But it's not."

Ward stopped twirling the lanyard and stood at the driver's door. She glanced at him across the roof of the Volvo and took new notice of the envelope he held and extended toward her.

"Picked up your mail for you."

"How?"

"Intercepted the mailman."

"Why?"

"Save you the trouble."

"Seeing as it's no trouble, please don't do it again."

"You really could be more grateful."

She leaned against the car and lay her arm across the roof, gesturing that he give the envelope to her. He dangled it above her open palm. She snatched it out of his fingers.

"Thank you," she said, hoping he would leave. She lifted the flap of her book bag, intending to cram the letter into the side.

"Open it."

"I will, when I get home."

"Now." Ward's keys cut the air on that whirling cord again. Rather than irritate her, the motion threatened. Those keys were weapons that could inflict serious pain if they hit her between the eyes with any momentum. She thought she saw them striking out at her and jerked back, then felt embarrassed.

"I read my mail without an audience."

"Add a little excitement to your life. Do it differently tonight."

"No."

"It's not a suggestion."

Lexi closed the third door and made her way back around the rear of the car to where Ward was waiting. She focused on maintaining a confident voice. "Ward, it's late. I'm going home. My daughter—"

"Molly. She's all grown-up and fresh to be picked by now, isn't she?" Heat rose up Lexi's neck. "I saw her at the school today. They're a bit lax over there about security, in my humble opinion."

The tears that rushed to Lexi's eyes were as hot and blinding as her anger. That level of offensiveness didn't deserve a response. In two long strides she reached the open driver's side door and, still holding the mystery letter, placed her left hand on the frame to balance her entry.

Ward's lanyard snaked out and struck her wrist, knocking her hand off the door, which slammed shut. The paper fluttered to the ground. She stared at it stupidly, not comprehending what was happening.

He stooped to pick it up. "Read the letter, Lexi, then I'll let you go home."

Her wrist bone ached where the keys had struck it. She took a step away from Ward, then turned the letter over to read the return address. The envelope was from the office of a neighboring county's district attorney. It quivered in her fingers. She held it under the light of the lamppost for several seconds. The beam flickered.

"The postmark on this is more than a month old," she said.

"Yeah, well, I didn't say I picked up your mail *today*."

Her perspiring fingers were tacky and warped the linen stationery slightly. Lexi tapped the short side of the envelope on the roof of the Volvo, then tore a narrow strip off the opposite side and let the scrap fall to the ground. She withdrew a piece of heavy folded paper, then spread it flat on the hood.

She thought it was a notice of Norman Von Ruden's parole hearing. She saw, at a glance, phrases like *your right to participate* and *verbal or written testimony*. But a red scrawl like a kindergartener gone crazy with a Sharpie obscured much of the text. A balloon poked by half a dozen arrows surrounded the date and time. Stick figures at the bottom of the page depicted a man coming out of an open jail cell, and a happy woman waiting for him.

Ward was breathing across Lexi's ear. She felt his body too close behind her.

"Isn't that nice?" he said, pointing. "That's Norm, and that's you!"

Lexi looked at the backside of the envelope to see if he'd tampered with the letter but it was still securely sealed. He knew. How could he know? She pushed off the car and shoved him away from her, leaving the letter behind. She snapped at him so that he wouldn't hear the fear she felt.

"You're sick, Ward. I'm going home."

"I'm entirely well, though I appreciate your concern. Aren't you going to ask me what it means?"

"It means you haven't changed one bit since the last time I saw you. I don't have time for your pranks."

She pulled the door open and dropped onto the seat without taking the book bag off her shoulder.

Ward picked up the letter and turned it over, holding it out to her. He propped his forearms on the open door and lowered the sheet, scrawled with another juvenile drawing, to her eye level. A red figure that looked like a child with *x*'s for eyes was visible through the glass door of an oven.

"No prank, Sexy Lexi."

Lexi felt blood rush out of her head. She took a shallow breath and lowered her voice.

"Okay. What does it mean, Ward?"

"War-*den*. *Warden*. Get it right."

There was no sarcasm in her voice now. "Warden. What does it mean?"

"That's my girl. It means—if you love your daughter like I think you do—that you are going to show up at Norm's hearing next Friday and testify on his behalf."

"What? Why?"

"Because you love your daughter."

"I can't do that."

"You can't love her?"

"No! I can't . . . Norman Von Ruden? He's insane."

"Not clinically."

"Don't do that. They diagnosed him with something."

"Nothing a fine shrink and a few bottles of pills couldn't handle."

"No." She shook her head. "No. I hate him."

"You loved him once. I'll wager there's still whore in you."

Lexi lashed out, clawing the letter out of his hands and scratching the skin of his knuckles. His keys fell onto the blacktop.

"How dare you!"

Ward seized both her wrists easily and shoved her back down onto the seat of the car.

"He killed my sister! He wrecked my family! My parents—"

"Will be mourning the loss of little miss Molly as well if you don't come to the party. So be wise about it, or I'll tell your secrets to everyone you love—and plenty of people you don't."

"Why are you doing this?"

"Because you should have chosen me, Lexi. All those years ago, you chose Von Ruden. But you should have chosen me." He crumpled the letter into a ball and tossed it across Lexi onto the passenger seat.

The light over the car died again. In the blackness, Lexi reached out and slammed the car door, punched down the manual lock, then contorted her body to hit the three remaining knobs in sequence.

"Save the date," he said through the glass.

She willed the wind to carry his words away, but the air was as still as her dead sister, bleeding on the sticky tiles of the mall floor.

{ chapter 2 }

Beyond the windshield of Lexi's car, the dark mountain range was a jagged saw blade that would tear the sky in two if the wind started blowing again. Crag's Nest slept, the few streetlights blinked yellow, and no other cars blocked the narrow stone bridge that separated her simple neighborhood from the flashy historic district and tourist traps. It took her only five minutes rather than the usual eight to race home. Ward's remarks about seeing Molly at school burned the back of Lexi's throat.

She spent every second of the drive regretting the choices she'd made that had led, however indirectly, to Ward's visit. On some level, his demand should not have come as a surprise to her. She'd known that he was a truly low man. After dragging her husband down into the sludgy gutters of meth addiction, Ward had vanished at the same time Lexi's world spun off its axis: it was the year that Norm killed Tara, that Grant drove away, that her father lost his mind.

Ward's departure from her life had been a weight lifted, though she couldn't take any credit for it. She had always believed that once Norm fell and Grant fled, Ward had no use for her. Which made his accusation about her rejection all the more confusing.

Ward's intentions regarding Norm's parole were a mystery. Her testimony couldn't guarantee the man's release and might even be called into question if the parole board learned the truth of her relationship with Norm. For a fleeting second she wondered if doing this thing Ward had asked of her might be the best way to keep her secret hidden.

How would Lexi explain a testimony to her mother?

The more pressing question was how to get through this with no damage to Molly. If her daughter was about to face the consequences of the most foolish decision Lexi had ever made, Lexi didn't know what she would do. There was no more precious child on the face of the earth than that little girl. All the love that Lexi had ever wanted to pour into another human being— love spilled out and lost over Grant's closed fists—had been welcomed by Molly's open hands.

Lexi pulled the lopsided Volvo into a gap that was not a parking space at the sidewalk leading to her apartment. The car creaked when she jumped out. She slammed the door and came around the front fender in a tight corner. Her foot connected with a metal object that tipped and then clattered.

"Oh no."

Painters who'd been touching up the flower boxes before spring planting had left a can behind. A small pool of black latex formed on the asphalt at the mouth of the can. Lexi stepped out of its reach and gingerly picked up the can by its handle, then carried it up the path toward her front door. She'd leave it outside, then take it to the manager in the morning.

The living room lamp shone through the window to her right. Lexi's roommate had likely fallen asleep in the old La-Z-Boy. Gina had her own bed, and her own desk for studying in her very own room, but the eternal student zonked out most nights with some massive university text on her lap.

Lexi made a mental note: *Window: closed. Sturdy dowel still in place in the track.* She hoped Gina was sleeping, or reading, and not doing something unimaginable.

Oh, stop it.

She blamed Tara's murder for her tendency to jump on runaway mental trains. If Ward meant what he said, he wouldn't do anything to her or Molly before Norman's hearing.

On the left side of the stoop, another window looked into the miniscule kitchen. A checkered café curtain covered the bottom half of the glass. The latches were in their upright, locked position. Gina knew better than to prop any window or door open. Lexi gave her an earful the first summer Gina lived with them until she caught on. Under the window, a planter box still contained the plants that had died months ago in October's first freeze.

The screen slapped against Lexi's backside while she shoved her key in the lock. It stuck, but she finally wiggled the dead bolt free of the jamb. The door glided open. The bottom of the screen clipped the heel of her shoe as she entered and passed through the short front hall.

Gina's recliner was empty. Her textbook lay open on the floor under an uncapped highlighter and legal pad. Her thick Bible balanced on the arm of the recliner.

Lexi closed the door, turned the lock, and headed straight for the room she and Molly shared.

The floorboards outside the door squeaked. She didn't try to avoid them this time, grasping the knob and pushing the door open, half hoping to wake Molly from a peaceful sleep so she could enjoy the good moment of tucking her back in again. The little girl's lava lamp night-light cast a pink glow over the shoebox room.

Molly was as she always was: snoring on her stomach, one arm hanging off the queen mattress. Her open mouth was all that was exposed by the thin sheet and threadbare blanket that otherwise covered her entire body. She slept kitty-corner across the bed and claimed this was because she wanted to keep Lexi's side warm for her.

Lexi's shoulders relaxed at this beautiful sight. She bent and kissed Molly on the back of the head, then stroked the girl's hair off her cheek. Circuiting the foot of the bed, Lexi lifted the curtain and checked the sliding glass door that led out into the back common area: latch secure, dowel in place. Two of the three lamps in the courtyard were out. The rest cast a weak beam across weed-pocked grass. No one was roaming at this hour. She dropped the window covering.

Nothing in the room was out of place.

Molly stirred and said something about noodles, then breathed heavily again.

Lexi returned to the hall to look for Gina. The women had known each other since they were sixteen, so when Gina needed a place to stay and Lexi needed someone to help look after Molly, they struck a deal: Lexi let her live in the second bedroom rent-free in exchange for babysitting Molly at night. Gina was six years into her late-started bachelor's degree and figured she could graduate next fall from the little Bible college down in Riverbend if she stayed focused. Her parents' decision to quit paying her way offered considerable incentive.

The desk lamp in Gina's room painted a stripe of yellow at the bottom of her door. Lexi knocked gently. When her friend didn't answer, Lexi took care to open it undetected.

Gina was bowed over her laptop on the desk, slumped forward in one of the chairs from the kitchen table. Her forehead rested on the touch pad, and her straw-blonde hair blanketed her shoulders. The glare of the monitor turned her white sweatshirt blue.

"Gina?"

Her hands, which seemed to have slid off the keyboard in the middle of typing, rested on the back of their wrists against the lip of her desk at each side of her bent head. Her relaxed fingers, turned upward, cupped invisible balls.

Lexi's heart interfered with her rational self, refusing to examine this scene rationally.

"Gina . . ."

She didn't want to, but Lexi reached out to lift the hair away from Gina's face.

"Gina, are you okay?"

Lexi's unsteady hand brushed her friend's shoulder.

They both screamed at the same time. Gina shot out of the chair, knocking it backward into her bed as she scrambled to get away from Lexi. The chair bounced off the mattress and came back at her, catching her bare foot midair and tripping her. Her wide eyes registered shock as she flailed, snagging the desk lamp with her fingers. The lamp teetered.

Lexi reached for her, missed. Groped for the lamp, caught it. Gina's fingers, tangled in the cord, nearly wrenched it away, but Lexi held on. The tilting shade cast angular shadows around the room. Gina's head smacked the closet's accordion doors, rattling them hard, and she landed heavily on her tailbone.

"Ooff!"

Lexi held her breath. Gina burst into giggles.

All her fear escaped Lexi in an explosive laugh of her own.

"Doggone you, Lexi. I'm having a heart attack!"

"Shh! We're gonna wake up Molly."

"That girl could sleep through the Second Coming."

Lexi set the lamp on Gina's desk and leaned over to help her stand, bringing her full weight to bear. Gina was a good six inches taller than she was, and half again as wide.

Her heart, too, was twice as warm and three times as generous, Lexi believed.

There were tears of laughter in her roommate's eyes and a red depression from the computer touch pad across her forehead.

"You've got to get more interesting classes," Lexi said.

"Shoot, Lexi, it's three in the morning. Nothing's *that* interesting." She wiped her eyes and tried to smother another outburst. Her effort sounded like a sneeze. "If you ever do that again I swear I'm moving out."

"You can't afford to move out."

"I won't be able to afford the therapy I'll need if I stay."

Lexi dropped onto the unmade bed. "I'm really sorry."

"I'll recover." Gina reached for her upended chair, and Lexi realized how grateful she was that Gina was here, with Molly. That they both were okay.

"How was Molly tonight?"

"Angel as always. Cooked us up some spaghetti for dinner."

"She's good at spaghetti. Any leftovers?"

"You bet. She said you'd want some for breakfast."

"You know it."

Gina straddled the chair and rested her elbows on the back. "She's learning blonde jokes."

Lexi shook her head, embarrassed. "I'll talk to her."

"Oh pooh. I'm teaching them to her."

"Gina!"

"Blonde walks into a library and tells the librarian, 'I'd like a cheeseburger with fries and a diet coke.'"

"Stop it! You're supposed to be tutoring her in division!"

"Librarian says, 'Lady, I don't know what you're thinking. This is a library.'"

Lexi shook her head.

"The blonde is mortified. She apologizes profusely, drops her voice to a whisper, and says, 'I'd like a cheeseburger with fries and a diet coke.'"

Lexi chuckled. "You're corrupting my daughter."

"She was in stitches for ten minutes. Honest-to-goodness, pure-kiddo funny bone."

"I pay you way too much."

"And I was going to broach the subject of a raise!"

Lexi drew her knees up to her chest and wrapped her arms around them.

"So everything was okay here tonight? No weird goings-on?"

"No more than usual." Gina's eyes shot away for half a second. If Lexi hadn't been looking right at her, she wouldn't have noticed. But when Gina caught her eyes again, Lexi found herself trying to remember whether looking away to the right or to the left indicated a lie.

After a lengthy pause Gina said, "Mrs. Johnson's cat got stuck up on 10C's balcony."

"Juliet must get stuck up there twice a week."

"And shall continue to do so until a tree surgeon trims that maple back."

"The manager won't spend the money. Especially not for a cat."

"'Course he won't. So the guys in 10A put on an impromptu performance of *Romeo and Juliet*'s balcony scene. Molly suggested we take our spaghetti out on the back patio to watch."

"Dinner theater."

"Exactly."

"Did it work—romancing the cat, I mean?"

"I don't recall that the original Juliet hurled herself from the balcony, but that's how the cat came down."

"You're pulling my leg."

Gina grinned. "Am I? Mort climbs up the tree, confesses his love and takes sweet Juliet in his arms . . . then the feline fatale claws him and gets dropped. I wasn't sad to see the cat go down."

"You're hopelessly in love with those guys."

Gina waggled her brows. "Just Mort. I told Molly she should save herself for Travis."

Lexi stretched, then rose. "Maybe I shouldn't leave you two alone so often. I'm not sure who's corrupting who."

"Not at all. We keep each other on the straight and narrow." Gina yawned.

"You want some tea?" Lexi rested her hand on the doorknob.

"I'll pass."

"Thanks for all you do for Molly and me."

"Oh gosh, don't mention it. She's a gem. And if it wasn't for what you don't pay me, you'd be gold yourself."

"And yet you live in palatial splendor!"

Gina guffawed. She never complained about the shabby apartment, though Lexi hated it. She hated it enough for all three of them and figured Gina knew this.

Lexi pondered telling her about Norman Von Ruden's parole, about Ward's freaky visit and more frightening demands. Gina had been compassionate toward Lexi and Molly when Grant fell into his drug-addicted ways, but she didn't know a thing about Norm except what the papers had reported of the murder. Lexi never spoke of him.

Gina stretched out on her bed, fully clothed, and yawned. The weight of the long night pressed down on Lexi's body. She'd have tea and ponder Norman Von Ruden privately, then go cuddle up with Molly.

"Good night," she said.

"'Night."

She pulled Gina's door closed. The living room light still shone into the hallway, crossing the strip of carpet and glancing off the cheap linoleum of the dark kitchen. Lexi went to turn it off and accidentally stepped on Gina's textbook, which she'd left on the floor exactly halfway between the chair and the coffee table. Lexi picked it up and shut it, using the highlighter as a bookmark. *Exposition of the Prophetic Texts.* She retrieved the legal pad as well and carried the bundle to the kitchen, which also served as an eat-in dining area. She flipped on the light and set everything on the table next to the crumpled letter Ward had delivered to her less than an hour ago.

Her eyes locked on the wadded ball of paper. She hadn't brought the letter in, had she?

Maybe she had, preoccupied as she'd been.

Lexi picked it up and lobbed it into the trash can at the end of the counter. It would be impossible for her to forget the date, only a week away. No need for the threatening, red-inked reminder.

She rubbed her eyes and circled the table, grabbed an old stainless kettle off the stove, then turned on the ball of her foot and filled it with water from the tap. The kitchen was so small that she and Molly often joked they could set the table, cook dinner, eat, and wash dishes without moving their feet.

The water made a drumming sound as it filled the empty pot. Lexi massaged the back of her neck with her free hand. She turned her head to the left, toward the window that looked out over the front walkway.

She saw black paint and heard the kettle fall into the sink. The water kept running.

Black paint dripped from a three-circle target that had been brushed on the kitchen window. The kitchen window she had passed on her way into the apartment not ten minutes ago. There had been no paint on the window then.

An involuntary shudder shook Lexi's body when she noticed that the paint had splattered her checked curtains. It was on the inside of the apartment.

Droplets of black speckled the countertop and the kitchen floor, leaving a broken trail that was smudged in front of the table. She must have stepped in it when she entered the kitchen. Her own shoe print led around the table and to the sink.

If Ward had followed her home and found a way in . . .

Lexi grabbed a knife out of her nearly empty knife block. It was short and dull but it was all she had. She held it out in front of her and followed the trail of black drops back to the hall. The carpets were worn from their original tan to a dingy gray, but as far as she could see, they were paint-free.

To her left: the bedrooms. Molly still snored. To her right: the front door. Closed. Both dead bolt and knob lock were vertical, secure. At eye level, though, a smudged row of four black stripes, rounded at the tips like fingers, gripped the door jamb.

Lexi's whole body was shaking. *Dear God, don't let Ward be in the house. Dear God, protect us.*

She tiptoed down the hall to the bedrooms, turning on the lights. Molly was okay, fully at ease in the rays of the lava lamp. *Thank you, God.* Gina faced her wall, breathing evenly. *Thank you, God.* Lexi checked the closets, the bathroom, the shower. She opened the linen cupboard. The bottom shelf was one of Molly's favorite hiding places.

No black paint in sight.

Better yet, no one wielding a paintbrush.

Thank you, God.

She didn't turn off the bathroom or hallway lights. She clicked on the only other living-room lamp and poked the knife into each side of the floor-to-ceiling curtains, which stayed open all the time. Cautiously lifting a slat at the far edge of the plastic miniblinds, she peered out into the complex.

Her square Volvo was half in gravel, half on the drive, at a haphazard angle. The parking areas that wrapped around the building opposite hers were nearly full. Her mind reviewed her encounter with Ward. Had his car been in the lot? She didn't remember seeing one. What was it he used to drive?

She couldn't remember that either.

That Ward knew how to scare a girl.

She decided not to call 9-1-1. What would she report? The ruckus of police arriving would lead to questions she wasn't prepared to answer. And she didn't want Molly to worry.

Leaving the lights blazing, Lexi pulled a kitchen chair out into the hallway where she could see in all directions, dropped onto the seat with her worthless knife, and planned to stay awake until dawn.

{ chapter 3 }

The exposed bulb in the ceiling fixture backlit the black target on Lexi's window. Warden Pavo leaned back against the front bumper of the Volvo and examined his work from the outside. He tried to be subtle most of the time, but every once in a while someone came along who deserved theatrics. Someone like Lexi Grüggen Solomon, the last man standing, so to speak, in the Grüggen family. Ward had been dismantling them for decades, and now, after seven excruciating years in which he'd had to bide his time, the moment for his coup de grâce had arrived.

He saw the shocked movement of Lexi's head and the jutting arches of her surprised brows when they rose above those cute little checked curtains. He congratulated himself for being in the right place when she lifted the slat of her living-room blinds to look for him, then dropped it. She couldn't see him standing right in front of her eyes. Wasn't that always the case?

Ward's fingers were still wet with the tarry paint. He dragged them up his exposed forearm, leaving four trails like jailbird stripes on his pale skin. He used his thumb and forefinger to bend the lines, smearing them apart from each other into crooked bars. Maybe that would have been a better illustration for the parole notice he'd given Lexi: Norman Von Ruden, busted out.

He cocked his head and considered painting something like this on the sliding glass door in Lexi and Molly's bedroom.

Fwack!

Warden swore and jerked upright off the bumper. His hand shot up to the back of his head where he'd been struck. By a rock, he figured. He snatched off his knit cap. Blood was running into the neck of his T-shirt.

An apple thunked onto the hood of the Volvo and rolled down, leaving a sticky trail. His fingertips came away from the injury sticky and smelling sweet. Juice, not blood, mingled with the smudged paint.

A voice he knew came out of the shadowy carport at the side of Lexi's building.

"You should have called to let me know you were coming," it accused. "I could have prepared a proper meal to welcome you."

The figure that emerged from the darkness was not fit to be seen even by moonlight. Craven was the most emaciated fellow Warden had ever known, though the creature fed endlessly on apples. He had lived at this complex longer than any other resident and used that fact to justify his disregard for good hygiene. His nails were greasy and his odor earthy. Warden had a strong stomach, but he had planned to steer clear of this stench.

"I hate baked fruit," Warden said.

He shifted his foot, which connected with the apple that had rolled onto the ground and sent it like a missile toward Craven, who failed to anticipate the move. The fruit hit him hard enough that his head snapped back.

Yet even with his eyes closed, even with blood spurting from his nose, he caught the ricocheting Red Delicious in his open claw and flung the food back at Warden so fast that he could not see it.

But he could sense it.

He tilted his ear to his shoulder and felt the displaced air as the apple whizzed past his throat. With his forefinger, he wiped juice spray from his chin.

A draw, for now. Warden snickered and Craven joined with his own low laughter, wiping his bloody nose on the sleeve of his threadbare army field jacket, which was about ten sizes too big for him.

"What brings you, Ward?" Craven asked.

"It's Warden to you."

"Waaaard."

Warden bristled. Craven sneered. "Your status as a jailer exists only in the black corners of your mind, Ward. Ward. Ward. Wardwardward."

He withdrew another fruit from one of his pockets. Warden envisioned himself seizing the apple and cramming it into Craven's jaws, then roasting him on a stick like the rodent that he was.

"So?" Craven asked.

"I'm back for Lexi Grüggen." He had always preferred her maiden name. It was truer to her real self. She might think of herself as a Solomon, but that didn't hide the facts of who she was and what she'd done.

"Ah." He licked his cracked lips and examined the Granny Smith as if he hadn't eaten all day. "What're you willing to give me for her?"

"Give *you?*"

"She's in my district."

"Well she wasn't when I started this job, so get over it."

"Nah. I'd rather have a cut."

"I'll give you a cut. Right across your throat."

Craven's laugh was a snort. "Ten to one she'll buck you. Again."

"Your disrespect is going to get you killed one of these days."

Craven bit into the apple's flesh and talked around the food. "They keep saying that. But here I am. Make it twenty to one, you lose."

"A hundred to one I'll succeed," Warden said.

"Stakes?"

"Your territories."

Craven stopped chewing and looked up at his eyebrows.

"Mine are worth more than yours," Warden said. "No need to calculate."

"If they were worth more, you wouldn't risk them for mine."

"I'm not the one taking a risk. You've wanted a piece of my traffic for eons."

"You'd like to think."

"Do we have a deal or not?"

Craven hesitated. "You steer clear of Mort Weatherby while you're here."

"Who's Mort Weatherby?"

Craven nodded at an apartment across the lot.

"I don't have any interest in him," Ward said.

"That's never stopped you before."

Warden grinned and leaned in toward Craven, getting a strong whiff of fruity sweetness mingled with sour clothing. "I'll take him when I take your territories and kill you, fool."

"We have a deal, then."

Craven stupidly stuck out his hand and Warden gripped it in a sticky squeeze that crushed the guy's knuckles. The tarry paint made a sizzling sound between their palms, then oozed out. A drop fell and hit the top of Warden's shoe.

He looked down at it. Craven matched Warden's grip and pulled, closing the small space between them.

"Friendly tip," Craven said, lowering his voice. His face was split by the grin of an adversary who thought he had the upper hand. Warden found the pretense tiresome. "The Grüggen girl has a sponsor."

"As you said, that's never stopped me before." Warden slid his hand out of Craven's easily and took pleasure in having dampened the impression his competitor had hoped to make. "In fact, if it's true, all the more reason for you to stay out of our way."

Craven wouldn't stay out. Warden could anticipate this without any lying words being spoken. Rule one of this business: every man for himself.

Warden decided he would have to keep an eye on this one, as he had on so many others he had bested over the years. That suited him fine. Tension kept his mind sharp and served him well.

Further words, being pointless, were unnecessary. Craven skittered like a walking stick back into the shadows, likely to find more edibles.

Warden turned his attention back to Lexi's apartment, which was ablaze with light, as if yellow beams begged the sun to rise early and meet them at the windows. Warden turned away. The light of the world would not come soon enough to prevent him from reducing Lexi to a sniveling mass of regret and bitterness. She would do anything he wanted.

Even if she did have a sponsor.

{ chapter 4 }

In Lexi's dream, she fell.

In reality, her body spasmed and slid off one side of the chair, and then she was fully awake.

What had awakened her?

A door, closing.

Her head snapped toward the front door. Her arm leveled the knife at it.

There was no knife in her fist! Where was it? Lexi quick-scanned the floor but couldn't see anything. She dropped to her knees, breathing hard, groping under the chair while keeping her eyes up, neck craned. *He might come down on me from behind.*

Who might?

Ward.

Her fingers closed on a serrated blade, which snagged her skin in the soft fold of the knuckle. Air stung the cut.

She finally found the handle and whirled with it, making a sweeping clockwise arc. On coming around, her wrist bone smashed into the cheap wood frame of the chair. The pain, tangible and immediate, restored her focus.

Nothing in the space was out of the ordinary, nothing but the sound of her own shaggy breath.

The room was empty. Sunlight had found its way through the down-turned slats of the blinds. What time was it?

What was the door she'd heard close? If that was not real, she'd go get herself a room near her dad's at the Mental Health Assistance Residence.

A faucet squeaked. Pipes groaned. The shower. Gina was in the bath-room. Of course. Her Friday-morning classes started earlier than they did the rest of the week.

Lexi dropped back onto her fanny and exhaled, guessing it was nearly seven. Molly would head to school in about an hour. She would drag herself out from under the covers before she was fully awake, cook herself a bowl of oatmeal on the stove—

The kitchen. The target. Lexi got to her feet. She had to clean up the mess before Molly woke up. She glanced at the fingerprints that were smeared on the door frame, but in the shifted lighting of morning, she couldn't see them. Hoping the paint was water-based, she decided to pull out the all-purpose cleaner.

She had the presence of mind to go look for her camera first, though. It would be a good idea to document the incident that she was about to scrub clean, especially if Ward continued to harass her into testifying on Norm's behalf. Between now and deciding what she would ultimately have to do, anything could happen.

Her point-and-shoot was a low-quality digital thing that she had found at a garage sale. It was good enough for occasions when a camera was required—birthdays, school events—but not so good that she ever brought it out for more than that. If the batteries had life in them, she'd consider herself fortunate.

She found it in its dusty black case in the bottom cabinet of the living room hutch. Its battery still had half a charge. For once.

Lexi powered it up and studied the digital display while walking into the kitchen. Deflected light made the pale blue area gray. The question of how to take a picture of a window without overexposing the shot crossed her mind.

This model didn't give her much in the way of bells and whistles, and even if it had, she wouldn't know how to use them. She'd try standing at an angle. Lifting the viewfinder to her eye, she framed the shot.

Then lowered the camera.

There was no target. No black paint. No spatters on the curtain or the counter.

Or the floor. The smudges from her shoes had vanished.

She heard water running. Not Gina's shower, but closer. The kitchen faucet was still open, spilling water over the hollow teakettle in the bottom of the sink.

Lexi reached out to shut down the tap.

The first thing that occurred to her was that she had been so exhausted the night before that her mind had fabricated every nonsensical event of the past twelve hours. What she really needed was a good sleep.

Challenging this notion, she walked to the trash can that stood at the end of the kitchen counter. A wadded ball of linen paper topped off the half-full bin. She could see the red ink bleeding through the fibers.

Her second thought was that Gina had risen early and preempted Lexi's cleanup efforts.

But why would her roommate bother? Lovely and loving though Gina was, she was only one dirty coffee cup away from being a slob. And if she'd *ever* go to such lengths to clean up, why would she erase the black paint but leave the spot of yellow cake batter there on the corner of the glass? That batter had escaped Molly's hand mixer a year ago and hardened into cement, though Lexi made a mental note to scrape it off every time she saw it.

"Why's there a chair in the middle of the hall?" Molly was up.

Lexi put the camera in the fruit bowl on the counter and tried to focus. For her child's sake.

"Hey, little kitty." She opened her arms and welcomed Molly into an easy embrace. Lexi ran her fingernails lightly down either side of Molly's spine. Molly draped her arms around Lexi's neck and made a purring sound.

Lexi thought of her daughter as a smaller, better version of herself.

Molly's brunette hair was thicker and shinier, her autumn-brown eyes kinder, her spirit warmer, her heart stronger. They had the same round face and short, athletic build, but Molly would one day become the woman Lexi could only aspire to be. Lexi believed this in the most private corner of her heart.

Molly's pink kitty-cat jammies were two inches too short, and her heels hung off the back of her slippers. Lexi mentally went through her own pajama inventory for something that would fit her daughter. They lived on nineteen grand a year plus tips, or Lexi would have bought her new ones long ago. Grant had never paid child support, and Lexi had no expectation that he would.

She and Molly would find their own way. She'd read in Gina's news-paper that Riverbend, the larger town half an hour down the mountain-side, planned to open two new grocery stores in the next six months. She'd apply for work at both of them. A union job with higher pay, ben-efits, and a chance for advancement would make the half-hour commute worthwhile. She might be able to work one job instead of two. Get better hours. Be home with Molly more often. Eat Molly's dinner creations hot off the stove.

The possibilities were a sweet dream.

Molly hung off Lexi's neck in a ten-second cat stretch, then shuffled across the kitchen to the cabinet.

"You okay?" Molly asked. She withdrew the round carton of oats and set it on the stovetop.

Lexi blinked. "Yeah. You sleep well?"

"Why's the kitchen chair out in the hall? And why are you still in your uniform?"

An answer for either question eluded Lexi. "Long story. Did you get your homework done?"

"Affirmative, Maynard." She got that from some TV show, Lexi thought.

"Ready for the big test today?"

"Affirmative. You want some of this?"

Lexi was ravenous but feared that eating anything then was a bad choice. "Thanks, sweetie, but I think I'll have some of your spaghetti later."

"Oh yeah. You'll like that. I used extra basil."

She went through the motions of filling her little pot with water, adding salt, waiting for it to boil. Lexi watched with her back to the window as if ignoring the target that wasn't there would bring sense to its unreality. Molly found the red box of raisins but passed over the brown sugar. She rationed that stuff like she was Ma Ingalls on the prairie, knowing it was the first thing Lexi would cut when the grocery budget was strained.

This kitchen was her daughter's domain. Her nine-year-old was a foodie. She'd bring home recipes from the newspapers her teacher discarded. At the library she'd go online and print out her daily five free pages, which she designated for homework assignments and Food Network ideas. She saved her meager allowance and periodically spent it on extravagant ingredients—pine nuts, hearts of palm, coconut milk—for special meals, which she tried out on her mother and Gina. Some were more tasty than others.

When Chuck let Lexi take home leftovers at the end of her shift, her coup sometimes felt anticlimactic. A bowl of mac 'n' cheese or box of chicken tenders never excited Molly like eggplant parmigiana.

Lexi loved that about her. One of many things.

Molly stirred the dry oatmeal into the simmering water.

"You should take a nap while I'm at school, Mom."

"I look that tired, huh?"

"No, it's just you don't want to get sick or anything."

"True. But I'm fine."

"You don't have to be to work 'til four, right?"

Her tone told Lexi that the question she meant to ask wasn't the one she voiced.

"Right." Lexi retrieved the chair from the hall and pulled it up to the table. She sat. Her other job—stocking shelves at the grocery store—was only four mornings a week, Monday through Thursday, while Molly was in school.

Her daughter stirred the oatmeal and tilted her head to one side. Molly's strong shoulders were pinched up toward her ears.

"I was thinking we could go rent a movie after school," Lexi said. "Maybe something to watch together tomorrow morning."

"We haven't seen a movie in ages! Is *Gobsmacked* out yet?"

"We can check."

"I want that one if it's out."

"Okay."

"And I can make pancakes." Her shoulders dropped an inch, and she glanced at Lexi for approval.

"Affirmative, Maynard."

Molly scraped her oatmeal and raisins into a bowl and set it on the table. Lexi was still waiting for her question-behind-the-question. Molly sat and spooned the sticky cereal into her mouth.

"Thank you, Lord, for this food," Lexi said by way of reminder.

"Ditto," she said around the spoon.

Lexi shook her head but let it go. A scolding at this moment could shut down the conversation.

"Mom, you know how you've said that some things you tell me are family business? Like I shouldn't be talking about it with my friends?"

"Mmmhmm." Their odd little family had plenty of history that didn't need to be broadcast to the world. Molly didn't know the half of it.

"Well, is family business something we can talk to other family members about?"

Confusion caused Lexi to squint.

"I mean, if you tell me something, is that something I can talk about with . . . well, with Grandpa when we visit him? Or with Gina? Because Gina's like family, isn't she? And she's your best friend, so she probably already knows our family business anyway is what I'm thinking."

Lexi's brain searched wildly for their most recent topic of "family business" and a memory of Molly's reaction to it. The mental file eluded her. Molly's grandfather had been admitted to a mental hospital several years ago, after his breakdown, and they visited him once a week. She never seemed troubled by those visits, and Lexi had never asked her to keep that piece of family laundry in the basket.

"You're going to have to give me an example of what you mean, sweetie."

Molly swallowed and pursed her lips before saying, "If someone talked to me and told me that our talk was private and I shouldn't tell you about it, would that be right?"

"Absolutely not!" Lexi bit her lip, sensing she'd been too forceful. "Except for some good secrets," she qualified. "Like birthday or Christmas secrets."

"Like when Gina got tickets for you to see the Switchfoot concert!"

"Exactly."

Molly looked doubtful. "Why would Grandma think you'd be mad about a good secret?"

"Grandma? She called you?"

"Uhhh, she came here."

Lexi's mother had dropped by the house. That's what Gina had been reluctant to tell her last night.

"When did she get into town?"

Molly shrugged.

"Do you know where she's staying?" Another no. "I take it you two didn't talk about food."

Alice Grüggen was a travel writer who focused on regional cuisines. She and Molly could go on for the longest time about how to cook pasta or what spices brought out the flavors of summer squash.

"Oh, we did, but that's not really why she visited."

"So, spill the beans."

"Are you mad?"

Lexi took a deep breath. "For now, I'm mostly confused."

"She said we should make it a secret 'cause you'd be mad if you found out."

Lexi sat on her true reaction to this news. Molly was not to blame for any of this. "Generally speaking, those would be considered bad secrets."

Molly sighed. "So I should tell you? I worried about this. If I tell, she'll be mad. If I don't tell, you'll be mad."

"No one's mad at you, Molly. I think you have a feeling you should let me know, otherwise we wouldn't be having this conversation."

"You and Grandma don't like each other."

Molly's powers of observation grew by the day. Lexi missed some things about the girl's earlier years, one of them being that it was easier to hide certain facts from her. "We *love* each other"—which was true, in its paradoxical kind of way—"but we don't agree on a lot of things."

"Like about my dad?"

Grant? This was about Grant? Lexi felt her neck flush. What was her mom doing? Lexi had never spoken a bad word about Grant to Molly, and she tried to answer her daughter's questions about him as truthfully as possible. But Alice knew Lexi had no intention of making him fess-up to being a father and play some halfhearted role in Molly's life. If he didn't want to, and that was as plain as his abandonment, who was Lexi to force him? She didn't even know where he lived. He hadn't contacted her since he left when Molly was two.

"What did Grandma say about your dad?"

Molly looked at her bowl of oatmeal. "Nothing."

Lexi was ten seconds away from shaking the information out of her daughter. She counted. Several possible questions danced around in her head. One saved her from doing anything rash: "Don't you think you'll feel better if you tell me what's bothering you?"

Molly looked at her, surprised, like she hadn't considered the situation so simply until now. "Yeah." She pushed her bowl away. "Yeah."

She left the table.

Itching to follow Molly, Lexi stared at the dish, which still had quite a bit of cereal in the bottom. Instead, she picked up the bowl, and the dirty pot that was on the stove, and put them in the sink, then filled them with water.

"Molly?"

"Just a minute," she called from her bedroom.

Lexi decided that if Molly opted not to open up, she'd call her mom later in the morning. She hated talking to her mother.

Molly's slippers slapped her heels as she returned to the kitchen a few seconds later and held out an envelope to Lexi. It was addressed to Molly, in care of her grandmother.

The envelope looked to Lexi almost as ominous as the one she had received from Ward. She took it.

"What's this?"

"It's a letter from my dad. You're not mad, are you?"

Lexi's fingertips felt electrified on the paper. She looked at Molly, who was wearing a combined expression of hope and anxiety. A letter from Grant to Molly. He'd never had any contact with her since he'd left. Molly's eyes were analyzing her, waiting to see if Lexi would allow her this unexpected joy of having finally connected with the man she must have dreamed of many, many times.

As much as Lexi resented Grant, she couldn't steal that from Molly. If he betrayed her, however, if he smothered this spark he'd lit behind Molly's eyes, Lexi would hunt him down.

"No. I'm not mad. Did Grandma read it?"

Molly nodded.

"What does it say?"

Molly hugged herself. "You can read it."

"Really? You'd let me do that?" Molly's openness shamed Lexi. The girl couldn't know that Lexi would have read it without permission.

"Yeah. Go ahead."

Lexi tapped the edge of the envelope on the table. "Okay. I will. Thanks for letting me. But I think I'll wait until I've had a rest." She couldn't read it in front of her child. It would be impossible to hide her feelings, toward Grant or her mother. Molly looked disappointed.

"We'll talk about it after school, before I go to the restaurant. You go get ready now. I'll drive you this morning."

"Why? I can walk. I still have time."

Still holding Grant's letter, Lexi walked into the living room. "The weather's getting colder."

"Mom, it's March. It's been cold."

Lexi raised the slat in the blinds again. Her little Volvo was where she had left it, and it didn't appear to have been tagged with a parking citation.

"All the more reason. I'm going to drive you to school for a while from now on, okay?"

"But you said driving me to school is a waste of gas."

True. It was terrible how the things parents said came back to bite them, Lexi thought. "Not anymore. Really, Molly, if you're embarrassed by me I'll drop you off a little ways out."

Molly rolled her eyes and tossed her hair as she went to her room to get dressed.

"Sheesh, Mom, of course you don't embarrass me."

Lexi looked down at the letter in her hands and wondered if Grant had anything to do with Ward's sudden reappearance and Norm's parole. The past they all shared was tangled enough that the possibility wasn't out of the question. She and Grant had not parted on the best terms, and she couldn't say what the last seven years had done to him.

Until she knew what was going on, she wasn't going to let Molly do anything alone.

{ chapter 5 }

Grant Solomon's feet drummed the dirt shoulder of the county road on the north side of Riverbend. His conscience had sent him jogging farther than usual this Friday morning.

Giving that letter to Alice had been a mistake.

There were only a few things that Grant was sure of anymore: He'd screwed up his life. He loved his daughter. And he should have delivered her letter *himself*, after talking to Lexi *himself*, instead of hiding behind the skirts of his mother-in-law.

The truth of this had kept him up all night. He was an idiot. Idiocy would hound his life no matter how hard he tried to outrun it.

Grant ran harder. It was seven thirty and he was due to work in an hour, with three miles of flat dry plains stretching out between him and home.

Home. A rat hole of a trailer in a deteriorated park, the only place he could find—even with Richard's good word—worthy of an ex-con on a janitor's salary. He let his gaze travel up the mountainside ahead. The home he really wanted was above him, out of reach in Crag's Nest, behind that ridge that the rising sun was touching. Lexi and Molly were living in an apartment now, Alice had said. Grant wondered who had taken over the old bungalow on Fireweed Street, and how much it might cost him to get it back.

All of it.

It was pointless, wondering. Lexi alone was unaffordable. Nothing he could dream up would buy his way back into her good graces. Not even the fact that she was still his wife.

He wondered if she'd found someone else by now.

Alice would have told him, wouldn't she?

Not necessarily.

Grant allowed himself a hope for Molly, though. Not that she'd ever look up to him as a real dad, but that they could at least find a way to know each other, maybe even like each other—grab a burger together now and then. Go on a hike. Exchange text messages. He'd get the two of them phones on one of those family plans.

Lexi's love for Molly might have allowed a guarded reunion, before this latest stunt. He cursed himself. Now, he'd be lucky if she didn't tell Molly he was dead. Maybe Molly already thought he was dead. Who knew what Lexi had been telling her over the years? Grant's foot shifted sideways over a loose rock. He caught himself and resumed his hard rhythm.

He'd call Alice as soon as he got back. If Lexi hadn't been home last night, there was a chance Alice still had the letter. He'd get her to hold off so he could do this right. For once.

Grant's shins took a beating as he knocked out the remaining miles in a race to his telephone.

As he left the road and turned up the gravel driveway that led into the trailer park, Alice was pulling out. She drove her late-model Beemer past the split-rail fence that was collapsing of dry rot and turned toward Grant. She rolled down her window.

Grant slowed to a walk and worked on catching his breath.

"When you didn't answer your phone, I decided to drive over," she explained when she reached him.

His forearm caught the sweat that was overflowing his eyebrows.

"Long run," he said between drags of air.

"Plenty of distance to go out here." Alice's gaze on him was steady. Wary.

Grant shook his head. "What? . . . Did you think . . . I'd split?"

"The thought crossed my mind."

He exhaled audibly. The morning sun glinted off Alice's sunglasses.

"You can't expect people to trust you just because you want them to," Alice said.

"I don't."

"Glad to hear it, because you're still earning my good faith. But Lexi has too much pride to accept my help, and that little girl needs a father, so I've extended you some credit based on what I know for sure. Don't default on me, now."

Still breathless, Grant bent at the waist and raised one hand, making a silent promise. There was little else he could do or say, short of staying the course, to convince Alice of his sincere intentions.

"How'd Lexi react?" he asked. "To the letter?"

"Lexi wasn't home."

Relief filled Grant's lungs with sweet air.

"I gave it to Molly," Alice said.

"What?"

"Molly and I had a good chat. You should have seen her face when I mentioned you. I couldn't not give it to her after that. I know I keep saying this, but you're going to love that girl to pieces." She saw Grant's expression. "Oh, it's not a big deal. Molly gets it. She won't say anything before we talk to Lexi ourselves."

"That was not the plan."

"We all have to improvise now and then. Look, Grant. She's working tonight at the Red Rocks. We'll go for dinner. It's a public place. She won't make a scene, and I'll be there as a buffer. Molly won't be there. What could go wrong?"

Grant could think of a hundred things, starting with the letter he shouldn't have written. He laced his hands together on top of his head.

"Molly will tell," he said.

"How on Earth can you say that? You don't know her half as well as I do."

He was successful in stopping the sharp words that almost left his mouth. "What time do you want me there?"

"I'll pick you up here at seven. Sound good?"

Grant stepped away from the car and lifted his hand in a wave. "Fine."

It was not fine. Lexi would not think it was fine. Grant stood on the packed-dirt drive, hands on hips, staring at the gravel. He decided to call his wife.

The decision prevented his heart rate from falling back to its resting level. His rusting trailer was at the back of the lot, and Grant walked there slowly. By the time he arrived he was still sweating, still short of breath. He entered the unlocked door, and the flimsy home, which contained nothing anyone would want to steal, groaned under his weight.

Because his hands shook so badly when he punched Lexi's number into the phone, he hung up and chose to shower first.

Ten minutes later, dressed in his janitorial blues, he completed the call. The connection went through. Grant looked at the clock. He had five minutes to get to work. After only a week on the job, he couldn't afford to be late.

He couldn't afford what might happen if he didn't explain that letter to Lexi.

She answered on the fifth ring. "Hello?"

"Hi, Lexi." He wiped a damp palm on his thigh. "How are you?" *Lame. I'm lame.* Grant closed his eyes.

"I'm sorry, who is this?"

"Yeah, it's been a while. It's Grant."

When she didn't reply, he realized he'd been bracing himself for a well-deserved torrent.

"This must come as a real shock. I'm sorry to catch you off guard. You must have a million questions."

She didn't ask one. He couldn't even hear her breathing, maybe because his own breathing was so loud.

"I had to call you this morning."

"This is not a good time." Her voice was level, calm.

"I know. I know. You have every right to be mad at me, Lexi. Believe me, no one is more angry at me for what I did than me. I'm hoping you might let me—"

"Mom, where's my spelling book?" Was that Molly in the background? Her voice sounded so much older than Grant had imagined, though Alice had shown him plenty of pictures.

"Under the bed," Lexi said, her voice muffled as if her mouth was turned away from the phone.

Grant swallowed.

"We need to go," Lexi said to him. "School."

"Yeah. Time really moves, doesn't it?"

Lexi didn't reply. Grant wished his fool words back and feared opening his mouth again. He could only make everything worse.

"I need to talk to you about Molly," he said.

"She's not your concern." Lexi spoke lowly, but with the growl of a protective mama bear. Grant wondered if Molly was within earshot.

"I'm sure I'm going about this all the wrong way, but I was hoping I could explai—"

"I don't need an explanation. For anything."

"But there's—"

"I don't care. Please don't call again."

Grant would do anything for Lexi. In light of all he owed her, he'd do anything. Anything but that. He covered his eyes with his free hand. He had never felt more pathetic or desperate. He could not let Lexi—could not let Molly—go.

"Lexi. Don't."

She hung up the phone.

Grant lowered the receiver onto the countertop. The Formica was riddled with gold veins that reminded him of a road map, and of all the highways where he could run and run until the horizon swallowed him up.

Lexi tried to hide her distress over Grant's call as she drove Molly to school. Though the intrusion stirred up a bitterness in her that she believed she had left behind some years ago, her greater fear was that Grant had more harmful intentions.

Such as reclaiming some paternal right to Molly.

The idea of spending the day camped in the school parking lot came to Lexi's mind, even though the air was as gray and cold as she'd warned Molly it would be. If Ward or Grant came by . . .

. . . what would she do then? She didn't even have a cell phone, had never been able to afford one. She couldn't afford one now, either. She was behind on her utility bill as it was. And she couldn't live in the school lot five days a week. Fridays were the only day she wasn't at King Grocery during school hours.

Feeling undecided, she cut the car's engine in the school parking lot and withdrew Grant's letter from her book bag. The temperature in the car dropped within minutes, and she pulled her jacket around her.

Lexi confessed to herself that she felt some irrational jealousy as she looked at Grant's familiar handwriting. He had written not to her but to their daughter, and although she had no desire to connect with him, his exclusion caused her some pain.

And his voice had filled her with an inexplicable combination of warmth and dread. She wondered about his phone call, an apparent afterthought to the letter. His insistent need to talk about Molly grated on her memory.

Lexi had parked facing the red brick school's main entrance. A man stood at the pay phone to the left of the front office, his back to Lexi, his ear and shoulder pinching the handset, his hips tilted so that all his weight was on one foot. The other foot tapped an irritated rhythm that caught her eye. A cigarette wobbled between the fingers of his left hand, burning like a slow fuse. Above his exposed elbow, partly concealed by his checkered shirtsleeve, a tattoo peeked out.

Warden Pavo, here, at Molly's school. Lexi put her hand on the door handle and prepared to confront him.

The man's chin turned in her direction, his eyes slanting toward the car and through the windshield as if he'd sensed her stare and was annoyed by it.

It wasn't Ward. Lexi dropped her eyes to Grant's letter, feeling on edge. No, not Ward—she stole a sly peek—but a handsome look-alike.

Ward had seemed handsome enough at first, when Grant first introduced her to him, but his good looks had paled against his increasingly offensive behavior, especially after Grant abandoned her. After Norm was sentenced, Ward hung around town, claiming that Grant owed him money. Ten thousand dollars or so, which he couldn't have extracted from Lexi even with all the PIN numbers in the world. She didn't even have five hundred, and what she did have wouldn't go to any cause but her baby's. Eventually she'd had to get equally nasty. He had suggested she could clear Grant's debt with a more lecherous form of payment, and she threatened to call the sheriff.

Lexi withdrew Grant's letter from the torn envelope and unfolded two papers, which had been torn from a wire-bound notebook. The ragged edges stuck together.

Grant's familiar printing filled every other line.

Dear Molly-Wolly,

Molly-Wolly. Years had passed since Lexi last thought of her daughter by that endearment. Grant used to string rhymes like train cars onto her name: Molly Wolly Polly Golly Jolly Dolly. Holly! He'd go on with this game until she was giggling.

All this was before the meth.

Lexi's hands were so cold. Her freezing fingers could barely hold the paper. And yet she was too frugal to keep the car and the heater running. Too cheap, Gina might have said. Well, maybe so, but she had less than half a tank of gas to get her through the month, and in this little mountain town, gas could be more expensive than it was in New York or L.A.

Dear Molly-Wolly,

Do you remember how I used to call you that? It was a long time ago and you're nearly all grown-up now, but I still think of you that way and guess I always will.

I expect you're angry at me for taking off and not being in touch for so long. But then, knowing your mom, you probably don't even remember me. In fact, I'll bet you have another dad.

The anger that flushed Lexi's cheeks took the edge off the chill. Her old resentment reared its head. Grant, not she, had removed himself from Molly's life. Right when they needed him most!

You might even have had several dads—*what!*—though I'm the only one who could legally lay claim to that title. I'd like to sit down and talk to you about what happened to make me leave. That's the least I owe you, but your mom will prevent us from getting together if she can. I suppose I might look back on this as a mistake, because I can only imagine what she's told you about me. She hates me, so you can bet none of it's true.

Lexi's mouth was open. Her mother had seen fit to pass this on to Molly? What was she thinking?

So I'm writing because I can finally set the record straight, Molly-Wolly. Now's the time, for reasons I'll explain when I see you.

"You won't be seeing her at all, buster." Lexi's words came out of her

NEVER LET YOU *GO*

mouth in a warm fog. She had never told Molly anything but the flattering truth about her father, unless one would call omission of the unflattering facts a lie. But really, what child needed to know her doting father blew his paychecks on a drug habit?

> Your mom is a bit blind about some things and might keep you from contacting me. But don't you think you deserve to know your real dad, or at least get your burning questions answered? She never loved anyone more than she loves herself, so we'll do what we have to for YOU, okay? If you think you might like to talk with me, send me a note back, and I'll work out the rest. No sense in getting your mom more lathered up than she usually is.
>
> > I hope it works out.
> >
> > Dad
>
> P.S. You can call me Grant if that's more comfortable.

This was followed by a Riverbend post office box address. He was so close?

And her mom was running interference for him. Why?

If not for the fact that Molly expected Lexi to give this document back, and her failure to do so would cause more damage than the letter itself, Lexi would have crumpled it and heaved it into the trash can that sat next to the pay phone. She would have chased it with a lit match!

Instead, the adult in her decided to rise to the occasion and figure out a way to speak with Molly about this, like . . . like an adult. She frowned, concentrating. How would she do it? Why should a nine-year-old be exposed to this kind of muck? Fortunately, Lexi thought, she had until three o'clock to calm down and choose a strategy. Perhaps she'd talk Molly into burning the thing herself.

Her mother would get an earful and a half and would be lucky if Lexi ever let her near Molly again.

{ chapter 6 }

When Molly emerged from the school at three, Lexi was cranky. She had left the car only for a ten-minute venture into the 7-Eleven across the street. She had heard they sold affordable prepaid cell phones there, without contracts, and Lexi thought she should have one for emergencies, all things considered. At least for now. But even those were out of her financial reach. She turned then to the pepper spray. It was time Molly started carrying it.

She left the store without one of those expensive items either, and planned to dig up the canister buried in the planter at the apartment.

For the rest of the day, she stayed in the school lot. To get her mind off the terrors of the prior night, and Ward's threat against Molly, and the decision she needed to make about Norm, she kept her eyes on the school doors and composed letters in her head to Grant, telling him to stay out of Molly's life. At some point, she switched to impersonating Molly. And then, overwhelmed by even these relentless thoughts, she'd rifled through the glove box in search of a napkin to write them on.

She emerged with a prestamped postcard, one of two she'd purchased for Molly to communicate with her grandmother. Sight of the stationery caused

Lexi to wonder what might happen if she actually mailed her thoughts, disguised as Molly's, to Grant. If he didn't think the letter had come from his daughter, he'd keep pestering until he got what he wanted. Addicts were like that. Sneaky and persistent.

Grant, thanks but no thanks. Don't bother asking me again. Molly. (Just plain Molly.)

Lexi wrote it, read it, and planned to mail it, then hesitated. Of all the adult ways in which she had planned to handle this mess, impersonating a child probably didn't qualify.

The letter should have gone in the trash, would go in the trash when she got home. And yet she didn't feel all bad about the exercise. It was good therapy to think she had done what she could to keep the man away from their girl. Her girl.

As she waited outside of the elementary school, she wondered if it was time she explained more to Molly, began to dismantle her daughter's romantic notions of Grant slowly. Painlessly if she could. That would be tricky. She was a child still, and would be for some time. What would be worse for Molly at this point: telling her the truth or letting her have her fantasy?

A minute later she saw Molly come through the wide double doors. One more year here and she'd be off to middle school. Murderous Middle School. That social scene had nearly killed Lexi and was probably ten times worse these days. She wanted her daughter to stay a grade-schooler forever.

She wanted Molly not to know the truth about her father.

She wanted Molly never to suffer.

Molly started walking home. Lexi honked, and Molly's head jerked in the direction of the car. Lexi waved, and the girl started jogging toward her, crossing her eyes and sticking her tongue out sideways.

She plopped herself onto the seat and kicked her backpack under the dash.

"I forgot you were coming."

"Goofy girl!"

"Do we have time to go to the library?"

"What do you need there?"

"Book for a report." She buckled in.

"When's the report due?"

"Monday."

"And I'm just now hearing about it?"

"It's a little report. About Indians. The Pawnee. At least I'm not waiting 'til Sunday night."

Lexi set her lips in a thin line. "I'll give you ten minutes to find what you need. Then I've got to get ready for work."

"So did you read it?"

Lexi was tempted to play dumb. She had hoped for a little more time to ease into this topic.

"You mean your father's letter?"

"Yeah. Did you?"

"Affirmative, Maynard." Anything to keep the discussion positive for as long as possible.

"And?"

Studying the rearview mirrors, Lexi pulled onto the street so she didn't have to look at Molly.

"Why don't you tell me what you think first?" she said.

"I really want to meet him, Mom."

"What?"

"I want to meet him. He sounds just like you've described to me—remember how you told me he used to make rhymes with my name? I always thought he never wrote because he forgot, but it sounds like that didn't happen, like something kept him from getting back to us, and I want to know what it is. I've been thinking about it all day."

Lexi's spirit groaned. It was not at all clear how Molly got that out of Grant's rude correspondence, but worse was that the mother and daughter were headed for a rare argument.

"Sweetie, adults sometimes make choices that don't make sense to kids your age."

In the silence that preceded Molly's reply, Lexi had no doubt her daughter's mind went through the paces of deciding exactly what her mother meant and whether the remark might be open-ended.

For a preadolescent, of course, everything was open-ended.

"That's okay. I mean, even if I don't understand it all right now, I'm sure he can tell me a lot. Don't you want to see him again?"

Lexi saw that her past attempts to take the high road in regard to Molly's memory of her father were about to backfire. Even so, she was unwilling to be perceived as the mean mom, which would be the only possible outcome of the discussion ahead, thus bolstering the claims Grant had made of her in his letter. She searched for a way to bring Molly to her own more accurate conclusions about Grant.

Sometimes, the strategy worked.

"He didn't sound like he'd want to see me, hon."

"What do you mean?"

"I mean . . . that he sounds like he's pretty angry at me."

Molly frowned as if Lexi spoke another language.

"What do you mean, angry? Where's the letter?" She spotted the book bag in the back and twisted between the bucket seats to get it. "I thought he was super sweet."

"Well, to you he was sweet." Lexi cleared her throat. "I'm sure he has never stopped loving you. But the way he talked about me was disrespectful, don't you think? That says something about him. The fact that he didn't even want me to know he'd sent the letter to you—"

Molly cut her off, reading. "'I haven't had the courage to go to your mom about all this yet, but I will. I suppose I might look back on this as a mistake, going to you first, I mean.' What's rude about that?"

"Where do you read that?"

"Right here." She leaned across the stick shift and pointed to some part of the page that Lexi couldn't study, not in the middle of traffic.

"See? 'Your mom is a smart woman and knows exactly what's best for you.'"

"Don't you go making stuff up, Molly. There was nothing like that—"

"Mom!" She stretched the word into three syllables. "This is a *big* deal! I'm not making up anything. You said you read this."

"I did. And I almost threw it away."

Molly held the letter to her chest and glared. "He wants to come back!"

"What about that garbage could make me happy? I'm starting to think we didn't read the same letter."

"Duh."

"Molly Amanda!"

"You're not being fair. To Dad."

Lexi made a left turn. "Read it again, then, so we can talk about this like women."

Instead, Molly read down to Lexi, pronouncing each word carefully and slowly, because it was clear to her that her mother hadn't understood the simple letter the first time through.

"'Dear Molly-Wolly,

"'Do you remember how I used to call you that? It was a long time ago and you're nearly all grown-up now, but I still think of you that way and guess I always will. I expect you're angry at me for taking off and not being in touch for so long. Maybe you don't even remember me, and that's okay. That'd be my fault.'"

"Molly, if your imagination is doing the talking right now, that won't help anything."

"It's not!" She poked at the letter with her index finger. "It's right *here*, and when you come to a stoplight I'll show you! I *knew* you wouldn't read this. You don't want me to meet him, no matter what he says."

What could Lexi say to that? The part about her wanting to keep Grant away from Molly was true enough, especially because it led to these kinds of delusions. Lexi glanced at her daughter as they continued. Molly gripped the letter with both hands and slouched over it.

"'I owe you some explanation for not being there for you. If your mom will let me, I'd like to sit down and talk to you about that.' See, Mom, that's not rude." She held up her hand so Lexi wouldn't reply. "'I haven't had the courage to go to your mom about all this yet, but I will. I suppose I might look back on this as a mistake, going to you first, I mean. It's just that I'm thinking your mom might not want me to see you at all, and this might be my only chance to say I'm sorry, Molly-Wolly. I'm sorry and I'm hoping maybe you can forgive me. If you can't, I'll understand, but I wanted to ask it anyway.'"

Lexi's heart was overcome by a sadness she hadn't known since Grant left. Their daughter had so much hope for a reunion with her father that could never be, and she was changing her father's lies to make her hope a reality. Why did she think she could get away with such a fabrication? What on Earth possessed her to try this trick after she'd given Lexi the original letter?

"'Your mom is a smart woman and knows exactly what's best for you,'" Molly read. "'She never loved anyone more than she loves you, so we'll do what she thinks is right, okay?'" *The girl is smart, she is. Her chances of getting what she wants always go way up when she puts me on a pedestal.* "'If you think you might like to talk with me, send a note back, and I'll take it up with your mom then. No sense in getting her lathered up over something you don't want in the first place. I hope it works out. I love you, Dad. P.S. You can call me Grant if that's more comfortable.'"

They had traversed the short length of town to the opposite side, where the library, courthouse, mining museum, and post office lined up at attention across the street from King Grocery. Lexi pulled into the library parking lot.

"I want to talk with him, Mom."

"Honey, I'm not sure—"

"You are *so* mean!"

Lexi sighed.

"You're still mad at him after all this time. You're mad and you want me to be mad too."

"No, Molly, that's not what—"

"I'm gonna write to him anyway."

Lexi raised her eyebrows.

"You can't stop me."

"I can ground you." Lexi immediately wished she hadn't said that. More than anything, she wanted to share Molly's heartache. She knew a thing or two about losing a father. There was so much about parenting she'd never get right.

"I don't care."

"Molly, give me the letter."

"No."

She opened the door and got out, grabbing at her backpack. The strap snagged on the manual window lever, and the letter crumpled in her palm as she yanked at her things.

"Honey—"

Molly freed her pack and slammed the door. Lexi sighed into the silent space of the car.

For several minutes her mind rehashed the conversation. She wished for a redo. Only twelve hours ago she'd raced home, fearing for Molly's safety, overwhelmed with gratitude to see her tucked in bed, and now here they were, hardly knowing how to speak to each other.

Lexi glanced at her watch—3:18. If only she didn't have to be to work at four. Then they could talk this through over supper. She hoped that tomorrow morning they could try again, after they'd both slept on it.

For now, though, she would do what was necessary to protect Molly. She withdrew the postcard she'd written to Grant and walked it down to the post office, then dropped it into the blue box at the curb. For a half second after the metal door snapped its jaws shut and swallowed her deception, she wished it back. Was sending it the right thing? She might never know.

But Lexi was resolved: if Molly tried to write a letter of her own, she'd intercept that too.

{ chapter 7 }

In a high-security detention center one hundred miles south of Crag's Nest, in a valley surrounded by a twisted mountain range, Warden Pavo was cleared for five minutes of visitation with Norman Von Ruden. He would be able to accomplish a lot in five minutes. A guard escorted the prisoner into the partitioned polycarbonate room where Warden had been waiting for ten.

The forty-six-year-old businessman—former businessman—had lost half of his golden hair and all of his self-assured, tall-man posture in the last seven years. The ski tan had faded to the washed-out pale of a sunless existence under fluorescent lighting. The broad chest had narrowed and fallen, thickening his waist slightly. The bright blue eyes had dimmed to the color of an iceberg.

Of course, the transformation had begun long before he thrust a knife up under Tara Grüggen's ribs.

"You look well," Warden said.

The man blinked as if to clear a head fog, then sat slowly, eyes on his old acquaintance. "I wasn't expecting to see you."

Warden smiled with only one corner of his mouth. "No one ever is."

Von Ruden frowned. "Can't imagine what brings you."

"Old stories. And new opportunities."

"That's the problem with you, Pavo." His voice was slow, fatigued. "You think you're a poet when all you've ever been is a hack."

"Right now I'm working on a little ditty I'm calling 'The Ballad of Grant Solomon.' When I'm finished you might change your mind."

"Huh?"

The man's lack of enthusiasm irritated Warden. Apparently he'd have to stir up the sediment of this man's sorry life.

"Solomon is out of jail. Been out a month."

"That right? What was he in for?"

"Nothing he ever did to you."

"That's justice for you."

"He's the one who deserved to be in your cell."

Von Ruden shrugged.

"C'mon now, that's not the way you really feel. That's your meds talking, Norman."

His eyes flashed. "Even if it is, what's Solomon to me? You don't get years back, once you lose them in here. The world is upside-down."

"And now, we have the opportunity to set it right."

The German sighed heavily.

Warden wagged his head. "This is no good. I have got to hook you up with something to drain that tar pit your brain is stuck in. Get the old Norman back in the game."

A light appeared in Von Ruden's eyes for the first time since Warden's arrival. They asked an unspoken question, which Warden interpreted as *Can you get me what I need?* Warden glanced at the guard and nodded gravely. The men lowered their voices.

"Next time I come," Warden promised.

Von Ruden filled his lungs with relief.

"Solomon's time has come," Warden said. "It's your turn with him."

"You say that like I'm Al Capone. What? I kill one person and you think I've got what I need to order a hit from my cell?"

This was the Von Ruden that Warden had been hoping to see today.

Warden grinned. "Wouldn't you rather do it with your own hands? You'll be out on your own soon enough."

"It's just a hearing. Not a guarantee." The inmate rubbed his eyes and sighed.

"You've been a good boy."

"That never mattered in this life."

"Lexi Grüggen will be speaking on your behalf."

A flash of regret crossed Von Ruden's face. "Grüggen? Did she remarry?"

"It's her maiden name."

"What's that all about?"

"Maybe you'll get the chance to ask her yourself."

The prematurely aged man sighed. "Lexi. More likely she'll be driving nails into my coffin."

"No. No. I have it on good authority. What do you say? When you're out of this place with Lexi's wind beneath your wings, you can have your justice."

Von Ruden was not smiling. He leaned in, matching Warden's voice. "Killers don't get paroled on a good girl's word."

"Watch it happen," Warden murmured. "You've got some time to fantasize about the possibilities."

Von Ruden dug a finger in his ear. "You still haven't told me what brings you here."

"A mutual goal. You want justice, don't you?"

"I'm not sure it exists in this world."

"Not in the courts. It's up to us," Warden said.

His old client took a deep breath and seemed to grab hold of the idea, if with little excitement.

"You never did anything out of the kindness of your heart, Warden. What's Solomon to you?"

"Ten grand. And some change."

Von Ruden whistled. "Must be a lot of change."

Warden stood and signaled to the guard. "My grandma always said if you look after the pennies, the dollars will take care of themselves."

"Isn't that sweet? And you want me to do it so you can keep your hands clean while you get your cash, is that it?"

"These are the hands that can keep you all lit up, you know. I'll be in touch."

When Molly dropped heavily into the front seat of the Volvo, stack of books in hand, a scent tickled Lexi's nose and she sneezed. Twice.

"What's that smell?"

She believed Molly saw the question as further justification to be contrary. "I don't smell anything."

But Lexi did, and the odor seemed to be coming from her daughter. She glanced Molly's way and sniffed. Molly shifted to face the window.

Her clothes reeked of smoke. Something thicker than cigarettes, and sweeter. The scent of an extinguished match.

The odor was gone by the time Lexi pulled into her carport, and she was thinking about calling in sick. Molly needed her, though she would have denied it. Hugging her library books and slouching as she walked, the girl sulked into the apartment without waiting for Lexi the way she usually did.

The events of the past twelve hours called for a serious rest. Lexi thought that if she could get a little sleep, maybe then she could sort out what to do about her mom's role in the Grant fiasco, patch things up with Molly, and weigh Ward's demand that she testify for Norm.

She picked up her mail on the way into the apartment and found a past-due notice for the phone bill, this on top of the already tardy utility bill. She didn't want to leave Molly with so many loose ends flopping around like live wires. But missing work, especially on the busiest night of the week, could mean the difference between phone service and cutoff. She hurried up the sidewalk at the same time Mort Weatherby passed the foot of the stairs adjacent to the building. The sight of him inspired an idea.

"Hey, Mort!"

The tall computer geek that Gina crushed on paused and ran a hand through his bushy curls. "Hey yourself, Lexi." He offered a smile, but it lacked his usual charisma. "Isn't the Red Rocks in the other direction?"

"Running a little late today."

"Happens to the best of us."

"You okay?"

He crossed his arms and planted his feet. "Fair to middling. That cat of Mrs. Johnson's died this morning, and she's got it in her head that me and Travis had something to do with it."

"Juliet?"

"She scratched me up good last night trying to get her down from 10C." He showed Lexi the inside of his forearm.

"I heard about that, Romeo."

He grinned briefly. "Yeah. We had an audience."

"What happened?"

Mort shrugged. "The cat was on my doorstep when I left for work this morning, stiff as a frozen washcloth. I took it over to Mrs. Johnson's place and she started yelling at me. Maybe I should've dumped it."

"Why would Mrs. Johnson think—?"

"Because she's crotchety and she thinks Travis and I scared the thing to death trying to help it. No good deed goes unpunished and all that."

"We all know you're good guys, Mort. It'll blow over. Maybe she'll even get a new cat."

"Maybe I'll *buy* her a new cat."

Lexi couldn't bring herself to say that was probably a disastrous idea. "Hey, can I ask you a favor?"

"Not if it involves taking your roommate on a date." He didn't smile when he said it.

"Now give me some credit. You know I'll never do that again. I only wondered if you'd keep an eye on my place tonight."

"What for? You all going out?"

"No, but I'd like a manly pair of eyes on my front door. Gina and Molly are home."

"Guy trouble?"

"You can see my front door from your kitchen window, right?"

He followed her eyes across the driveway between their units. "Yeah. Yeah, I guess I can."

Lexi took two steps toward her front door. "So maybe whenever you grab a snack or a drink or whatever tonight, you can take a peek."

"What am I looking for?"

"I don't know. Anything out of the ordinary."

"Anything out of the ordinary happens here, it'll be front-page news."

Lexi sure hoped not.

Inside, Molly had set up camp in the living room. She surrounded herself with library books, her back to the entryway. Nanopod something-or-other earbuds plugged her ears. A Christmas gift from Lexi's mother.

A copy of the *Gobsmacked* DVD Lexi had intended to rent earlier lay on the kitchen table. Gina wore sweats and slippers and was making Ramen on the stovetop. Lexi picked up the movie, an English comedy starring some teen heartthrob who made girls Molly's age swoon.

"Thought Molly and I could watch that tonight," Gina said.

"Yeah. She's mentioned it." There went their Saturday-morning movie. Lexi sighed and put it down, fearing Gina's thoughtfulness might widen the gap between Lexi and her daughter. "I'm sure she'll love it."

"Her and every other fourth grader in the world." Gina rubbed her eyes. "It's right up my alley."

"You look flushed. You okay?"

"Nothing but a headache. Long day. But I can't complain. Your day is just starting."

As it was going on thirty-six hours since Lexi's last honest rest, the day felt pretty old.

"Thanks for cleaning up the paint this morning," Lexi said. "You were probably wondering—"

"What paint?"

"There was paint on the kitchen window."

"From what?"

Lexi paused, all answers out of reach. "It was gone this morning."

The window glass was as clear and bright as ever in the winter afternoon glare. Gina stirred the pot and looked from the window to Lexi and back again.

"You'll never believe what happened to me last night," Lexi said.

"You're late for work."

"I should tell you now."

The music from Molly's earbuds was loud enough for Lexi to hear, which meant the girl wouldn't overhear what her mother planned to say. She watched Molly while telling Gina about the Volvo, Ward, the painted target. The sweet smoky smell on Molly.

Precious Molly.

She left out the parts about Grant and Norm.

When she finished, Gina said, "All I smelled on her was cafeteria fish." Gina was sitting at the table now, sipping soupy noodles off a large spoon. Her glassy eyes told Lexi that she found the tale far-fetched. Or maybe she didn't feel well.

"You said the paint was on the curtains too?" she asked.

"And the doorjamb." Lexi leaned back into the hall to look at it again. Clean. "I can't explain it."

"And you think Ward was responsible?" Skepticism threaded her words. "Why?"

Wishing she'd made a more compelling case, Lexi shoved her hands into her jacket pockets. Her right hand closed around a plastic bag filled with soft contents. She pulled it out.

Her life with Grant had exposed her to enough marijuana to recognize the crushed tealike leaves. Gina must have recognized it too. Her noodle-filled spoon paused halfway to her mouth, then her eyes darted to her bowl. In half a second Lexi decided not to wonder aloud where the bag had come from. That could only make this moment worse.

"You've been working hard," Gina said, examining her spoon. "It's been a long winter. I think you're tired, Lexi. You close late tonight, don't you?"

Lexi couldn't explain why the reply hurt her feelings, even though she wished all those crazy experiences were nothing but the result of an exhausted, warped perception.

"Why didn't you tell me that my mom came by yesterday?"

Gina stirred the soup. "I didn't think it was newsworthy."

"You didn't think it odd that Mom would drop by when I wasn't here?"

Gina talked around the spoon in her mouth.

"I didn't realize you'd banned her from the apartment."

"I haven't *banned* her. But why didn't you tell me?"

"Because I knew you wouldn't sleep if I told you."

"You're not responsible for making sure I sleep, Gina."

"Sure I'm not. But I try to help."

Lexi snatched back *I don't need your help* from where it teetered on her tongue. There was no point in leaving tonight having broken bonds with both Molly and Gina.

"My mother doesn't know how to make decisions that don't hurt people," she said. "She brought Molly a letter from Grant"—Gina's mouth popped open in surprise—"and now Molly's got it in her head that she should meet her dad. If my mom starts poking her nose in my daughter's life, I want to know about it."

"Got it. She comes by tonight, I'll tell her no one's home."

"Be serious, Gina."

"Alright, alright. Lighten up."

"If Molly talks about Grant—"

"I'll fill you in in the morning."

"And please make sure everything stays locked up and—"

"Lexi! You're late for work."

{ chapter 8 }

When Lexi arrived at the Red Rocks Bar and Grill, she parked in the spot
closest to the rear door, then threw the bag of weed in the Dumpster on
her way into the kitchen. She trusted that the disposal service would haul it
away before anyone found it. The presence of the bag was as disturbing as
everything else that had surprised her lately. Who had put it in her pocket?
And when? She'd worn the jacket all day. Even though the bag was no longer in her possession, could a dog smell it in the lining? She worried about
what that might mean for her. For Molly.

The path of her thinking led her straight to Ward, the dealer who had
snared Grant and Norm into his web all those years ago. He was building a new, sticky trap—for her, apparently, and for reasons she didn't yet
understand.

The cool air prickled her skin with goose bumps.

The manager, Chuck, gave her the evil eye when she blew in through the
rear door ten minutes late, but he didn't say anything, and so Lexi pretended
not to notice. In a passageway that doubled as a closet and pantry, she hung
up her coat and her book bag. Lexi had never exchanged her high school book

bag for a purse, partly for financial reasons and partly because she intended to get to college one of these days. The satchel was a hopeful reminder.

When had it turned so grimy and brown? For a second she stared at it and thought the time might have come to give up her dream. Maybe until Molly was grown. Lexi needed money more than a degree right now. That was a wicked catch-22: no degree, less money. Less money to pay for school, no degree.

Lexi sighed. She'd drive into Riverbend before her shift Saturday and fill out applications for the new stores going in. Maybe she and Molly could move.

"Order up!"

The cook's call pulled Lexi back into the kitchen. She tied on her apron, shoved an order pad and pen into the front pocket, and stuck her head out into the dining room. Mr. Tabor had already arrived. She smiled and waved at him. He grinned back, nodding his head in that slow, regal way of kind kings.

She shoved a gigantic red plastic cup against the ice dispenser, then filled it with orange soda and took it to Mr. Tabor with a straw.

"You be blessed today, lovely Lexi!"

"How are you, Mr. Tabor?" The man's aging coffee skin and foamy white hair reminded Lexi of a skinny mocha topped with whipped cream. He was an old soul with a frail body and a Herculean spirit. He'd been a defense attorney until his recent retirement.

He patted his stomach. "Got myself a big ol' hole right here that needs filling."

"I can fix that for you. Who'll be joining you today?"

"Whoever God brings my way."

"Should I go ahead and put in the Reuben for you, or do you want to wait?"

He stuck the straw in the sugary drink and took a long draw. "You'd better feed me, child, or I might evaporate."

Lexi laughed. "Can't have that now, can we?"

"Oh no. That'd be bad news indeed."

"I'll get that right out for you."

Lexi found their daily exchange to be a warm comfort in her routine. She put up the order for his favorite sandwich, then dished his side of sweet deli coleslaw into a Styrofoam cup, sealed it, and dropped it into a paper bag. He liked to take that home for dessert.

A few minutes later she was cramming a paper filter into the industrial-size coffeemaker, asking God how her sister's killer could possibly be up for parole a mere seven years after her death, when the brass bells attached to the front door tinkled against the glass.

Another waitress, Simone, nudged her with an elbow. Lexi followed her eyes, which were scanning the frame of the tallest man Lexi had ever seen. He was broad also, and from where she stood seemed too wide to have come through the door square on. He scraped his boots and removed his gloves.

Through the glass pane of the front windows, Lexi saw a pickup truck parked in the dusty lot. She noticed it for two reasons: First, because it was a bright shiny thing that looked like it had a bazillion horsepower and an engine larger than her living room and a bed big enough to park her rattle-trap Volvo in. It had to be his, judging by size alone. Second, it was painted a deep shade of magenta, a color she'd never seen on any car, let alone a man's.

"Table for one?" Simone was asking him, her hip jutted out to one side. Lexi found herself agog over his towhead and unusual eyes, which were a russet-green, like oxidized copper. He was Norwegian fair. She had a split-second vision of him in plaid flannel and suspenders, felling trees in one of those strong-man contests that aired on late-night cable TV.

"Actually, I'm looking for someone." He said this to Simone but was looking at Lexi. She was annoyed to sense herself blush. She heard coffee grounds hit the linoleum at her feet and realized she was filling the filter without watching. She turned back to her task.

"There he is," she heard him say. "Thanks."

Lexi shoved the coffee basket into its compartment, punched the illuminated red switch, and turned to rescue the Reuben sandwich from the heat lamps.

"Hubba hubba," Simone crooned under her breath as she passed Lexi and entered the kitchen.

The blond giant had taken a seat opposite Mr. Tabor but was too tall to fit his knees under the table. He'd wedged his body into the vinyl booth and left his feet in the aisle. Lexi stepped over them.

"Sorry about those," the man said to her.

She found his apology unnecessary but accepted it with a smile and set the hot plate in front of Mr. Tabor, then put his packaged slaw on the end of the table.

"My dear, you are a doll like my sweet Beulah, God rest her soul." He slipped three ones under his unused spoon and she pretended, as always, not to notice. "This here is my friend, Michael."

"Everyone else calls me Angelo," the stranger said to her.

Lexi chuckled and thought of the custom-colored Chevy. "Are you a self-named artist, or does someone in your family have a sense of humor?"

"My father," Angelo said. "And you are?"

The fear that gripped Lexi when he extended his hand couldn't have been more irrational or unexpected. The sight of that palm, as large as a salad plate, shot an indecipherable warning through her stomach. Her throat filled with regret that she had remarked on his name. Even if a good sense of humor did run in his family, her laughter felt woefully inappropriate.

She wiped her hands on her apron and let him wrap his fingers around hers. He pumped her arm once in a firm greeting.

"Lexi." She jerked her hand away, blushing again. "Get you anything?"

"How about some coffee and hot apple pie?"

"À la mode?"

"Absolutely."

Mr. Tabor laughed and slapped the table. "You'd better bring him the whole pie plate and a bucket of ice cream. One slice won't even whet his whistle." Angelo grinned.

In the awkwardness of not knowing whether the old man was serious,

Lexi hesitated. When Angelo turned his eyes on her, still beaming, she realized he was going to leave her to guess, if she didn't dare to ask.

"You take your coffee black?" she asked.

"Never."

"Maybe you'd like a scoop of ice cream in it too?"

Angelo looked at Mr. Tabor, who was lifting the corned beef and sauerkraut to his lips. "Now how come I've never thought of that?"

"Because she's the brains in this trio, isn't she?" Mr. Tabor bit into the sandwich.

"Apparently so."

Lexi turned away, high stepping over Angelo's feet and considering how to deliver his order.

When she returned minutes later with a mug, a carafe, a slice of pie, a scoop of ice cream on the pie and another in the coffee, and a whole pie (minus one slice) in a box, Mr. Tabor and Angelo had a good laugh.

"Now that's what I call service," Angelo said, eyeing the spread.

"She earns her keep, she does."

Angelo ate four slices of the pie over the three hours that he and Mr. Tabor sat there, talking, and though she couldn't say why, his appetite pleased her. She refilled his carafe twice and wondered at how calm he seemed after what must have been eight cups of coffee.

When the men departed around seven, Angelo pressed the pie box into Mr. Tabor's hands, then left her a tip that was the same amount as his bill. She watched him climb into the pickup and drive out of the lot as she cleared the table.

"Bug's gonna fly into your mouth if you don't close it," Simone said to her as she passed by with a full load of steaming plates.

Lexi snapped out of her stare, embarrassed to have been noticed. She rolled her eyes at Simone.

From the corner of her eye, she caught sight of a patron at booth eleven in the far corner, head bowed into his open menu. How long had he been waiting? Couldn't have been long, or else Chuck would have kicked her in the behind. She'd get to him next if Simone hadn't already helped her out.

The metal-framed glass doors of the restaurant swung open as Lexi stacked the plates, and the cold draft that was the lion's tongue of March licked Lexi's ankles. Two people entered the dining room.

At the sight of them, she walked straight into the back of a chair that protruded from its table and almost lost her load. The collision made furniture and flatware rattle. She caught her balance and prevented a mess. The pair looked in her direction.

Her mother, Alice Grüggen, stood in front of the door, flanked by red vinyl booths and overshadowed by a grim figure tailing her. Grant Solomon, Lexi's estranged husband.

{ chapter 9 }

Lexi and Grant had met in high school, became pregnant with Molly as soon as they graduated, and did the shotgun thing. But those drugs got in the way of their happily-ever-after. There were Grant's drugs and then her sister's murder, and misery came at Lexi like an unavoidable, slow-motion car wreck. Two years after the wedding, she followed Grant out of their little one-room bungalow, clutching a wailing toddler while her meth-cooking husband tried to explain why he couldn't stick around anymore.

To this day she couldn't recall what he said.

What she did remember was how quickly it became clear that she was the only sane Grüggen living and breathing in their little town. Her father's descent into mental illness was more like a free fall, and her mother created a tidy little fantasy world of her own to deny what was happening to their picture-perfect family. Alice ran away, taking up life as a traveling food critic.

Lexi had not forgiven her mother for abandoning her father, no more than she had forgiven Grant for abandoning Molly. If either departure had been about her, Lexi would have put it all behind her. She would have handled it, or at least turned her back on the offense. But her father, Barrett

Grüggen, didn't deserve his wife's neglect. And Molly . . . Grant might have thought the little girl would forget him. Lexi knew the truth firsthand, though: no daughter ever, ever forgot her need for her daddy, even if she couldn't remember his face.

Because Lexi was such a daughter, she believed Alice should never have turned her back on Barrett, no matter how much it hurt to see him change. He'd never done anything to deserve that. Alice's pain wasn't his fault.

Lexi tried to hold them all together, for a few months. She told herself repeatedly that her failure was not worth revisiting. Eventually she gave up. There was only so much a daughter—a wife, a mother—could do or be. So she put all her eggs into a basket called Molly and faithfully visited her father down in Riverbend.

That she had coped at all, even in this unremarkable, my-life-is-still-limping-along kind of way, was due in large part to Gina. And Jesus. Gina and Jesus. Lexi thought the two went together like Ben and Jerry, like Fred and Ginger.

"Lexi and Jesus" didn't roll off the tongue as nicely, but at the time, she figured that was to be expected. Gina introduced Jesus to her the day Barrett was given permanent residency status at the mental hospital, the day Alice listed the home Lexi grew up in, the day Lexi had to admit she'd failed. At everything. Jesus didn't mind that, Gina said. He was all about second and third and fourth and fifth chances.

Lexi needed another chance. Because she loved Molly and Barrett so much.

It was this same love—Lexi was convinced of it—that today spun her away from Alice and Grant and propelled her into the kitchen, where she dumped her load of dirty dishes into the bus bin so carelessly that one of the plates chipped. She took a deep breath, almost not caring if Chuck noticed.

How dare they come here? *Here*, where she worked, on the busiest night of the week, where enough witnesses would recognize Grant to keep the gossip mills churning out stories for months?

How *dare* they?

She decided to let Simone seat them. Lexi headed back to take care of the customer who'd been waiting.

It was impossible not to see them from the corner of her eye when she reentered the dining room. Lexi felt the skin of her neck warm up. Those faces, eyeing her like a specimen in a jar, were the portrait of gall.

"Get you something to drink?" she muttered to the man in booth eleven, fishing in her pocket for the notepad. She glanced back to Alice and Grant, who seemed to be deciding whether to seat themselves. Simone was headed in their direction.

"I'll have me a Blue Devil," the man said.

The voice. The drink. Lexi's gaze snapped to him.

"Ward. Warden." It was a toss-up as to whether facing her mother and her ex would have been more enjoyable than this.

"Hey there, Sexy Lexi."

"You know I hate that."

"Deep down, you don't. Good seeing you again."

Lexi huffed. "What do you want?"

"All I ever wanted is you, you know that." He leaned in, neck long, chin up, then laughed low at his joke that wasn't exactly a joke.

"I mean to eat."

"Your little girl cooked up some mighty fine spaghetti last night. Got any more of that?"

Lexi leaned forward and placed her palms on Ward's table, more to hold herself up than to appear intimidating, which was impossible. "You stay out of my house."

Warden grinned so big that his eyebrows disappeared under his knit cap. He threw one arm across the back of the booth.

She backed away from the table and escaped through a pair of swinging doors into the bar, trying to make sense of the storm that was brewing out in the dining room. Her palms were sweaty. After seven years of routine, how was it possible that everything could be reduced to chaos in a matter of hours? Next thing she knew, Norman Von Ruden would barge in and order a basket of French fries.

She gave the bartender Ward's drink order, then leaned on the bar and pretended to watch the TV, wondering how love could disintegrate into resentment. There was a time when she'd cared for all of them deeply: her mom, Grant, Norman, even Ward, whom she never loved but found to be a decent fellow once upon a time. How could she feel such extreme opposite emotions toward the same people?

The answer to that came easy: *Because they failed. Spectacularly. They failed me. They failed Molly.*

Of course, she'd failed many times in her life. She'd even failed people, but this is what set her apart from the adults out in that dining room: she had never failed someone and then abandoned them. She had never failed them and then tried to meddle in their lives as if she knew what was best for them.

As Lexi stood at the counter and watched the bartender mix a strange brew, the arrival of her mother and husband took on new clarity. If she had any hope of extracting this wedge that had come between her and Molly, she would have to put her mom and Grant, these failures, in their place. Which was not here.

Ward was a different kind of animal, though. She didn't know what to expect of his reappearance. Would he stalk her until she agreed to testify? She wondered if Grant had noticed Ward.

She wondered if they had stayed in touch all these years.

Lexi set the highball glass full of swirling blue alcohol on a round tray and swooped it up, heading back for the dining room.

She pushed through the double doors with one hand and saw that Simone had seated Alice and Grant in the nearest booth, to the right. Something told Lexi they'd requested this seat, maybe the fact that their eyes were on her as she returned. Grant, sitting with his back to the bar, had to twist his head nearly off his neck to get a look, but he was as focused on Lexi as her mom was.

He slipped out of the booth, gripping a pair of gloves with both hands, and placed himself right in her path.

"Lexi," he said. He looked at his feet, and she was glad he had the decency to look ashamed.

She matched him toe-to-toe. "What are you doing here? You have no right." Lexi's fury contained itself at a low, discreet volume. The restaurant was busy, though not packed, and she wouldn't make a scene. Not here. She looked at her mother. "*You* had no right, sending Molly a letter like that behind my back."

Grant said, "I tried to explain—"

"Did you even read it, Mom? You're supposed to protect her, protect *us*, from that kind of poison. And you"—she turned back to Grant—"you don't have any idea how to handle the heart of a nine-year-old girl. What were you *thinking*? How could you do that to Molly? What did you expect would happen?"

Grant blinked. His eyes darted to Alice, then back to Lexi. She saw Molly's profile in the shape of his jawline. Her anger roiled, but her memory traced his attractive features, his light blue eyes that contrasted with his dark brown hair. She used to tell him that his slight build and intense expressions reminded her of a young Sean Penn.

Grant used to stand straighter. His shoulders were square once upon a time; now, everything stooped. He looked older, and thinner.

"A letter 'like that'?" Alice asked, then sighed. "I worried this would happen."

Why did she insist on these games?

"You're right," Grant said. "I shouldn't have put Molly in that position. I called this morning to try to sort that out. I'm sorry, Lexi."

Her mouth fell open at this. It took a long moment for Lexi to give words to her shock.

"You've been gone for seven years, and you're apologizing for that letter?"

"I owe you more apologies than I can count," he said.

She dropped her voice to a whisper.

"You left us, stoned out of your mind, with five dollars in the checking account and a brick of cheese in the refrigerator, and you think—"

"I'm so sorry. Please. Forgive me."

Forgive him? *Forgive* him? Just like that? No explanation, no excuse, no can-I-make-it-up-to-you?

"Is this a joke? Showing up *here*, and *now*? As if you can trap me under some fluorescent lights and brainwash me into forgiving you for . . . for . . . a slanderous letter?"

Grant looked confused. "Slanderous?"

Alice spoke up. "It seemed wise to have our first meeting in a public place."

"Yes, I see how that might prevent a *murder*."

Her mother flinched. Alice recovered with, "Like I said."

"I can suggest a dozen other public places in this small town where I'm not employed."

"And I don't suppose you would have actually shown up at any of those places, would you?"

"No."

Alice put her hand over her heart and picked up a menu. "Do they still make that rosemary meat loaf here?"

Lexi scowled and bit her lip, because she could feel tears rising in her eyes. Grant's eyes glistened, too, and she couldn't fathom why. "Please, just go," she said.

"When can I talk to you?" Grant asked.

"You've said all I need to hear." Lexi leaned in toward her mother. "And *you'll* be lucky if I ever let you near Molly again."

Alice waved off the threat as if she didn't have time for the drama anymore. Having been reduced to the status of an immature child, Lexi chose to act like one, making her exit in the form of a sharp turn away from the table.

"Lexi, please." Grant reached out to stop her.

His fingers touched Lexi's elbow and she jerked it away from him. He was faster than she was, though, more desperate. He seized her wrist before she retracted it too.

Grant had never been a violent man. Even when his mind was completely clouded over by the meth, he'd never raised anything more than his voice against Lexi or Molly. So she couldn't have said why his touch made her cower as if he was going to hit her. She wasn't consciously afraid of him. But when his fingers closed like a handcuff around her wrist, her body reacted.

She felt the cold puff of March wind on her legs again, as if the front door had been reopened. She smelled a hint of that sweet smoke. She turned her eyes away, sank into a crouch, and raised her opposite arm to cover her face.

The tray carrying the Blue Devil tilted, and the glass hit the chrome corner of a table before bouncing off and shattering on the floor. The gin and Blue Curacao and who knew what else splattered everything on the aisle. The little round tray took off like a downhill snowball, rolling on its side the full length of the dining room, until it clattered to a stop against the rear wall. The whole restaurant turned to look.

Lexi straightened, not daring to catch anyone's eye.

Grant was bent, picking up glass.

Simone, who never moved anywhere slowly, was already using bar towels to wipe the mess into a contained disaster area.

"Thanks, Simone," Lexi muttered, taking over her towels.

"What was it?" she asked.

"A Blue Devil."

"I'll get you another one. Where was it supposed to go?"

"Booth eleven."

Simone missed a beat, and Lexi thought she'd gone. But her feet were still planted.

"You sure?" she asked.

"Yeah I'm sure." The cold floor hurt Lexi's knees. Her mom was still looking at a menu as if none of them existed. Grant had stepped aside for Chuck, who appeared with a mop in a wheeled yellow bucket.

"Well, take a look around, hon, and tell me who ordered it. There hasn't been anyone in booth eleven since last weekend."

"Simone . . ." Lexi craned her neck and gestured toward the booth in the corner of the room. It was empty.

She sighed, stood, and glanced around the dining room.

"Forget it," she told Simone. "He must've left."

"Lucky you. Chuck'll be sticking you with the tab, you know."

He would. Chuck was scowling at the mess. This was exactly the kind of stunt Ward loved to pull. Lexi sighed again and got off the floor, then walked over to the empty booth. The menu was still lying on the table. If Ward had any decency, which he didn't, he would have left her a few bucks before taking off. It was irrational of her to hope for it, and yet she did. She dropped the sopping wet bar towels in a bin under the drink station, then took three steps to number eleven and picked up the menu.

Instead of cash, there was a photo. Lexi knew the photo well. It was of her and her daughter, a snapshot taken at a Mother's Day tea Molly's class had hosted back when she was in first grade. Another mom offered to take their picture, then sent them a copy. Lexi kept it in the Volvo, tucked into the plastic panel that covered the speedometer.

Her hand shook as she lifted it off the table. Ward had drawn on the print, bold black concentric circles forming a target. The bull's-eye obscured Molly's sweet face. A message was printed on the outside ring, one line of handwritten block letters.

"Come and get her."

Lexi felt her fingers go cold. The message made no sense, but the writing . . .

The writing was hers.

Turning, she scanned the dining room a second time, wanting Ward to explain this to her. No sign of him. She shoved the photo into her apron pocket.

One of the cooks leaned out into the dining room from the kitchen. He was waving a cordless phone receiver over his head.

"Lexi, call for you."

As one, Mom, Grant, Simone, and Chuck turned her way. The cook interpreted Lexi's surprised expression correctly. She never took calls at work unless . . .

"It's an emergency."

{ chapter 10 }

When Lexi took the receiver, Molly's agitated voice came over the line. "Mom, I'm going to the hospital!" she announced.

"Are you okay?"

"I'm fine, Mom, but Gina's super sick."

"She's driving you?"

"No. Mort's driving me. He let me use his phone."

Lexi tried to stay calm. "You're going to have to start at the beginning, hon. What happened?"

"Mort saw the ambulance come, and he helped."

"An ambulance, huh?"

"Gina threw up, and she was shaking, and she wouldn't talk to me. I don't know if she could hear me. She was in the bathroom, but she left the door open."

"So Gina's with the paramedics?"

"I called 9-1-1."

"You did good, Molly. That was really quick thinking. I'm proud of you. Are you scared?"

"Nah," Molly lied. She hadn't hit the age where she was good at hiding things from her mother, and Lexi was glad for it.

"Don't worry about a thing, okay? They'll take care of Gina. They know what they're doing. Which hospital are you going to?" She was already in the pantry-coat-closet passageway, shrugging into her jacket. Molly turned her mouth away from her phone and asked Mort.

"St. Luke's," she said when she came back on.

Lexi stayed only long enough to call Debbie and beg her to take over the shift, then she was out the door and driving down the mountain in her lopsided car toward St. Luke's, which was a good thirty minutes away in Riverbend.

With some guilt, because her relief came at Gina's expense, Lexi felt like she'd escaped a worse situation.

Somehow, she reached the hospital before Molly and Mort did. She found Gina but wasn't allowed to see her. They were stabilizing her, the staff told Lexi, and running some tests. That was all the information she got. No one would say whether Gina would be okay or what was wrong, and Lexi accused a nurse of being an undercover secret service agent preventing her access to the doctors.

Separated from Gina by a brigade of scrubs and several secure hospital doors, she paced the floors looking for Molly and Mort, wishing she had his cell phone number. She couldn't imagine what was taking them so long. They should have arrived ahead of her, if not at roughly the same time.

The clerk who sat at the front of the ER admitting patients watched Lexi out of the corner of her eye. Lexi made a triangular trek around the floor, meandering from the main desk, to the door that separated her from Gina, to the emergency room entrance, expecting to see her daughter and friend. A fluorescent light fizzled out, turning the sea-foam green carpet a darker shade of gray. An elderly man, the only other person in the waiting room, who had not moved since she arrived, held a cup of coffee that he did not drink and watched an infomercial.

Twenty minutes passed, and Lexi's anxiety rose. If Mort didn't show up in the next five minutes, she decided, she'd get in her car and drive the route from the hospital to her home.

Her mind went to Angelo's great big pink truck. There was no doubt in her mind, though she knew nothing about him, that he would have been happy to drive around looking for Mort and Molly. Lexi figured it was wishful thinking and left it at that.

On one of her return trips to the front doors, a siren drew her outside.

Two sirens, belonging to two ambulances whose flashing lights slapped her face and reflected off the ER windows. She watched them drive into the bay twenty feet to her right and park next to each other.

Their arrival was followed by a practiced scurrying of medics, quick but not frantic, self-assured, assessing information at a rate that outpaced Lexi's tired mind. Two gurneys came out of the first ambulance. An EMT started rambling to a nurse as the gurneys were pushed toward the swinging doors. Lexi thought it was a nurse—nurse, doctor, PA, resident; she couldn't tell the difference, no more than she could understand all the lingo.

The other vehicle's rear doors parted, and a sheriff's deputy emerged first.

A sheriff's deputy?

He was almost as large as Angelo, and he helped pull the gurney out of the back of the first vehicle with one hand.

Lexi was pondering the incongruity of an officer in the back of an ambulance when a small voice lit a fire under her feet.

"Is my mom here?"

Molly's voice. Molly's voice, coming from the gurney that was being wheeled into the hospital. *Dear Jesus, my daughter's on a gurney.*

Dear Jesus, we're uninsured.

Lexi was horrified for thinking it, but there it was—the truth of her fears rearing up before anything else. Just as quickly, the ever-present reality of never having enough money for what was necessary vanished, and she was running, chasing that bed on wheels into the emergency room.

"Molly!"

"Mom!" The girl tried to sit up and managed to get propped on an elbow. She had a bandage on her cheek but she looked to be in one piece. She wasn't even bloody. *Thank you, Jesus.*

Lexi grabbed her outstretched hand and Molly smiled, then started sobbing. The person pushing the bed had the kindness to stop so Lexi could embrace her. She glanced at the tech, a soft-cheeked woman who probably could shush wailing infants with that tender gaze. That she had been the one with Molly was a balm to Lexi's sick heart.

"This brave soul busted her ankle up," the woman said, "but she's otherwise fine. It could have been so much worse."

"What happened?"

Lexi didn't get the story right away, but piecemeal from Molly, and eventually from Mort, who almost didn't make it. It was an unbelievable story made simple by Molly's childlike point of view, in which life happens without question.

Lexi found it to be a story that was hard not to question, though witnesses confirmed it.

After Molly called her mom, she handed the phone back to Mort as they passed through a major intersection six blocks from the hospital. A call came in before she'd even handed it off, and Mort flipped the phone open. He did not see, though Molly said she did, the government-licensed Suburban that ran the red light and came right at them.

Molly even claimed to have seen the driver, and she remarked on this to Lexi because she said his long narrow face and sunken cheeks reminded her of Cruella De Vil driving her motor car at reckless speeds.

The Suburban T-boned Mort's SUV precisely at the driver's seat. Mort suffered all manner of injuries that the doctors said would take him many months to recover from, including a ruptured spleen and six broken ribs, one of which punctured his lung.

Molly was thrown from the car, squirted like a grape from its skin out the passenger-side window. She swore she was wearing her seat belt, and the investigator who examined Mort's car confirmed that her belt buckle was firmly latched. The strap, however, was snapped apart in two places, across the shoulder and across the lap, frayed as though it had been chewed in two by a mouse.

He'd never seen anything like it in his twenty-year career, the detective said.

As if the same force that broke her seat belt also broke glass, Molly's window was snapped off at the door frame, broken clean, though it was rolled up, snug against the chilly evening in its tidy little window seal. Apart from this being a physical impossibility, the detective said, the safety glass should have shattered when Molly hit it. She should have been severely injured. And yet investigators found the pane lying in the street, whole, twenty-five yards away from the point of impact.

Strange, all of it, but inconsequential compared to what happened after Molly flew out of the car.

A truck driving parallel to Mort's SUV was approaching on the inside lane and was entering the intersection when the Suburban hit. There was the impact, then Molly flying out the window, then her hitting the windshield of the truck as its momentum carried it through, swooping her away from disaster. The truck that caught her accelerated and shot out of the way, while the Suburban plowed Mort's car across all three lanes and into oncoming traffic, where an eighteen-wheeler shaved off the passenger side like a potato peel. The passenger side. The side where Molly had been sitting, where she had been securely belted in.

When Lexi heard this story she vomited into a trash can. There were so many ways Molly should have died within that five-second span. The weight of them all landed like a virus in her stomach.

Lexi hated hospitals. She hated the death-defying smell and the colorless rooms and the squeaky floors. And she especially hated hospitals at night. They were eerie as the dead, with those unnatural lights and cryptlike halls and staff moving around like zombies.

The only thing she hated more than hospitals at night was being at the hospital at night with a loved one. Two loved ones.

By twelve thirty Friday—make that Saturday morning—she'd been sitting in the molded plastic chair of the emergency room bay for hours, disbelieving the impossible chain of events that had put her there.

Lexi waited for Molly to be splinted and discharged, and then they waited together for news of Gina and Mort. Holding hands, they sat in the desolate waiting room with the same lonely, head-bowed man, Molly finally collapsing into sleep, breathing noisily through her open mouth, her foot propped up in the wheelchair.

Gina's mother rushed in at twelve forty with uncombed hair and a wild-eyed expression. She hugged Lexi and promised to bring whatever news she could get. At five minutes to one she returned to the waiting room and said Gina was slipping in and out of consciousness.

"Could it be the flu?" Lexi asked. "She wasn't feeling well when I left her today."

Mrs. Harper was holding her purse to her chest as if it were a comforting pillow. "If it's the flu, it's the worst case I've ever seen."

"What are the doctors saying?"

"They don't know. They just don't know."

Lexi took Mrs. Harper's hand. "I'll stay with you tonight."

"No, no." She shook her head and squeezed Lexi's fingers, then looked at Molly. "You get that little girl home. She needs rest. And she needs you like Gina needs me."

Lexi nodded, relieved but also worried. Mrs. Harper went back to Gina.

Molly stirred as Lexi prepared to leave, and a detective entered the waiting room. His name tag said Reyes. He was taking a report of the accident and asked if he could speak to her. During the conversation, the detective speculated that Molly broke her ankle because it snagged Mort's window frame as the truck caught her and barreled through.

A Chevy truck.

A magenta Chevy truck.

Angelo's truck.

Lexi gripped the arm of Molly's wheelchair.

"I know that truck," she said. Detective Reyes and Molly seemed surprised. "It's Angelo's."

Reyes checked his notes and allowed himself a half grin. "Michael."

"Right. I just met him today—yesterday. Where is he?"

"We released him at the scene. He isn't implicated in anything except a little heroism." He winked at Molly.

"You can take me to work with you tomorrow to meet him, Mom," she said.

"Or you can meet him yourself right now," Lexi said, rising, because with the same kind of timing he had demonstrated in saving Molly's life, Angelo approached the emergency room doors and caught her eye while he was still outside.

He waved, then ducked slightly to come through the entrance without hitting his head. Molly gave Lexi a wide-eyed "wow" look.

Angelo nodded at Reyes and extended his hand for a shake.

Lexi crossed her arms over her aching stomach and cleared her throat, then took a step toward him. "I think I should say thanks," she said, itching to know how he'd come to be where Molly was right when he was most needed. "Except that it seems inadequate."

"You don't have to say anything. How are ya, Molly?"

She grinned, uncharacteristically shy. Her right cheek was bruised. Lexi looked back at Angelo. "I have a million questions . . ."

She stopped midsentence, because she didn't realize until that moment that two people had come into the hospital behind Angelo and now stood a short ways off.

Grant and Alice. Again.

Her mother made a beeline for Molly, who lifted her arms for a hug. Grant stayed put.

"What are they doing here?"

"You'll need their help," Angelo said.

"You don't know anything about what I need," she said without think-ing, then closed her eyes, overcome with embarrassment. "I'm so sorry. I didn't mean to snap at you."

"I understand."

"How can you possibly understand? I just met you. You don't even know these people."

"Your mother, your husband," he said, possessing all the kindness and patience exhaustion had stolen from her.

"My ex-husband."

"You're still married."

"Good grief! How do you know that?"

Angelo placed his forefingers at his temples and closed his eyes. "I can read minds," Angelo said. He opened his eyes. "Of course, it's much easier to do that when people tell me what I want to know."

Lexi didn't know whether to feel grateful or ticked. This man was sticking his nose into her business. Considering he was the hero of the day, though, and the fact that her gratitude was at an all-time high, she didn't dare accuse him. She wasn't sure she had the right.

"Grant told you," she said.

Angelo nodded.

She intentionally avoided looking at the people she'd only recently escaped. Molly was holding Alice's hand but looking at Grant, who was the obvious question in her mind. Lexi had never shown Molly a picture of him, having burned them all after he left. She had tried to compensate by preserving a decent image of him in her mind.

"Having them here, now, doesn't help me at all," Lexi told Angelo.

"You might be surprised."

Another detective came in through the secure doors to join Reyes.

"I've had enough surprises for one day."

Angelo glanced at the ER windows, reflective like black mirrors against the night, as he said, "Then brace yourself."

There was no time to ask what he meant. The man who joined Reyes was named Matthas, according to his name tag.

"He's still unconscious," Matthas told Reyes. "It could be awhile before we get his take on things."

"Mort's unconscious?" Lexi said. He was sedated but aware when she'd seen him an hour earlier.

"Not him," Reyes said. "The guy in the Suburban."

"The driver?" What a terrible night this was turning out to be. Lexi sank back into her chair.

"Passenger. Driver's fine—a walking testimonial to seat belts and airbags, which says a lot for a penitentiary transport."

"A what?"

"Guy's a felon," said Matthas. "They were transferring him to the prison downtown. He was cuffed but not belted. Bounced around inside the cab and split his head open."

Lexi cringed.

"Don't waste your sympathy on this one. Like I said, he's a con."

"Even so."

"A killer," Reyes said. "You might have heard of him a few years back."

"I don't follow the news too closely," Lexi muttered, ready for everyone except maybe Angelo to leave her alone with her daughter. "No time."

"Murdered a young woman at a shopping mall," Matthas said. Angelo caught Lexi's eye, and his gaze alone held her upright. That was when she understood he'd seen this coming. "Name's Norman Von Ruden."

{ chapter 11 }

Warden Pavo stood on the outside of the ER looking in, seething, his hot breath fogging the glass.

Blast that Craven! A car wreck, of all things. If bodily harm was his aim, he should have sent Mort Weatherby skiing off a mountainside, or brought the dead cat's grieving owner after him with a shotgun. That flimsy twig had no idea what he was messing with, no idea what he had set in motion.

Warden snatched his knit cap off his head and wrapped his left fist in it, condemning Craven with every vile curse he knew. He would not allow the creature's insignificant business with Mort to interfere with his own plans again.

Grant turned away from the hospital scene where he was not welcomed and stared at his reflection in the black glass of the hospital waiting room, pretending to look outside. For many years Grant had wondered what Lexi told Molly about him. Life in a cage had given him more time to think than he wanted. He'd spent weeks beating his head on the cinder block trying to create enough noise to drown out the truth: he was a waste of a man. No matter what terrible things Lexi might have to say about him, they couldn't be worse than that fact. There could be no kind way of stating the kind of man he was, the kind of husband who'd failed his wife, the kind of father who'd disappointed his only child.

Once, he tried to die. He took the relatively simple approach of starving himself, which was ridiculous in hindsight. When lack of food made him weaker than he was in the first place, all the authorities had to do was pick him up off the floor of the cell and stick a feeding tube in his stomach.

At the time, Grant believed that resurrecting a dead man against his will was worse than the death penalty. Because even in something as selfish and simple as suicide, he was a complete failure. And he'd proved his idiocy again by letting Alice take that letter to Molly instead of going to Lexi himself first.

He willed his thoughts to stay under control. If he let them run on like this they'd only take him right back to where he started, which was at the bottom of a tar pit that would suck him down for good next time.

Take every thought captive.

That's what Richard had said, wasn't it? Grant planned to look it up when he got back home.

Take every thought captive. Richard must have known how brainless that directive would sound to a man sitting in Terminal Island prison for four years. As if Grant's thoughts weren't already captive, banging like a riot on the bars of his head, demanding to be heard, cursing him and condemning him to die.

Richard said that wasn't what the saying meant. You gotta take command of those thoughts, he said. You have authority over them and not the other way around, he said. If you don't corral those guys and keep them in their place, you won't be able to sort the lies from the truth anymore, and then whadya think is gonna happen?

What did Grant think was going to happen? Nothing worse than what had already happened, that was for sure.

The sound of Richard's voice willing Grant's accusing thoughts to be silent made him smile now. But back then, Grant thought the guy was just another wacko, like him but high on a different kind of drug. A religious one. And Grant sure couldn't see how that was any improvement over his own choice of anesthesia. He figured religion did as much damage, killed as many people or more, triggered far greater wars than a few cartels ever managed to pull off.

Maybe that was true on some level. But eventually Grant came to see that it was beside the point.

Because what was going to happen was that Grant was going to die. Either way, he was going to die. He'd die if they let him out at the end of his five years, because he'd go back to his bongs and blades and papers and syringes and cookstoves and off himself right that time. And if he couldn't, if he was still such a failure that he couldn't do even that, he'd die behind bars, where a second round of cold-turkey withdrawals would do what he was too weak to do himself.

Grant decided he'd rather not die alone. Richard was a little off in the head, but he was a warm body and a decent listener. So when he'd come to Terminal Island twice a month with his ratty paperback Bible, Grant went to hear him talk in the drab room where cons with nothing better to do would trickle in. Then after he was done and the men all filed out, Grant would hang around to have someone to talk to, and Richard would listen to him.

They sat on a worn blue utility carpet that had been unrolled on the concrete slab. The prison didn't allow folding chairs, which only begged men like Grant to pick them up and hurl them at each other.

Sometimes Richard pointed out Scriptures that he thought would interest Grant. Sometimes he'd loan Grant the good book.

It was something to read.

Grant started dreaming about Richard between his visits. He'd dream they were in a boxing ring and Richard was Triple H, even though the only similarities between the two men was their long blond hair and their weight. The match was never fair, as Grant had never even qualified for the lightweight wrestling class in high school. Richard would beat Grant until he couldn't see out of either eye, then scoop Grant up by the armpits and tell him to fight, that he couldn't do it for him.

You gotta fight your own demons, Richard kept shouting.

Once, Grant told Richard about this recurring dream and the minister laughed. That'd be a sight, he said, you and me on WWF. Richard was almost sixty, at least three twenty-five and paunchy, and four inches taller than Grant. He kept his receding hair tied back at the base of his neck.

Grant had wanted to know what the dream meant.

Richard said he didn't know, but maybe it had something to do with how Grant felt about their meetings.

I don't feel like I want to beat you up, Grant said.

Good, Richard said, 'cause if you can't even do it in a dream you're in a world of hurt.

That was the first time Grant had laughed in . . . well, the first time that he could remember he'd laughed since he hadn't been blitzed.

Then he told Grant maybe he was getting ready to do some mortal combat with the truth. Those were his very words: "mortal combat with the truth."

Grant crossed his arms and slouched over the thin carpet.

"What if all these months we've been talking, you've actually been hearing me?" Richard asked.

"Of course I've been hearing you."

"You been listening, but hearing? No, that hasn't happened quite yet."

"You're splitting hairs."

"No, no. I'll tell you the difference: You listen, you can tell me what I've been saying. You hear, you do more than that. You take what I say to heart. You think maybe it's true. You think maybe you should quit arguing with it and give it a try."

"Well then maybe I don't believe it's true yet."

"I think you're coming up on the idea."

"I'm a hard man to convince."

"What if it's true, then? What if everything Jesus said is right? What if a man can change?"

"No offense to Jesus, but I haven't seen much proof of it in me or anyone else."

Richard guffawed at that. "You're still a kid. You haven't even hit thirty. What do you know?"

"I'm just saying."

"Would you *want* to know if you could?"

"Maybe."

"Well, *what if*, then? What if? That's all you have to ask yourself."

"And then what? Abracadabra? Poof?"

Richard smiled. "That'd be step one, or something like it."

"And after that?"

"When's the last time you had contact with your wife?" he asked.

Grant got up and left. He skipped Richard's next visit.

Lexi probably had divorced him—should have divorced him—on grounds of abandonment. The possibility stayed in the front of Grant's mind like a splattered bug on a windshield. If she hadn't divorced him already, she would when she learned why he'd left.

There was also the possibility that his little girl had become another man's daughter. He wasn't sure what the worse failure would be.

Grant lived the dream two more times before seeing Richard again.

The first time, Lexi and Molly, still a toddler, were standing in the corner of the spotlit ring, watching Grant fall under Richard's devastating fists. You gotta fight your own demons, Triple H kept saying. You gotta *want* to.

Lexi picked up their daughter, who hid her face in her mother's shoulder. Lexi looked away, disgusted, when Grant took a hit to his groin. He woke on his cot curled in a fetal ball, feeling humiliated.

The second time, it wasn't a dream at all.

On a blistering summer day out in the yard, where Grant had no friends and, therefore, plenty of enemies, he was jumped by a rookie who had something to prove for a gang initiation. The guy was no Triple H, but he was bigger than Grant anyway and probably in for something like armed robbery rather than drug possession. He hit Grant from behind, driving between his shoulder blades and pinning his arms. Grant landed on his nose, breaking it. His mouth filled with blood and dry yellow dirt. The dude landed on Grant's back, held his wrists in one hand and grabbed his hair with another, then started pounding Grant's face into the ground.

He sensed more than saw the men in the yard clear a circle.

He tasted liquid copper while his forehead beat a small crater into the dust. A black fog rolled in over his mental landscape, and he relaxed. This would be a good way to die.

But Richard was shouting at him.

Darn that Richard, Grant couldn't get him out of his head even then. The one-voice riot was louder than any of the crowd's cheers, rooting for the sake of small-minded entertainment.

Prove it, Grant thought. He wasn't sure if he was talking to himself or to Richard.

Grant freed one arm and rolled out from under the attacker, trapping the guy's hand by lying on top of it. Grant held him in place and kicked the side of his head.

The kid swore and dropped to the dirt, clawing at Grant's neck. His knees fired like pistons and the men tumbled, a mass of sweat and teeth, and blood from Grant's nose.

Grant still wasn't sure how long the fight went on, nor how it unfolded from there, but when it finished they were both in the infirmary and the other guy had a dislocated shoulder and was crying. He was just a boy in spite of his size, and scared to death about what had happened. Grant wasn't sure what consequences he faced as far as his little gang was concerned, but it seemed clear enough that the kid was afraid of him.

That was a change.

"Please don't kill me," he blubbered. "Man, I'm sorry."

Kill him? Grant thought he'd been fighting for his own life.

NEVER LET YOU *GO*

"Relax," Grant said. "I'm not going to kill you."

A nurse was taping his nose, and the agony of it was a knife into his eyes. Grant yelled at her and gripped her wrist to release the pressure of her fingers.

He opened his eyes and saw it was Molly standing over him with gauze and a calm expression. His brain's manifestation of a grown-up Molly, who looked so much like Lexi the day he married her, looking at him like he'd never do her any wrong.

"Relax," she said. "I'm not going to kill you."

The pain shot into his skull.

"I'm sorry," he whispered. "I'm so sorry." And he gave in to the overwhelming ache.

The next time Richard came to the prison, Grant asked him for help. Help without Jesus needing to be part of the deal. He wasn't ready to commit to something he wasn't a hundred percent sure of. Truth was, he doubted God's willingness to forgive him. Some things were too wrong. Too big.

Richard seemed to understand but stuck with him anyway. Ten months later when Grant got out, Richard set up the trailer arrangements in Riverbend and got him three job interviews and a used car.

Today, Grant still had no answer on the question of Jesus, though he'd recently taken up the habit of praying—in an eyes-open, send-up-your-random-thoughts kind of way. A thank-you-God-my-daughter's-safe kind of way.

Grant had recognized Molly the instant he saw her at the hospital, her ankle propped up on that wheelchair. He would have recognized her on the street. She was so beautiful, like her mom. The sight of her punched him in the gut. He was overcome with relief that her injuries weren't worse. He felt the strangest combination of pride and heartbreak and protectiveness and shame.

She saw him, too, and he thought she might have known who he was. There was no hate in her eyes, not that he could see. She was young enough that he figured maybe he could repair the damage he'd caused without terrible lingering effects. He needed something in his life not to fail, and he saw the greatest hope of that in Molly.

Her mother was a different story. Still, he'd try to fix those problems too. He'd try and try.

As much as he'd wanted to say something to Molly there in the hospital, there was no appropriate moment. Lexi stood between them, and then, by way of announcement, Norman Von Ruden was there in the room too.

In the reflection of the dark hospital window, Grant watched the officers speak with Lexi. He turned around at the sound of Von Ruden's name and saw Lexi blanch. She tucked her hair behind her ear, then rested her pointer finger on her lips, a gesture he recognized as belonging to frayed nerves. The news that her sister's killer was here, tonight, could only add to her stress.

His eyes met Lexi's for half a second. The anger in her glare at the restaurant had been replaced by anxiety, he thought, and he wondered why. Grant took a step toward her without evaluating whether he should.

She spun away from him and took hold of Molly's wheelchair.

"I need to get my daughter home now," she said, pushing with the full weight of her small body.

Alice said something. Grant didn't hear the words, nor Lexi's terse reply, because Molly was looking at him. She lifted her fingers off the arm of the chair in a barely perceptible wave.

Grant waved back. Lexi didn't seem to notice.

{ chapter 12 }

Saturday morning Lexi woke with her arm slung across Molly's flat narrow belly. She hadn't let her daughter out of reach since she'd been discharged.

Oh God. Thank you for protecting her. Thank you for not taking my precious girl from me. Please tell me what to do so Ward can't touch her.

The doctor expected Molly back for a cast when the swelling went down. A pillow propped up her braced foot, and a cardboard-box tent surrounded her ankle to protect it from the tug of blankets. She snored.

Miraculously, Lexi had been able to sleep a few hours. But she awoke with the churning mind of a woman who did not know how to untangle the sheets of the bed she'd made for herself.

She woke thinking of Norman Von Ruden. When Grant and Lexi had been married one year, and Grant's attention was riding away from her and Molly on a wave of methamphetamines, Lexi had an affair with Norm—an affair that no one ever discovered, an affair that she never broke off.

His murder of Tara was what finally ended things. Not some courageous act on Lexi's part. Saturday morning she woke with no feelings toward him except hatred and hostility. The morning marked no change in what she'd felt toward him for years now, except that circumstances had split open her tidy storage of feelings like a rotten, fermenting melon. He had destroyed everything she held dear. Everything except Molly, and Grant was doing enough on that side of things to make Lexi want to drop the fetid melon on his head.

She held Grant responsible for the whole mess. He was the one who brought Norman and Ward into their home. While Lexi held Molly on her hip, Grant told her to fix up some supper for them while they took care of some business.

Business. The business of death. Ward, as it turned out, was Grant's supplier of far more than meth ingredients. Though she didn't know it at the time, Grant could get anything from Ward. Anything illicit. Which was why Norman, a sensible businessman of good means, had come out of Riverbend to find Grant. He needed antidepressants, which shouldn't have been hard to come by except that he and his wife were going through adoption proceedings, and if he'd gone to a physician for any diagnosis that warranted such pills, their application would have been blacklisted.

Lexi knew none of this about Norm until after the trial.

It was a strange and backward world, she thought afterward, that Norman would go to such pains on behalf of his family and simultaneously dash it to pieces by getting involved with Grant and her.

When Ward told Grant he could get Norman something more effective than the standard Prozac, Norman decided to look into it. Lexi never knew why. Nor did she know why Ward agreed to meet Norman.

What she did remember about that first night when Grant brought them home was how stunning Ward was. *Handsome* was not an adequate word. *Beautiful, imposing, perfect* came to mind. It was hard for her to reconcile this memory of Ward to the greasy-haired smart aleck who showed up at her car like a sloppy valet Friday night. But when Grant first ushered him into their little one-room house all those years ago, Lexi stared too long at Ward.

"You're a gorgeous woman," he said when he noticed, extending his hand. Grant had failed to introduce them.

Lexi blushed and returned his grip without looking into his eyes, inexplicably embarrassed about her plain, underfurnished home. His hand was cool and dry. She couldn't imagine what she'd dig up to feed these men. Glancing sidelong at Grant, she wondered if she should refuse.

Ward and Norman both acted like white-collar professionals who were out of Grant's league somehow, all politeness and good manners. Molly started to fuss. Grant and Ward moved into the living room.

Norman smiled at the baby and waved. She reached out for him.

"She likes you," Lexi said, holding on to Molly.

"For now," he said. He looked at Lexi the way she imagined she'd been looking at Ward.

He played with Molly's pinkie finger. "Kids love unconditionally, but not forever," he said. "Enjoy it while you can."

"You have kids?"

He shook his head.

She noticed a ring on his left hand, then wondered why she'd looked.

"She's happy," he said like a man full of envy. Molly's fussing was almost a genuine cry by then. Lexi's gentle bouncing had no effect.

"Apparently not."

"No, I mean you can tell by looking at her. Under the complaining." Lexi had no idea what he meant. "You must be a good mom."

She cleared her throat. Grant had never said a word to her about her mothering.

"Ruden," Grant called from the living room.

"Keep being a good mom," Norman said to her before joining her husband.

Lexi's memory of their strange introduction was interrupted by a pounding at the front of the apartment. She threw back the sheets, hoping whoever had come knocking wouldn't wake up Molly. She pulled a sweatshirt on over her pajamas as she hurried down the hall.

Through the peephole, she viewed her mother.

Lexi groaned inwardly and opened the door.

Alice pushed past her and entered the house.

"Lexi."

"Mom."

She carried a large suitcase, which she steadied against the living room wall. Lexi glanced outside to see if her cohort had joined her yet again. No sign of Grant this time, though.

Alice Grüggen had started dressing up more since she left Crag's Nest. The L.L.Bean look of the town's mountain ways had fallen beneath her. She ran away from this place wearing sneakers and khakis and had come back in wide-leg trousers and pointy-toed shoes. Today, she topped the look with a denim jacket. She'd cut her hair into a short windblown style that looked nice on her. It softened her heavily lined brown eyes.

"You're going to need help with Molly," she announced.

Lexi closed the door and leaned against it.

"We're getting along fine."

"What are you going to do when you have to go to work? And she'll miss a few days of school until—"

"Yeah, I know. I haven't exactly had time to figure that out, Mom."

"So let me help you. I worry about you two. And with Gina laid up, you need me."

"You worry too much."

"I'm taking some time off. I'm not going to travel for a while and I have my car. I can get her to doctor's appointments, to school."

Everything she said was true, but Lexi didn't care. She didn't want to need her mother. Not now. She sighed. "Can I make you some coffee?"

"I've given up coffee."

"Well, I need some." Lexi turned into the kitchen and flipped on the light. Her eyes involuntarily went to the window. Still sparkly clean.

"What kind of food writer gives up coffee?" Lexi asked as she reached for the can of grounds on the top shelf of her cupboard.

"You have no idea how many coffee substitutes there are these days." Alice followed her into the kitchen. "So much better for you, too, without all that acid and caffeine and chemicals. There's Teecino and Yerba Maté and several different varieties of chicory and barley . . ."

Lexi thought drinking toilet water might have been more pleasant. "I'm sure Molly will be dying to hear about them."

"There's no need to get snippy."

Her mother's defensive tone shocked Lexi. While holding a scoopful of coffee grounds she twisted her neck in Alice's direction. She was standing near a chrome and vinyl kitchen chair with one hand resting on the back, the other hand balanced on her hip, her chin jutted forward, and her eyes brimming wet.

"I didn't have to come here, you know," she said. "You've made it clear you don't want me around. But this isn't about you."

Lexi set down the coffee and looked her mother in the eye. "Mom, I'm sorry. It was really good of you to come. Molly will be ecstatic."

Alice returned her gaze for a minute. She seemed so sad. Lexi imagined her saying, *There was a time when you would have been ecstatic too.*

The unspoken accusation rankled Lexi enough to test her mother.

"Molly and I go see Dad on Saturdays."

"Go, then. Go. Don't let me stop you." She looked away and pulled out the chair she'd been hanging on to.

"Maybe you'd like to come."

"I'd rather not get into this right now, Lexi."

As she'd thought. Grade: F.

But Alice's pained expression caused Lexi to wonder if she was too hard on her mom. She'd tried on many occasions to empathize with Alice's decision to leave Crag's Nest and traipse around the world writing articles about crème fraîche and bruschetta and whatever else she was willing to sample. She'd tried to imagine how she'd behave if someone killed Molly and then she'd lost her beloved husband of thirty years to mental illness. The beloved-husband part was difficult for Lexi to conjure up, but she didn't think that was the only reason why she judged Alice for abandoning him. He was in a good facility, at least. And Alice paid for it somehow, though she refused to see him anymore.

ERIN HEALY

Lexi had wondered many times if the sight of Alice might restore in her dad something of what he'd lost.

Within seconds Alice's sadness was gone, replaced by the perky, confident self she created for the benefit of outsiders.

"Molly might want to stay here with me today," she said.

"You two can work that out, okay? I'm glad for the help. But you and I need to clear the air about Grant before Molly wakes up."

Alice folded her hands on the table. "Nothing's clouding the air but your own stubbornness."

The coffeepot gurgled in its final attempts to suck all the water out of the reservoir. Lexi poured her coffee black.

"If you're serious about getting some quality time with Molly, you won't push my buttons."

"You don't have a whole lot of choices, Lexi. You can't afford a sitter. She's not old enough to be left alone. You can't take her to—"

"Mom!"

Alice looked at Lexi, eyebrows raised, defiant.

"You came into my home when I was not here, and you gave my daughter a letter that cut me down—"

"I don't know what you're talking about."

"If you're going to act this way, the door is there." Lexi pointed.

"No, I mean I don't understand how the letter cuts you down. You said something last night about slander. That was a bit of an overstatement, don't you think? Grant would never—"

"I'm pretty sure I know what Grant is capable of."

"People change, Lexi."

"People want others to *think* they've changed. Seven years ago Norman Von Ruden claimed during his trial that he'd had a conversion experience. Maybe he did, maybe he didn't. It doesn't mean I should go strike up a friendship with him."

She'd said too much. She hoped her mother didn't read anything into it.

Alice said, "You had a conversion experience."

"I had nothing to gain or lose publicly from that. Not the way Norman did. All I know is that the damage is done. That goes for Grant especially."

"But his letter was perfectly nice."

"Nice? He left Molly and me to fend for ourselves all these years and I'm supposed to cave because he's nice? And by the way, that letter of his was *not*."

"Let's have a look at it."

"What?"

"Where is it? Let's read it together and then maybe we can understand each other."

Lexi set her coffee cup down on the counter so hard that the liquid sloshed out. She had no idea where Molly had stashed that letter. How had her mother so efficiently commandeered the conversation? Now they were on an off-road journey, far away from the main point, which was that she and Grant had subverted Lexi's role as Molly's mother.

Lexi couldn't have overstated the anxiety she felt.

She rifled through the backpack Molly had left on the living room sofa. Not there. Then she scanned the library books Molly had left scattered across the floor. A piece of notebook paper with a ragged edge peeked out of a book about Pawnee Indians. She snatched it out of the pages and strode back into the kitchen, reading aloud.

"'Dear Molly-Wolly . . .'" Lexi read the opening lines in one breath, then plopped down at the kitchen table with her mother.

"'I expect you're angry at me for taking off and not being in touch for so long. Maybe you don't even remember me, and that's okay. That'd be my fault. I owe you some explanation for not being there for you. If your mom will let me, I'd like to sit down and talk to you about that.'" She paused and reread the words silently. They were not what she remembered. Alice watched, her chin resting on one hand.

"'I haven't had the courage to go to your mom about all this yet, but I will. I suppose I might look back on this as a mistake, going to you first I mean. It's just that I'm thinking your mom might not want me to see you at all, and this might be my only chance to say I'm sorry, Molly-Wolly. I'm sorry and I'm hoping maybe you can forgive me . . .'"

Scanning the letter quickly, Lexi could see that it was the same letter Molly had read aloud. It didn't make sense. Where was the copy Lexi had read? Why were there two versions? She rubbed her forehead.

"So, tell me your objection," her mom said.

Lexi flattened the letter on the table. "My objection is that you went behind my back."

"I'm sorry about that. Truly, I am." She pointed to the letter. "But Grant was right, don't you think? You wouldn't have let him see her before this, would you?"

"That's not the point. Why did Grant involve you in this anyway?"

"I guess he thought it would help his odds."

"How long have you been in touch?"

"Awhile."

"Awhile. What does that mean? Where is he now?"

"He's been living in Riverbend."

"How long?"

"A week or so."

Lexi picked at the ragged edges of the notebook paper and counted to five before speaking again.

"Let's be clear on this, Mom. If Grant is going to meet Molly—and I haven't decided on that yet—they'll meet on my terms. That means they'll meet where and when I say they can, and I will be there, and you will have nothing to do with it. Is that clear?"

"I'd be happy to make sure—"

"When I say nothing, I mean *nothing*. If you can't respect that, I won't be able to let you stay here. I won't be able to let you and Molly hang out together."

Alice set her lips in a line and nodded once. A curt nod.

"Your mind is whirring around up there looking for loopholes."

She frowned. "Is not."

"There are no loopholes, Mom."

"A girl needs her father."

Lexi stood and took three steps to Alice's suitcase, then started toting it toward the front door.

"Fine, fine." She lifted her hands off the table and looked around. "I can take the sofa while I'm here."

Lexi returned the suitcase to its place against the wall, confident she'd made her point.

"There's no reason you can't take Gina's room. She'd insist."

"How long will Gina be out?"

"I don't think they even know what she's got yet. I'll call the hospital this morning."

"I might be here for a time after she's home."

Lexi took a calming breath and waited for her to explain.

"I plan to stay through Norman Von Ruden's hearing," she said without looking at her daughter.

Their feelings toward Norman were one of the few things they had in common anymore. The thought crossed Lexi's mind that Norman's injuries might postpone his hearing. What then? She and Alice could possibly endure a week in this small home without having to erect a wall down the middle of the apartment. After that . . .

"Did you hear how badly he was hurt?" Lexi asked.

"No. Too bad he didn't die."

It seemed best not to reply to that.

"In any case," Alice continued, "Anthony says he's been earning Brownie points for good behavior."

Anthony had been the prosecuting attorney in Norman's case.

"Brownie points can't do a convicted killer *that* much good. Has Anthony asked other people to testify against him?"

"Of course."

"Will you testify?"

"Just as sure as you will!"

Lexi turned her back on her mother and topped off her coffee.

"Actually, I was thinking of writing a letter."

"There's no reason you can't honor your sister by showing up at his hearing in the flesh, Lexi."

Lexi shook her head, exhausted all over again and wrecked afresh by Ward's demands. "Yeah, alright, Mom. You show up to honor Dad in the same way, and I'll consider it, okay?"

{ chapter 13 }

Lexi almost didn't go to see her father. It was the Volvo's second trip down into Riverbend, and at the rate she was going she'd burn through her gas budget in two weeks rather than four. Then there was the fact that Molly agreed a little too readily to stay home with her grandma. If Lexi hadn't thought Molly really needed to stay off that ankle, she wouldn't have let it be an option.

There was also a chance Dad wouldn't recognize her, even if she did go. Sometimes he thought she was Tara, or a complete stranger. It was hit-or-miss with him.

If pressed to tell the truth, though, Lexi wasn't ready to spend the morning with her mother and daughter, two against one on the matter of a certain delinquent husband. The apartment was too small for that kind of dynamic.

So when she pushed through the glass-paneled doors into the high-ceilinged, sunlit common room of the Mental Health Assistance Residence, she saw her father dressed and napping in a recliner beside a tall paned window and was glad she'd come. His button-down shirt and clean-shaven face indicated a good day.

She took the love seat opposite his recliner and weighed whether she should wake him.

Barrett Grüggen was only fifty-nine and still handsome. He didn't look like the stereotype of a mentally ill person. He was trim and his tidy hair was still more charcoal than ash. He should have had a lot of sane years left in him. Lexi blamed Norm for stealing those away along with her sister.

Her dad was the only person besides Norm who knew about the affair. Last year she'd finally confessed it to him, because the Bible did say she should confess her sins to other people and not only to God. She hoped her confession counted on that point, because there wasn't anyone else she could bear to know about that particular moral failure. If it had been an affair with anyone other than Norm, she might have told Gina. Or even Simone.

But Norman Von Ruden. Of all people.

Because Barrett didn't acknowledge her confession and never brought it up, she couldn't say exactly what he understood about it, and that was a can of worms she choose not to open, not to mention part of the reason she chose him as her priest. He wasn't responsible to forgive her for that sin; God was—and he had, she was confident of it—and so she left the rest alone.

Barrett slept with his glasses on, even at night, the nurses told her. They were askew, so Lexi leaned over to straighten them. She cupped his cheek with her hand when she finished, the way she used to cup Molly's when she was a dozing infant. He stirred and blinked a couple of times, then lifted his head.

His eyes alighted on Lexi and brightened.

"Tara! I didn't know you were going to drop in today."

"Hi, Dad."

He lowered the footrest of the recliner.

"Where's your little sister, eh?" Lexi thought he meant Molly. "I saved the kiddie page out of the newspaper for her yesterday." He looked around the chair as if he'd misplaced it. It would be the same comic page he'd been reading and refolding for six months now.

"She's with Mom. I'll take it to her, though."

"Good. Good. I'll find it and send it home with you. Or . . . well . . . I'll keep it until your next visit. You'll come by tomorrow?"

"You want to go for a walk, Dad?"

"No, no, no. This sunshine here's enough for me. I went on a walk yesterday."

"You did? How did that go?"

"Fine, just fine. Had a friend with me to talk to, and that always makes for a nicer walk."

"Tell me about your friend. I'd like to hear it."

"Big guy." Dad raised his hand up over his head to demonstrate. Lexi recalled his mentioning a linebackerish orderly who sometimes helped him in and out of bed.

"Joe?"

"Who cares about names anymore, Tara? Joe, Moe, Schmoe. I don't remember."

"Okay. Where did you walk?"

"To the river."

As far as she knew, the river wasn't within walking distance of the Residence, but there was no point in saying so.

"Awfully cold to be by the river," she said.

"Not yesterday it wasn't. And he was big enough to block the wind. It was warm anyway. Worked up a sweat just talking."

That made her smile.

"And what did you talk about?"

"Your little sister." Dad gazed out the window and drew his eyebrows together. "She's lost. I don't know how we'll find her."

"She's not lost, Dad. She's okay. She's with Mom, like I said."

"But she is. Wandering around. You know, she was always a smart tack when she was a kid, smarter than you sometimes." He nodded at her. "Don't be offended. It's only the truth. But then she grew up and seemed to forget so much. Like the way I forget names."

At this point, Lexi wasn't sure if he was talking about her or Molly. "Well, who cares about names anymore, right?"

"Oh, I do. I care. He told me she's going to end up in jail if she doesn't find her way home."

"Who told you? Joe?"

"Jail."

Lexi took a deep breath. Maybe a change of subject would help.

"I saw chicken piccata on the dinner menu when I came in."

Dad leaned forward and rested his elbows on his knees, then grabbed her hands. "The jailer is after your little sister. You have to help her get home again."

A twinge of unease poked Lexi over her heart. Dad's glasses were still slightly crooked, but his eyes were more clear and probing than his mind. She decided to roll with this one and hope she ended upright when he was finished.

"If she's done something wrong, maybe she should go to jail," Lexi said. "I mean, if she's really lost, like you said."

"How can you say that? Who would want that for her own flesh and blood?"

"I don't *want* it, Dad. Nobody wants it. But it's just. That's the way it works. That's the way it *should* work, or else this world would be a mess."

"But she's been pardoned! She confessed!"

"Confessed to what?"

"Being lost." He began to shake his head, a fearful wobbling.

"Oh, Dad."

Lexi slipped her hands out of Barrett's grip and rubbed her thumbs over his knuckles. His skin was soft and more knobby than she'd noticed before.

"I'll find her, okay? I'll find her and everything will work out. Don't worry anymore, please. I don't want you to worry."

"There is no worse place to be than in jail."

Lexi smiled at him. "It's not the end of the world."

He didn't reply.

"I'll talk to Joe," she said. "Maybe he can help me."

Dad nodded slowly. "You do that. Yes, that would be a good idea. He'll know what to do. In fact, go for a walk by the river. That'll clear your mind. It did me good."

He leaned back in his chair, taking his hands out of her reach. He closed his eyes again. Lexi took this as her cue to start a monologue.

"Grant showed up out of the blue yesterday. And Molly wants to see him. I'm not sure what to do about that. She was in a car accident, but she's okay, except she broke her ankle and'll be hobbling around for a long time . . ."

She went on like this for several minutes until it seemed to her that her father was asleep. Usually at this point Molly and she would leave. Today, though, Lexi felt the urge to stay.

It occurred to her that this kind of ease might be the very thing Molly longed for in Grant. Even at nine, she might understand what she was missing. Lexi questioned herself. *Would I dare withhold such a relationship from her? Even for her own good?*

When a nurse headed toward them with the bearing of someone about to dispense of medical orders, Lexi rose to go. She bent over her father's resting form and kissed him on the cheek, then turned away.

He lifted his arm and touched Lexi's hand.

"Tell your mom I love her, Lexi."

Lexi's cheeks were still wet with tears when she stepped outside of the Residence. She stopped in the covered breezeway, wanting neither to go nor to stay. Her mind reeled through the current agony of her most important relationships: Molly, Mom, Dad. Maybe Grant.

She felt pain, but concrete thoughts eluded her.

She considered going to see Gina and Mort. Maybe she'd go get something to eat. Maybe she'd—

"Care to walk by the river?"

She gasped and spun. Angelo stood behind her. "If you think you're being cute, I'm seriously freaked out. What are you doing here?"

"Following you around."

"No kidding?"

"I'm teasing. How's your dad?"

Swiping her cheeks with the heels of her hands to make sure they were dry, Lexi wondered what he knew about that, then started walking toward her car.

"I don't know you well enough to say," she told Angelo.

"He seemed well when I saw him yesterday. Took him out for a walk."

She pulled up and decided to stay close to the building in case she needed to run for help.

"How do you know my father?"

"When I'm not eating out, I'm here."

"Getting treatment, you must mean."

He laughed. "I work here."

"Doing what?"

"Nothing medical or professional. They need me for my brawn, not my brains."

"How come I've never seen you before?"

"You're only here once a week. And on Saturdays I'm only here 'til noon."

She swallowed. "If you're here so often you should know better than me exactly how my father is doing."

"Well, maybe that wasn't a fair question. I wanted to know how *you* thought he was doing."

Lexi raised both her hands like an officer stopping traffic. "I'm not comfortable with this," she announced.

He paused. "With what?"

"You. This . . . asking all these personal questions. What do you want with me?"

"I don't want anything from you, Lexi."

"Then what's with the stalking?"

He chuckled, friendly enough. "I'm serious. You don't need to be afraid of me."

"You're not very good at calming people down, then. Were you the one who got my dad on this kick about jailers and lost little sisters? Because that was unkind. I could hardly talk to him."

"You'll have to tell me what he said."

"No. I don't have to do anything."

"Okay." Angelo's face sobered, and Lexi thought that his expression was sympathetic. "I heard you got a letter about Norman Von Ruden yesterday."

He *heard*? How? From whom?

"How do you know about that?" She held up her hand and took a step toward the parking lot. "No. Don't answer that. I don't want to know. I really don't want to know."

The truth was, everyone in Crag's Nest knew about Norman Von Ruden and the poor Grüggen family, how they'd collapsed and dissolved after the beautiful young Tara Grüggen was so unbelievably slaughtered in public. The tragedy made the national news the day after it happened, then was forgotten everywhere but in this cozy little mountain town.

Maybe this strange giant had kept tabs on the story.

A creepy option. The fear that had swirled in her stomach yesterday when he first introduced himself flared again.

"I don't want to talk about it." And she didn't. Not about the past two days, not about Norman Von Ruden, not about how Angelo knew as much as he did.

"Alright," he conceded. "How's Molly's ankle?"

"I'm surprised you don't already know." She sounded rude to her own ears. A breeze swept past the front of the stone building, which was meant to look more like a spa than a treatment center, she supposed. She shivered and overlapped her jacket across her chest. "I'm sorry again. I'm always doing that. How did you happen to be right were she needed you to be last night?"

Angelo scratched his head.

Lexi nodded. "Ah. I see. You're Batman and can't reveal your secret identity."

He gazed out into the parking lot. "Somehow I don't think Batman would go for a cranberry Batmobile."

Lexi didn't know what to make of his easy, self-deprecating reply. She relaxed a little. "What's with the pink?"

"It's not pink, its *cranberry*. And I love that truck. The paint job wasn't cheap, either."

"It's magenta, fuchsia."

"I refuse to let a woman drag me into an argument about color." He smiled as he said it.

"Call it what you want. It's Mary Kay on steroids."

"Nothing unmanly about steroids."

She had the distinct sense he was messing with her. Maybe it was the way the corners of his copper eyes crinkled. She took one step back. *What an odd duck.* "Maybe you should tell me the truth."

"Here it is: I thought you'd like an ally right about now."

"That's it?"

"In the simplest terms."

The simplest terms were immensely appealing, but also inadequate, and strangely put. "Why would I want an ally?"

"Like I said, I heard Norman Von Ruden came up for parole. I knew your dad was here, unlike when Von Ruden was on trial. Your mother was out of the country until recently, and I gather your relationship with her isn't on the best of terms."

It was hard for Lexi not to be offended by this. "And how do you gather that?"

"She told me a few things before we connected with you at the hospital last night."

Lexi shook her head, disgusted with her mother's inability to hold her tongue.

"How's Molly handling all this?"

"I'm sorry, but I just don't see why you—"

"Molly's getting older. Old enough to have new questions, give you some new anxieties. What does she know about her aunt's death?"

"Not as much as you do, I'm sure."

"And then you have Grant, coincidentally out of prison at the same time—"

Lexi reached out behind her for something to lean against, but found nothing. "Grant was in prison?"

Angelo looked at her and let the truth sit out there for a few seconds. The news burned her throat like a pending illness. What did Alice know about that? And how did it figure into her whole "people change" campaign?

"This is crazy. Nothing's private anymore. Did you tell my dad? About Grant?" She wondered if that would explain what triggered his jailer remarks.

"We talk."

"You shouldn't worry him with that kind of thing. When he's not lucid he makes all kinds of irrational mental connections."

"That's true for any of us, don't you think?"

Lexi glared at him. "I should run far, far away from you right now."

He waited for her to go, and when she didn't, he said, "But you could use some support."

"We have Gina." Had Gina. Even if she were well, Lexi wouldn't have leaned on her with the full weight of her burdens.

He said, "True," and Lexi got the unnerving sense he was answering her thoughts rather than her statement.

She cleared her throat. "You're saying all this like I'm supposed to believe in old-fashioned altruism."

"So you're of the chivalry-is-dead opinion," Angelo said.

"No, I'm a card-carrying member of the pepper-spray club."

Angelo laughed again, a belly laugh that cut through all her cynicism and fear, right against her will. "You asked me to tell you the truth."

"It's harder to believe than I expected."

He nodded. "Most truth is."

She softened. Just a little.

"I still think you're strange," she said. "Or desperate for a date. Or both."

"I wouldn't object to having lunch with you."

"I thought I'd go see Gina," Lexi said.

"Can I join you?"

She thought about it.

"Okay. But only because you asked. Next time you sneak up on me uninvited, I'll transform back into my chilly, rebuffing self."

He removed his keys from his pocket and jangled them midair. "I'll follow you in the Batmobile."

{ chapter 14 }

Mort Weatherby, St. Luke's Community Hospital, trauma center, south building, fourth floor, room 406.

Warden entered the man's room wearing a white coat and a laminated photo of himself clipped to his pocket. Even with all the hullabaloo about increased security, he found that walking into a hospital room was one of the easiest things to do, so long as there wasn't a dinosaur nurse at the front desk who knew the name of every doctor and patient she'd ever met in the last fifty years. But he'd been doing this kind of thing awhile.

He had the vial; he had the syringe; he had the sleeping body.

This would only take a minute.

Mort. What an appropriate name.

"What are you doing?" Craven was already in the room. His eyes widened and he came off the wall where he had been slouching.

"Accepting your invitation to join the party."

"What?"

Warden filled the syringe and tossed the empty vial into the trash can on the other side of the room. This was his preferred method: hide the evidence in plain sight and almost no one ever sees it.

"You're not going to *kill* him?"

Craven, a foot taller than Warden but half his weight, stood beside him, avoiding his eyes like some poor noodle of a high school boy who couldn't hold the gaze of the star quarterback. His cheeks were flushed and his nose was running. He wiped it on the heel of his hand.

Warden lowered the needle to the crook of Mort's elbow.

"I'll file a complaint!" Craven protested.

Warden lifted the needle off the skin and cast an unconcerned glance at Craven. "Don't whine. You should have anticipated this when you involved my girl in your little escapade last night."

Craven's bloodshot eyes were glassy. "What are you talking about?"

"That little girl you almost killed."

"You said the Grüggen woman was yours."

"That's her mother, imbecile."

The cackle that rose out of Craven's throat at this news was most grating. It started low like an angry cat and crescendoed into a full chicken cluck. Warden had met hyenas with less agonizing expressions of pleasure. He restrained his annoyance. There was no point in wasting it on a worm like Craven.

"I would have liked that very much," Craven said. "If the little one had died."

Warden returned the needle to the vein pulsing weakly beneath Mort's skin, silencing Craven.

"You can't kill him. It's against the rules."

"Not even you play by the rules."

Craven was a weightless thing, but fast. His arm lashed out and his knuckles struck the inside of Warden's wrist, knocking the syringe out of his hand. It slid across the floor, spinning as it went, right under the vacant bed next to Mort's. Craven dived for it.

Warden pulled the bed on wheels away from the wall. It rolled over

Craven's outstretched hand. Warden sat upon the bed, pinning his opponent's palm to the floor. Craven snarled. The situation couldn't possibly hurt, but Warden was sure he found it inconvenient.

The needle rested in a cloud of fuzz, having stabbed a dust bunny clean through the heart. "Someone should tell Mort that this place isn't sanitary," Warden said.

With his outstretched foot, he kicked it out of Craven's reach while the man tried to extricate his hand from under the wheels, cursing as if Warden weren't already cursed.

"Relax," Warden said. "I'm not going to kill him."

Craven still wriggled, but less vigorously. He spat on Warden's shoe. "I don't believe you."

"Fortunately, belief doesn't change facts. Of course I won't kill him. I need something to keep you occupied and out of my way. If Mort dies, I have a hunch you'd become an even bigger pest than you presently are."

"Then why come here at all?"

"To remind you of your place."

Warden jumped off the bed, landing on Craven's forearm. A bone cracked, and Craven cried out, spitting and writhing more. Taking two steps, Warden bent over to pick up the syringe, gingerly, without spilling his little bacteria sample everywhere.

Craven descended onto his back, all arms and legs and teeth. He flailed and bit and, in spite of Warden's conscientious effort, managed to knock the piston out. It rattled to the floor and rolled under Warden's heel as he tried to pry the octopus off his body while keeping the syringe upright. He heard the plastic snap as his weight ground down on it.

Warden imagined what this scuffle looked like to dear Mort, lying there, thinking he was dreaming. He couldn't prevent a chuckle from escaping him. Craven swung at his head with renewed gusto.

Still holding the syringe, Warden kept the needle pointed at the floor in order to preserve the contents of the tube. Craven's bobbing head connected with the precious cargo, driving the needle like a nail into Warden's opposite hand. This made him laugh harder. The sensation of pain, such as it is, was invigorating. And he had a firm grip on the bacteria now.

Staggering only slightly under his furious burden, Warden returned to Mort. At the edge of the hospital bed, he raised his arm over Mort's peaceful face and upended the separated syringe. The germ-ridden fluid splattered, hitting the patient right between the eyes. It pooled in the corners and ran into his ears and baptized his nose and mouth with an unholy sprinkle.

"That'll do," Warden announced.

He shook Craven off. The greasy figure slid off his back like water off the proverbial duck, landing on his feet, staring at Mort.

"What is it?" he asked.

Warden gripped the hollow plastic tube and yanked the needle from his hand. It was a fine needle, slender but strong, and still intact after the scuffle. He waved it in front of Craven's eyes, breaking his concentration.

Then he brought his arm down hard and shoved it into Craven's back, into the soft tissue between his shoulder blade and his spine. Though if he had to guess, he would say Craven had no spine at all.

Craven winced and grabbed at it, but the thing was out of his reach.

Warden made to leave the room.

"If you're lucky," Warden said, "he'll live."

Lexi and Angelo arrived at St. Luke's within ten minutes. Gina was still in intensive care, though her condition had been upgraded from critical to serious. Her room, which was third from the left on the bleach-white U-shaped ward of St. Luke's, was partitioned off by a sliding glass door so that she, like every other bed on the floor, could be continuously within sight of the staff. Lexi wouldn't be allowed to see her, a nurse on duty said, but when Gina's mother saw her through the glass, she came out and grabbed Lexi in a bear hug. Angelo hung back, a gesture Lexi perceived as kindness.

"You give that little girl of yours this hug from me," Mrs. Harper said into Lexi's hair. "I'm making Molly my honorary grandbaby." She leaned back to look at Lexi. "They told me what happened. How's Molly holding up?"

"She's good. I don't think she knows how bad it could have been."

"And you?"

"I'm okay."

"I asked after Mort this morning. Gina has a thing for him, you know." Lexi smiled. Mrs. Harper shook her head. "They say he's taken a turn for the worse."

Distress for the man who'd only tried to help her family filled Lexi's stomach.

"Oh no. I'll check in on him. How's Gina?"

Mrs. Harper let her go at the shoulders but grasped Lexi's hands. She shook her head. "A virus of some kind maybe. One wicked germ. There's so many tests to do. Far as I can tell they've only just started."

"Not food poisoning or something basic like that, huh?"

"Oh no. They ruled all that out pretty quickly, not that I know how." She faced Lexi.

"Has she woken?"

"In and out," Mrs. Harper said. The women walked arm in arm to Gina's room without going in. She lay in bed on the other side of the window-wall, looking unearthly pale but at rest. An IV was hooked up to her hand. "Her oxygen's not what it should be, you know. And her blood pressure is low. But they're good people here. They're looking after her alright."

"Can I get you anything?"

"Oh no. Gina's dad is on his way down and he's bringing my things. The two of us'll do fine."

"What about Gina? Maybe I could bring her pajamas or something."

"That'd be nice. I'm sure she'd like that."

"Next time I come then. In the meantime, you'll let me know how I can help?"

"You pray, dear, and we'll do the same." Mrs. Harper smiled at Angelo, who lingered by the nurse's station, and patted the back of Lexi's hand.

"I'll do that. Molly will too. I assume you've got our number at home?" When she nodded, Lexi said, "Please tell Gina not to stay down too long. Molly wants to learn some more blonde jokes."

"We'll kick her into gear as soon as she's sitting up."

"Okay then." Lexi kissed Mrs. Harper's cheek and waited until she was beside Gina again before turning to go.

Without taking in any details, her eyes scanned the other rooms on the ward. She probably wouldn't have noticed anything had an orderly in green scrubs not pulled back a privacy curtain in one of the rooms on the opposite side of the unit.

Through the sliding glass door, she saw a uniformed police officer standing in the corner of the room and a patient with a bruised face lying in the bed. His left arm was in a cast and his head was wrapped in gauze over his right eye.

A slim doctor about Lexi's age, perhaps Pakistani or Indian, was walking into the room while engrossed in a chart. The officer walked out and took up post by the door.

The man in bed turned his head to the doctor and in so doing caught sight of Lexi.

Norm.

He smiled. A light, casual, corner-of-the-mouth, isn't-it-a-crazy-day kind of smile.

That scythe of a smile cut Lexi's heart. That smile, which had once knocked her senseless, aroused in her every fiery arrow of flaming emotion she had ever felt over the death of her sister. News of his pending parole had made her angry, but this unexpected encounter transported her to the day she had learned Tara was murdered and Norman charged with the crime.

The blackest day of her blackest year.

Tara had visited Lexi the day before she died. She arrived while Molly napped, bearing hot cinnamon rolls and a thermos of fresh coffee because she knew both were Lexi's weakness. They sat and ate and laughed and licked their sticky fingers, and she waited until Lexi bit into her second roll before ruining the mood.

You need to end this thing with Norman, she said. You need to cut him off because he has a wife and they want a child and he needs them the way you need Grant. Norm won't make you whole.

You'll shatter his family into a million pieces, Tara said. And yours. If you and Grant can't hold it together, you'll kill Molly.

Lexi found that last bit to be over the top. Grant is the one who'll kill Molly, she shot back. He'll kill her by ignoring her or by hooking her on his drugs—if he doesn't kill himself first. Tara didn't have any idea what she was talking about, Lexi announced. She couldn't possibly. She wasn't married. She wasn't even dating.

Neither Tara nor Lexi budged in their positions, Lexi because she was stubborn and Tara because she was right. Lexi sent her away with her thermos but kept the leftover rolls and devoured them all within the hour.

They turned to a rock in Lexi's stomach and sat there for weeks, months even, after she understood she would never see Tara again.

Barrett was the one who called with the news. He was in the morgue and couldn't speak for a whole minute after Lexi realized it was him on the other end. He sobbed and she imagined him with his free hand tilting his forehead so that his face turned up toward God, groaning the questions that had no answer.

"Your sister's dead, Lexi. A random, freak accident. They've arrested someone."

Lexi was at home, tethered to the kitchen phone by a cord too short to reach a chair, and by the time he finished she was on her knees on the cold, sticky floor, pressing her brow into a cupboard door and gripping the overhanging counter above her head.

Grant came home in a drugged-up stupor. He found Lexi on the floor, still holding the phone receiver, which by that time was droning on with a recorded message about what to do if she'd like to place a call. Molly was crying, but Lexi only noticed because Grant demanded she hang up the phone and do something about it.

Now, there he was, Norman Von Ruden, getting the same professional medical care that her best friend was receiving. What he deserved was a third-world, flea-infested armpit of a disreputable clinic.

No, he didn't deserve even that.

There he was, getting patched up to be released a mere seven years after he killed Tara in a haze of what experts believed was undiagnosed bipolar disorder.

There he was, smiling at her, after he huffed and puffed and blew down her family and left her standing in the rubble.

You should have died last night! Lexi's screams bounced around inside her brain. *You don't deserve to lie in that bed! They should dump you out on the street!*

She was aware of a presence by her right arm, touching her at the elbow.

Even in prison you can't leave my family alone! Molly almost died! It's your fault! You don't deserve to live!

The hand on her elbow took hold of her, squeezing hard. The brown-skinned doctor in Norm's room turned to look at her. A nurse at the station was staring. The sheriff posted at Norm's door was headed in Lexi's direction.

Her body quavered. Norm's smile faltered. She heard the sound of her own voice and realized she was shouting.

I'll kill you myself! I should do it right now!

The physician took two steps and yanked the privacy curtain closed.

Angelo gently pulled Lexi from the ICU before the officer reached them.

{ chapter 15 }

The cloudy-gray post office boxes seemed to darken as Grant stood in front of his open cubby and read his daughter's note. He hadn't expected a reply so soon, though the reply itself wasn't a great surprise.

> Grant, thanks but no thanks. Don't bother asking me again. Molly. (Just plain Molly.)

It wasn't the rejection that disheartened him, but the fact that Lexi had written it. She hadn't gone to great lengths to disguise her handwriting, which made the impersonation that much stranger. He hadn't thought she'd use Molly that way. Ever. For any reason. Grant tossed Lexi's fakery into a freshly lined trash can and stood there a minute, trying to sort through what this meant for him.

"Can I help you?" A postal worker stood at Grant's elbow. The man sounded worried, and Grant didn't look at him. Sometimes Grant figured he looked like a con, with his tired eyes and scruffy hair, and it was hard for him to tell if people who approached when he was pondering life were more concerned for him or their own well-being.

"Sorry. No. I was just leaving. Thanks."

Grant pushed out the door into the afternoon glare and thought he saw, from the corner of his eye, the employee leaning into the trash can where he'd tossed Lexi's letter.

What first struck Grant as strange sorted itself out with an easy explanation. The cans had to be emptied at some point, didn't they?

As he pointed his rusty Datsun back toward the trailer park, Grant picked the course of action that seemed most insane. He decided to try seeing Lexi at the bar and grill again. He was nuts, sure, but at this point, what more could he possibly lose?

He took a back road home, swerving casually across the double yellow line on the carless road, back and forth, weighing his options. An unexpected fear caused him to linger on the wrong side of the stripes. If Lexi wouldn't forgive him, what hope did he have that God ever would?

In the St. Luke's hospital parking lot, Angelo sat with Lexi on the open tailgate of his Chevy while she calmed down. She found him to be nothing short of the ideal man in that moment: he didn't leave her, and he didn't try to talk to her. She tucked her hands under her legs because they were cold, and he got her jacket from the Volvo and brought it to her.

"It shouldn't have surprised me to see him," she said after several minutes. "I knew he was there."

It was almost one o'clock and she hadn't eaten anything yet that day. Her stomach was making small clenching jerks.

"Did I say all that? I mean, was I really shouting?" Angelo rested his huge hand on Lexi's shoulder. "They must think I'm crazy. Except . . . I guess they wouldn't know me from any plain Jane down here. But he *is* a con. Do they know who he is? What he did? I wonder if it's hard for doctors to patch up guys who have killed other people, no matter what their oath says. I could have killed him." Lexi stared at the asphalt several inches beneath her dangling feet. "If we'd been alone, I think I might have done it. Does that make me like him?"

Lexi didn't want Angelo to answer that question, and he didn't.

The discomfort of concealing truth from another person came over her then, between her stupid question and Angelo's gaze.

She shook off her unease. Angelo couldn't have had any inkling of her past relationship with Norman. Still, his compassionate silence also seemed to judge her. She wished he would speak and dispel that notion. She wished he would say anything to make her feel better.

"What would you have done?" she asked.

"What would I have done, or what would I have done if I were you?"

Lexi wasn't sure.

"The way people hurt each other is a terrible thing," he said.

"That man did more than hurt my sister."

Angelo nodded once. "He did."

"You can understand why I feel the way I do."

"I can."

Rather than justify her anger, his agreement stirred a well of grief in Lexi.

"That yelling, ugly screamer is not who I am. It's not the way I want to be."

"Of course it's not."

"But his offense was so . . . huge."

"It has you by your hair," he said.

"What?"

"His sin. It's got a hold of you."

"No it doesn't." She wasn't angry at his observation, but confused. "I've done fine moving on with my life since it happened. You know my husband left me that same year? What a double whammy! But I put that behind me. I had to. If I hadn't, I probably would have lost my job *and* Molly and who knows what else. I don't think it has a hold of me. It's just the stress of everything that's happened in the last day or two. I'm tired. I snapped. That's all."

Lexi sat on this claim for a few seconds. Wasn't it bad enough to have lived through Tara's murder and Grant's abandonment? Why heap on the possibility that Norman and Grant still had some psychological influence over her? An unbidden image of Norman's fist gripping her hair at the roots made Lexi shiver.

"Anyone in my shoes would have done the same thing," she said. "It's normal." Lexi slid off the back of the tailgate. "I should go."

Angelo followed her home without offering to, perhaps to avoid the risk that she'd refuse him. As they climbed the mountain between Riverbend and Crag's Nest, Lexi pondered what the protective gesture might mean. Brotherly love or something more? She tried not to overanalyze it. After all, she'd invited him to lunch, and they hadn't eaten yet.

She planned to invite him in. Angelo's presence would be a buffer between her and her mother. Maybe even between her and Molly, depending on whether Alice had stirred up Molly's need to see Grant. Lexi wondered what her mother had been saying about that in Lexi's absence.

If Angelo could handle this dynamic, Lexi would take a closer look at the merits of his friendship. His visit would be something of a test. It couldn't hurt to have a man of his size and apparent devotion nearby, considering the present company she seemed to attract. On the other hand, if anything could send a man running, the collective effect of Warden Pavo, Grant Solomon, Alice Grüggen, and Norman Von Ruden should have been it.

Thinking of the pancakes that Molly had wanted to make, Lexi swung into the Crag's Nest Safeway to splurge on a pint of blueberries while Angelo waited in his truck alongside her Volvo. By the time Lexi pulled into the carport in her apartment complex, the berries sat on the passenger seat looking like an insignificant gesture. She hoped Molly would accept them anyway.

Angelo seemed glad for the invitation to come in. Lexi promised him a hot chocolate but avoided mention of blueberry pancakes until she talked to her daughter.

When Lexi opened the front door, the sound of Molly and Alice laughing spilled out onto the walkway. Angelo held the screen door open and she turned to smile at him, glad to start this thing on a positive note.

But he was scowling.

Lexi felt confused. She glanced around the entry. The place was decently clean, no doubt Alice's doing in Gina's absence. Nothing smelled bad. In fact, the welcoming aroma of bacon floated out of the kitchen. Her mother and daughter had been cooking.

Lexi moved down the short hall and took one step into the kitchen before realizing what was wrong.

Warden Pavo sat at her kitchen table.

He was laughing. And Molly was laughing. Her head was thrown back over the top of her seat, and her brown hair shimmied with her giggles.

"Lexi!" Alice gushed. "We have a guest!" She stood at the stove, using tongs to turn bacon. Molly sat with her leg propped up on a chair. She had a bowl of spinach leaves in front of her, and a pile of stems sitting on the edge of the table. She straightened when Lexi came in, then looked away.

Warden's jack-o'-lantern grin faltered when he saw Angelo, but he recovered quickly enough.

Alice said, "Molly and I are making spinach salads, and here he comes, knocking on the door." Mom gestured to a photograph lying on the table. "When he told me he was an old friend of yours, I invited him to eat with us. Figured you'd be back soon in any case." She caught sight of Angelo and brightened further. She set down her tongs and wiped her hands on her apron, then held her arms out to him as she walked around the table.

"Our local hero!" she announced, and he bent into her overexuberant hug. "Angelo, right? Well, this is going to be one happy luncheon. Good thing I boiled extra eggs. You could have let me know you were bringing him home with you," she scolded.

"I don't have a cell phone, Mom."

"I'm sure he wouldn't have minded if you borrowed his," she said.

Considering Alice's poor judgment in allowing a complete stranger into the house, Lexi decided she was entitled to ignore the remark.

"Are those blueberries?" Mom took the pint from Lexi's hands.

"They're for Molly," Lexi said. Molly glanced up but let her grandmother keep the fruit.

"We'll have them for dessert," Alice said. "With cream."

"I don't have cream," Lexi mumbled, picking up the photograph.

It appeared to have been taken several years ago. Grant, Warden, and Lexi stood in front of their tiny bungalow over on Fireweed Street. Molly, who was still a toddler, hugged her mother's neck. The men flanked them. A much younger and more handsome version of Ward goofed off by making devil's horns behind Grant's head.

Lexi had no recollection of posing for this picture, but that didn't mean anything. She wondered if Norman had taken it. She tossed it back onto the table.

Ward spoke up, "You're the only one of us who hasn't changed since then." He nodded at Alice. "It's obvious now where you get your good looks."

Alice blushed. Lexi bristled.

"You owe me some money for that drink you ordered last night," Lexi said, hanging her keys on the hook by the phone.

"Oh, right. I'm so sorry about that. Had an emergency call and had to go, and I couldn't find you to tell you." He fished in his back pocket for a wallet and withdrew a five-dollar bill, then extended it to her. "Please. Take it. I won't be indebted to you."

"I thought you took off when you caught sight of Grant."

Ward scratched his neck. "Grant's in town?"

Ward was a liar. He had pulled off this play-dumb skill of his more than once in that short era when he and Grant and Norman were a trio. Its obviousness now spooked Lexi. What else did Ward know about her that he pretended not to? How long had he known?

How would he use it against her?

She tried but couldn't come up with a reason why Ward, Norman, and Grant had all reemerged in her life within a twenty-four hour period after being wonderfully absent from it for all of seven years. It couldn't be coincidental.

When Lexi didn't take the bill, Ward laid it on top of the discarded photograph.

Alice kept looking at Angelo, who was a hulk under the low ceilings of the old building. "Aren't you going to introduce your friends?" she asked Lexi, returning to the bacon.

Lexi shrugged out of her jacket, then made appropriate hand motions. "Warden, Angelo. Angelo, Warden." Introductions hardly seemed necessary, however, because Angelo completely ignored Ward, and Ward didn't seem to mind. His posture relaxed slightly.

She glared at him, told him with her eyes as loudly as possible that he was not welcome here. The presence of her mother and daughter prevented her from vocalizing it and exposing her twisted dilemma. Ward lifted the glass of iced tea in front of him and raised it to Lexi, with a nod, a toast that thumbed his nose at her.

"How's the ankle?" Angelo asked Molly, taking the seat between her and Ward.

"It hurts. A little."

"That's all? If that were my ankle I'd be saying it hurts *a lot*." He rested his elbows on his knees so that he didn't tower over the girl. She responded with a light giggle.

"Grandma's made me stay off it."

"Good grandma."

"Make yourself useful, Lexi," Alice commanded while smiling at Angelo. "Peel some eggs." She nodded toward a colander full of boiled eggs by the sink.

"Mind if I have a look at that splint?" Angelo asked Molly. "It's quite a contraption."

"I think it looks like a launchpad for a rocket ship," she said.

"And your leg's the rocket!" Angelo said. Lexi moved to the sink to wash her hands, feeling Ward's eyes on her back.

That high-tech splint might as well have been made by NASA, for all that it was going to cost Lexi. This one time, she might have to ask her mom for a loan.

She turned on the water faucet to wash her hands. The water that came out of it was gray, like the water Molly drained off a can of olives. Lexi waited, thinking some minerals had built up in the pipes, although when that had happened before the water came out brown. Instead of clearing up, the gray darkened to a watercolor black, then thickened to the consistency of the tempera paints Molly and she had used for a school project.

When it became the consistency of motor oil and started falling from the faucet in burping bubbles, she shut off the tap and watched the greasy liquid slither into the drain.

"Problem with the water?" Lexi flinched at the sound of his voice. The space they shared was not made for two people.

"No," she said.

"You have other problems." His voice was low. Ward's breath caressed her neck and smelled like eggs. Or maybe it was the pot on the counter. The scent of wood smoke came off his clothes.

"You're at the top of my list."

"That's right."

From the corner of her eye, Lexi saw Alice lift bacon onto paper towels. She didn't seem to notice Ward standing so close. Molly and Angelo continued to chat.

Lexi couldn't bring herself to turn around in the crowded quarters and face Ward. With so many people in the room, he'd have to back off soon enough.

Her legs were shaking, even though her voice was level.

"If you're here about Norm—"

"One of many things."

"I'll give you my answer in a few days."

"Mmm. I'll need to know sooner than that."

"Why?"

"Five letters: M-O-L-L—"

"Okay." Lexi snapped around, holding a boiled egg. Her toes knocked Ward's. Bitterness toward Norm clogged her throat, but fear for Molly's safety overcame it. She'd say anything to make Ward leave her life forever. "I'll testify," she whispered. "I'll put in a good word for the snake."

"No you won't."

Confusion made Lexi frown. "What do you mean? I will."

"You say you will. You'll say what you want me to hear. But it's not the truth."

Lexi swallowed. She'd make it the truth. She would do it, no matter how distasteful. She didn't know how, only that she would. No matter what she said about Norm at the hearing, she didn't have to mean it. She would need a way to explain it to her family, though.

"I'd do anything for Molly."

"That's what you'd like to think."

"But you said you wanted me to—"

"I do."

Lexi stared at Ward. He was not wearing his knit cap today, but his hair would have benefited from one. His greasy black curls made his forehead shiny, and he appeared to have skipped shaving. Ward's nose was too wide for his narrow face, and his eyes, which she had remembered being clear blue in striking contrast to his hair, were like midnight.

She shoved him out of her way, reaching the living room and a place to breathe in four long strides.

"Eggs, Lexi!" Alice called.

"In a minute," Lexi said.

Ward followed her, as she expected.

"What are we really talking about?" she asked him. "Is this about Norm, or about Molly, or me, or something else entirely?"

"Yes." Ward was grinning.

Lexi put her hand on her forehead, then dropped it.

Ward said, "I heard Grant wrote you a letter. A nasty letter. Or was that for Molly?"

"This is about Grant?"

"Everything's about everything." His lips formed a smug line.

"What do you know about the letter?"

He laughed, a breathy chuckle. "More than you do."

She crossed her arms. "Then there's no need for me to explain it."

"That's right. So I'll explain a few things to you."

"Please."

Lexi figured it was possible that Grant and Ward had coordinated this return to Crag's Nest, that they were still in some kind of business together, but why?

Her mind lit up with sense. So Grant could get custody of Molly. Or kidnap the girl. Or do something just as crazy. That's why Ward would demand she testify for Norm—he was doing this at Grant's prompting! He must have found out about the affair. Grant could have his revenge, rub Lexi's face in her own poor judgment. Lexi felt her heart pounding all the way up in her temples.

Ward said, "Grant still owes me some money."

Lexi blinked. What did that have to do with anything? "You can rest assured I don't have any of it."

"As I've said, you don't have to pay me with cash."

"Shut up, Ward. I don't owe you *anything*."

"You and Grant are still married. Legally, his obligations are yours."

"Since when did you care about the law?" she challenged. But the walls of Lexi's living room felt close and thick. In the kitchen, Alice was saying something and Angelo was listening, but the big man's eyes were on Lexi. His gaze emboldened her.

He got up from his chair and responded to Alice. She laughed. Angelo turned, tilting his shoulder to lean against the wall that separated the kitchen from the hallway and living room, blocking Lexi's view of her mother and daughter. And vice versa.

Lexi kept the conversation at a low volume. "*I* don't owe you anything," she repeated to Ward.

"That's a common misconception among people who know me."

"It's the truth."

"Did you ever wonder, Lexi, why the law didn't come after you when Grant left—why they didn't see to it that Molly had the chance to be raised in a more . . . privileged home?"

She released the wall. "Because I had nothing to do with Grant's moonlighting. The 'law' never knew about that anyway."

"Ever wonder why? It's a small town, and your name was on the title of that sweet little house where Grant built his meth lab."

"It was your lab."

"Not the way it looks to an outsider. *I'm* the reason they never dropped in on you."

"Am I supposed to thank you for that?"

"It wouldn't hurt."

Lexi glared at him. "Maybe my *husband* would be more grateful."

"Is he your husband still? After what you did, Sexy Lexi? I mean, I suppose you still have a piece of paper saying you're still a Solomon, but are you? Do you deserve that title?"

All words left her. The smoky aroma of his clothing hit her fresh then, and the tones of Molly telling a joke reached her ears. This was the scent that had covered her daughter at the library. Lexi balked.

Ward asked, "Did you see him today, when you visited your friend? Did you see Norman?"

"Were you with my daughter?"

"While you were with your lover?"

"He's not—!" Lexi controlled her volume and closed the space between her and Warden. "That was a mistake. It was years ago. It doesn't matter anymore."

"Is that permission to tell?"

"Of course not!" Her thoughts went directly to Molly. "What is this all about?"

"Grant owes me money, and you're going to get it for me."

The paper-thin foundation under Ward's claims infuriated Lexi. She couldn't lay hands on that money any more than she believed Grant owed it to Ward.

"Do you want a testimony or do you want cash? Because I'm having a little trouble keeping up with all the demands."

"You're going to give me both."

"Get it yourself."

"The reason you're going to get it for me is because Grant came back to Crag's Nest for a reason, and that reason is you. And his daughter. He'll give what he owes to you far more easily than he'll give it to me."

"It's a bad idea to work with people you don't know very well."

"He owes me twenty-five thousand—"

"He never owed you that much!"

"Interest accrues. In exchange for collecting this money on my behalf, you'll get to keep your daughter. How hard can it be to take money from a man you already despise?"

"You think I can just ask for it on a paper plate?"

"You have until Norman Von Ruden's hearing to collect."

The smell of boiled eggs and the confusion of what was happening made a nauseous combination in Lexi's stomach. Frustration and desperation brought tears to her eyes.

"You tell Grant I'm done with this," Lexi said. "If he wants money, he's going to have to get it from someone besides me. And if he wants to rub my face in the Norman mistake, he can come do it himself. I don't know what he's talked you into or what you think you're going to get out of it. Twenty-five thousand dollars to split? Well, you're the idiots. You can't steal from someone who doesn't have anything."

"You have Molly."

"You will never, ever get close enough to my daughter again to even *touch* her. Neither of you."

"I have been closer than that already," he whispered. "She's the point of this fine mess, isn't she? She's the prize, the cost, and the consequence all rolled into one."

The skin of Lexi's neck started to tingle where Ward had breathed on it. "None of this makes sense."

"When the parents have a debt to pay, the party that always, always pays it is the children. I don't care who you think you are or how you think you're going to cook the books of your life, Lexi. When it's time to settle accounts, the money's coming out of your children's pockets. Molly's pockets."

"Grant is the one who owes you."

Ward shook his head, a gesture of false pity. "I'm never gonna let you go, Lexi. You're in debt to the bottom of your soul. You just don't know it yet."

{ chapter 16 }

Ward left. Angelo stayed. Molly and Alice seemed unaware of Lexi's exchange with Ward, and her gut told her that Angelo's powers of distraction were responsible for that. Powers of protection, she thought. She wondered then if maybe he could protect her family from her past. From Grant. From Ward. Maybe that was why he was really here, sent by God, even though he couldn't have known it.

Lexi's anger toward Grant grew after Ward's departure. He had put her in this mess by abandoning her in marriage even before he left. Her animosity toward Norman intensified too. She blamed him for seducing her, and then her self-loathing expanded as well, for allowing him to. She spent the afternoon in a haze, wondering what she could have done differently to prevent Molly from ending up in so much danger.

She boldly asked Angelo to stay with her mother and daughter while she went to work. The thought of Alice and Molly alone, and Alice being so willing to let Ward in the house, frightened Lexi. Angelo reacted enthusiastically, as if he'd been waiting for her to ask because he feared offending if he offered first.

"For all you know, Ward's a serial killer," Lexi whispered to her mother so Molly wouldn't hear. Angelo had left the room to wash his hands before eating.

Alice looked shocked. "He's not," she said. "He's completely decent."

Lexi's mind went to Norman. "Killers usually are, don't you think?"

"For heaven's sake, Lexi. What would you know about that?"

"You're the one who spends so much time worrying about what's going to go wrong, Mom. Just this once, it would have been nice if you'd been completely paranoid."

"Okay, so tell me what's wrong with Ward. He must have told me the truth about you guys knowing each other for a long time. He had a photo! Tell me his big bad secrets."

Lexi looked at Molly, who was fishing around in her salad for the bacon pieces, listening in spite of Lexi's low voice. There was no good answer to offer up at this moment, no answer that wouldn't lead to the truth about why Tara had died. Lexi wasn't prepared to expose her own blame to anyone. There had to be another way.

"He's bad news, Mom."

"Now that's helpful." She went to the sink to wash her hands.

"Mom, wait," she said, fearing the black ooze once again. Alice lifted the lever on the faucet. The water ran clear.

"Seriously, Lexi, I'm more frightened of that Angelo."

"You've got to be kidding!"

"I'm not. He's huge. Monstrous. He could squash me with his thumb. And he's not half as good-looking as your friend Ward."

Lexi blinked. *Good-looking* and *Ward* did not belong in the same sentence together. This was her reason for trusting him? "Well, handsome men have never been responsible for any evil in the world, have they?"

Alice shook her hands dry and reached for a dish towel. The black water in the pipes—gone like the paint on the window. Lexi was quickly learning not to trust her eyes any more than she trusted Ward.

"Don't be sassy. If we're going with our guts here, Lexi, I have to listen to mine. That Angelo makes me shiver inside."

"He saved Molly's life!"

"By accident. Keep your eyes open. I hope he hasn't turned your head."

"Mom!"

"You've known him all of what? Two days?"

Either confirming or denying it was a losing proposition. How long had she known Ward? Eight years?

Molly looked at them, and Lexi hoped she didn't know the phrase "turned your head."

"Are you going out with him?" Molly asked.

"No!"

Lexi thought her answer might have been too quick, too emphatic, because when Angelo returned from the bathroom, Molly frowned at him.

A pint of blueberries could only do so much.

"Did you and Gina get a chance to watch the movie before she got sick?" Lexi asked.

Molly shook her head and stabbed a spinach leaf.

"Maybe we can watch it tomorrow morning." That would mean skipping church. There was a time when all of the Grüggens had trooped to church on Sunday mornings, because that was their routine. At some point they must have decided they preferred newspapers and coffee to church bulletins and potlucks. Lexi still preferred newspapers and coffee, honestly, and she and Molly didn't get to Freshwater Church of the High Country much these days—9:00 a.m. came early after a 3:00 a.m. bedtime.

Molly shrugged. Lexi sighed.

Besides the possibility that Ward might return while she was gone, Lexi asked Angelo to stay in case Alice got any ideas to invite Grant over. It wouldn't take much pleading from Molly to talk her into it. Grant was scary enough without Ward in the picture. Now that Lexi believed the two men had never parted ways, she needed to be that much more wary.

Tomorrow, if Molly slept in, Lexi would put her mother on the proverbial witness stand. She intended to find out why Alice was feeling so supportive of Grant. Maybe because he was still so handsome.

Lexi cried all the way to work. And prayed. And when she arrived at the Red Rocks Bar and Grill she sat in her car in the parking lot until the last possible second before her shift started. Her eyes were bloodshot from tears and exhaustion, but she couldn't rest. If she was late two days in a row, Chuck might fire her.

The wind and the grasses were still that Saturday afternoon, and the sky was such a pristine blue that Lexi wanted to float up and away in it.

Lexi had never thought of herself as being good at praying. She didn't do it regularly and doubted she had the right words. Most of the time she figured God knew what she was thinking and needing without her having to say it. But periodically they did have one-sided conversations.

God, what's happening?

He tended not to reply, and she thought that was because he didn't have much to say or because she wasn't a good listener. In any case, she tried not to demand.

Gina said you'd put my past behind me when I started over. So why is it about to run me over? Why Grant, Ward, Norman, Mom—all here, now, all wanting something from me?

Molly and I didn't need anything but a fresh start. Was that too much to ask? Was it only a temporary arrangement?

Ward's remark about Molly paying for Lexi's debts poked into her thoughts. No child deserved that weight on her shoulders. Though she hadn't confessed all her sins to Gina, her friend knew a few of them, and Lexi was sure God knew the rest.

I thought that whole bit about you pardoning me meant I wasn't going to be punished for my mistakes for the rest of my life. I'm not saying I got that right, but if you would set me straight as gently as possible, I'd appreciate it.

And if you have any ideas about how I should handle Ward and Grant, I'll take those too.

Protect Molly. You've got to protect Molly. Please. Do what you want with me, but Molly doesn't deserve this wreck that's about to happen.

She didn't see any way to prevent it.

At 3:59 she locked the Volvo and plodded into the kitchen, head down. The question of how to come up with twenty-five thousand dollars was second only to the question of whether to confront Grant.

Lexi paused at the hook in the pantry/closet. Why would Ward demand cash from Grant if he intended to split it with Grant?

She rubbed her eyes and had no answer.

There was so much she needed to ask Angelo that she hadn't had time for yet, beginning with what he knew about Grant's incarceration. She also wanted to know about the strangeness that had passed between him and Ward at the house. Did they know each other? If so, how? What was their story?

Lexi hung up her book bag and jacket as she had Friday night, before her life started falling apart. She shoved a notepad into her apron pocket and it hung up on something.

The dog-eared photo Ward had left at his table last night, with black targets covering Molly's pretty face. Last night, right before . . .

Lexi shuddered and crammed the picture into her book bag. She entered the kitchen, trying to put the confusion out of her mind, and walked by a bucket of carrots that Chuck would expect her to dice if the prep cook got busy.

Mr. Tabor was the only warm body in the restaurant so far. He was reading the newspaper. When she took him his orange soda, he folded the paper and set it aside, smiling at her. The wide, toothy grin was one of the dearest, most authentic gestures of human kindness she'd ever known.

He patted his stomach.

"Still got that hole there?" she asked.

"That I do, child. It seems to be bottomless."

"I'll top it off for you, then. At least for a little while. Who'll be joining you today?" She asked so that she could be comforted by his answer.

"Whoever God brings my way."

Lexi wondered if God actually worked like that, brought certain people into the lives of other certain people, or if the world was more honestly random. For some reason, she liked that Mr. Tabor believed God had a plan, even if she didn't believe it.

"I'll go ahead and put in the Reuben for you."

She took a few orders, and about ten minutes later she picked up Mr. Tabor's sandwich with a napkin for a hot pad and walked it to his table. Someone sat opposite him in the vinyl booth. Lexi marveled. Mr. Tabor never ate alone.

"You be blessed today, lovely Lexi," Mr. Tabor said, slipping three one dollar bills under his spoon. "You bring me life on a plate, like my own sweet lady used to do."

It was impossible not to smile at this man, no matter how sour her mood.

"I forgot your slaw."

"All in due time. Dessert can never come too early or too late now, can it?"

"I guess not."

She turned to the other guest at the same time Mr. Tabor said, "May I trouble you to bring my friend here something to drink?"

Her eyes closed slowly, deliberately, as she did when she had to draw upon every reserve of her strength. Grant.

She opened her eyes and lifted her eyebrows. "Of course."

"Just coffee." He didn't meet her eyes. "When you come back. Don't make an extra trip."

As she wasn't willing to slight Mr. Tabor's kind heart by neglecting his table, Lexi returned immediately with a pot of black coffee, an empty cup, and a handful of creamers in her apron pocket.

Mr. Tabor was saying a blessing over his sandwich, and Grant had bowed his head. Lexi couldn't bring herself to set the cup on the table until they finished. In the whole of their brief romance and marriage, she'd never seen Grant bow his head to pray.

His hair needed a trim. It was wispy behind his ears. His denim shirt was worn out at the elbows and seemed a size too big in the shoulders, which curved forward under some invisible weight. He used to carry Molly on those shoulders when he was clearheaded. She'd throw her arms around his neck and hold on like a cape while he flew around the living room of their little Fireweed bungalow until he collapsed, blaming her for choking him to death.

"That coffee's growin' cold in your very hands," Mr. Tabor said, smiling before he took a bite of the Reuben. Lexi snapped out of her trance and poured the coffee without apologizing. Grant wouldn't look at her.

She left.

Grant and Mr. Tabor talked for an hour longer than Mr. Tabor usually stayed. She had no idea what they discussed and did only what was necessary as their server, clearing the dishes and keeping the coffee and orange soda topped off. Then, after Mr. Tabor left at six, Grant continued to sit. He had the old man's bill but didn't seem in a hurry to pay it.

Lexi smoldered. The only good thing about his being here was that it meant he wasn't trying to visit her home. She wondered where Ward was.

She wordlessly refilled his cup twice before mustering the nerve at six thirty to ask him if he wanted something to eat. When he declined, she suggested he give up the table for a paying customer. It was a slow Saturday, though, and at least three booths were unoccupied at the time. He allowed his eyes to pass over these without remark, then he withdrew his wallet from his back pocket and placed a five under the spoon that held Mr. Tabor's standard three-dollar tip in place. She walked away feeling both angry and ashamed.

At seven he paid the bill and Lexi returned his change. Between then and nine forty-five he examined the stain that had formed around the inside rim of his cup after asking her not to refill it anymore.

At ten, of her own accord, she took him a glass of water and the bowl of clam chowder that would have been hers to eat if she'd had any appetite. She set it on his table without saying anything. After she left the table, she saw him place a ten-dollar bill on top of Mr. Tabor's ones and his five. She wished she hadn't said anything about paying customers.

By eleven, the restaurant was empty except for a few people who'd probably stay in the bar until closing. Some of them might order a bite to eat. She had wiped down tables, swept the floor, refilled the salt and pepper shakers, and married the ketchup jars.

Lexi couldn't stand it anymore.

She dropped into Mr. Tabor's seat.

"What do you want, Grant?"

"I want to talk to you."

"So talk."

He placed his hands palms-down on the table. "How's Molly?"

"Good, considering."

"How bad is the ankle?"

"She broke it in three places and fractured six bones in her foot." Lexi erected a barbed-wire fence around her heart to separate the physical facts from the worse emotional truth: her daughter was in pain and Lexi couldn't rescue her from it. "We won't know what that really means until the swelling goes down. A couple months in a cast at least. Maybe surgery."

"But she's getting around?"

"There isn't too much that can keep her down."

"No?"

That was the first time she had the conscious thought that Grant didn't know anything about the girl his baby had grown into. She opened her mouth to tell him how headstrong Molly was, and all the ways that was a beautiful thing, then hesitated. Knowing a child the way she knew Molly was a privilege Lexi had earned. Why should she slice it up and serve it to Grant like one of Molly's carefully prepared meals? He didn't deserve it.

"She's a determined girl," Lexi said. She pulled the night's receipts out of her apron pocket and began to sort them, to give herself something to look at.

"She looks like you."

"Prettier," Lexi said.

Silence stopped them up for half a minute. She was aware that she was making this difficult for him. A part of her wished she could get over it. The stronger part insisted he be held accountable for the problems he'd caused and granted her permission to be a jerk.

"I imagine you have some questions about why I left," Grant said.

She neither confirmed nor denied it.

"I owe you an explanation."

"I'm not looking for one, Grant."

"Still."

"What will an explanation change, really? Why go through it? So please, let's not. Not tonight. It's late."

"I need to tell you, though. I'm hoping . . . I need you to forgive me, Lexi."

"You *need*."

He exhaled loudly.

"*You* need," she repeated. Her fingers closed on a stack of receipts. "Seven years without a thought of me or your daughter—"

"That's not true."

"—and your first words to me are about what *you* need." Lexi slid out of the booth, sweeping the white slips of paper into a pile. "Don't throw words like *true* at me. If you want me to forgive you, Grant, I'm going to need at least another decade."

Grant reached out but didn't touch her as she stood.

"Lexi, wait."

"Why?"

"Please hear me out."

"You know what? I don't want to. In the space of twenty-four hours my ears have been chewed on by my daughter—who's furious with me because of that letter you sent, by the way—and by my mother, and then I find out you have some royally twisted partnership still going on with Warden Pavo—"

"Ward?"

"And Molly almost died and my father's out of his mind and my best friend's in the hospital practically sharing a room with Norman Von Ruden."

"Ward's in town?"

"Funny, he said the same thing about you, and just one day ago you were both standing in this very dining room within spitting distance. He told me why you two are here, and honestly, I don't get the joke. I'm not laughing."

"You're mad about the note. I'm really sorry about that. It was one of the dumbest ideas I've had in a long time. Your mother thought—"

"Stop. Just stop it, Grant. Take responsibility for your own actions for once."

Grant swallowed.

Her anger simmered, but she didn't leave the table. She was searching for a way to convince him to leave, forever this time, while fearing what might happen if he and Ward *weren't* working together. Would Ward follow through on his threat to Molly if Lexi didn't make an effort to pull together some money?

The possibility loomed too large for her to ignore.

She picked up the cash he'd left and crammed it into her apron with the receipts.

"Ward told me about the money. About Molly. What do you have to say about that?"

The frown lines between Grant's blue eyes deepened. He shook his head. "I don't know what you mean. What about Molly?"

"Fine. We're done. That's all I need to know."

He got out of the booth and planted himself in front of Lexi before she'd taken a step. "Is he threatening Molly?"

"You're the one who's threatening her!" Lexi's voice was nearly a shout. "You're trying to take her from me, and you're going to use your mother-in-law and an old drug dealer to get her! Of all the low—"

"That's not even close to what I—What did Ward say to you?"

Lexi's mouth fell open, but nothing came out. It was the shock of believing him that silenced her. All he'd ever done was lie to her, but right now she believed his own fury, paternal and protective.

"Where is he? When did he get to Crag's Nest?"

"I thought you knew."

"I haven't seen that con since the day I left you."

A headache shoved memories around Lexi's head like a ransacking burglar. Hadn't Ward said he and Grant were together?

"Do you still owe him money?" she asked.

"A fair amount."

"He wants it back."

"Well I don't have it."

"Are you working?"

"Yeah."

"Where?"

"Janitorial stuff down in Riverbend."

Grant was probably earning less than she was. If he wasn't also dealing drugs on the side. Lexi weighed this possibility. Grant's return to the business could be the only reason Ward thought he could collect on his debt. If Grant had money that could get Molly out of a difficult spot, he owed it to her.

Would Grant offer it?

"Sounds like it's time for the two of you to work something out," she said.

Grant picked his wallet up off the table and crammed it back into his pocket. Ward's threats came to the front of her mouth, but she bit them back, unsure if it was in Molly's best interest to tell Grant what was at stake. He might use it against her, her folly with Norm in particular, a reason to shoehorn himself rather than his money back into Molly's life. Play the hero, the great defender.

Lexi looked at the receipts in her hands, wondering why she hoped that Grant would never learn about the affair.

He walked out without saying good-bye.

{ chapter 17 }

When Lexi got home, Angelo was sitting in the chair Gina usually studied in. The reading lamp was the only light on in the house. She opened the door and he stood, casting a burly shadow across the entire room. It touched her feet.

"Thanks for staying," she said.

"Happy to do it."

Lexi leaned her book bag against the wall.

"That's surprising to me. That you'd be happy to babysit. I hardly know you."

He nodded, as if he understood the strangeness of that fact but didn't find it strange at all. Lexi almost blurted that she would have slept more easily if he'd stay awake in the living room all night. Instead, aware of how awkward that would have been, she struck up a conversation, intending to get him to stay without asking.

"It's very hard for me to understand your interest in my family. As much as I appreciate it."

"That's alright."

She thought he'd say more, but he didn't.

"Everyone's good?" she asked.

"The swelling in Molly's ankle is almost gone."

This was perplexing news. The doctor had said she should expect it to be puffy for more than a week, maybe two.

"My days are filled with inexplicable events," she said.

Angelo smiled and took a step forward. He reached out for Lexi's jacket, and when she gave it to him, he hung it in the closet. She sat down on the sofa and he returned to the chair.

Lexi felt oddly like she was in his home rather than her own. This felt good to her. This felt . . . relaxed. Like the responsibility for life wasn't all hers.

"You okay?" he asked.

"Tired. But yeah. I'm okay."

"Ward didn't look like a friend," he said.

So much for that warm fuzzy feeling. Tension reappeared between her shoulders. "You dive right into the heart of a thing, don't you? He's one of the many reasons I asked you to look after Mom and Molly tonight."

"What did he say to you?"

"Oh, please. Angelo, I've taken advantage of you today. You don't want to waste any more time on my problems."

"It's not like that."

"What's it like, then?"

"Tell me what he said."

She wanted to. For the next hour she told him everything, finding safety in his being a virtual stranger. Somehow it was easier to disclose herself to a person she might never see again than to a close friend. Here she was, telling Angelo about things she'd never mentioned to Gina. Maybe the pain of his potential judgment was less frightening. The prospect of losing him was less severe. The cost lower.

She told Angelo about Grant's drugs, about his entanglement in Ward's web, about Norman's appearance in their lives, about the escape she'd found in his distraction until Tara died. Lexi told him about Grant's abandonment and her father's descent into a mentally safe place and how Alice abandoned him in the same way Grant abandoned her—even though her mother denied it. She explained how Gina had reconnected her to God and how after all this time she still didn't understand what God wanted from her. By the time she finally told Angelo about Ward's threats against Molly, she was sobbing.

"I don't know what I did to deserve this," she cried. "I've worked so hard. What Grant did to Molly by leaving is . . . if he'd done it to me, that would have been different. But he did it to his daughter. That's unspeakable. That's . . . I can't let him near her, do you understand? If he left again it would kill her. And now this! From both sides—Grant wants her and Ward is threatening her." She shook her head. "If I lost Molly too . . . if anything happened to her I'd die. It would kill me. I can't let anything happen to Molly."

Angelo had reached out and placed his warm hand on Lexi's shoulder, as he had after she fell apart at St. Luke's. She tried to remember the last time someone had touched her so kindly. Except for Molly's hugs, she couldn't remember.

She said, "What should I do?"

"I'm better at listening than advising, unfortunately."

Lexi sniffled and laughed. "At any other point in my history I would have preferred that in a man."

He chuckled. She tried to take a calming breath, but it got hung up in her throat. She covered her wet eyes until she was breathing evenly again.

"Molly showed me the letter from Grant," he said.

Lexi shook her head. "Don't take it as a compliment. I told her she couldn't see Grant and then brought you home with me. She sees you as competition."

"That's normal for a girl her age."

"She wasn't rude to you, was she?"

"Of course not. She's defensive of her dad, that's all."

"You mean her idea of her dad."

"That's all she has."

Lexi leaned back against the sofa cushions. "That was some letter, huh?"

Angelo didn't offer his opinion.

"Let me ask you something," Lexi said. "Friday morning I read that letter, and then I read it again yesterday morning, and it was a completely different letter. How's that?"

"It was probably the same letter the whole time."

"My eyes played tricks on me, then? Or my tired mind?"

"Based on the story you've told me, I'd blame it on a tired heart."

"What's that?"

"You've done a lot for Molly since the two of you were left alone. You want to protect her and do what's best for her. Then along comes something you see as a threat, something that you believe could undo all your hard work, and you're going to read trouble into it."

"That doesn't explain my first impressions of that letter."

"Maybe that's all they were—impressions. Perceptions."

The theory wasn't an adequate explanation for Lexi. She didn't like the idea that she might not be in complete control of her own mind.

"The love you have for Molly is very powerful," he said.

"What can love do against men like Ward and Grant?"

"Against them?"

"Love your enemies, right?"

"I guess bludgeoning your enemies with love could work in some instances. But that's not what I meant."

She waited for him to explain.

"Your love for your daughter will show you the best way to protect her."

"That's a nice thought, Angelo, but it's not something I can grab hold of, you know? It's not money I can take to Ward or use to buy a plane ticket out of Riverbend."

"You're right. But look at all the emotions competing for your mind right now: you have anger and resentment and confusion and—"

"And hatred," she supplied.

"And love," he said. He spread his hands, palms up, a gesture inviting her to listen carefully. "Let that one inform you. Not the others. Hatred is especially dangerous."

She stared at his large hands, doubting. "I can't make it go away."

"Maybe not right away, but while you're working on it, you can consult any of the emotions you want for advice."

"Can't I consult flesh and blood like you, Dr. Angelo?"

"Flesh and blood is soaked with imperfection."

"And my emotions aren't."

"Only love isn't."

"I don't know about that. I fell in love with Grant, didn't I?"

He lowered his voice and smiled like a wise older brother. "Falling in love isn't Love with a capital L."

"Okay. This conversation is getting a bit woo-hoo for this hour of the morning." She waggled her fingers. The gesture didn't tickle his funny bone as planned.

"Go with flesh and blood then, if you dare. Who are you going to talk to?"

That silenced her. If not Angelo, then who?

"Where do you think love comes from, Lexi?"

She couldn't think of a bright answer.

"C'mon. You know. Every good and perfect gift comes from above," he said.

"You mean God."

"I do."

"You and Gina speak each other's language," Lexi said.

"You speak it too."

"Are you suggesting I need to pray more?" Defensiveness crept into her voice.

"I'm suggesting you need to consult love on this one. That's all."

"I'm going to have to agree with you about being a better listener than adviser," Lexi said.

"I'm sorry," he said.

"Don't be. I'm tired. It might make more sense to me in the morning. Later in the morning."

Angelo smiled his understanding. "Daylight does wonders," he said. He rose and took a piece of paper out of his breast pocket. She noticed, after all this time, that he was actually wearing flannel. Her lumberjack. If she wasn't so drained she would have teased him about it.

"Someone called while you were at work," he said. "Asked you to call back."

There were two seven-digit numbers on the paper. "Who?"

Angelo was reaching for his own jacket, slung across one of the kitchen chairs. "Love," he said, grinning.

"Very funny. Who was it?"

"Just call." He shrugged into the sleeves and his arms spanned the hall from kitchen to living room. "Maybe he can give you clearer advice than I can."

"He."

"The number on the bottom is mine. In case you need anything."

She wasn't ready for Angelo to go.

His bright truck had exited the parking lot before she realized she'd forgotten to ask him, the kindest man she'd ever met, why he'd been so cold toward Ward.

The sunny window by Barrett's chair was being spray painted with black targets while Molly placed hundred-dollar bills into a skillet that Ward then lassoed with his key chain. The money caught on fire. Angelo's incredible arm span cast a shadow that looked like eagles' wings over the lawn. The shadows pulsated and fanned Ward's flames into an inferno. Grant walked through the fire toward Lexi like the dark man in Nebuchadnezzar's extra-hot furnace, invincible.

Lexi reached out for Grant and woke up sweating.

At the end of such oppressive nightmares, she was surprised and grateful to open her eyes and see at the back of her mind a much more beautiful memory. One that involved Tara.

When Lexi was nine and her sister thirteen, Tara was selected by the dance instructor at their ballet studio to be photographed for promotional materials the school was having produced. Tara's limber, svelte figure was so different from Lexi's more husky form. Lexi was built for gymnastics, but being in awe of her big sister, she wanted nothing more than to follow her every step, which was nuts. Two years later Tara would have the role of Clara in *The Nutcracker* and Lexi would have dropped out, too old for the beginning classes and too unskilled to advance. At the time, though, their parents allowed Lexi's copycat behavior and Tara tolerated it, because everyone thought she'd eventually outgrow her foolish yearning.

But when Tara was selected to dance in front of a camera, Lexi insisted that she be included and was denied. Rather than be happy for Tara, Lexi felt the rejection personally. Tara was talented, and she was a klutz. Tara was grown-up, and she was still a child. Tara was pretty, and she was not. As a nine-year-old who was not merely young but also immature for her age, Lexi was overtaken by jealousy.

The night before the photographs were scheduled to be taken, Lexi sneaked into Tara's room with dull safety scissors and patiently severed every wisp of the shiny fawn-colored hair that spilled across her forehead and pillow.

What surprised Lexi most about her plot to bring her sister down from that high cloud was that Tara's horror did not make her happy. Instead, they both were miserable.

Lexi's misery lasted longer than Tara's. That morning, after ignoring Lexi entirely, Mom rushed Tara to her own hairstylist instead of the usual kiddie barbershop. Tara emerged with an adorable pixie cut that wowed the photographer and became the trendsetting style for every girl in her eighth-grade class. Tara never wore her hair long again.

What was beautiful about this memory was what happened three days afterward. Lexi sat on the concrete driveway of their home, her legs sprawled out in front of her, heavy with roller skates that anchored her feet to the earth—except when she wanted to stand upright. Her tailbone ached.

Sitting on the porch, Tara had pretended not to notice Lexi's fall. Tara hadn't spoken to her little sister since "the vandalism," as the family came to call it, and Lexi missed her terribly. Usually Tara held her up on her skates. At the moment, Lexi doubted Tara would ever hold her hands again. She bowed her head and tried to work up the courage to apologize for real, and not begrudgingly, as she had when their dad required it.

While Lexi still stared at the sandpapery surface of the driveway, Tara left the porch and sat down next to her.

"I'm sorry for being so angry at you," she said. "I miss you and I hope you'll forgive me. Can I help you back up?"

Even today, as an adult, it was hard for Lexi to comprehend the magnificent size of Tara's heart at an age when hearts seem prone to selfish shrinking.

Lexi remembered leaning into Tara's arms and hugging her shoulders, too overcome to look her sister in the eye.

The memory was beautiful and devastating.

The door of the bedroom Molly and Lexi shared was closed, and the room was gray with the morning light filtered by thin curtains. The radio mumbled low in the living room and the scent of cinnamon Pop Tarts drifted over the bed. Molly only ate Pop Tarts when she was gloomy. At any other time they'd be beneath her. Lexi thought she should go see how her daughter was doing. Check her ankle. See if the swelling was as low as Angelo had suggested.

First, a few more minutes to doze.

Her hair and pillow were damp with sweat. She tried to get comfortable again but couldn't. She flipped the pillow over to the cool side, and when she dropped her cheek into the cotton worn thin by a thousand vigorous washings, she encountered a crinkling of paper and a gravelly lump.

Lexi sat up and ran her fingers over the surface of the pillowcase.

Something had been shoved inside it. Turning sideways, she dangled her feet off the edge of the bed and lifted the cushion onto her lap, then inserted her hand and retrieved a piece of crumpled paper scrawled in barely legible handwriting.

Don't make me call the cops, it said.

She slipped her hand back into the case. Her fingers touched a small plastic bag. She pulled it out.

The bag, barely two inches square, was filled with small pinkish chips that looked like plastic rocks.

Crystal meth.

{ chapter 18 }

A man of Norman Von Ruden's dubious social status need only be stabilized, not healed, before being discharged from a hospital and readmitted to prison. This happened Sunday morning, thanks to his vigorous constitution. Warden was glad for it, because the longer Norm stayed at St. Luke's, the higher the chances that Craven would retaliate for the whole episode with Mort Weatherby.

Sunday, Warden showed up as an EMT assigned by the prison to accompany Norman to the facility where he'd await his parole hearing. In other words, Warden would take Norman where he had been destined to go in the first place, before the accident. Getting this gig was a little more difficult than the man-in-a-lab-coat stunt Warden had pulled off on Mort's behalf, but not impossible. Warden had a gift for making people see what they wanted to see—in this case, a highly competent substitute provided by the state for a coworker who had called in sick. It was very rare that Warden had to force people to see what *he* wanted them to see. So often, their visions coincided. That was what made his work so easy.

He and Norman rode alone in the back of the ambulance.

"Warden," Norman said, not entirely clouded over by a haze of pain-killers. "Imagine seeing you here."

"I'm not here. I'm merely one of your Percocet hallucinations," Warden said, examining the IV bag. These things were fantastic, providing direct access to the bloodstream as they did. It used to be that he had to get more creative when he needed to slip somebody a little something.

Like that bag of goodies he left for Lexi before she and Gigantor showed up at her home the day before. Warden thought it too bad that she wouldn't actually consume any of it. Maybe someday he'd talk her into trying some. Or finagle a way to get her hooked up to a bag like Norman's. That would be rewarding—but less rewarding than if she decided she wanted to get high all by herself. Forcing a person's hand in anything didn't really do it for Warden. He much preferred to watch people fall down and believe the failure was entirely their own doing.

As Norman did. All Ward's bets about Norman Von Ruden had paid off years ago. Warden wouldn't need him much longer.

Norman's eyes were on the bag. "Did you bring me more? Because what they're giving me now is as worthless as hillbilly heroine."

"That's because they don't know how much you really need."

"Fix me up, then."

"Patience, friend. I know what to do." Without following hygienic procedures, Warden thrust a cannula into Norm's IV port and loaded it up. "I've seen your girlfriend," he said.

Norman grunted. "Saw her myself."

"No kidding." Warden was sorry to have missed the encounter. "That must have been a happy reunion."

"She brought me roses and passionate kisses. And a death threat."

"And to think you parted on such good terms."

"Not what I expected from a gal who's supposed to be talking me up in a week."

"You know women. They so rarely mean what they say."

"You don't know squat, Warden."

"Tell me, what don't I know? That you loved her like an insane man? That you were a fool to meet her sister? You would have made a lot more headway if you'd killed her husband instead."

Norman swore.

"C'mon. You've got to give me a little room to rib you. You provide me with such good material. It's what friends are for, right? What's a man who can't laugh at himself?"

Norman tried to take a deep breath, which couldn't feel good considering the broken ribs and punctured lung. But Warden sensed the morphine taking some effect. Norman's agitation dropped a notch.

"What are you going to say to her at the hearing?" Warden nudged.

"Nothing."

"That's your bruised ego talking."

"She turned her back on me after the trial and hasn't contacted me since."

"She couldn't. You know what it would have looked like. She still has feelings for you. You've got to know she does."

Norman frowned, a fleeting, doubtful frown. "Even if she didn't mean what she said, not even a monkey would have heard love in it."

"No. No. Listen. Seven years of her never breaking off her relationship with you—"

"You're that man women love to hate because you don't understand the word *no*, aren't you?"

Warden laughed once, a loud bark. "Yes! That's me. And I'll tell you why it works. But before that, let's get the truth straight. There's no point in talking about these things if we can't talk about the truth."

"Fine words from the boldest liar I ever met."

"Which is why you can trust me. You know what I'm about. So here it is: you are still, after all these years, crazy in love with Lexi Grüggen."

"Solomon. She never divorced him."

"Aha! So you don't deny it!"

"Me setting you straight about her name doesn't mean anything."

"It's you that needs to be set straight. She's a Grüggen. She can't help herself. She wants to live without that beast of a husband."

"Yeah. Whatever. If all this works out, you and I will get our revenge and she'll get what she wants. Grant, dead. Everyone, happy."

"She could also have you back."

"I'm telling you, she doesn't want me back."

Warden leaned over Norm, commanded his eye contact. "You have to tell her."

"Tell her what?"

"It wasn't your fault, Norman."

He turned his face away.

"The death of Lexi's sister was not your fault. She has the right to know it."

Norman yanked on the straps that kept him anchored to this hospital bed. "What do you care, Warden? What are we really talking about? Because my case is not up for appeal, and there isn't any new evidence in the works, and it was my bloody knife that killed that woman. There's no need to rehash all this."

"It was Grant's fault. It was his fault for giving you those placebos. He used you to make a buck. If you'd got what you needed to get better—if you'd got what I sold to him—"

"Shut up."

Warden leaned back against the bouncing ambulance seat. "You need to tell her that everything that happened is Grant's fault."

"Why?"

"Why protect her? Why keep up the charade? You protected her *and* her lousy husband through the trial. You could have brought him down if you'd had the guts to point your finger at Grant and name him."

"What would that have gained me? Nothing—no reduced sentence, no co-conspirator—"

"Have you *no* imagination, man?" Warden smacked the addict on the head. "You could have nailed him as a low-down dealer, a jealous husband, a mastermind who framed you—"

"That would have killed her."

"She deserves to know the truth."

"The *truth* is that I killed her sister."

"NO! Grant did it! Don't you see! Grant is wholly responsible, regardless of who held the knife."

Norman shook his head.

"You're an idiot in love," Warden said. "How much more are you willing to give up for her? All these years!"

"I thought if I protected her from being connected to the murder through Grant, she might . . . come around."

"Brilliant. You have the patience of a *saint*, apparently." Warden sputtered his disgust. "You should have told her how Grant completely messed you up. How you weren't in your right mind when you agreed to meet Tara. That if you'd had the medication he promised you, nothing would have happened. *Then* maybe she would have actually divorced him."

Norman seemed to chew on this new way of seeing. Warden gave him some space to ponder.

"You're right," he mumbled.

"Yes, I'm right. I'm always right. I was right the day I told you to cut Grant out and work straight with me. The middleman killed you, Norman. He's still killing you, seven years after he's forgotten your name."

The road noise of the ambulance sounded like a hypnotic hum.

"Lexi can still be yours," Warden said. "You can keep her for yourself and keep her out of Grant's reach."

"You still don't know what you're talking about." But Norman's heart rate on the monitor picked up a few beats per minute.

"Ask her to meet you."

"What?"

"Tell Lexi you want to speak to her before the hearing."

"So she can scream at me some more?"

"No, no. For something much bigger than that."

After a contemplative silence he said, "For what, then?"

"Ask her to forgive you."

The ambulance hit a pothole and caused Norm to cringe. Or maybe it was Warden's suggestion. But then he started laughing, a cynic's laugh borne by weariness. He placed a hand over his wounded lung.

"If it's not my fault, then there's nothing to forgive, is there?"

"Now, don't get cynical on me. You're a man of vision, Norman. You can understand what I'm getting at here. Ask her to forgive you."

"She won't."

"She might. And if in her forgiving you she learns to love you, you win. But even if she won't forgive you, you win. The moment she refuses, you own her."

"How is that winning? That's not love."

"I never promised love. But that's the beauty of this, see? I can promise you obsession, which is even greater. She will never let you go."

Bitterness, Warden believed, was the most stunning of all human emotions. It was multidimensional, multifaceted, multifunctional. It was the most effective emotion he could call upon in his line of work, the emotion that brought him the most success.

"What do you want out of this, Warden?"

"The satisfaction of helping my friend extract a little well-deserved revenge."

"I don't believe you."

"You'll have influence over her *forever*," Warden whispered.

"I never wanted influence. Just happiness. Was that so much to ask?"

"Not at all, friend, not at all. But we take what we can get. Let me tell you what I've set up."

{ chapter 19 }

Lexi's hands shook as she poured the rock crystals into the toilet, then dropped the plastic bag in too. A little water had splashed onto the rim, and she wiped it down with a piece of toilet paper. She flushed, then opened the window and turned on the fan and flushed two more times. The street value of the tiny packet probably would have taken care of a few bills, a thought that sickened Lexi almost as much as the existence of the bag itself.

She tore apart her bedroom looking for more. One anonymous tip to the authorities was all it would take for them to sweep through here with dogs to smell what she couldn't see. She imagined them barking at light fixtures and floor vents and dusty ceiling fans, then receiving rewards while their handlers slapped cuffs around her wrists and dragged her off, away from Molly. Lexi wondered how much time Ward would have had to hide more yesterday while Alice let him wander the apartment. She wondered if she could afford to wait until her mom left or Molly went back to school before she searched the other rooms.

She had a little less than week, if Ward stuck to his word. A week before Norm's hearing, a week to talk Grant into producing twenty-five thousand dollars. This truth calmed her a little. Warden was only showing her that he was serious. It was likely that there were more drugs hidden around the little apartment in places she'd never think to look.

For now, she decided, she would spend her energies on getting that cash.

Lexi leaned against the edge of the bathroom sink trying to figure out next steps. Ward's demand that she get the money from Grant still didn't make any sense. How was it that he thought she had more influence over Grant than he did?

She could make a plea directly on Molly's behalf. Did he want contact with her badly enough to pay for it?

The implications of that arrangement frightened Lexi.

Ward's accusation played itself over in her mind. *You should have chosen me.* Even this made little sense. Ward had never made a play for her that she could recall. Unless she was so blinded by her attraction to Norman that she never noticed it. That possibility was unbelievable to her now, repulsive even. Clearly, she'd been blinded to so much more during those months. So, even though she couldn't make sense of Ward's motive, if he meant what he said, he would take pains to make her life difficult, rather than Grant's.

How was she going to talk Grant out of twenty-five thousand dollars? Maybe it didn't all have to come from him. Maybe none of it had to come from him.

There was Alice.

Lexi sighed.

Her mother. Lexi would have to tell her some of what was going on. The fleeting thought that she could talk Alice into taking Molly away from Crag's Nest for a few days crossed her mind. If only Molly were more mobile. She might be safer anywhere but here.

Lexi went down the hall. Alice was sitting on the sofa, reading the paper.

"Where's Molly?"

"Gina's room. She was up for a bit and ate something, then said she was tired. I set her up in my bed rather than disturb you."

Lexi detected disapproval in this information, as if she should have gotten up with Molly much earlier.

"She misses you," Alice said. "She's growing up without you."

"I have to pay the bills."

"There are other jobs. Jobs that wouldn't make you stay out so late. It's danger—"

"I get to take her to school and pick her up. I'm with her during the day on weekends. I do what I can."

"When a child is sick, her mother is the only one who—"

"We need to talk about Grant," Lexi said, leaning against the wall. "Seven years ago you were the first person to tell me it was best that he left, that he wasn't good for me or Molly. Next thing I know you're passing notes to her from him and having dinner with him where I work. I want to know what that's all about, Mom, because what's really going on with Molly right now has nothing to do with my job or my hours."

Alice folded the newspaper and set it next to her on the seat cushion. She removed her reading glasses.

"Five years ago I was in Los Angeles covering the Chinese new year— they had a related food festival going on in Chinatown. I was sampling something from a street vendor, I can't even remember what it was now, when I noticed a man carrying this beautiful little girl who looked exactly like Molly when she was about three." Alice gestured at her hair and face. "That thick chocolate hair and full cheeks. She was crying her eyes out, and the man was trying to calm her. It was Grant."

Lexi had often wondered where he'd gone after he left Crag's Nest, but Chinatown had never occurred to her. It wasn't hard to imagine him being paternal, though, in spite of what he'd done in leaving.

"The girl had been separated from her parents, and he stood with her in the same spot until they found her again. He kept saying, 'The best way to be found is to stay where you are. They'll come back. I won't leave you.'"

Alice put her reading glasses on the end table. Her story made Lexi ache. Molly had been that little girl once. She wasn't old enough to ask about her dad until a couple years after his departure. By then, Lexi didn't dare suggest he might ever come back, because she didn't trust herself to know what to do if he tried it.

She still didn't.

Alice shook her head. "I didn't know what to make of the scene. After what he did to you. I didn't know whether to talk to him, and the girl's parents came back before I decided. The mother was hysterical and the father . . . I don't know. It was so clear what Grant was doing, but when parents are afraid for their children they don't think straight." She caught Lexi's eye briefly, then lowered hers to her lap. "I thought at the time the father believed Grant had something terrible in mind. He grabbed his girl out of Grant's arms and punched him in the face. Grant blacked out I think. Everyone was shouting or crying." She shook her head. "The man gave the girl to his wife, and she ran off. Then he bent over Grant and went through his pockets. He pulled out Grant's wallet, pulled everything out, then threw it on the ground. Who wants to get involved in a situation like that? People watched, including me. More people turned away. No one wanted to interfere. It wasn't clear what was going on. Someone must have called the police, though.

"Grant was out cold for a few seconds. Half a minute at most. When he started to come around, this man was kneeling over him. He pinned Grant's shoulders with his arm, like this, and he was holding something over Grant's face. A bundle like a sachet. It was white and tied off with a wire twist. The guy was shouting. Not in English. I don't know what it was. Something Slavic."

"In Chinatown."

"He wasn't Chinese."

"Grant doesn't speak anything but English."

Alice shrugged. "Anyway, they stayed like that until the police arrived, and when they did, this guy switched to English, said he was a private investigator who'd been tracking Grant and found him in possession of cocaine—apparently that was what was in the bag."

Lexi rubbed her eyes and took the seat that Angelo had occupied, Gina's reading chair.

"He accused Grant of trying to kidnap his daughter," Alice said. "I thought the guy was crazy."

"Did you say anything?"

"I'm ashamed to say I didn't."

"Ashamed?"

"Don't look so incredulous. It was an awful thing to witness, no matter what he did to you."

Lexi supposed that separating victims from offenders was sometimes a matter of perspective. But this was her mother talking. Lexi managed to hold her tongue.

"I should have spoken up. Instead I found out which police station they were taking him to, and I followed. He was more than a little surprised to see me."

She fell silent, maybe remembering, maybe deciding how much to say. Questions ricocheted around in Lexi's head.

"I posted his bail on the condition he tell me why he left you and Molly, and what he'd been doing in the meantime."

"That's the biggest waste of money I could have dreamed up."

"You didn't tell me he'd been dealing, Lexi."

Lexi leaned forward in the chair. "There was no point in telling you. What were the chances you'd see him go down in a deal gone bad? Don't make your choice to bail him out my fault. You saw enough yourself. Did you think the guy who knocked him down was making it all up? After what Grant did, Mom, couldn't you believe he was capable of anything? Molly doesn't know. I don't want her to ever know."

Alice extended her hands in a gesture meant to calm Lexi down. "I wasn't blaming you. I heard how he spoke to that child when he thought no one was listening. He wasn't there to take her away. He was helping her. It was a fifty-fifty chance from my point of view that this so-called PI had set Grant up."

"What did Grant tell you?"

"That the man was a client, not a PI. They'd completed a deal that morning, and it was a beyond-bizarre coincidence that Grant happened upon his lost daughter that afternoon. When the man saw Grant with her, he lost it. He thought Grant was going to use her as a pawn in some unfinished business—I don't know what that was all about. It doesn't matter anyway."

"If he was a client, he wouldn't have testified against Grant."

"He didn't have to. Grant pled guilty to everything. Didn't even have a trial. I think he wanted to go to prison."

"Of course he did. Free room and board, probably greater access to all the illegal substances he wanted."

"Lexi, stop." Alice's gentle voice chastised her daughter without judgment. "Listen to you."

She did stop, even though she felt no less justified in her opinion of what Grant had done. Why should a criminal have every need met in prison while his victims scraped by on the outside, barely pulling together a living?

Lexi wondered how much the bail was but couldn't bring herself to ask. The number, no matter how great or small, would only have made her more upset.

"How long did he stay with you?"

"Three days."

"And this was enough time to change your opinion of him."

"Yes."

The answer grew big in the silent room. Lexi felt betrayed by it. She wanted to know the details and yet she knew they'd crush her. Her own mother, allied with her drug-dealing husband!

Lexi finally said, "You shouldn't be upset with me for not telling you he was a dealer, not after all you've withheld from me." She meant it to be an accusation, but it sounded more like a pout. "Have you kept in touch with him all this time?"

"No, not the whole time. He was sentenced to five years, and when he went in, he cut ties with me. I tried to see him once or twice, but he refused. And I was working. Traveling. I meant to get back to Los Angeles in time for his release, but he got out early. Everything's overcrowded there, you know. They don't keep the small offenders as long as the rest."

"I thought drug dealers got tougher sentences than killers," Lexi said. "Not that Norman and Grant are any indication."

"I think that's changing."

"So he looked you up when he got out?"

"He found me in Las Vegas a few weeks ago."

"Why? Did he tap you on the shoulder and say, 'I want my daughter, will you help me get her?'"

"First he wanted to know about you. If you'd remarried. How much you despised him. He used that very word, *despised*."

"Did you tell him I'd welcome him back with open arms?"

Alice got a short laugh out of that remark. "I discouraged him at first. I told him you weren't even on speaking terms with *me*. That gave him pause." Alice hadn't looked at her more than a couple times during the course of this conversation. Now she gave Lexi her full attention. "I've never seen a man more convinced he was in love with somebody."

"I have," she said. "Dad was always that way about you. He still thinks he is."

Alice stood and walked to the front window. "He's not in his right mind."

"He might be, if you hadn't run away from him like you did."

Lexi knew which words would bring out the upset mother in Alice Grüggen, and she selected them as her way of getting even for her unbelievable betrayal. Once Alice was angry with her, the conversation would be easy enough to end without having to take any blame. Lexi waited for her "how dare you" or "watch your tone of voice, young lady."

Instead she broke down.

"I did. I turned my back on your father because it hurt too much to see what Tara's death did to him. What he'd become." She still could not look at Lexi. "I know you feel you lost them both, but I did too, Lexi. And then to have you so angry at me! I always thought you didn't understand, but

I realize you were only going through the same loss. When Grant found me, he woke me up. Here he was, trying to find his way back to you, and I realized I was no different from him, the way I'd run off." She sniffled and looked helpless without a tissue. Lexi got up and fetched the tissue box from the kitchen, not knowing how to respond to this side of her mother. The transparency scared her a little. Lexi offered the box and Alice took it.

"The thing with Grant . . ." Alice dabbed at her cheeks. "He's changed. I believe him with my whole heart. Something has changed in him, and I was so convinced by it that I encouraged him to write to Molly. I thought she'd be more . . . open than you. But me, I haven't figured out how to change yet, Lexi. I don't know how to go back to your father."

"He'd take you in an instant," Lexi said, groping for something kind to say to stop her from saying more. She shifted her weight on her feet and looked out the window "He doesn't have a clear sense of time. He probably doesn't realize how long . . ." The lame remark didn't deserve to be finished.

The pair stood there for a few minutes.

"I'm angry at you for going behind my back," Lexi said.

"I know. I'm sorry."

"I don't believe Grant has changed."

"You haven't spent any real time with him."

She almost said, *I don't want to*. But Lexi could see a new argument regenerating itself out of that. Also, she wasn't sure anymore what she wanted. Instead she said, "How do you know he's not still dealing?"

Alice frowned. "Grant's been testing every three weeks for everything under the sun. Just to prove himself to me. He's clean."

"Who's paying for that?"

"I am."

"How?"

"Your dad took very good care of me before Tara . . . he was a good long-term planner. That's how we're paying for Dad's care, Lexi. You knew that, didn't you?"

"Have you loaned Grant money?"

"A little."

"Has he paid you back?"

"Are you worried about Molly's hospital bill? Because the state will take care of that. The accident was their fault, after all. But even if they don't, I can help out. I can—"

"No, Mom. I mean, I'll have to see what it is when I get it." If the state somehow dodged its obligation, there was no way Lexi could pay the bill, not after having lost hours Friday night, not while other modest bills were beyond her means. The fear that struck Lexi then was the emerging truth that Grant might not have two quarters to rub together for Ward. And if he didn't have it, and she didn't have it, and Alice was taking care of everyone else . . .

"Give Grant a chance, Lexi."

She didn't know how. She didn't know if she dared. After all these years, her distrust would not budge. "I can't," she said.

Molly's voice came out of nowhere. "What's this?"

Alice and Lexi both jumped. Molly balanced in the hall on crutches. How long had she been there? She looked tiny and fragile and lopsided by the splint that was nearly the diameter of her waist. A white postcard was collapsed in her fist. She held it out to Lexi. "Did you write this?"

Lexi took the paper from her hand.

Grant, thanks but no thanks. Don't bother asking me again. Molly. (Just plain Molly.)

Her skin went cold. She looked at her daughter.

"You wrote that, didn't you?"

How had it gotten into Molly's hands? Lexi's mind explored several possibilities in half a second.

"Molly, you have to understa—"

"I *hate* you," she screamed. Her arms were rigid, her hands clenched into fists at her sides. "I hate you more than anyone else in the world!"

{ chapter 20 }

Scrubbing toilets at a facility where most of the people who used them had lost their minds wasn't the career Grant aspired to. He'd been in prison-based detox centers that required less elbow grease. But it was work.

And work was what Grant needed, especially after his disastrous weekend. If he couldn't come here, God only knew where he'd be, and what he'd be doing. So he tried to drum up some gratitude in spite of the voice in his head that said he belonged here among the mindless droolers.

He'd only worked at the Mental Health Assistance Residence for a month, Monday through Friday, and after the first week he'd adopted a hokey little ritual that would have looked ridiculous to anyone but meant something to him.

Every day in the residents' common room, in front of a south-facing, two-story window, the morning light passed over a sun-bleached strip of carpet. And every day before his shift started, he'd stand in the insulated sunshine for a minute, close his eyes, and hope the warmth would give new life to whatever weakened resolve kept him putting one foot in front of the other.

Most days he thought about Molly and what it was going to take to be her father again. Now that he had a face to go with her name, the possibility seemed more real.

Or less, taking into account his encounters with Lexi.

On this particular Monday, though, after a miserable Sunday holed up in a trailer that he didn't have the courage to leave, the sun failed to resurrect anything in him.

He was a complete idiot. Less than a half-wit. What had he thought? That Lexi would welcome him back with open arms and tearful hugs? That he could overcome the sum total of his lifelong stupidity in a couple days?

His one mental snapshot of Molly—in a wheelchair at the hospital, eyes on him—fell away from his mind's eye like a special effect in a Hitchcock film.

A cloud passed over the window and Grant's skin rippled with goose bumps. He kept his eyes closed, expecting the image of Molly to come back.

It didn't.

He thought about putting this era of his life behind him. He could start over clean. New job, new city, maybe a new wife if anyone would have him. Why keep going back to his own vomit?

Grant stopped himself. He'd come back to Crag's Nest for his kid, not some fix. He would have come back for Lexi, if she'd have him. That she wouldn't was a downer. The kind of downer that drove alcoholics back to their bars after months or years on the wagon.

His mind flashed to Ward and why he might be in town.

And what he could hook Grant up with.

He tried to snuff that thought with a technique they'd taught him in one of his rehab stints: replace bad ideas with good ones. Untrue notions with true ones. A spin on Richard's take-every-thought-captive advice, which wasn't quite as clear.

Where had his sight of Molly gone? He willed his mind to call her back up again. The only thing worth doing in this life was worth doing for her.

He couldn't do it. She wasn't there. All he could see was Ward, standing smug in the middle of this black mass of failure his life represented, palm outstretched, offering Grant a hit.

Grant jerked his eyes open and made an abrupt turn to his janitorial cart. He shoved the cart because he had to shove something, and it was there. The wheels moved half a yard and then jammed, and the mop bucket sloshed onto the dingy blue carpet.

They hadn't jammed, really. They had plowed into someone's shoe. One massive, humdinger, Shaquille-O'Neal-is-a-little-pixie monstrosity.

"Sorry," Grant said. "Aw, I can't believe I did that. Here, here, let me clean that up for you."

"Relax, man, I'm not gonna kill you."

The friendly words paralyzed him for half a second. This chorus kept resounding in his dreams, in a senseless but significant repetition. He looked into the man's face.

"Holy cow, it's you. Angelo, right? You work here?"

The big man who'd saved his daughter's life, miraculously they said, was wearing a set of enormous green scrubs.

"Grant Solomon," he said. "Yes, I do work here. Good to see you."

Angelo didn't seem at all surprised to see him. Grant handed him a clean rag out of his bin. "I bet that's never happened to you before. You're hard to miss."

His laugh was low and soft, but his whole body rolled with the joke, which relieved Grant. Angelo bent over to blot up his wet pants leg.

"Hey, there was so much going on the other night, I didn't thank you the way I should have," Grant said, staring at the top of his head. He wondered for a split second what size hat the guy wore.

"No thanks needed."

"You were in the right place at the right time."

"It happens every once in a while." Angelo handed the rag back but kept hold of the edge a second longer than necessary. Grant had to pull it out of his fingers.

"Molly's recovering well"—Grant hesitated, unsure how much Angelo knew or needed to know about him—"I hear."

"She is. The swelling's going down fast."

That simple remark pricked a jealous spot in Grant that he hadn't known existed. Molly had been talking to Angelo? Of course she had. Why shouldn't she have a few conversations with the man who pulled a Hollywood-worthy rescue out of his supersize magic hat? Had he been to see her since the accident? Grant hated Angelo and idolized him in the same second.

Angelo's eyes were unreadable.

"I'm curious," Grant said. "How the timing of all that managed to work out. How you managed to be right there, right then, going the right speed so that it all . . ."

Without warning, he was overcome by images of everything that *could* have happened if Angelo hadn't passed through that scene when he had, going the precise speed that he was, in the correct lane.

Images of Molly hurtling through a dusky sky and hitting Angelo's fender instead of his windshield . . . of Molly breaking the window of Mort's passenger door and falling headfirst onto asphalt . . . of Molly being halved by the truck that shaved the SUV as it barreled along in the opposite direction . . .

All this came over Grant like an upended bucket of mop water, and he choked on his own question. "So that it all . . . you know."

"Some things are too big for the mind to grapple with," Angelo said.

Grant exhaled and managed to keep his grip. "Yeah. A miracle's a miracle, right? No point in dissecting it."

"I was talking about all the what-ifs."

Grant shrugged off the awkwardness of his insight. "I don't spend too much time worrying about things that never happened."

Angelo nodded.

"Thanks, just the same. It's not enough for what you did, I realize that." Grant cleared his throat. "I don't know if you know this, but I hadn't seen Molly for several years before Friday. The sight of her sitting there with only her ankle injured, that was something. I can't describe it." He was embarrassed by his own display of gratitude. And he was sick all over again, still unable to call up that picture of her. There was only that blackness and Ward, and his offer to numb Grant's loss.

He extended his hand, trying to put an end to the encounter. "I appreciate what you did."

"Don't mention it."

Angelo enveloped his fingers in a crushing grip and pumped once. A pain shot up Grant's arm the way it did when he whacked his crazy bone. Instead of dissipating at the shoulder, though, it wrapped around Grant's collarbone and then zinged up his spine and straight into his head.

Then there she was, exploding into the front of his mind in such sharp clarity that Grant thought the image of her would be burned there forever: Molly, laughing, happier than he'd ever seen her. Molly, nine, laughing her heart out the way kids should spend their whole lives laughing. And he knew he'd never seen this image before in real life. It wasn't a memory, but a hope. He didn't know what else to call it.

Molly-Wolly, splitting her sides, busting up over something he'd said, a blazing sun in human form.

Grant thought he must have looked like one of the poor souls who was treated at the residence, standing there with a slack mouth and blank eyes. He cleared his throat and shoved his hands into his trousers' pockets and noticed that Angelo had already moved on.

The giant walked right past the two-story window and Grant knew then that he'd never be able to tell this story to anyone: the clouds parted for Angelo and the whole room lit up. Yellow light bounced off his white-gold hair and warmed Grant where he was standing.

He heard Molly laughing aloud.

{ chapter 21 }

Warden stood behind the book stacks of the adorable elementary-school library and watched Molly, admiring her spirit. It was young and unscarred and still capable of hope. For a little longer, anyway.

She sat at a low round table working on a report, waiting out P.E. and recess, with her sausage of an ankle propped up on another chair. Except for the fuzzy stuffed bookworms wearing horn-rimmed glasses as they dangled over bookcases, she was alone. The librarian had stepped out for a smoke. She couldn't withstand the temptation, Warden knew, because Molly was a responsible girl who needed hardly any supervision.

He was only a little surprised that Lexi hadn't kept the poor child home, but the woman had to choose her evils, didn't she? Go to work and risk that Grant or he might drop in for a visit on dear old mom and daughter, or push Molly off to school where unauthorized grown-ups weren't supposed to have access.

She couldn't have known that never stopped Warden.

Molly was working on the project that was due today, the one that was derailed by the unexpected events of her weekend, a report on an Indian tribe.

She was assigned the Pawnee, a piece of trivia she kindly offered Warden during his visit to her home last weekend.

He had come here to suggest a volume she might be interested in. The books she had access to didn't go into great detail about his favorite of the Pawnee ceremonies, the Morning Star ritual, because parents and librarians who wore their underwear a size too small believed children didn't need to know the gruesome details of a practice long forsaken. These same people preferred to whitewash history.

The tradition was so appropriate for Molly's present circumstance, however, that Warden located an old text with captivating illustrations and captions. As he paged through the old book, he found himself wishing he knew the man who had created it. Here, a young maiden of, say, ten, was captured by the enemy Pawnee; here, she was stripped, then painted black and red; here, as the sun rose, she was shot through the heart with arrows and bludgeoned to death by warriors with sacred clubs as her blood spilled to the earth.

A riveting story for a nine-year-old girl.

He approached Molly with the load of books in his arms. "Excuse me."

She startled, then recognized Warden and relaxed. She put her hands in her lap and lowered her eyes. Demure. Submissive.

"Hi, Mr. Warden."

"How's your report coming?"

The ruled notebook paper in front of her was half filled with neat penciled handwriting and a border of fine eraser dust. "Okay."

"Found something that might help." He took the book off the top of the stack, then placed it on the table beside her right hand. On the cover was a map of the stars, the sun and moon, the heartbeat of the Pawnee religion. In the illustration, these astrological bodies had faces. Fierce warriors and striking, strong women.

Molly only glanced at it, but Warden was unconcerned. She'd study it later. And she wouldn't show her mother. In his experience, children were intuitive about that kind of thing. The innocence in them understood when it was being strangled. Yet it was what they wanted, a perverse desire to grow up by killing their own childhood.

Warden pulled out the seat across the table. Molly tapped the eraser end of her pencil on an open book, where a warrior hunted a buffalo.

"I didn't know you work here," she said.

"Just volunteering today. You ever volunteer at a library before?"

She shook her head.

"Try it sometime. You'll learn more there than you'd ever pick up in a classroom."

She pursed her lips and looked Warden in the eye as if to gauge whether he was lying. He decided to work up to his own lies by starting with the truth.

"You're a brave girl to be back at school so fast after an accident like the one you had." He nodded at her elevated ankle.

"I wanted to stay home today."

"But the parental units said no, eh? I know it doesn't seem like it, but they do that because they love you."

This was as unpersuasive as he'd meant it to be.

Molly frowned. "It's just my mom."

"Your dad said you could stay home? Wow. When I saw him I didn't make him out to be that type."

"That Angelo guy wasn't my dad."

"No kidding? Okay. Well, he seemed nice enough."

She held the pencil horizontally with both hands, staring at the book Warden had picked out. "I don't really know my dad."

"Really."

"Mom says I have his jawline. I don't really know what she means, but she says it sometimes."

"So where is your dad?"

"Dunno. But he wrote me a letter."

"Cool. What'd it say?"

"That he wants to meet me."

"And do you want to meet him?"

"Yes, but Mom won't let me." Her eyes caught Warden's again, but this time he detected they were calculating whether he could be of use to her in this desire.

Yes, my dear, I most certainly can.

"My mom doesn't like you," she said.

"She doesn't know me as well as she thinks she does."

"My mom's usually right about people."

"Is she right about your dad?"

Molly shrugged again. But it lacked definition this time. "She doesn't say very much about him."

Warden leaned in as if to whisper a secret, even though they'd been talking at a low decibel level the whole time. "She doesn't like your grandma either, but you and I both know how wrong she is about that."

Molly tipped the pencil eraser to the corner of her lips and applied slight pressure, giving her a lopsided, joyless grin. Her eyes hadn't left Warden's face. For a fleeting second he worried he'd failed to convince her.

It happened now and then, especially with children, which bothered him a little. On the other hand, he could afford a failure occasionally. The risk was worth it. When it came to the measure of his success, stripping the souls of children doubled his returns almost automatically.

"Do you know your dad?" she asked.

"I do."

"Do you like him?"

"I do."

"Some dads aren't so good."

"How do you think yours measures up?"

Molly's uninjured foot started swinging under her chair. Her heel hit the chair's leg in even rhythm. "His letter was real nice."

"There you go. So tell me, Molly, why a bad guy would write such a nice letter."

A tiny line appeared between her brows. Warden dived into her moment of doubt.

"I think I could find out where your dad lives."

The line disappeared and her eyes widened. "You could?"

"You want me to try?"

She nodded, but then caught herself. "Mom still won't let me see him."

"I'll talk with her about it. See if I can change her mind."

"Okay, but I bet she won't change it."

"You leave that to me, Molly. I'll let you know how it goes." Warden pushed his book toward her, stoking her curiosity in the unearthly illustrations. "You take care of the important stuff, and I'll deal with your mom."

{ chapter 22 }

Mondays and Thursdays were always the most grueling days of Lexi's week, the days she worked from nine to three at King Grocery, picked up Molly from school, rushed home to change clothes, then waited tables from four to two at the Red Rocks Bar and Grill.

She didn't see Angelo at all Sunday after the 3:00-a.m. pep talk. She hoped he'd gotten some sleep before he went to work. She didn't even know what shifts he kept at the Residence. By the time her ten-minute noontime break arrived Monday, she was missing his lumberjack presence and the sight of that crazy pink truck. Both put her at ease in a way she hadn't noticed until then, when they'd been absent more than twenty-four hours.

Lexi stocked six dozen cans of Campbell's soups in the wrong dispensers before finally deciding to call him. Maybe she would talk him into dinner at the restaurant, if he didn't already have plans to be there with Mr. Tabor.

The slip of paper with his phone number on it was in her book bag in the break room, a filthy ten-by-ten Sheetrock box painted with cigarette smoke and grime. Five lockers that were shared among whoever was on duty lined one wall. Over the coatrack, the bulletin board displayed yellowed announcements dated nearly ten years ago.

Lenny King, the owner of King Grocery, didn't mean to be sloppy, he just had more important things to do.

The break room had an equally old and dirty phone on the wall. The receiver was connected to the base with a spiral cord so twisted that its six-foot length had been reduced to one. But it worked for local calls, and Lenny didn't mind his employees using it for that purpose so long as they kept an eye on the round-faced clock directly above it.

At 12:02 Lexi went into the room, washed her hands, then wiped them on the olive green apron that, worn over a white button-down shirt and khaki slacks, was her uniform. She lifted the flap of her bag and ran her hand down into the slim pocket that usually held the checkbook and several sticks of Trident. Her fingers brushed the slip of paper.

Not until she withdrew it did she remember that Angelo had taken down someone else's number for her to call. In the wake of Molly's Sunday outburst and ensuing silent treatment, she'd forgotten.

Lexi wavered between which number to call first. There wouldn't be much time between jobs. She also needed to call Gina's mom and check on her friend. Her work schedule would prevent her from getting over to the hospital today.

She decided to call Angelo, the least uncertain of her options. She pulled an antibacterial wipe from a dispenser on the counter and used it to pick up the phone receiver.

Was this his home number or his cell? Would he be at work?

Was she a fool to call him, a virtual stranger even after such a strangely intimate weekend? Lexi paused, trying to quantify how much more he knew about her than she knew about him.

She punched the number in and contemplated whether to leave a message or hang up when he didn't answer.

"Yeah?"

"Uh, Angelo?"

"Lexi! Hi there."

"I hope I'm not interrupting."

"I'm in the middle of an open-heart surgery with only a licorice rope and a thumbtack. This had better be important."

All her nervousness about calling him vanished. She hoped he could hear her lighter heart and understand that he was responsible for it. And what then? If he knew the effect he was having on her, would he run off? The men she knew were always running off.

"How's Dad today?" she asked.

"Did you know the man can put away three peanut-butter-and-mayonnaise sandwiches in one sitting? I watched him myself."

"I'll bet you a fat-free dinner that he polished off each one with a glass of whole milk."

"So that's something he used to do at home?"

"Only when he was in a really good mood. When his time comes, I hope he dies while eating something like a cheese soufflé. He'd be happiest then."

"I don't think he's going any time soon. He has the metabolism and blood pressure of a teenage boy."

"And how's his mind?"

"He thinks my name is Angelina Jolie."

Lexi cracked up. "You're pulling my leg."

"Just to hear you laugh."

"I probably shouldn't be laughing at his expense."

"You of all people should know he'd be telling you these jokes himself if he didn't have peanut butter stuck to the roof of his mouth."

Lexi leaned against the wall. "Molly would throw a fit if she knew what that man loves to eat."

"How'd she do yesterday?" Angelo asked.

Thoughts of Molly sobered her up. "The ankle is nothing compared to the wounds I've inflicted. She hates me."

"That's a strong word."

"Her word."

"I'm sure you said the same thing to your mom once or twice when you were a kid." She thought she might have said it as an adult, too, now that he mentioned it. "You didn't mean it."

Lexi had to stop and think about that. He was right, of course. She didn't really mean it, not in any eternal way. There were times, though, when it was the most succinct description she had for the way she felt.

"Molly should hate Grant if she hates anyone, but she can't even do that. Oh my. Did I just say that aloud?"

"She's still a kid," he said. "Kids are great that way. Their emotions are so pure but impossible to manage. All this love she has for you is being threatened by her love for her dad. She doesn't know what to do with that."

"You sound like a psychologist," she accused. It was defensiveness. Was he saying she had threatened Molly? Had she? No. Grant had. "I mean, a really good psychologist."

"And I'm very affordable!"

"Let me repay you, then. With a meal. I don't cook—and I have a hunch Molly wouldn't think it's a great idea to have you over for dinner right now—but I'm working tonight. Come in? It's on me."

Angelo hesitated long enough for Lexi to think she'd misinterpreted his friendliness, or he'd misunderstood her invitation.

What was her invitation about, anyway?

It was a simple thank you, for all the moral support.

It was a desperate plea not to be left alone.

It was a wish.

She wondered why she hadn't thought to ask her mom and Molly to come over to Red Rocks. For dessert if not for dinner. The thought of Molly's sullen posture bent over a piece of limp chocolate silk pained her.

She loved Molly so much. Love should be the easiest, strongest, clearest message in the universe to send between human beings. So why wasn't it?

"It's last-minute," Lexi said, trying to give Angelo the out she thought he needed. "I'll understand if you—"

"That's okay. I'll be there. Do you care what time?"

"Any time."

"See you at any time then."

"Okay." She hung up before the awkwardness took over, then dialed the other number on the slip of paper. She glanced at the clock. 12:07.

"Hello and you be blessed today!"

She knew that voice, heard it every day.

"Mr. Tabor?"

"The one and only, child. At least in Crag's Nest. Who might this be?"

"It's Lexi. Lexi Solomon. Someone said you tried to call me?"

"That I did."

"So what can I do for you?"

"That is the question of the day, now isn't it? You remember I was a defense attorney for fifty-two years, yes? I do believe I told you that story some day past."

"That's right." It wasn't a story, per se, but she remembered.

"I've been spending some of my free time these past few months looking into my history, wondering if I should take up that mantle again, Lexi. What do you say?"

She would have said she was perplexed. Why had he called her at home with this personal question? Why couldn't it have waited for the delivery of his four o'clock Reuben? "I didn't realize you were looking for something to do, Mr. Tabor."

"No, no. I've got me plenty to do. And it happens that I found just the right thing down in Riverbend, something not straying too far from my old line of work. About six weeks back I decided to become what they call down here a prisoner's advocate." Lexi stiffened. "So here we are. It's a bit of a new program, and I suppose we'll figure out what's needed as we go. But today I am giving you a personal call as a friend. See, child, I'm calling on behalf of one Norman Von Ruden."

Lexi groped for the nearest grimy chair and sat hard.

"He'd like to request a meeting with you."

"I don't have any reason to meet with that man."

"I'm sure I don't know whether you do or not, but he did seem to think you'd say that. He asked me to tell you that he has some information you might want to have. Something about your husband, Grant, that you'd want to know. For Molly's sake, he said."

"Mr. Tabor, if you're calling as a friend . . . you know what that man did to our family. He has a parole hearing coming up. I can't meet him."

"I won't be saying what you can or can't do, now."

Something about his tone chilled Lexi. It wasn't unfriendly, but knowing. As if Norm had told him about their affair. Older people had that way about them at times, she thought. There was such a fine line between wisdom and knowledge.

Lexi spoke cautiously. "You spent several hours with Grant Saturday night. Maybe I should meet with Grant instead."

"If you think that would help."

"Help what?"

"Lexi, child, I'm not an attorney here. I'm not a counselor either, just an old man with two perfectly decent ears for hearing people talk about their woes. And what goes into those receptacles on the sides of my head almost never comes out my mouth. So you won't hear me speaking out of turn. But it seems to me that you and Mr. Von Ruden might have some things you need to clear up before this hearing."

"Is he threatening me?"

"Not in so many words, lovely Lexi. It's what he's not saying that has me worried on your behalf. Those silences are what set him apart. I thought you might be knowing him well enough to read between the lines, if you catch my meaning. Especially if he's talking straight about your little girl."

Her little girl was awake when Lexi got home, though she pretended to be asleep. The cardboard box that encased Molly's broken ankle made it impossible for her to turn onto her stomach. She shifted positions when

Lexi tiptoed into their room. In the glow of the lava lamp night-light she saw her daughter put her arm up over her eyes. Tears wet her cheeks.

"How's your ankle?" Lexi whispered. Molly didn't answer, but her breathing wasn't right for sleeping. "Is it hurting, sweetie?"

She shook her head. Alice would have given her something for the pain before she went to bed. The next doctor's appointment was set for Thursday, which seemed a long way off.

Lexi started to undress in the dark. She tossed her greasy clothes into the hamper by the door, then pulled on a T-shirt and cotton shorts before climbing into bed. She lay on her back looking at the dark ceiling.

"How was school today?"

No answer.

"Did you get your report done?"

Molly sniffed.

"I know you're still mad at me, honey. I wish I could explain everything in a way that would make sense to you."

"I'm not stupid, Mom."

"Of course you're not. I didn't mean that."

"What did you mean, then? I'm almost ten. I know a lot of stuff you don't know."

These were the moments when words failed Lexi as a parent, when Molly was both wiser than Lexi would ever be and so innocent that she wanted to wrap her daughter in her arms and hold her forever. The most painful reality of all was that no words could ever reveal this truth to Molly.

"You shouldn't have written that note," she accused. "It's a good thing Dad didn't see it."

Lexi wondered if he had. How had it gotten from that little blue library mailbox into her daughter's hands? If Grant had received it, even if he'd given it to Alice, she wouldn't have shown it to Molly. Not that note.

Unless Molly had gone snooping in her grandmother's things.

Or . . .

Ward.

That didn't explain how Ward had come by it, though.

Molly turned her head away. Lexi reached out for the hand at her side. She was holding a stiff piece of paper, which she jerked out of Lexi's reach.

"What's that?"

"Nothing."

"Molly, show me."

She didn't move.

"Show me. Please."

Her arm came back at Lexi in an arc, and a corner of the paper poked her mother in the cheek. Molly let it go. It was a photograph, bent in the center and damp from her fingers.

Lexi, Molly, the black target.

"Where did you find this?"

"In my pajama drawer. Where you left it."

"I didn't do this, Molly."

"Why didn't you just cut the picture in half, if that's the way you really feel?"

"Molly, I love you. I *did not* do this." Shaking, fear and anger working in tandem within her mind, Lexi got up and threw the picture in the trash.

Lexi knelt by Molly's side of the bed to look her daughter in the eyes, silently asking God to show her the way out. Angelo's advice that she "consult love" came to mind, without any clarity about what it actually meant. She would have preferred three-step instructions.

"I love you." If Lexi said it enough, would it penetrate?

"I know." Her voice softened. "Dad loves me too."

"Yeah. I think he does." In his own strange way.

"But you wrote the note."

"It was wrong of me to write that note to your dad. I did it for all the right reasons, but it was a mistake."

"The biggest mistake *ever*."

If only she knew. "It was a whopper for sure. I'm sorry."

"I know, Mom."

"Are we going to be okay?"

"Yeah."

"You won't hold it against me? My dumb mistakes?"

Molly shook her head, sniffled, and wiped her face. "So are you going to let me see him?"

Lexi laid her hand over Molly's heart. In children's minds, everything was so simple. Everything was connected and straightforward. "I'll think about it, okay? That's all I can promise tonight. I need some time." Molly stiffened and rolled over.

There was nothing Lexi could do to hold her close.

{ chapter 23 }

Lexi had never been in a jail before visiting Norman Von Ruden. Her notion of them included little cubicles, monitored telephones, glass partitions, orange plastic chairs, and security cameras in every corner of the room.

Except for the security cameras, nothing else about Lexi's visit to the Riverbend prison met her expectations. It was a minimum-security facility, which was not where convicted killers would normally be held, except the statutes for victims' rights in the state required that public hearings for parole be held within a one-hundred mile radius of the victim's or nearest survivor's residence, or at the closest facility, which was why Norman had been transferred here. Mr. Tabor had explained all this to her during his Monday evening meal.

Norman was not considered a flight risk, Mr. Tabor said. He was a one-time offender, and the bipolar disorder believed responsible for his crime—that being the murder of her sister—was being "successfully managed." With his potential for parole so close, he was statistically unlikely to do anything that would jeopardize his chances. And then there was the fact that it would be a few weeks before he was back to his usual healthy self. The car accident had taken its toll.

None of this mattered to Lexi, though she listened to the information patiently.

When she arrived at the prison Tuesday afternoon, she surrendered all of her possessions at the check-in desk and was searched for weapons and contraband as if she were going through airport security. She found the process uncomfortable and unnecessary, as if facing Norm after all these years and everything that had transpired wouldn't be shameful enough.

Lexi followed a guard to the hospital ward. Norman had his own room, as she supposed most injured convicts did. It wouldn't be good for prisoners to get into a scuffle in a place where they were supposed to be healing.

It was like any other hospital room except for the lack of furnishings and the fact that the door locked from the outside. The smell was off too. There was nothing antiseptic in the air. Nothing that smelled of blood or bandages or bacteria. The only scent was earthy and slightly damp, the way her air vents smelled when the furnace kicked in for the first time at the end of a warm summer.

The guard brought in a cheap wooden chair for Lexi, then left.

She didn't sit right away. Instead she stared at Norman, whose face was still purple and slightly puffy from the wreck. One of his eyes was swollen shut. He studied her with his other, squinting. The room was dim, curtains drawn over one small window and lights low.

It was strange, she thought, that she didn't feel the outburst now that had risen in her in the ICU. Emotions in her duked it out beneath the surface, anger throwing punches at grief, loneliness taunted by a faint rumbling she recognized as long-dead yearning. Something that once was love. Or an imposter of love.

A silent prayer for clarity formed in Lexi's mind. A plea to escape whatever danger she'd walked right into.

"Where's your attorney?" he asked.

It was not the question she had thought he'd ask first, not after the screaming she'd done the last time she saw him. Lexi reached behind her for the chair and sat, wary of the war within her and the unknown threat that had summoned her here. It wasn't that she hadn't thought she should bring a lawyer, but that paying for one was out of the question.

"Where's yours?" she asked.

"Not here 'til the hearing. He would have advised me against this meeting if he knew of it, but I'm not worried about you."

"You're not? I might beat you to death with this chair."

Norm chuckled.

He said, "Do you really wish I was dead?" His voice was smooth, the voice she'd loved once, the voice unchanged though his body was older, bruised, tired. Lexi couldn't sort out her multiple and conflicted responses to his question, so she didn't answer.

He said, "I'll let your silence feed my hope."

"You know that's not what I meant."

"Set me straight, then."

"Mr. Tabor said you need to tell me something."

"Lexi, love—"

"Don't."

He licked his lips. "I have so much to say."

"If you don't know where to begin, maybe I should come back another time."

"No, please. Please stay. Lexi, you were a lifeline to me when my world was falling apart."

"Obviously I didn't have any influence on your ability to keep it together."

"You and I were stronger than what happened. We could have made it. We could still."

"We didn't, though, so I don't see the point of revisiting that."

"The truth will set you free, they always say." Lexi cringed at this, a quotation from the Bible coming out of Norman's mouth. She was pretty sure his interpretation of it wasn't exactly what Jesus had in mind. "I'm talking about putting the facts out on the table. Getting a fresh start, you and me."

"Nothing can repair what you did."

"Because you don't want what we had anymore, or because you don't believe we can reach out and take it back for ourselves?"

Lexi hesitated before she said, "Both."

"You don't know what really happened. What came out at the trial, that's only half the story."

"My sister died. You killed her. What else do I need to know?"

"It wasn't my fault."

"A jury said it was."

Norman lifted his hand off the sheets. "All these years—I've needed someone to believe in me, Lexi. I'm not talking about what I deserve. I know I deserve this punishment. I'd lie in a bed of hot coals for twenty years if it would make things right for you."

Nothing would make anything right in this matter, and she didn't have to say it. She could see in his eyes that he knew this already.

"Let me touch you, Lexi. Let me hold your hand."

She stayed put.

He sighed and lowered his arm. "I expected you to write me a Dear John letter after the sentencing. Why didn't you?"

"No one knew about us. If I'd written, someone would have found out."

"We didn't want that, did we?" An edge crept into his voice, cautioning her. She tried to direct the course of conversation carefully.

"You had a wife and child."

"Only a wife. We weren't approved for the adoption. It probably goes without saying. She left me anyway. An exposed affair wouldn't have changed a thing." His words revealed Lexi's selfishness.

"Thank you for protecting me during the trial. And Molly."

"I did it because I love you."

Lexi gripped her hands like a prayer, wishing this meeting were over, wondering if she should walk out.

He repeated, "I did it because I love you. Do you still love me, Lexi? I think you do, on some level, even though you've tried to bury it. I think you've stayed here in Crag's Nest because you can't move past me. Is it true?"

Panic fluttered in her chest. It wasn't true, was it?

"If you can't tell me you love me, tell me you hate me. Say it out loud and I'll leave you alone."

Lexi's confidence faltered. "I've already said that. In the ICU."

"No, no. You were shocked to see me. I understood that. Forgive me? Please? We never had the chance to talk about what happened."

She couldn't reply.

"Of course you would feel as angry as you did. It's only natural, especially if you've kept our connection bottled up all these years."

"Only a shrink would say that."

"But it didn't kill everything, did it? Please, if you'd only forgive me."

What did that mean, exactly? That she could say *sure* and they'd get a do-over? Was his request even an apology? And if it was, could she accept it? Offense made her sneer. How could he think of patching this up like that?

He said, "I believe your love is still—"

"Stop it. Please, stop."

"You never ended our relationship because you didn't want it to die."

Lexi hadn't consciously examined her love for Norman since the day of his sentencing. She had wrapped it up in a bundle of resentment and buried it deep in an untouchable cavern of her soul. Was it still there, thunking rhythmically like a man buried alive, desperate to be saved before the oxygen ran out?

No. It absolutely was not.

She shoveled as much dirt onto the open grave as quickly as she could.

"You have one minute to tell me why you asked me to come here today"—she pointed to the door—"and then I will leave and never speak another word to you."

Norm's breath came out in an airy laugh. He sing-songed, "I just called . . . to say . . . I love you."

Lexi's palms broke out in a sweat. She stood so quickly that the chair scraped the cold floor and bumped the wall in the close quarters. She took two steps toward the door and raised her fist to beat it.

"Molly," Norman said, his voice level again.

She turned around.

"I asked you to come here because I know how you feel about Molly. You might love me or love me not, but you would do anything for your little girl."

"Spit it out."

"I hear Grant is back in town, that he wants to have a piece of her."

Her arms folded themselves across her chest.

"You're not going to let him have her, are you?"

"No court will, either."

"Just because a man's an ex-con doesn't necessarily mean he loses his rights to play daddy when he wants to. Not in this state anyway."

"I'm not worried about Grant. Why are you?"

Norm's good eye darkened as he shifted it to look at Lexi in the poor lighting. "How much longer do you think he'll be patient, before he swoops in and takes her right out from under you? What does he have to lose?"

She shivered.

"What do *you* have to *gain*?"

"Love, Lexi. True love." He lowered his voice and beckoned her to come closer to the bed. She allowed her feet to return. "You need your knight in shining armor."

"No, I don't."

"I know something about Grant. He's the one who killed Tara."

"Don't insult me."

"Okay, I'll say it as plainly as I know how. Grant wasn't just a dealer, he was a crooked dealer."

"What other kind is there?"

"I went to him for the meds I needed to take care of this precious little organ of mine." He tapped his skull with an index finger. "I knew what was wrong. I knew I was a danger to everyone but you. You, Lexi, are my only true stimulant."

Lunch churned in her stomach as if it had begun to ferment. Norm's easy manner, his precisely cut words, belonged to a stranger. The man she'd had an affair with was never so cocky. She wondered if it was the medications or the illness that had sharpened his edges.

"He told me I was getting the cocktail I asked for—a cocktail to take the edge off my mood swings. Extra elastic to keep my mind from snapping." He clapped both hands together and Lexi flinched at the sharp sound. "You know what I really got for my good greenbacks? Placebos. Sugar pills. Snake oil."

At first Lexi didn't want to draw this line between Grant and her sister's death. Then she immediately wondered if it would absolve her own guilt. Then her guilt deepened because of the thought.

"I wasn't of sound mind the day your sister asked me to meet her."

"That much has been public for a long time."

"The truth, though, is that it wasn't my fault. I thought I was okay, that we'd have a pleasant adult conversation, but . . ." He raised his eyebrows and tilted his head. "These things come on without warning. I don't even remember the moment."

Lexi gripped the rail of his bed.

"All I needed was the right medicine. But your husband needed a few extra bucks." He wagged his head. "Grant is not a man you want around Molly."

"Noted," she murmured.

"I don't think you're hearing me. I'm only going to say this once. Warden says you'll come Friday, speak on my behalf at the hearing. You'll do that, won't you?"

Their eyes locked together.

"Tell them you've met me and seen for yourself that everything my doctors are going to say is true: I'm not the man who killed your sister. I'm reformed. I'm . . . a fine, upstanding, medicated citizen. Do that for me.

Give our love a second chance. When I'm out, I'll take care of Grant. He won't cause you this confusion anymore. It's his turn to be punished."

"You'll take care of . . ." Whatever she had thought Norman might promise, it was not this. Even in his right mind, he was murderous. She stepped away from the bed.

"I won't. I can't do that. In fact, I'll tell them what you've—"

"You do that and I'll make the affair public. I'll tell them everything, including that you were in partnership with your dear old man. I hear that you have carried on without him."

Warden's planted drugs flashed in Lexi's vision.

"I'll implicate you in Tara's death," he continued. The muscles that ran from his jaw to his ear flexed. "I'll give them a very compelling reason why I needed to protect you all these years. And I'll tell them you still operate. What do you think that'll do to your stupid efforts to give Molly a good life?"

She gasped. "Why would you do that?"

"Because I can. And because I have support. Warden's got designs on Molly, too, doesn't he?"

"But why? I don't understand. You . . . we . . ."

"Have changed in the last seven years," he said.

She struggled for words. "They'll never believe you," she finally cobbled together. "This is about Grant. Why me? What did I ever do to make you turn on me?"

"You turned on me first, didn't you? Just walked away from what we had."

"You murdered my sister!"

"Don't try me in this, Lexi. I have always been a man of my word. It's one of the reasons you fell in love with me in the first place."

Lexi spun and hit the door with her entire body, and she pounded on it with both hands until the guard set her free.

{ chapter 24 }

The off-balanced Volvo took Lexi straight to the Mental Health Assistance Residence, a mere five miles away. Not to her father, but to Angelo. It wasn't quite six o'clock. She thought he should be close to getting off his shift. The winter sun had set behind the mountains moments earlier, turning the world into purple and gray shadows.

Lexi doubted that love would be a part of any solution Angelo might offer for this latest dilemma. She laughed aloud in the car. She was about to tell a man she was interested in all the ways in which she had wrecked every relationship that ever mattered to her. Lexi doubted that Angelo would be interested in her crisis-filled life much longer, but who else could she turn to?

When would she have to tell her mother she'd had an affair with the man who killed Tara? What would happen when Grant and Molly found out?

When. Not if, but when.

The realization that she feared what Grant might think gave her pause.

It didn't matter that the extramarital relationship was short-lived and had happened almost a decade ago. Lexi had hoped this moment of reckoning would never come. Prison had separated Norman and her; his mental illness had overruled their bond. She had no proof he had ever been of sound mind, or was even now. How could he blame anything on her?

A rhetorical question.

Her regrets over the affair blossomed.

Molly. Molly. Molly. Her daughter's name was the only prayer Lexi was capable of. She trusted God knew exactly what she was begging for.

Angelo might not have any idea what she should do. She wouldn't blame him if he hightailed it out of her broken family circle as suddenly as he had entered it. She would regret it, though. He made her feel safe. But if he wasn't going to be a permanent fixture in her life, she thought it would be best to know sooner than later.

Could one ever be sure of these things? Did it matter, considering her marriage was still legally sound, if not otherwise shattered?

God hated divorce, she'd been told, and for Lexi that truism was a twisted justification for her inaction against Grant, and a repellent to more relational disasters. It protected her from everything she never wanted to face.

Including her easy attraction to Angelo. She drove into the Residence's parking lot. His truck hulked at the end of the lot near a bare ash tree. She decided to park next to it.

Was she a glutton for punishment? That must be it. She pulled into the slot and gripped the steering wheel in both hands as if it could direct the course of her life and she could actually control it. Then she let go.

The fear that Angelo had triggered in her the first time she saw him came to mind. That might have been something instinctive, or spiritual. A warning.

Lexi ignored it and got out of the car. She beat it off the back of her mind as she traversed the dim parking lot, making for the lights of the Residence.

The sprawling facility, a monument to insurance dollars and mental-health lobbyists at work, was built on an eye-poppingly gorgeous, densely wooded property. It had been donated to the state by an elderly man who'd lost his wife to dementia back in the day when her only care options were more medieval than modern. The building that served as the visitors' entrance had once been their home.

She approached the main walkway, a broad swath of cobblestones.

A tiny grunt, the kind a pitcher might exhale when he released a baseball, caught her ear and she turned her head toward the pink line of horizon west of the building. A black orb aimed for her head triggered all of Lexi's reflexes: She gasped. She threw up her hands. She averted her eyes.

"Ow!"

She didn't see the projectile that hit her cheekbone until after it fell to the pavement and rolled to a stop several feet away. With one hand on the side of her face—it was wet and sticky, but not bloody—she bent and saw a small apple, with a white bite cut out of its side. The skin near this had split from the impact of hitting her, she assumed.

Someone had thrown an apple at her?

A wandering resident. That was her first thought. The shadows didn't give up a human form.

She groped for her book bag and pepper spray, but she'd been so upset by her visit with Norman that she'd left them both in the Volvo.

Keeping her head turned in the direction of the apple's launch, she moved in the direction of the building, which seemed farther away than it had a second ago. The sky's blue had darkened to purple. If there ever was a time for Angelo to make an unexpected appearance, she thought, this would have been it.

After two quick steps she collided with a body. A treelike, lanky body attached to one of the ugliest heads ever to crawl out of a gene pool. His face was the shape of a lightbulb. The eyes, squinty and mean; the nose, small and piggish; the cheeks, bony and sunken.

"I'm sorry," she muttered, lifting her hands to separate them.

He gripped her arm with fingers that were strong talons. His touch was fiery, hot through the sleeve of Lexi's jersey shirt like a terrible fever, and sweaty. With his free hand he crammed another apple into her lips, grinding them against her teeth. "Eat," he said. She struggled but couldn't break his hold.

When she wouldn't open up for the fruit, he started banging it on the top of her head while holding her upright. The pounding should have hurt, but the apple was soft, as though the heat of his palms had baked it.

"Help!"

"Eat, eat, eat, eat . . ." he chanted. Her thrashing hands tangled in his greasy hair. Her fingernails scraped his face. After a dozen hits, the juice started running onto her scalp, and the bruised flesh slipped out of his fingers. She heard it hit the asphalt of the parking lot.

He released her arm and grabbed the hair at the nape of her neck in a split-second motion. Her head snapped back involuntarily, following the pain. He lifted Lexi so that she had to stand on her toes. She tottered.

Somehow he had another apple and she imagined the pockets of his oversize army field jacket full of them. She grabbed his collar, as much to balance herself as to hold him off. He held the fruit close to her mouth and nose as he leaned over her face.

"We leave each other alone," he muttered. Lexi shut her eyes against his hot breath, his terrifying displeasure and babble. "Alone to be. Me, myself. No interference. That's all I ask for, to do my work in peace. But he can't stay out of anything. The only us is I and mine, which you are *not*. He is *not*."

What was he talking about? Lexi was gagging on her own breath, hyperventilating around the close, sweet-scented fruit. His grip on her hair paralyzed her neck. She raised a knee into his groin but he didn't seem to notice. Her supporting ankle wobbled.

"You're not my subject, as he was not his subject. We don't interfere in each other's work. Eat. *Eat!*"

"Help!"

She coughed and gasped, opening her mouth enough for the man to jam the tennis ball–size apple into her mouth. She swiped at it. He blocked her arm and her teeth snagged the fruit unwillingly. She spit it out, jerked her head, and felt hairs release at the top of her spine.

He pinched Lexi's jaw, tucking the flesh of her cheeks between her molars.

"He has to go. If I remove you, he'll have to go."

When he released Lexi's head and face, he shoved, and she fell backward, tailbone hitting first, then the heels of her hands, bracing her from going over. He snatched one of her wrists out from under her, twisting her shoulder. She turned into it protectively, then rolled as he dragged her, screaming for help, across the asphalt. The rough surface tore into the skin of her hip. His scalding fingers were bony handcuffs.

"Shut the apple trap," he ordered.

Lexi's body bounced over a curb and met dry winter grass. The parched branches of a shrub snatched her hair and scratched her face. With a free hand she tried to ward off abrasions. Her forearm burned from scrapes. Grass came loose as he pulled her over it and packed itself down into the waistband of her jeans.

She kept screaming.

Darkness came quickly in the mountains, and the lunatic hauled her into the deeper darkness of an evergreen stand on the east side of the Residence. Twisted bristlecone pine trees and ponderosas crouched like old, bored men. Snow from a fall of two weeks ago still lay under the trees; the sun didn't shine there even during the day.

He let go of Lexi and the side of her head caught a rock, sending streaks of red and purple behind her eyes. She slid off it, coming to rest in a patch of ice that brought a brief, strange relief. She rolled onto her back, gasping and crying, clawing at the ground. He towered over her, straddling her ribs, fishing in his pockets. Dropping his knees down onto her arms, he pinned her to the dirt. If he'd weighed a few pounds more he might have broken her bones.

God, please help me.

He clamped a hand over her lips and withdrew a handful of something from his pocket. More apples?

No, something smaller. Hard and spiney, inedible gobstoppers. He gripped them in a fist and a sound like a popcorn kernel landing in oil passed through his fingers. The objects in his grip started hissing.

One of them cracked. Then another.

He pinched her nose and, when she struggled for air like a gaping fish, he began stuffing the spiderlike shells in. They cut into the tender lining of her cheeks.

"I and me and mine and not him, no, not him or you . . ."

Lexi flopped her head from side to side, trying to keep him from putting the shells in her mouth. He hit her in the temple, the same place struck by the rock, stunning her into stillness. Her lungs convulsed, needing to cough. She couldn't breathe. She would inhale and slice up her throat on the strange rocks.

They were hot and dry.

"'If you're lucky, he'll live,' he says. If you're lucky. Well I'm lucky. Luckier. And smart enough to know when you have to kill them. You'll die slowly while my man lives slowly. Justice."

Lexi's lungs demanded air. Her head buzzed as if it were about to shut down. Instead, the weight came off her chest. Her attacker was lifted off of her. Not pushed or tackled or yanked, but lifted. Levitated. A rush of cold air swooped in over her clothes, cooling all signs of his body.

The chill shocked her eyes open, and she saw him, hovering over her, grimacing and swearing, swiping at her furiously, kicking out his bony knees and feet. One of his arms lashed out like a striking snake. His fanglike fingernails missed her by inches.

Inside Lexi's mouth, one of the tough shells split open and expelled something hard into the back of her throat. She couldn't prevent the coughing then. Rolling onto her side, she heaved and sputtered, emptying the sharp contents onto the contrasting snow—tough shells, split open and covered in curling spines; small marbled seeds, black and beautiful. Her tongue tasted blood.

The man who'd attacked her was shrieking at a pitch that brought her hands to her ears.

And then he fell. From a mere five feet, he hit the ground as if he were a skydiver whose chute failed to open. His shrill cry stopped. Logic told Lexi he should have smashed her, and yet he crashed at her side, scattering a layer of dead pine needles. The bone-crushing impact might have killed him.

Might have killed *her*.

Her body reacted by snapping into a curled position, defensive, cowering. She heard him snarl and she looked.

He was, inexplicably, standing. Crouching, defensive. His skeleton fingers open and shut rhythmically. He paid her no attention.

She weighed whether to play dead or make an escape.

Her knees got themselves up under her. The balls of her feet pushed off the cold ground, and she was running, staggering blind away from the scene. A branch caught the corner of her eye as she weaved through, unbalanced. When her foot hit a thick pile of dead needles, the earth was pulled out from under her. Lexi grabbed a branch on the way down and prevented herself from collapsing completely, but in the swimming gray light, she was still disoriented.

There was cursing and yelling close by, the hissing of expletives sliding past teeth. Then the shrieking started again.

She heard heavy feet pounding, coming in her direction.

The tree she clung to, a crooked bristlecone with branches like bottlebrushes, began to tip.

At first she thought she was passing out, or falling, or dizzy. But when the branch was wrenched out of her hand and she found herself still upright, she scrambled to compute a different explanation. Her palms burned from the stabbing needles.

The tree groaned and the earth broke, giving up the roots. Clods of dirt and snow showered the ground, but the pine shuddered and stilled when it was only halfway over. Ten feet away, a figure dropped out of its bent form and crouched again. Lexi could feel the heat coming off his body.

She turned and ran back the way she had come.

Lexi might as well have been pickled drunk. She couldn't see where she was going and couldn't have followed a straight line if it glowed in the dark. So when she crashed into a solid mass, she was only half surprised.

But when the mass surrounded her with bulky arms and picked her up as if she weighed nothing, she put all her remaining strength into wriggling free. She hit and kicked and punched. She sank her teeth into what was in front of her mouth.

"Work with me, Lexi. Quit fighting."

Angelo. *Angelo*.

She cried out, so frightened, so relieved. She threw her arms around his neck, smacking his chin in the process, and gripped his collar in her fists. He would have to cut it out of her hands if he wanted her off of him.

The piercing howls of Lexi's stalker sliced the darkness in half.

"What's happening?" she gasped. "Did he get out of the Residence?"

"Hold on," Angelo said.

"Where's security?"

There was no time for stupid questions.

She pressed her face against his shoulder. Angelo had one hand on her waist. She didn't know what he was doing with the other one. Clearing tree branches as they plunged into the depths of the wooded property maybe. She didn't care.

It seemed to her he ran for hours; it seemed only seconds. When they stopped, though, they were on a hill above the Residence. She recognized the spot.

A walking path snaked through the rolling glade at the bottom of the slope. Her dad loved to be out on that path.

Angelo set her down and her tennis shoes crunched into an icy layer of old snow.

She still clung to his flannel shirt.

"Let go," he ordered.

She couldn't disobey that tone.

His body was turned to the east, alert.

She didn't ask what he was waiting for.

It came through the trees like a bullet, too fast to be seen as much as sensed—a snarling, leaping form that lunged for Angelo's throat. They connected in a wrestling match that became unnaturally quiet.

Lexi dropped to the ground mere feet away, groping for rocks to throw, or a heavy branch to swing. Her hand closed around a stone as heavy as a paperweight, and she tore her gaze off the entangled fight to dig it out of the compressed dirt.

The silence of the fight gave way to brief shouting.

"Mine mine mine mine mine!" the man screamed.

"You don't have any power here," Angelo declared.

"Mine mine mine . . ."

The screech ended like a man falling off a cliff.

The tips of Lexi's fingernails turned black as she dug into the cold earth. In three seconds, maybe four, she palmed the mass and hefted it over her shoulder to throw it. Her eyes locked onto her target.

But she let the rock fall to the ground behind her.

On the crystal slope, Angelo was bent at the waist, hands on knees, heaving, still standing but spent.

Fifty yards downhill, in the grassy depression between Angelo and the path, all that was left of the man who'd attacked her was a tattered army jacket, lying in a circle of melted snow and a cloud of rising steam.

{ chapter 25 }

Grant was leaving his shift late, thanks to a flooded laundry room, and making his exit through the kitchen delivery dock when Angelo came up the outer stairs with Lexi. His wife was holding Angelo's hand. Clinging to his hand with both of hers. Her eyes were wide under her frowning brows.

She didn't seem to notice Grant standing there. Her temple bulged under her hairline, and her clothes were filthy, her pretty brown hair tangled. There was blood on her lips.

Grant reached back to keep the door open.

"What happened?"

Lexi registered the sound of his voice and turned her face toward him, looking stunned. It occurred to Grant that he'd forgotten to mention *where* he was employed as a janitor.

"Can you get her some ice?" Angelo asked.

"How bad is it?"

"I'm fine."

"She's not fine."

Grant moved quickly to the freezer in the back. When he returned to the kitchen, Lexi was leaning against a stainless-steel table while Angelo examined the gash on her head.

"Some maniac attacked me."

Angelo stepped away and let Grant apply the ice pack he'd made out of a dish towel. The fear that ripped through him was unfamiliar. What if Lexi had been killed? What would that have done to Molly?

What would that have done to him?

Grant supported the back of her head with one hand and applied the pack with the other. Her head was warm, her hair as silky as ever. He could smell the scent of lotion on her skin, the same cheap drugstore brand that she'd asked him to pick up for her once with a pack of diapers.

She smelled like almonds. Their sweetness brought back good memories. Newlywed happiness.

Her shoulders relaxed.

Grant cleared his throat. "Someone from the Residence?"

She and Angelo exchanged a look he couldn't interpret. "It seemed that way," she finally said.

"I'll drive you to the hospital," Grant said.

"No."

Angelo took his side. "Yes." The huge orderly opened his hand above the shiny table and upended several objects that looked like sci-fi models of viruses enlarged to a million times their actual size.

"What's that?" Grant leaned over them while keeping pressure on Lexi's head. A few of the hard, nutshell-like things were whole. A couple had split in two. Mixed among them were three black beans.

"These were in her mouth," Angelo said. He pushed them around with an index finger.

Grant grimaced and looked at Lexi again. She was wiping the blood off her lips. "They cut you? The inside of your cheek?" He tried to look.

"It's not a big deal," she said, twisting her neck away.

"It's a huge deal," Angelo said, fingering one of the black beans. He held it up for her to see. "Castor beans."

"Castor beans." Her smile was weak. "So he thought he was a doctor—about a hundred years behind the times."

"Or a killer," Angelo said. "The oil's a decent remedy for some things, but these beans are one of the deadliest plant poisons around."

Lexi paled. "How deadly?"

"How many did you swallow?" he asked.

"None. I didn't swallow anything." Her tongue traced the insides of her mouth.

"The pods burst when they warm up," Angelo said. "Usually in summertime. One or two is deadly enough."

He seemed to be talking to himself, examining the hulls. He inserted his thumb into the hollow of one, then broke off the spines on its outer side.

"There must be more efficient ways to kill someone," Grant said, then wished he hadn't.

"There are faster ways," Angelo said.

"I didn't swallow anything," Lexi repeated, maybe to convince herself.

"Open your mouth," Grant ordered. He directed her yawn toward an overhead light and this time she complied. It was hard to see anything. After a second she jerked her chin out of his hands and wouldn't meet his eyes.

"You ought to see a doctor," Grant said.

"No. No hospitals." She walked toward the door, but when Angelo and Grant didn't follow her, she paused and crossed her arms. Then she stared at the black rubber mat under her feet.

"Can we clean it somehow?" Grant asked Angelo. "A saltwater rinse or something?"

Angelo's eyebrows went up and Lexi clapped her hand over her mouth.

"Right. Dumb idea."

"Sterile saline might work," Angelo said. "I know where I can get some. Stay with her."

He left the kitchen, carrying the freaky little castor beans and their pods away with him. A brief flash of annoyance came over Grant. How could a man like him compete with a sunshine boy like that? It was Hades versus Hercules.

Lexi continued to avoid his eyes, her hand still over her mouth. Grant put his hands in his pockets. A warming ice cube cracked in the bundle that had been abandoned on the table.

He spoke first, out of desperation to connect with her. "I'm glad you weren't hurt. Worse than you are."

She nodded.

The old analog clock over the sink ticked.

He said, "Did you notify security? About the—"

"Not yet. It just happened."

"Where's the guy?"

Lexi shook her head.

"What if he's still—"

"He's not," she said. Grant waited for an explanation. She didn't offer one.

"Lexi—"

"You didn't tell me you worked here." It was an accusation that rubbed Grant the wrong way.

"You didn't tell me your dad was a patient."

She glared at him.

"I'm sorry," he said. He sighed. The refrigerator hummed. "You come to visit him tonight?"

Lexi looked at the door Angelo had exited. Grant understood in an instant. It seemed he was going to have to stand there and take one hit after another.

But then, he deserved each strike.

She said, "I saw Norman Von Ruden today."

Norman Von Ruden. Norman Von Ruden? The only man in the world Lexi probably hated more than Grant.

"Why?"

"He asked me to."

"Why?"

"He had . . . news for me. About you."

"Did he, now?"

Her eyes were knives.

"He says the meds you sold to him back before the incident were blanks."

"What?"

"Don't play deaf."

He wasn't playing deaf. His question was a reaction to the past sneaking up on him from behind and taking a bite out of his neck.

"He doesn't know what he's talking about," Grant mumbled.

"He's blaming you for . . . for Tara."

"You can't believe him."

"Why shouldn't I?"

"Because he was found guilty! He was on tape, for crying out loud! The jury took less than an hour to reach their verdict!"

"I don't mean he didn't . . . that he wasn't the one who . . ." She huffed. "His head wasn't right, and that was your fault!"

"How could it be my fault?"

"What did you sell him?"

"Exactly what he paid for."

"What does that mean? That he paid for sugar pills?"

Grant realized then that he had been sucked into an argument he'd been making for ages: that he wasn't to blame for anything, that others' lives weren't his responsibility. His whole point in coming back to Riverbend had been to prove he could quit this way of thinking. Her very question begged him to live up to his self-promise that he would find a way to make things right. So when Lexi stood there looking pained and beaten and disbelieving of his worn-out lines, all smug defenses drained out of his heels.

"Yes," he said.

She blinked, and her lips parted.

"I sold him fakes."

"Why? What did you think? That he wouldn't know? That he didn't really need them?"

Grant couldn't remember what he thought back then. What he thought now was that everyone medicated themselves with things that didn't cure their sicknesses. A man who went to the street to find help he could have gotten from a doctor's office was probably looking for something no one could give him. In that sense, no, Grant would say Norman didn't need those pills.

But Lexi would misunderstand him if he said that.

"This is why I left."

"What?"

"When the manic-depressive thing came out in court . . . when they said he'd failed to be diagnosed or treated . . . I figured he'd point the finger at me. At us."

"There was no *us* in your schemes."

"No, there wasn't. But if I'd stayed . . . you and Molly . . . it's a small town."

Her arms dropped to her sides.

"You left us for something that never happened?"

Grant cleared his throat.

Lexi's steeliness returned. "You could have taken us with you."

"You wouldn't have come."

"I wou—"

"Lexi, we shouldn't lie to each other anymore."

Tears coated her eyes and she looked away.

"I was the one doing the lying," Grant confessed. "You don't know half of what I was into. When your sister died, everything I'd told myself about how my ventures with Ward were harmless, good money . . . I was the fool. I thought, what if it had been you he'd run into? What if you'd seen him and stopped to be friendly, and he snapped? Tara was a complete stranger to him. It was such a freak coincidence."

Lexi stood in profile to Grant with her head bent and both hands clutching the back of her neck. Her eyes were closed. He shouldn't have brought up her sister, but he didn't know how he could have avoided it. Grant rushed to say everything before he chickened out.

"Everything seems wrong now. Leaving was wrong. Staying was wrong. At least, staying while dealing was, but I didn't know how to get out. It's taken me years. I did some time, which was a backhanded gift. Lots of time to stare my mistakes in the face. Your mom probably told you."

Lexi didn't move.

"I don't expect you to excuse me from being an idiot. But at the time I honestly believed I was protecting you and Molly. I did. I'm sorry. You have no idea how sorry I am, how badly I want to make it up to you."

She shook her head. Grant didn't know how to interpret that.

"I'm totally clean, Lexi. Going on two years." He sounded pathetic, so he shut up.

A long minute ticked by over the sink.

"You can make it up to us," she finally said.

"How? Tell me. Anything."

"Ward wants his money."

Grant didn't see the connection but said, "I'm working on that."

"He wants it by Friday."

"Well, he'll have to wait."

"He won't wait."

"What does that mean? I don't have it. It takes a while to save up ten grand when you're working at minimum wage."

"Ten?"

"I owe him ten thousand dollars. That might not seem like much, considering how much money used to pass through our hands every day, but legally earned cash is hard to—"

"He says twenty-five."

Five years ago, Grant would have laughed at that and cursed. In the face of Lexi's expression, though, his stomach flipped.

"That's twice what—why is he talking to you about what I owe him?"

"He wants Molly."

Grant shook his head. It was impossible to follow the turn of this discussion.

"He wants me to get the money from you in exchange for Molly's safety."

"That doesn't make any sense."

"Who cares about *sense?*" The volume of her voice rose. "I've raised my daughter in spite of you; I've been her mother *and* father for seven years, and we are still paying for your stupid, stupid choices! Tell me that makes sense, Grant."

"Why would he want Molly?"

Lexi threw up her hands. "The question is, do *you* really want her? Or if that means you have to pay up, is your daddy-dearest plan going to turn out to be a farce?"

"Hey!"

"Don't pretend to be offended."

"Look, I screwed up. I've been trying to apologize. I don't know how many more ways to say I'm sorry. But if I didn't care about you and Molly I wouldn't be here. You've got to know how hard this is for me."

"I don't care how hard it is for you. If you loved Molly—"

"I do! You don't know a thing about what I feel. I love Molly more than I ever—" He clamped his teeth down and exhaled slowly.

"More than you ever loved me," she said.

There was nothing to say about that. It didn't matter that he'd never stopped loving Lexi, that he loved her more now than when he'd left, now that he had a crystal clear understanding of what he'd abandoned. When it came to a wife, no words could shout louder than actions, and Grant's history was very, very noisy.

"What is he saying?" Grant asked. "What is Ward telling you he'll do?"

"He says he'll take her."

"That's it?"

"Isn't that enough? He didn't exactly lay out his plans, Grant!"

"Where is she?"

"With my mother."

"Your mom can take her somewhere until we sort this out."

"Sort what out? You either have the money or you don't."

"Ward's a negotiator."

"Molly can't travel right now."

"She'll be traveling with Ward if we don't do something!"

Lexi put a hand on her forehead. She looked as though she was about to tip over. Grant moved forward to support her by the arm, but she wrenched it out of his reach.

"You mean if *you* don't do something," she growled.

All the ancient arguments Lexi and Grant had waded through failed to prepare him for the intensity of her anger now. Somehow, detached from her for so long, he'd accomplished the amazing feat of downplaying her fury. His memories of her anger were varied: pleading with him to stay home, giving him the silent treatment if she was really upset, or—above all other images—standing speechless in his rearview mirror, holding their toddler, when he drove off for the last time. But never worse than that. The intervening years had turned her into a fierce she-bear who would kill to protect her child, and Grant was her most-hated enemy.

"You know Ward better than I do," she said. "You're not so unlike him. Do you think he won't kill her, if that's what he wants?"

"He wouldn't kill over such a small amount," Grant said.

But he failed to convince himself. He couldn't deny the possibility. Just as he couldn't deny his role in putting his wife and child in this situation. He had knocked over a heavy domino years ago and he could not stop the rest of them from crashing down. And at the end of the line: a beautiful little girl, the only human on the planet whose love he had a chance of regaining, was about to be crushed.

She, too, was beyond his reach.

Grant covered his face with his hands. His shoulders started to shake. And in the ensuing saline bath of his own, those tears washed the dirt off the folds of his mind and revealed exactly what he needed to do.

{ chapter 26 }

The decrepit Datsun Richard had secured for Grant strained at fifty-five miles an hour and started rattling at sixty. He pushed it to sixty-five and clattered down the north-south thoroughfare into downtown Riverbend, irrationally certain of the haunt where he would find Warden Pavo.

Riverbend, population one hundred fifty thousand, was part of the larger Rawson County. Big enough to sustain its own brand of drug dealers and runners, but too small for taxpayers to support any full-time legal force devoted to this particular line of crime. The Riverbend sheriff's department was tied up in the dubious distinction of having to manage a city with a per capita murder rate second only to Detroit's. As far as Grant knew, that hadn't changed in the years he'd been gone.

Warden Pavo had been particularly successful in this region during the time Norman and Grant did business with him. Chances were good Warden was still king of his usual places of business.

What made no sense, though, was why he would try to extract the money from her. Warden could have come after him easily enough. How hard could it be to find an ex-con who'd come back home?

The Datsun complained all the way to the south end of town, where Grant careened into the parking lot of the Blue Devil's Nightclub and sped around the building. The absence of lights on the backside was intentional and brought to mind a more sinister interpretation of a place where the sun don't shine.

Grant got out of the car and slammed the door so hard that a rear hubcap fell off.

He made his way to the basement rooms by memory rather than sight. Twelve jogging strides to the metal rail, seventeen cement steps down to the grate that covered the drains. Three steps, then through the door into the bunkerlike hall that glowed with a golden yellow light.

Inside, a skinny punk dressed in a business suit greeted Grant. He went by the name of Rayban, like the shades. He sat behind a rusty desk and was eating from three boxes of Chinese takeout. Rayban would have seen Grant coming through the night-vision security camera and could have locked the door if he'd wanted to.

He said around a mouthful of noodles, "Been a few years, Solomon."

"I'm here to see the Warden."

"Not sure he wants to see you." He slurped the lo mein.

This guy barely broke one twenty-five or five-and-a-half feet. The business suit gave him the appearance of a boy in his father's clothes. Grant wouldn't test the man, though; he was nasty like a weasel.

"He'll see me," Grant said.

Rayban gestured to the elevator doors in the wall behind him. "Don't let me stop you."

He couldn't have, not this time, though Grant was glad he didn't make it difficult.

Grant stepped into the elevator and pushed the button for the lowest level. The ride down took nearly half a minute. The doors opened and he stepped into the room.

The air in here was strangely sharper than the mountain oxygen outside, oxygen that he'd been deprived of during his years in Los Angeles. Grant recalled his first visit to this room and his surprise, back then, over the showiness of the place, the Las Vegas glitz of it. It was the Casablanca of nightclubs, a place where those invited by friends of friends could thumb their noses at the blue-collar Blue Devil patrons drinking beer above ground, and they could pretend for a few hours that they didn't live in a small, inconsequential Rocky Mountain city.

Tonight, though, he stepped into the room and was caught off guard by the stench of smoke—some from substances other than cigarettes—and the frayed look of all the glamour. The lights were up, footpaths were worn into the carpets, and the mirrored walls were foggy. The eyes of guests who bothered to look at Grant were vaguely dazed. One of them held an opium pipe in his left hand.

Ward didn't run the place but knew the people who did. At least that was what he told Grant years ago.

Grant scanned the room, looking for him, and when he came up empty he passed among the tables to a hallway on the opposite side of the floor. A curtain of black beads separated the bar from the rooms where business was conducted privately. In the days when Ward had suppliers for Grant to meet, they usually conducted business here.

The beads rattled when he pushed them aside and entered the bloodred hall. There were six offices, for lack of a better word, three on each side. Each door marked the bull's-eye of a black target. The targets' rings arced over the doors, overlapping the adjacent lines.

Grant threw open each one without announcement. Empty. Empty. Empty. Occupied.

Two men exchanging bundles of money and cocaine glared at him. Grant held up a hand in apology and pulled their door shut.

In the fifth room, Ward sat alone. His feet, crossed at the ankles, were propped on a glass-topped square table. His chair stood on its two rear legs. He chewed the end of an unlit, hand-rolled cigarette.

"Thought you might drop in, old friend," he said.

Grant took two steps into the room and leaned on the other side of the table's glass top. The fact that Warden appeared to be waiting for him was disorienting. He had expected to interrupt an exchange.

"Why go to Lexi for the money you want from me?" Grant demanded.

"I don't want the money from you. Ergo, Lexi."

"Why did you tell her to get it from me, then?"

"Doesn't matter to me where it comes from."

"I'm the one who owes you."

"I've got what I need from you, Solomon."

A frown pinched Grant's brow. He would readily admit he owed Ward ten grand. For Molly's sake, he was willing to make a deal to pay Ward whatever he wanted, twenty-five grand if it came to that. This dismissal of Grant's obligation was wholly unexpected.

Ward extended the homemade cigarette to him.

"For old times?" he invited.

Grant swatted it out of his hand. "Explain this. Lexi doesn't owe you anything. And using Molly as a pawn is beneath even you."

"Oh, nothing is beneath me." Ward balanced on his tipping chair and wiggled the fingers of his right hand like a magician. A closed fist, a flick of the wrist, and a fresh cigarette appeared between his fingers.

Grant shook his head. "Don't distract me."

"Already have."

Another roll of tobacco appeared in Warden's other hand. He touched the ends of the two cigarettes together, and each one began to smolder. When the tips glowed orange, he pulled them apart and handed one to Grant. A thread of smoke rose under his eyes, making them burn. The vapor smelled like the decaying leaves of fall.

Grant took it, then dropped it on the floor, grinding it under the toe of his worn-out cross-trainers.

"Let's sort it out, Ward. You stay out of Lexi and Molly's way. That's all I'm asking."

"This is all so noble of you, Grant. I'm touched, really I am. But it's also irrelevant."

"What do you want with them?"

"Money. Sins. Souls."

Grant stared at him until he continued.

Ward lowered his chair to the floor and leaned onto the tabletop, speaking slowly. "Lexi has money. Lexi has sins. Lexi has a black, black soul, and I'm entitled to her."

"Entitled to her *what*?"

"No, idiot. Entitled to *her*."

"She's not a piece of property."

Ward laughed at that. "Call her my collateral, then."

"Then what does Molly have to do with it?"

"Molly is the only thing Lexi has that she doesn't want to lose."

Grant clenched his jaw. "The debt is *mine*," he said through his teeth.

"Oh believe me, she has her own. And she has the ability to pay it too."

"How?"

"The same way you did, old friend."

Stupefied was not too strong a word for what Grant felt at this claim that Lexi had entered the rotting world of drug runners and dealers.

"Lexi doesn't deal. She hated me for doing it."

"You've been gone a long time, brother."

"I'll never believe it. Not so long as she's got Molly."

"We all must face our disillusionments."

Grant let his hand fall hard on the table, slapping it with a flat palm. "Only when they're based in facts."

Ward shrugged. "Pay her a visit, then. She's got stashes of great stuff all over her home sweet home."

"What's the street value of it?"

"Enough to pay me back."

Grant cursed and came around the table. "Then let her pay you back and leave her alone, if it's true!" He shouted. "Take her inventory. She doesn't have cash. She never did, and you know it. What's the point of putting her through all this on account of what I did?"

"No man is an island," Ward said. He leaned back in his seat, all four legs of the chair earthbound this time. "Our sins are never only ours to bear."

Grant's fist came back over his shoulder, then swung out in an arc toward Ward's jaw. He blocked the blow easily, locking Grant's forearm in his grip. The ease of his move sobered Grant up fast.

Ward didn't release him.

"Let me own what I owe," Grant said. "Let me take what Lexi owes, too, even though I'm sure you're making all that up. I'll find a way to pay you back for both of us."

"No."

"Why *not*, man? Name your price!"

Ward yanked his arm so that it nearly came out of its socket. Grant's head snapped back, then came forward so that it was nose-to-nose with Ward's.

"My price is the price of innocence, Solomon, and you have paid every last dime already. You don't have anything that I want, not anymore. The only person who has more than two pennies to her name is your dear little Molly."

Grant jumped on Ward then. He launched all his weight toward Ward's chest, hitting him square so that he tipped backward on the seat. His grip on Grant's forearm tightened and twisted, burning the skin.

They tumbled over the chair. Ward's throat rumbled with an unrestrained laugh. Grant got the clear sense that nothing that was about to happen would be his doing. Everything that transpired in this room, before and after his arrival, was purely for Ward's entertainment.

Ward allowed Grant a few punches to his ear, a few frustrated sprays of spittle. When he was done with Ward's ear he aimed for the man's greasy hair and locked on, expecting to come away with fistfuls of charcoal-gray tufts.

He came away empty-handed.

The room rolled, and from his new position underneath Ward, Grant kneed him in the ribs, then kicked at his kneecaps.

"You finished?" he taunted as Grant clipped his shins with his hardest kicks. Back when Grant was an inmate at Terminal Island, he once fractured a guy's leg this way.

Grant kept kicking, hyperaware of his strange impotence on Ward's turf, trying to clear his head and reevaluate his weaknesses.

What was going to happen to Lexi? To Molly?

He let loose with his three free limbs. He thrashed and twisted at the waist, bent at his hips, butted with his head.

Ward twisted Grant's arm until he cried out and flipped onto his stomach. Ward pressed the struggling fist between Grant's quivering shoulder blades. The odor of dead tree leaves clogged his throat.

"My turn," Ward said.

Grant believed Ward let him off lightly. He ended up with a swollen jaw and a sprained wrist, a bloody nose and more bruises than he could count afterward. Ward crushed two of his fingers and dislocated Grant's shoulder. Grant passed out from the pain. When he came to, he lay panting on his back while Ward lit another cigarette. He wasn't even breathing hard.

Ward bent over and blew smoke up Grant's nose, triggering a coughing fit.

"There's nothing you can do to save your daughter," he said. "You had your chance, years ago. You made your choice. Now it's all Lexi."

Grant spit in Ward's face and missed entirely. Gravity had a wicked sense of justice.

"I can't accept that," he groaned.

"Nothing I can do about that," Ward said. He grabbed Grant's twisted arm and yanked again. Grant screamed. His shoulder popped back into its socket.

"Now, listen carefully, old friend. The only thing you have worth living for anymore is the life you wish you had. And in case that doesn't feel very satisfying to you, you are welcome to join my guests in the nightclub out there who are living for the same reason, drunk and dumb on their own fantasies. Join the crowd. It takes the sting out of the regret. You understand me?"

Grant didn't understand a word of it, but he couldn't say so. Ward had placed his large hand over Grant's mouth and nose and pressed down, cutting off the air. Fight left his body, but not his mind.

"Let's talk about regret for a minute. You lost your wife seven years ago. You know who stole her out from under you? Norman Von Ruden. That's how weak a man you are. That's how little she regards you."

Grant's chest seemed to collapse. All these lies! What Ward had in store for Lexi was beyond Grant's imagination. She needed his help. He had to get Lexi to listen to him before—

"That's the mistake you people make more than any other I've seen," Ward said. "You think you have more time. Time to love, time to make things right. You fools. And Molly? You never had her to begin with. So move on, brother. And don't look back. Because when you do, I'll be the one snorting down your neck until my scalding breath singes every nerve at the surface of your skin. If you want to go through that, it's your call. At least when I'm through with you, you won't feel a thing anymore."

The seal that was Ward's hand tightened. In this basement clubhouse where the oxygen once had seemed so pure, Grant found himself suffocating.

Ward snarled. Grant's starved brain saw sharp incisors behind his black lips, and a forked tongue.

His eyes closed.

The sleep that followed was a relief.

{ chapter 27 }

Lexi was sucking blood out of her finger on the cereal aisle of King Grocery when Alice found her Wednesday morning. She'd been unloading cases of cereal and got the mother of all paper cuts from the corrugated Rice Krispies shipping box.

The slice drew tears as well. Not because it hurt, but because it showed how powerless she really was. She needed to be out saving Molly, to be finding money, to be telling the sheriff that Norman had threatened her, to be finding the drugs Ward had planted in her home, to be fleeing the state on the tank of gas in her car and the twenty-six dollars in her bank account.

Instead, she was paralyzed in routine, working because of all her options it seemed the only one that could buy time to think. Norman's hearing was in two days. She had two days to figure out how the planets that were Norman, Grant, Ward, and her precious daughter had aligned so swiftly and catastrophically. Two days to decide how she was going to save Molly's world.

The sight of Grant weeping over Molly had undone Lexi. His brokenness confronted her. His tears humbled her. She believed he was contrite for every mistake he'd ever made.

Had she ever shed tears like that? No. She'd turned her regrets into defensiveness. Grant could not have known she was upset over her role in Molly's danger. He could not have known Ward wanted Molly for jealous revenge against Norman and her. How could she tell him? What would she do if Ward told him first? Grant's eyes would dry up fast enough when he learned just how much of their family mess she was responsible for.

For the first time since Grant walked out, she considered whether her own wrongdoing was more offensive than Grant's. So what if he had driven her to it? Was that a valid excuse anymore? Had it ever been?

Lexi's finger would not stop bleeding.

The brisk clicking of high heels drew her attention from her cut. Alice was coming up the aisle, looking sharp in an aubergine pantsuit. Lexi stuck her finger back in her mouth.

"Let me get you a Band-Aid for that." Alice produced a travel-size first-aid kit she carried in her purse, then applied a bandage.

"What are you doing here?" Lexi asked. "You promised me you'd stay with Molly today."

"I lasted twenty minutes. What fourth grader can stand to have Grandma sitting in the back of her classroom? I couldn't torture her that way."

"Then go get her out of school. Take her home. I shouldn't have sent her back this week anyway."

Alice put her hands on her hips. "You said yourself that school is the best place for her to be right now, with everything going on. I agree. It keeps her mind off—"

"Please. Go get her." The only decision Lexi had been able to make so far was that Molly should not be left alone, not even in a crowd of friends and teachers. The scrapes on Lexi's face were too real, the cuts inside her mouth from the castor bean shells too raw. The attack on her might have been coincidental—when trouble rains, it might as well hail, her father used to say—but she wasn't willing to believe it yet.

"Lexi, we need to talk."

"Not here, Mom."

"There's no better time."

"This afternoon."

"I want to talk to you about Molly. Not when you're both home together."

Lexi grabbed two boxes of cereal and set them on the shelf. One tipped over and hit the floor. She sighed. "What do you want to talk about?"

"She's not herself."

"Of course she's not. None of us is, not after a week like this."

"You need to let her see her dad."

Lexi averted her face by collecting the fallen carton. "And what will that help, Mom?"

"You should give Grant a chance," Alice said. "I'm not saying you should sign over custody to him, alright? I'm just saying see what happens. Molly doesn't understand all your reasons, and she shouldn't, but she needs to know you're on her side."

"I am. There is no one *more* on Molly's side than me."

"You're not the only one."

Lexi took a breath and handed Alice a box of Chex, then pointed to the shelf.

"Ward came to our house the other day because Grant owes him money," Lexi said. "He wants it."

"Why's he coming to you?"

"Because Grant doesn't have any money."

"Neither do you."

"But I have Molly."

Alice's blush brightened as her cheeks paled. "You can't be serious."

"No, Mom, I'm making up stories."

"He's threatening *Molly*?"

"Don't ask me to explain it."

A woman with a baby girl sitting in the seat of the shopping cart stopped near them and picked up a happy yellow carton of Cheerios. Lexi put up two more packages of Chex. The woman rolled on. Alice lowered her voice.

"How much money are we talking about?"

"Twenty-five thousand."

"Gracious. I might be able to scrape that together."

Lexi cleared her throat, rushed with shame.

"How soon could you get it?" She couldn't look at her mother.

"I don't know. It's in assets, not cash. A week or two?"

"We need it Friday."

Alice placed her hand at her throat. "We'll go to the police."

"I can't. Not yet."

"For heaven's sake, why not?"

"For one, Ward doesn't exist as far as the police are concerned. He's a phantom dealer. He's been dealing drugs for who knows how many years and he's never been caught. Do you think it's because no one's tried to sell him out?"

"For one?" Mom murmured, still holding her box of Chex.

"He's planted drugs around my apartment. *If* I rat on him, and *if* he's found, he can say that nothing I claim is true, that I'm a fellow dealer with a grudge. In fact, they don't even have to arrest Ward for him to start that rumor. That'd be easy enough for authorities to believe, don't you think, considering my history with Grant?"

Alice's mouth went slack. "He seemed like such a nice man. Oh, honey, this is terrible." She straightened her shoulders. "I'll call my accountant. And we'll find the drugs first. Tear the house apart if we have to."

"I spent all night last night looking."

"I know this man who has a dog—"

"Mom . . ." Lexi touched Alice's soft hand with her own callused fingers. "They'll take Molly away from me. I'll go to prison."

"You didn't do anything."

"No, I didn't, but proving it will be hard."

Over at the butcher counter, Lenny King belted out an announcement that pork shoulders were on sale for ninety-nine cents a pound.

Alice raised her voice. "I said, you can run away."

A man passing by at the end of the aisle glanced their way. Lexi returned to stacking the shelves with refreshed speed.

"This isn't the place to have this conversation."

"It doesn't sound like we can put it off, either. I have friends, Lexi. Ward will forget you. What's twenty-five grand to a drug dealer, right?" Alice looked hopeful. "You have until Friday?"

"Right."

"There, you have two days' head start. On Friday—oh, the hearing is Friday, isn't it? Well, you can miss that. I'll understand. It's crazy for you to stay for that now."

Lexi studied the full cartons cluttering the aisle.

"I need to be there Friday," she said.

"I can be there for both of us."

"It won't be enough."

"You are the most aggravating girl sometimes, Lexi. Out with it. Please, explain why you have to be there now after you told me you wouldn't go."

There would be no more avoiding this. She tucked her hair behind her ear and brought her finger to her lips for a moment. Her heart was beating so fast.

Her mother would hate her for this. Hate her. And then Lexi would have lost more than she could bear.

Lexi's voice shook. "Norman Von Ruden and I had an affair." She cleared her throat. "Before Tara died."

Alice stared at Lexi for long seconds, burning a hole in Lexi's heart. Then she looked at the box she held and placed it back in the case as if it were breakable.

"I'm sorry," Lexi said.

Alice zipped up the pocket of her purse. "Molly doesn't have to know."

Lexi shook her head. Her eyes burned, but she lifted them to her mother's face. "You don't understand, Mom. Tara tried to tell me what a mistake I was making. She tried to stop me. I wouldn't listen. So she went to Norman—"

"They met?"

"That night, for the first time."

"Norman knew her?" Lexi let Alice add up the facts up without interrupting. Alice's body stiffened, and Lexi thought she was restraining herself from screaming, or maybe from lunging. "Tara was there for you. She died for you." She placed an unsteady hand on the purse strap over her shoulder. "You killed your sister."

A sob burst from Lexi's throat. "No, Mom." *Norman killed my sister*, she wanted to say. *And if I don't show up Friday, the last threads that are holding me to life as I know it will be cut with the sharpest of scissors.*

Her tears ran in tiny rivers and dampened her white shirt around the collar.

Alice averted her eyes. She was gazing at boxes of wheat and rice and oats. Lexi could hear her breathe.

"I'm so sorry," Lexi whispered. "Please forgive me. Please. I had no idea what he would do." To her own ears she sounded like Grant. Her husband, the man she had loved. Her daughter's father. "Please," Lexi repeated, expecting Alice's response to be no different than hers had been.

"You don't deserve Molly," Alice said. Then she left.

Tuesday night, after sending Grant on his merry way, Warden started heating up.

It had been decades since he'd smoldered. That restraint had taken him some years to perfect. It was too easy to slip into fury at times like these, and fury never ended well. He considered what had happened to Craven. The incompetent frog shouldn't have been so upset over something as insignificant as Ward's bacteria. If he'd had more self-control, Mort Weatherby wouldn't be unattended now.

Warden himself, though, was too heated up to dress until late Wednesday morning, when he finally brought his temperature low enough that steam wouldn't rise off his head when he stepped out into the cool mountain air.

The reason for his rage? Revelation. Stinking, spiritual, humbling revelation, of the variety that turned lives around. The hundred-eighty-degree change. Grant Solomon and Lexi Grüggen had gotten far too much of it in the past three days.

He decided to move up his timetable. Intervene himself, before his plan collapsed. The choice helped him to chill, and by the time he reached Molly's school he was feeling almost cool again.

It was recess, and there was Molly, so let down by her shortsighted parents that she was too glum for her friends to endure. They had left her on a bench against the wall where the playground fence met the red brick. He approached like a confident cat.

"Healing up nicely," he said.

She jumped and grabbed the crutches leaning next to her, to prevent them from sliding to the ground.

"You scared me," she said.

"What's life without a few surprises?"

Her smile was halfhearted. Which was all it ever should've been.

"Brought you some good news," he said.

She turned her face up to him. Children, he'd found, were always so hungry for good news. Of any kind.

"What?"

"I found your dad."

Molly turned her whole body on the bench. She lifted her swaddled ankle onto the seat in front of her.

"Where is he?"

"Well, he's working right now, but he gets a lunch break in a while and I thought we could meet up with him."

"Really?"

"I told him what a good chef you've become. There really isn't time to do any cooking today, but maybe you could plan a meal for him. For next time."

She chewed on her lower lip.

"Here's the best news of all: your mom said it was okay to visit him."

Still no smile.

Warden sighed and pretended to be found out.

"Can't slip anything past you, can I, Molly girl? You shouldn't have been born so smart."

He could paste a pained expression on his face as well as the next actor. "I'm sorry, sweetie. But I'm sure you understand what's going on here."

Her eyes dropped. The kid was totally in the dark!

"Your mom and that guy I first thought was your dad? What's his name?"

"Angelo."

"He's kind of spooky, don't you think? Anyway, sorry, don't need to go there. But he and your mom . . ."

Molly's eyebrows came together, working on the puzzle pieces he'd set in front of her mind.

"Your dad isn't going to get to be part of your family again, Molly. And I think that's a crying shame. If we do this right, though, maybe you and your dad can be friends anyway. Who needs old Angelo? Look." He stuck a piece of paper between the fence pole and the rough bricks. "She wrote a note excusing you to come with me. Actually, I wrote it. Pretty good, you think?"

Molly read the note, written on a sheet from a gas station notepad that Lexi kept by her phone. Warden had the foresight to tear off a few sheets when he last visited. The request was in Lexi's hand. He'd practiced well.

Come and get her, for starters. He spent quite a bit of time on that one.

But this one said, *Please excuse Molly at lunchtime today for a personal family matter. Our friend Warden Pavo will pick her up. Sincerely, Lexi Grüggen.*

"What about Grandma?" Molly asked.

"Can't come for lunch today, but she says you should have a good old time with Dad."

"Are you gonna eat with us too?"

"Nope, I'm just your chauffeur. I'll take you down to Riverbend and then get you home afterward. Your mom will want you there when she gets off work, you know."

Mom would be busy after work with other matters, which he'd set into motion in about an hour, when Molly was safe with him. Ha! Safe with him. One anonymous tip would be all it took to expose a hardworking single mom's dual life. Warden clapped his hands together.

"This'll be fun, right?"

Molly looked doubtful.

"You shouldn't worry about a thing, Molly-Wolly. Dads love their little girls to pieces, and you've grown up into the most beautiful girl in the world. There's no way he won't love you."

He was finally rewarded with the white teeth of her smile. Truth, after all, was the slickest axle grease a wheel of lies could spin on. And this one was rolling right along.

{ chapter 28 }

Visions of fanged serpents striking at Grant's eyes woke him. He hollered and slapped at them. The snakes morphed into lightning quick arms and fists. Triple H was pounding him into the mats.

"Hey! Relax!" Triple H commanded.

The voice belonged to Grant's old friend Richard, from Terminal Island. Grant opened his eyes. The man's blond pigtail dangled over one shoulder above Grant's face.

In the space of seconds, he crab-scrabbled out of Richard's reach, aggravating his sprained wrist. His hands hit the hollow base of some flimsy metal steps. Where was Ward?

Where was he?

Home.

These steps led to the aluminum door in the trailer Richard had rustled up for Grant when he landed the job at the Residence. There were a dozen decrepit trailers in this dusty park, and none of them had the shade of trees. Grant craned his neck to see around Richard's bulk. The Datsun was there, two wheels on the asphalt strip and two in what was supposed to be a flower bed. Nothing but weed-choked pavers. How did he get here?

What was Richard doing here?

Grant relaxed enough to sit. "You're a long way from Los Angeles, Richard."

"Conference in Riverbend. Starts tonight. Remember? You and me were gonna have some lunch."

They were?

"Sorry."

"Doesn't matter." Richard was squatting, his elbows resting on his knees. He pointed at Grant's swollen face. "What have you been up to?"

His encounter with Ward came back to him easily enough. Most of them, anyway.

"I wish I could remember." Grant ran a hand over his morning stubble.

"That's no good."

"It's not what you think."

"No?"

"I test every three weeks, Richard. I've been clean since before I got out. You can ask my PO." He rolled his eyes. "And my mother-in-law."

The sun was high enough to make Grant squint. He slowly stood, then stomped into the trailer, skipping the bottom two steps. Richard followed him, holding up his hands.

"I'm not here to keep you in-line. Just a friend dropping in on a friend, okay?"

Grant's head was throbbing. His jaw and shoulder ached. His whole body ached. He stepped into his sorry excuse for a bathroom and knocked through the stuff on the counter until he located the bottle of aspirin. He took three without water, then braced his hands against the basin, looking in the mirror.

His cheek was purple and the size of a plum. There was dried blood on his lips. He grabbed a length of toilet paper and moistened it under the tap, then started dabbing at his face.

Richard was leaning against the door frame.

"What demons you been fighting to work yourself up into this frenzy?" he asked.

The word *demons* bridged some connection in Grant's brain. He lowered the tissue and looked at Richard in the mirror.

"What do you do when someone's been lying about you?" Grant asked.

"Depends on the lie. Most are best ignored. Truth speaks for itself in my experience. Who's been telling lies about you?"

"They're not about me. Or maybe they are. I have no idea what he's been telling her."

"You're gonna have to bring me up to speed, friend."

"My former big man. He says my wife is dealing."

Richard nodded.

"Said she had an affair too. A long time ago with a friend of ours. Someone who . . . forget it. It's a long story. None of it's true, though."

"And how did that get you a fat lip?"

"Because his fight's with me, not her. I tried to make him see that, but . . . it's confusing. Why would he use an old gripe with me to go after her? Why not stick with the source?"

"Especially when he can take you down so easy," Richard mused.

It wasn't funny. "He's got Molly in on this, Richard."

"Your little girl."

Grant threw the wet, blood-tinged toilet paper in the trash.

"I'm sure I don't know what's going on, or what lies have to do with any of it, but the truth as I see it is that you're still the husband. You're still the daddy."

"What's that got to do with anything?"

"Well, if your wife is having to take on your old mistakes, you'd better remedy that."

"I told you, he won't—"

"Not him, her. What's the lady's name? Alexis?"

"Lexi. She doesn't want my help."

"Does she know she needs it?"

Grant started to say *of course*. Lexi was the one who'd told him about Ward's demands. But Grant's words got stuck on Ward's claim about the inventory Lexi kept at her house. If it wasn't outrageous enough that Lexi was in the business, it was even more ridiculous that she would keep a supply so close to Molly. Grant didn't believe a person would change *that* much in seven years.

Then again, he hoped *he* had.

What did he know?

Ward's lie about Lexi's affair with Norman Von Ruden had come on the heels of this claim. Why bother adding insult to injury unless he'd expected it to turn Grant against her?

It was the first thing that had made sense to Grant in a long time. Ward would turn him and Lexi against each other. He'd load her up with Grant's debts and make her resent him. Ward would fabricate some lie about an affair to make Grant throw up his hands.

Why?

Grant thought on this. Why? Why would Ward bother?

To have her for himself.

Grant snorted a laugh at this thought—Lexi wouldn't have Warden Pavo any sooner than she would have run off with Norman Von Ruden! Angelo was more her type. Grant wondered if they were officially an item. Could he blame her? Yes. *Yes*. He and Lexi were still married, and he didn't care what anyone had to say about that. She was his *wife*.

In fact, their marriage was reason enough for Ward to lower the boom on them. Divide and conquer. Keep Grant from playing the hero. Ward must have been ticked off at Lexi about something other than jealousy.

What better way to harm the parents than to harm the child? And what better way to harm a child than to come between her parents? Worse, what would happen to Molly if Ward convinced authorities Lexi was up to no good? What if he'd planted drugs at Lexi's place and she didn't know about it?

A drug dealer for a mother and an ex-con for a father. A grandfather in a mental institution and a grandmother who traveled the world on a hit-or-miss income.

They'd take her away.

Grant wasn't sure that Lexi needed him, but Molly did. He pushed past Richard out of the bathroom and searched for his cordless phone. It sat on top of a pile of junk mail in the kitchen.

He punched in Alice Grüggen's cell phone number. "Take a rain check on lunch?" Grant asked Richard.

"Sure. Looks like you need to get to work."

"Not today I don't."

Alice didn't answer.

It was nearly noon. High noon. Grant looked at the front door of Lexi's apartment and saw it as the last opportunity he had to make things right. Because if he messed this up, if Ward hadn't hidden any drugs here—if Lexi and Molly didn't need protection from anything—Lexi would call the cops on him herself.

Of course, the whole thing could be a lie. That was his risk, wasn't it? Better to risk himself than Molly, he decided.

Lexi wasn't one to keep a spare key anywhere except maybe in the glove box of her car. Nevertheless, Grant checked. He sifted through landscaping rocks under the front windows. He ran his fingers along the top of the door frame. He knocked on the siding, looking for a loose or hollow panel.

She shared walls with neighbors on both sides, so when Grant exhausted his search of the front, he had to jog down the sidewalk a few hundred yards before finding an easement that led into the rear common areas. He counted units until he reached Lexi's. Two plastic chairs sat on a six-foot-square concrete slab under a small awning. Behind the chairs, a sliding glass door led into the master bedroom.

The curtains were drawn, the door locked at the handle and bolted at the seam. A sawed-off broom handle lay in the track.

The window of the second bedroom was six feet down the wall. Grant moved one of the chairs under it to get a better look.

It was open three inches. Lexi would never have left it unlocked, but Alice . . . That must be the room she was staying in. Well, Grant thought, if he wasn't the hero of the day, there was a slim possibility that Lexi might be more angry at her mother for giving him this opening than she would be at him for breaking and entering.

He used his car key to slice an access in the screen, then stuck his hand through to shove the window open. He lifted the metal miniblinds and crawled in.

In seconds Grant was standing on Alice's bed. He closed the window and studied the other apartments within sight of Lexi's unit. Nothing caused him to think he'd been spotted. At midday in the middle of the week, it was possible he'd been lucky. Or everyone was at work. Regardless, he needed to move quickly.

Working in Grant's favor was the size of the apartment. Seven, eight-hundred square feet. Also working in his favor was the fact that hiding drugs was a bit old-hat for him. He could make a few assumptions:

One. Neither Lexi nor Ward would hide drugs anywhere that Molly might accidentally find them. Laundry, out. Video and DVD players, out.

Two. If Ward hid this stuff and Lexi didn't know about it, he'd spread it out, reduce his chance of her finding the whole lot. Grant, however, knew at least some of Ward's favorite spots.

Three. On the downside, Grant had no way of knowing exactly how much to collect to clean out the stash.

He started in Alice's room, which did not appear to have been shared by Molly. Someone else lived here. The clothes and shoes in the closet were too grown up for a nine-year-old, too youthful for a travel writer in her late fifties. Grant checked the heels of the shoes, and the insoles too. He patted down every item of clothing that was lined and looked in every box on the shelves. He checked the carpet for loose corners. Nothing in the light fixtures, in the computer software jewel cases, or in the books on the shelf over the bed.

He lifted framed pictures off the walls and checked the backs. One of the pictures was of Lexi with her old friend Gina. Maybe all the stuff was hers. He opened two framed pictures on the desk—nothing but cardboard and photos inside. He went through all the dresser drawers. A suitcase—he assumed Alice's—stood in the corner of the room, and Grant touched every square inch of the inner and outer surfaces, looking for telltale padding in the lining.

Fifteen minutes into his search of this one small room, he had found nothing. Grant began to wonder if he was a bigger fool than even Lexi had presumed.

His eyes went back to the window, and the blinds that covered it. They were a bit battered, and the string ladder on the left was frayed. The center string was completely undone. Grant pulled on the cord to raise the slats. Friction caused it to drag.

The blinds' hardware was rusty, but the box flaps moved easily enough when he lifted them on each end and slid the blinds out of the window. The tube where the strings were threaded was hollow. Or should have been hollow. Grant landed his first find: a plastic bag of weed, maybe two or three ounces.

This small discovery refreshed his sense of urgency, and he moved into other parts of the house. He couldn't remember what time Lexi got off work. If Alice barged in, she'd be more understanding.

Within a half hour, Grant found packages of weed, crystal meth, and cocaine in the bathroom and Lexi's bedroom: in the base of a lamp, in the elbow of a floor vent, in the toilet tank, and in the spring-loaded rod of the toilet-paper dispenser. There was more taped to the bottom side of Lexi's headboard.

Eventually, Grant thought he had maybe three or four thousand dollars' worth of merchandise—more if the coke hadn't been cut. If there was truly twenty-five grand in this little place, he had a lot more to unearth, but it wouldn't be much longer before someone found him here.

He gave himself two minutes to check one more place. Withdrawing the pocketknife he carried, he flipped open the screwdriver and removed the faceplate from the light switch in Lexi's room. Another bag of rocks had been stuffed into the wall there.

When he repeated the process with the electrical outlets in the bedroom, the discovery repeated itself too. Grant broke out in a sweat. It would take him hours to go through the house like this. If he'd hidden this stuff himself he doubted he'd remember all the locations he'd used—and so far he'd gone through only the bedrooms and bathroom.

Grant had amassed quite a pile of merchandise on the bedroom floor. Surely it was enough to convince Lexi to let him come back in and finish the search later. She'd see he was trying to help her, wouldn't she?

He grabbed a pillow off the bed and stripped it of its case, then dropped what he'd found into the makeshift bag.

Someone pounded on the front door.

Sweat broke out at Grant's hairline.

"Ms. Solomon? Sheriff's department. May we have a word?"

Not too bright, these guys, if they thought she was home instead of at work. Or maybe, Grant thought, he was the dim bulb and she had left the store awhile ago. Or a neighbor had ratted on him.

He looked out the sliding door. No cops back there.

Across the narrow strip of brown lawn that covered the residents' shared open space, another sliding door opened. A heavy-set, middle-aged woman stepped out with half a sandwich in her hand. She took a seat on her concrete step next to a pet's water dish and bit into the bread. The name Juliet was painted on the side of the bowl.

A foot-high headstone stuck out of the dirt near the woman's feet.

Choices: Run with the stash straight past a witness. Risk getting caught. Dump the supply. It would take awhile to flush this stuff. Risk Lexi disbelieving him. Risk that Ward would do this right next time. Leave the supply here and tell Lexi where to find it. Risk the officers coming in with dogs.

Couldn't anything be easy?

It was a small town. More than likely these guys would leave and come back later, or keep an eye on the place. But if they had a warrant—and Ward could have given them enough for one, however he managed that—busting the door down to search and seize wasn't out of the question. They didn't seem either stealthy or equipped for that kind of a move, though.

If they didn't have a warrant, Lexi might invite them in, overconfident in her own innocence.

Impossible to say.

Grant tiptoed to the kitchen at the front of the apartment, keeping his head below the checkered curtains that covered only the bottom half of the windows. Two officers stood at the end of the long walk between Lexi's front door at the gravel-edged driveway, talking to each other. Maybe they were going to wait for her after all.

The sink had a garbage disposal in it. Grant lifted the tap and flipped on the motor, then emptied the pillowcase onto the counter and started dumping what he could. Several precious minutes ticked by.

He threw twist ties and rubber bands into the trash and hoped no canine units would be involved in searching her home, if it came to that.

A bigger problem was what to do with the plastic bags. Clogged plumbing would be a giveaway.

Grant slipped out of his cross-trainers and yanked the insoles out, layered folded bags in the bottom of the shoes, then replaced the linings. The material shifted around under his weight. Not a foolproof hiding place, but it might buy him some time.

In the bedroom he replaced the pillowcase, then returned to the sliding door. The rear yard was empty.

Grant scurried to make his exit then. His PO was going to apply to be reassigned when he heard about this one.

He struggled to get the broom handle out of the track. The peg lock on the bottom of the door jammed. The lever lock on the door handle was broken. He wondered if Lexi ever opened this door.

When the door finally came loose, it screeched.

Silently apologizing to Lexi for not being able to lock the door from the outside, Grant exited, dropped the curtain behind him, and ran.

Straight into a brown-shirted beanpole of a sheriff.

{ chapter 29 }

At noon, out of habit rather than hunger, Lexi went to the deli and scooped a few spoonfuls of macaroni salad into a plastic tub. Fifteen minutes wasn't long enough for lunch, but Lenny allowed her to help herself to the lower-end salads because she never took much.

Lexi stared at the sallow pasta and couldn't imagine eating it.

You killed your sister. You killed your sister.

Her mother's voice would not leave her alone. Lexi considered taking a few of her sick hours and going home early.

A cute couple was at the counter ordering sandwiches. They had the tan raccoon faces of skiers and were laughing with each other. The girl put her arm in the crook of the guy's elbow and leaned on him. He was tall and blond.

Lexi's thoughts went to Angelo, who was both a practical stranger and the closest friend she'd had in a long time. *Close friend* wasn't quite right. It was more like he was the husband she never had. The protector she needed. A miracle worker.

It was a miracle how he'd gotten rid of the crazed resident who'd attacked her. Angelo had been tight-lipped about the incident, refusing to answer her questions about his perspective on what had happened, in particular how the lunatic had gotten away so fast. She would have said he vanished, but that didn't make sense. The image of steam rising from that discarded jacket wouldn't leave her alone. Even now, she shivered.

Whatever the explanation was, Lexi owed Angelo her own life now, in addition to Molly's.

Someone was calling her name from the direction of the break room. Rachel, she thought, the head cashier.

"You got a call," she yelled. King Grocery's small-town, mom-and-pop version of a PA system. Lexi hurried around the counter and down the aisle to the back of the store. Rachel stood there with the old cord stretched out the door behind her.

"New boyfriend?" she whispered, waggling her brows.

Lexi must have looked as shocked as she felt, having not dated for nearly a decade, because Rachel said, "You'll have to introduce me to him, 'kay?"

Lexi frowned and held out her hand. Rachel placed the receiver in it.

"Hello?"

"Sexy Lexi, how are you?"

At the moment she was wishing she could avoid the last person she wanted to see, think of, or speak to.

"What do you want, Ward?"

Rachel mouthed, *Ward?* Lexi turned her back.

"What have you decided about Norman's parole?"

"I thought I had until Friday to decide."

"Don't kid yourself, Lexi. You know what you're going to do already. Most people know and never change their minds, no matter how long they think about it."

"I need time."

"You've had seven years. A couple of days isn't going to change anything."

Lexi let the little plastic cup of macaroni salad fall into the large trash can under the phone.

"I heard you went to see your old flame yesterday," Ward said. "How is he?"

"How did you know—"

"Ready to take you dancing as soon as he's out of the slammer?"

"Stop it."

"You're a heartbreaker, Lexi," Ward said. "Probably drove Grant right back to his sordid past. You and Norman, you and Angelo . . . he was all broken up."

"You told Grant." She meant to ask it as a question but it came out as a fact. Lexi hoped Ward was messing with her.

Probably not. She wondered if the news had wounded Grant.

Wounding Grant, getting back at him for his hurtful actions, should have been satisfying on some level. So why wasn't it? She realized she didn't want to hurt him again. The anger she'd felt toward him at the Residence was what she'd conditioned herself to feel but not what she wanted anymore. They'd both suffered enough.

"Sure I did. You haven't gone soft on your old man now, have you?" The sharp tone of Ward's voice recaptured her attention. "Your bitterness is what gives you your edge, Lexi. You don't want to lose that, do you?"

Wariness crept into the corners of her mind. What edge? "Ward, get to the point or end the call."

"My point is that you don't need until Friday."

Lexi's knuckles went white on the receiver, she gripped it so hard.

"You already know, for instance, whether you will let your sister's killer go free or protect your own reputation. What's it going to be, whore?"

It took some courage for Lexi to say, "I haven't decided."

"You know. In your heart of hearts, you know."

"For the sake of everything that is holy, Ward, deal with me straight."

"Straight? Straight? All that I know is crooked, Lexi. Your crooked little ways in your crooked little heart, acting like you drew your life map with a ruler! Let's stop and talk about what is *bent*, why don't we?"

His lips were close to the phone. Lexi could hear him breathing.

"Let's talk about all the ways you could have saved your sister from dying."

"What do you know about that?"

"All that I need to. Tara's death was your fault."

"No."

"Blame it on whomever you like. She wouldn't have made arrangements to see him if you hadn't crammed her pleas down her throat and turned her away. She wouldn't have tried to save your marriage if you hadn't prostituted yourself to—"

"It wasn't my fault! Norman was . . . I can't believe I'm having this conversation. It's over. Now."

"Yes, we're done."

"Don't call me again before Friday."

"Oh, I won't be calling you again, Sexy Lexi. It's been a pleasure knowing you."

She blinked. What was he saying? "What? But what about . . . Did Grant give you the money?"

"*You* were supposed to give me the money. Too late for that, though. I have what I need from you now."

Her heart rate kicked up as if she were running. "I don't understand."

"I thought we were finished with this conversation."

"Do you want the money or not?"

"As I said, *no.* I have secured something far more valuable. Superior collateral. We'll call it even, shall we?"

Dear God, please, not Molly . . . Her mind couldn't form any more coherent thought than that. Lexi's eyes started to burn. She screamed without thinking, "Warden Pavo! This was not what you said would happen!"

Rachel was frozen over a coffee cup at the break room sink, staring at Lexi.

"You'd like to keep talking? We can go on if you like. Let's talk about all the ways you will not be able to save your daughter from dying."

"You monster! Where is my daughter?"

"She's with me."

"You *will* give her back to me, Ward."

"Whether you get her back will be up to her, honestly. But I can promise you one thing: when you find her again—*if* you find her—she won't be the Molly you know and love today."

Lexi reached out to brace herself on a locker. "What do you want?"

"From you, nothing more. I have it."

"You must want something. Name your price."

"She is my price."

"But what about the money?"

"Don't you get it, Lexi? This was never about money."

Her mind was spinning around Ward's twisted logic. She could not untangle it.

"This was always about you," Ward said, "and what you owe everyone else. For betraying Grant. For killing Tara. What you really deserve for all your sins."

"What's that?" Her voice was a whisper.

"The same thing you think everyone else deserves. Grant, Norman, me: justice."

"Why should Molly have to pay for my sins?"

"All children do."

"My sins aren't against her. Or you."

"True enough. She's just an innocent bystander. I'm only the justice of the peace."

"Who gave you the right?"

"Authorities more powerful than you or I. It's the way of the world, Lexi."

"You wouldn't know justice or peace if they offered to buy you a drink."

"Ha-ha! You have a sense of humor in a time of crisis. I admire that."

"I'll call the police."

"I have no objection. I've been eluding police for longer than you've been alive."

"I'll find you!"

"You do that. You make me your life's work. It'll be the only thing worthwhile after this."

"Ward."

"Warden. Say it."

"Warden." His name was a petition on her lips.

"That's right."

"You must have a ransom of some kind."

"I don't."

"She's all I have."

"That's what justice calls for, isn't it? Paying what you owe with what you've got? When the time comes, no one ever wants to pay. It's why you can't forgive Grant for walking out on you. It's why you want Norman to stay in prison. Someone has to pay, and you think it shouldn't be you."

"No, I think it shouldn't be *my daughter*."

"Listen carefully to me, and maybe one day you'll understand: I punish the children for the sins of their mothers. In the year of my jubilee, I collect all debts. Molly is your debt."

"Let me talk to her!"

"There is no time for that."

"Let me know she's okay!"

"But she's not. She really is not."

{ chapter 30 }

When Lexi realized Rachel was trying to ask her what had happened, she was hyperventilating and chanting, "He has Molly. He has Molly."

"Who has Molly? That guy Ward?"

"Call the sheriff! I need the sheriff." Lexi was still holding the phone receiver as if hanging up would disconnect her from her daughter forever. Her hands were shaking so badly that she couldn't dial 9-1-1. She kept hitting the 8 and 9 keys together.

Rachel depressed the switch hook, then dialed for her. The cashier's slow, intentional gestures brought Lexi's focus back to center even though she couldn't stop the shaking.

"Emergency operator. What's your emergency?"

"He has Molly! He's going to kill Molly!"

"Who is Molly, ma'am?"

"My daughter. He kidnapped her and said he's going to kill her!"

Rachel gasped.

"And your name?"

"Lexi Solomon."

"And you know the person who took her?"

"Warden Pavo. He's an old . . . friend. *Was*. Please hurry. Put out one of those alerts!"

"Where did you last see your daughter?"

"I was at . . . it was this morning . . . we were—he took her from school." Her mother should never have left her. Never. Never.

"What school, ma'am?"

"Wasson Elementary."

"Up in Crag's Nest."

"Yes!"

"Where are you now?"

"At work! King Grocery."

"In Crag's Nest?"

"*Yes*, I told you. Are you sending the sheriff? Are you—"

"How long has she been gone?"

"I don't know. I haven't called the school . . ."

Oh God, what if she's already dead?

"Do you have reason to believe your daughter is in imminent danger?"

Lexi started screaming at this operator, whose questions were taking too long. "What does *kill her* mean to you? *Yes!* She is going to die if you don't—"

"Law enforcement is on its way to the school, ma'am. How soon can you get there?"

"In seconds." She could probably get there before the sheriff did. Lexi hung up and blew past wide-eyed Rachel. There was no time to tell Lenny.

She jumped into her Volvo and took off without latching the seat belt.

Where would Ward have taken her? Lexi didn't know any of his haunts. She didn't even know if he'd been in Riverbend all these years or had only come back since Grant's release.

Oh God, please keep my daughter safe. You've got to bring her back to me.

The two-mile drive to Molly's school seemed to take hours.

Without warning, three men collectively responsible for destroying the life she had wanted so many years ago all reemerged from their rats' nests at the same time. The consequences of their arrival were too dramatic, too profound, not to have been . . . what? Planned. Calculated.

Her head ached. Her grocery apron was covered in wet spots from fallen tears.

She took the last corner to Molly's school without downshifting and going about fifteen miles an hour too fast. She clipped the curb. Lexi bypassed the parking lot and pulled right onto the sidewalk closest to the admin building.

She realized as she burst into the school offices that she was expecting to find Molly sitting on one of the chairs lining the wall. Her daughter wasn't there, though, and the sight of one of Molly's classmates brought fresh tears to Lexi's eyes. The girl was swinging her legs and studying the split ends of her long red hair.

Lexi unloaded her fear on the woman behind the desk.

"What happened to Molly?" she demanded.

The tone of Lexi's voice caused her hands to stop moving over the keyboard. She looked at Lexi over the computer monitor. The nameplate on the front of her desk said Sue Jacobs.

"Where is my daughter?"

Sue stood without taking her eyes off Lexi, apprehension in the frown lines between her eyes. "You're Molly Solomon's mother."

"Please tell me that there's been a ridiculous misunderstanding and she's still in class!"

A counter separated the women. The little redhead stared, her whole body still.

Sue Jacobs withdrew a green three-ring binder from under the counter and opened it. She licked her middle finger and flipped through a few pages. Her silence was choking Lexi.

She paused on a page of handwritten names, dates, and times, and ran her finger down the list. She shook her head.

"He signed Molly out a half hour ago," she said.

Lexi grabbed the book and looked.

Molly Solomon. *Time out: 11:40. Time in*: blank. *By: Warden Pavo.* This, signed with a smiley face in the *O*. Lexi studied the signature. It was her own handwriting. *Reason: unpardonable sin.*

Unpardonable sin?

Sue had been reading the book upside down. "He said it was a family emergency," she said, seeming as perplexed as Lexi about what he'd written. Lexi grabbed a tissue out of the box on the counter and swiped at her wet, snotty face. Sue cleared her throat and moved to a file cabinet.

"Molly had a note. I could have sworn you wrote it."

"Where is it?" Lexi yelled. *"Where is it?"*

Through the bank of windows on the other side of the office, Lexi saw the sheriff's cruiser pull up behind her car. She'd left the driver's door open.

Lexi ran back outside without waiting for Sue.

Sheriff Dawson and his deputy, Crystal Ames, were still unfolding themselves from their sedan when she reached them. They were moving so slowly that she wanted to inject them with adrenaline. At this rate Molly would be dead before Crystal got her clipboard off the backseat!

Why couldn't anyone understand how urgent this was?

Sheriff Dawson nodded at Lexi, all squinty because he never wore sunglasses, just a cowboy hat with a rim not quite broad enough to protect him from the brutal sun of the high-desert climate. He also never wore a uniform, but blue jeans, a black chamois shirt, and that silver star. His square face sported a gray mustache and graying wavy hair that almost brushed his shoulders. If he hadn't felt the need to bring Crystal, he probably would have shown up on his cruising bike.

Crystal was young enough to be his daughter. Lexi's age, but fairskinned, copper-haired, and mean as a copperhead.

"Lexi," the sheriff said, glancing at the Volvo. "Haven't been up to the grill for a while. Guess I'm due for some of Chuck's chicken-fried steak here pretty soon."

"Molly's been gone more than a half hour," Lexi said. "We have to hurry."

"Who ran off with her?" he asked.

"Warden Pavo." Crystal wrote this down.

"Someone you know?"

"From a long time ago. He and Grant used to . . . work together."

"Well, now. Isn't that interesting?" he said to Crystal.

"What? What's interesting?"

"Seems Grant's back in town," the sheriff said.

Lexi nodded. "He's working in Riverbend."

"Not today, it seems."

Grant's whereabouts didn't interest Lexi. Except that the last time she'd seen him, he was clearly upset about Ward's threat against Molly.

"He owes Ward some money," she said.

"Is that why you think this guy Ward took Molly?"

"He told me he doesn't want the money."

Crystal stopped writing. Her eyebrows arched up over her dark glasses.

"Ward's contacted you?" Sheriff Dawson asked.

"He called me at work. Eight, ten minutes ago."

"Why you instead of Grant, if it's about money?"

"I don't know. But like I said, he told me—"

"What's he demanding if not money?"

"Nothing. He said he doesn't want anything."

"Maybe you've got something else he wants," Crystal muttered. Her tone made Lexi feel like a suspect in Molly's disappearance.

"Please, I need to find her."

"Any idea where he would have taken her?"

Lexi groaned and shook her head. She had no idea.

Sheriff Dawson crossed his arms and planted his feet wide. "Crystal, why don't you have a talk with our school people in there"—he nodded to the offices—"and then we'll go have a word with Mr. Solomon."

Crystal moved like a sloth up the sidewalk. Lexi bounced on the balls of her feet.

"I don't know where Grant lives. I'll need to call my moth—"

"Grant's down at our office," Dawson said. "Deputy Garrison picked him up about five minutes ago."

"Picked him up?"

"At your place, I hear. Anything you want to tell me about that?"

Ward appreciated the simplicity of children. For them, the world was a small, ordered place run by basic desires—to know one's daddy, for example. For that reason alone, disrupting their lives should have been easy work for him. And yet they were too innocent to be easily disrupted.

Therein lay the challenge. He had to admit he enjoyed it.

She sat on the passenger seat of his truck.

Ward figured he had a couple hours before anyone would track Molly to the food court of the Bedrock Mall, depending on how long it took the sheriff to sort out the details of Lexi's distribution operation and her daughter's abduction. The self-imposed time limit gave Warden a little thrill.

Mere hours to ruin a little girl—mind, heart, and soul. It used to take him months.

"Sophisticated kid like you probably doesn't like mall food," he said to her.

"That's okay."

"How long's it been since you had a greasy burger?"

Molly wrinkled her nose.

"Oh, girl. You've gotta live a little. What's your favorite food that your mom won't let you have?"

"Uh, nothing."

"Nothing? She lets you eat whatever you want?"

Molly looked confused.

"How about dessert before vegetables? You get away with that?"

She grinned then, and giggled a little. "No."

"Then Dairy Queen it is. And they have greasy burgers, too, if you want one afterward."

"I think Daddy should decide where to eat."

"Well sure. But we'll probably get there before he does."

"Are there lots of choices?"

"Millions."

"I've never been to the mall before."

"That's a crime! Why not?"

"Mom says there's nothing there worth seeing."

"Really. Well what do moms know? There's a pretty fountain right in the middle of the food court."

"Are there fish in it?"

"Just pennies. And quarters for wishes worth making. You want some quarters?"

Molly shrugged.

"What do you wish for?" Ward asked.

She shrugged again and looked at her lap.

"You can tell me."

"That's okay."

Ward laughed. "Bet I can guess?" Molly looked at him. "You wish your mom and dad would get back together."

"Maybe."

"What? You think if you say it, it won't come true?"

"Isn't that how it is with birthday wishes?"

"Well sure. If you're four or five. But you're all grown up, little lady. Those rules don't apply to you anymore."

She pieced this together in her mind, maybe deciding whether it was worse to be four or five or to have had the rules change without being told.

"Do you mean I can just say wishes and they'll happen?"

"No no no. I mean wishes don't come true anymore. You turn six, and slam-bam, thank-you ma'am, wishes aren't worth the quarters you pay for 'em."

Molly looked like he'd told her that Daddy wasn't coming to lunch.

He wasn't, but Ward would mention that later.

"You're teasing me." It was a question.

"Wish I was, little lady. But telling the truth is part of growing up and being responsible. You know what else I wish? I wish moms and dads always told their kids the truth so I didn't have to keep doing it for them."

Molly blinked.

"Tell you what. Let's not let a little thing like spoiled wishes ruin our day. I'll make it up to you. When we get to the fountain I'll tell you the truth about why you've never been to the mall, and I'll give you a hundred bucks to throw in the fountain for the heck of it. Trust me, it'll make you feel better."

{ chapter 31 }

Grant understood that drug investigations could take years before they amounted to anything, so he felt half lucky that this was the sheriff's first visit to Lexi's home. Luckier that they didn't find the bags lining the bottom of his shoes. On the other hand, his breaking and entering gave them permission to go into her apartment and have a look around.

Grant didn't know if they found cause to keep an eye on her place until Lexi walked into his cell. She was the last person he'd expected to visit. For a split second he feared she'd been arrested too. The sheriff, a mustached man in a black shirt, watched them.

She grabbed hold of the bars near her face. There were no cuffs on her wrists.

"Lexi, what are you—"

"Ward's got Molly," she whispered.

Grant swallowed. "How?"

"From school."

"Why?"

"I don't know. I must have done something." She started to cry.

"No. No, you couldn't have." Grant's visit to the Blue Devil reared its head in his mind. "What does he want?"

"He won't tell me. Nothing, he says."

Grant put his hands over hers. She leaned her forehead into the gate, and he reached through the bars and stroked her hair. She let him. The sleek locks fell over his fingers. Touching her filled him with confidence.

"We'll find him in time," Grant said.

"How?"

"I might know where to start looking."

"Where?" Lexi straightened and wiped her eyes with the back of her hand.

He looked at the sheriff. "The Blue Devil. A nightclub down in Riverbend. On the south end of Parker Avenue. He's got a place in the basement."

"I know it," the sheriff said.

Grant described how to get into Ward's operation from the back of the building. He also mentioned the inside elevator in case the rear door was locked. The elevator was located on the main floor behind a sliding panel near the restrooms.

"I can show you," Grant offered.

"You can stay right here," the sheriff said. Grant put a lid on his frustration for Lexi's sake. "We'll check it out. Got a couple other leads from the school. And an Amber alert sighting of his car headed north. Those come first."

The opposite direction from the nightclub.

"They said you broke into my home," Lexi said. She didn't seem angry about it, though.

The sheriff took a step toward Lexi, appearing to encourage her to leave with him. Grant thought he wanted to eavesdrop, though, so he didn't say anything.

"What were you doing?" she asked.

"I needed some money," he lied, then chanced a look into Lexi's eyes. He'd always believed she was smarter than he was, and he hoped this moment was no exception. They could be of more help to Molly if they were out there together. Would she acknowledge that? Would she believe he loved Molly more than his own life?

She said so the sheriff could hear, "But I gave you a key."

His heart rose into his throat. "I lost it."

"You didn't say anything about a key," the sheriff said.

"Would you have believed me?"

Lexi looked at the law man. "You told me you had a drug tip."

The man nodded once.

"Did they find anything?" she asked.

"Not yet," he said, still studying Grant.

Lexi's grip on the bars eased enough for her fingertips to turn pink again. She returned her gaze to Grant, and her lips parted. Something like stunned understanding passed between them. Had she known Warden had planted merchandise in her home?

"Of course they didn't find anything," she said. "Where did your tip come from? Warden Pavo himself? Doesn't the timing of all this seem strange to you, Dawson?"

"More than you know."

The innuendo shocked Grant.

"You don't think I had something to do with Molly's disappearance?" Lexi said.

"Anything's possible right now."

"Anything but that," Grant said.

"I'll bet that sighting of Ward's truck isn't legitimate," she blurted. "He wants you to think—"

"Lexi, let us do our job," he said.

She pursed her lips, and Grant knew she didn't care what the sheriff planned to do.

"I don't want to press charges against Grant."

"That might not matter."

"He could help us find Molly."

"Us?"

"You can't stop me from going to the Blue Devil."

"Don't hamper my investigation, young lady, or I'll lock you up too." But he smiled at her.

"Let my husband go." *My husband*. Grant took a deep, hopeful breath. "I promise you he won't leave town while Molly's missing."

"Or after we find her," Grant said.

"There's paperwork to be done first," Dawson said.

"Do it later!" she said. "Our daughter's out there!"

"I'm by the book. How do you think I keep getting reelected?"

"We need him! He knows where this guy goes! How he thinks! We have to check everywhere."

"And we will. But we've got limited manpower and limited time. We chase the hottest leads first."

"You've called the FBI, right?" Grant asked. "How long will it take them to get here?"

"Couple hours."

"What did you mean by limited time?" Lexi asked.

The sheriff frowned.

"He means every minute counts," Grant said to Lexi, fearing he meant something else.

"He meant something else," she said, looking at Dawson. "How much time?"

He held her eyes. "Statistically, abductors who intend to kill do it within three hours," he said. The air left the room. "You coming?" he asked Lexi.

"Go," Grant told her. "I'll come as soon as I can." He grabbed her hand as she pulled away. "Don't go to the Blue Devil by yourself. Let the sheriff do what he has to do, but I don't want you there alone. Wait for him."

"I can't wait," she said.

"Then at least get Angelo. Take him with you."

She nodded.

"Lexi, I'm so sorry. For everything. If I could change it all . . ."

Her arm fell to her side. "I forgive you," she said.

"I love you."

She didn't answer.

{ chapter 32 }

Lexi wouldn't have taken the time to fetch Angelo except that Grant's warning scared her. The Residence was located directly between the sheriff's office and Porter Avenue. If Warden was disinclined to surrender Molly on request, Angelo's brute strength would be more convincing.

She pulled in at the facility as she had at Molly's school, taking a handicapped spot instead of a piece of lawn this time. She flew over the cobblestone walk into the stunning lobby—the only portion of the building that had been built to impress with its skylighted indoor garden, fountains, and solid oak furniture.

Her feet sprinted past the reception desk and down the north wing toward the nurse's office. They would know where Angelo was.

Lexi yanked open a glass door embellished with frosted peacocks and pounced on the closest nurse, who was carrying a cup of coffee to her desk.

"Where's Angelo? It's an emergency!"

Her eyes went wide. "With one of our residents? We have proced—"

"No! I need him for something else."

A man in scrubs who was typing at a computer spoke without looking away from what he was doing. "Angelo went to lunch more than an hour ago. He should have been back by now."

"Where would he be?"

He looked at a door in the rear of the office and pointed. "Check the dining room. Third shift is passing through about now. Downstairs, second door on the right."

Lexi pushed the door open before he finished, hit the stairs in five strides, and clattered down to the lower level, making as much ruckus as a basketball team on a shiny arena court.

Please be there, please be there . . .

There were plenty of people in the dining hall, which reminded her of a high-school cafeteria.

No Angelo. Could he be sitting down?

There were only three rows of tables, and two aisles. Lexi speed-walked through, looking for the broad crown of white-blond locks.

She was out of time. If only Grant could have come with her!

Lexi spotted her mother. The sight of Alice hit her like a car.

Here?

She sat next to Lexi's father and stared at his plate of food, her head tilted as if to hear him better in this noisy place, her hands folded in her lap. His face was rosy beneath his glasses, and his food was untouched. He beamed and talked, animated as Lexi had never seen him since before . . .

Alice looked up and saw her daughter, then attempted a dim smile.

Questions were popping out of Lexi as she hurried to their table, but she couldn't linger. Even if she could, she'd ruin their moment.

"Have you seen Angelo?" Lexi asked them, bending over the bench seat.

Alice turned to her purse and lifted the flap. "After he brought your father in from his walk. Yes."

She wouldn't look Lexi in the eye. Still angry about her confession, Lexi thought. She withdrew a folded piece of paper from the side pocket.

"Angelina Jolie took me for a walk today," Barrett said. "Pretty day. Pretty as your mother."

"Mom, I have to talk to you."

"It can wait."

"It's Molly, Mom. Ward took her."

Now Alice looked at her.

"I need to find Angelo. He can help me find her."

"He had to go." She handed Lexi the page from her purse. "Asked me to give this to you."

"What is it?"

"I don't know. I didn't read it. What is the sheriff doing?"

"Looking for her, of course."

Lexi unfolded the paper. A handwritten note.

Lexi, I will not be here when you need me most, but all this will make sense later. Listen: when I said the other night that you need to consult love about Molly, I don't think you understood what I meant. Love always protects, always hopes, always perseveres. Love will never fail you.

Don't listen to Warden Pavo. Listen to love, which keeps no record of wrongs. Choose love, and it will save you even now. Molly too.

Angelo

Barrett said, "I told you to watch out for that jailer," and shoved his spoon under a mountain of mashed potatoes.

Lexi's eyes snapped to him. She'd forgotten her dad's babbling during their last visit. "Did he get your little sister?" he asked. "She's lost."

"Dad, are you talking about Molly?"

How was it possible that Angelo and Dad could have known about her abduction before it happened?

"Course not! Silly girl. Molly is your niece. I've been saying plain as day that I mean your little sister. Lexi, baby. Did he get Lexi?"

She slowly shook her head, wondering if she should be nodding. Barrett mirrored her movement. They were a picture of solemn worry.

"Well, he'll get her soon enough. She's lost, you know, and no one's looking for her."

Alice placed her hand over his, and her eyes glistened.

Before leaving the Residence, Lexi told her mom about Grant and made Alice promise to go hold Sheriff Dawson's feet to the fire until that paperwork was finished and Grant could be released. Alice had pressed her cell phone into Lexi's palm and insisted she take it. She said she'd buy a prepaid one and would call as soon as she had news about Grant. Lexi told her where she was going and promised to call every twenty minutes.

Sitting in her car, she tried to call Angelo's cell phone three times. He did not answer.

Lexi had sacrificed fifteen minutes by the time she drove away from the Residence with Angelo's note crumpled between her palm and the steering wheel. She'd read it four times and still didn't understand it. Couldn't he say anything plainly?

For the first time, she was angry at him. Her daughter's life depended on speed and clarity. Was that so much to ask for?

She needed her husband out and helping as soon as possible.

Her husband.

It had been years since she'd thought of him that way. It had been years since he'd acted like one. Until today. Lexi knew she would not be out looking for Molly if Grant hadn't intervened in Ward's attempt to frame her as a dealer.

She had so many questions: how Grant had known there was trouble, why he'd bothered to get her out of it, how he knew where to look for whatever Ward had stashed, how he'd gotten rid of it. It would have cost him dearly to be caught in possession of those things!

When he said he was sorry, when he said he loved her, it was so easy to believe him. The things that had prevented her from forgiving him before seemed like nothing compared to what they faced with the potential loss of their daughter.

She did forgive him, because she had to. She had to cut herself loose of her anger toward Grant because it took too much energy to stay attached to it. It zapped her heart and her mind of the agility she was going to need to save Molly. She couldn't afford a grudge right now.

Did that make forgiving Grant an act of selfishness? Maybe. Just maybe.

She pushed her Volvo to its limits and made it to the Blue Devil by ten after one. The parking lot was empty.

The building, low and long, had a steep wood-shingle roof and poorly applied brown clapboard siding. No windows. Ads spray painted directly onto the walls of the nightclub advertised *Girls! Girls! Girls!* and two-for-one drinks on Tuesday Ladies' Night. The plastic *D* in the electric sign was shattered, exposing the broken bulbs.

Grant had instructed them to look in the back of the building. Lexi drove around to the rear, looking for stairs. Cement steps and an iron rail, he'd said, going down.

When she didn't see any, she pulled the car into a U-turn and drove back, close to the building, leaning over the passenger seat.

Nothing.

Lexi felt sick to her stomach. Would Grant have lied?

She got out of the car. There was a door in the back of the club with no knob on the outside. A Dumpster sat by itself ten feet from the door. She found a pile of whiskey bottle boxes and a lot of sticky stains on the asphalt that ran the length of the building. No stairs.

She would try to find the elevator inside.

Lexi jogged around to the front of the building and tried the main entrance. It opened.

The interior was dark and reeked of unappealing smells. She switched to breathing through her mouth. Loud music from a jukebox that had been pumped through a higher-tech sound system vibrated through her internal organs.

Her eyes adjusted to a pretty typical bar scene. Small tables and chairs. A dance floor. A stage. A neon-lit bar lined with mirrors across the back.

The bartender was drying glasses, eyeing her. The music was too loud for talk. She saw a sign for the restrooms and signaled that she was going to use them, mainly to prevent him from following and asking questions.

Lexi stepped into a narrow hall and banged her elbow on the pay phone. The walls were papered floor to ceiling with flyers held in place by staples: posters, advertisements, glossy concert announcements, pictures of scantily clad women scrawled with mustaches and horns and Web site addresses, handwritten for-sale signs, beer ads. Between the men's and women's rooms, she looked for one that Grant had described: "E Ticket Rides Didn't Die with Elvis! Thrill Seekers, Apply Here."

It covered the elevator call button, Grant had said.

There was too much. Too many sheets of paper separating Lexi from finding her child. She ran her hands over the mess, trying to focus on each flyer.

"Help you find something?"

Her heartbeat stumbled once and then recovered. The bartender was standing close enough to touch her. He was shelling peanuts and letting the skins fall on the floor.

"Some*one*," she said, shoving her hand into the pocket with the cell phone. "Warden Pavo."

"Never heard of him."

"He and I go way back."

He talked and chewed at the same time. "Whatever you say."

"I was told I could find him here. That he runs a sort of . . . bonus operation downstairs."

"Ain't no downstairs in this building."

"Of course there's not," Lexi said, hoping to convey that she could keep a secret.

"So now that the plain-as-day has been firmly established, can I get you a drink?" He held out a peanut to her between his first and second fingers. Lexi turned back to the cluttered wall.

"When I find Ward, I'll order one for each of us," she said. She put her hand on the largest poster and jerked it off the wall. It was grimy. The paper tore in half.

The bartender laughed. "You think he's hiding under that mess? He'll have a few staples in him."

Lexi grabbed papers with both fists and pulled off as much as she could at once, hoping he'd get mad enough to show her what she would surely find out by being destructive.

"Let me get you a trash can," he said.

She followed him back into the main room, her fists full of torn papers. "Please. I really don't care what you and Ward have going on here. You can trust me to be utterly blind, deaf, and dumb. I'm not police, I'm just a mom. He's got my little girl and I want her back. That's all. I swear it. I'll get her and you'll never see my face again. You can keep doing whatever it is you do."

He glanced over his shoulder and kept moving toward the bar. Then he lifted the hinged section of counter that allowed him to pass through, bent over and disappeared beneath the bar top, and came up with a small lined trash can, which he handed across to her. She stared at it.

"People who talk like that usually need something pretty stiff. Sure I can't make you reconsider?"

"Talk like what?"

He leaned his elbows on the bar and scooped a few more peanuts out of a bowl in front of him. Lexi shoved the papers into the can.

"I'm a good listener. And you sound like you've been through a tough time with your daughter. Maybe I can help."

"The only way you can help me is by taking me to Warden Pavo."

"I honestly have never heard of the guy."

"I have it on pretty good authority that he's a regular here."

"Maybe he goes by another name?"

Lexi closed her eyes and bit her lip to keep herself from falling apart. Then she said, "Scrawny guy. Five nine, five ten. Greasy black hair, a little too long. A hooked jaw."

"That's about fifty percent of my clientele."

"Key ring tattoo on his left arm."

"Ah. Skeleton keys? Like an old jailer?"

"So he has been here?"

"No." The word was a hammer. "But you're not the only one who's been asking about him."

"It would have been nice if you'd said so."

"How was I supposed to have put the name and the tat together?"

"Who was looking for him?"

"Nasty-ugly dude. Face shaped like an alien, all pinched in the eyes. Bony skull." The bartender screwed up his face and squinted, hunched his shoulders and drew his hands up like claws. His voice was high and breathy, "'I hear this is the warden's playground. Seen the warden? Where's the warden?'" He returned to his peanut-crunching self and gestured to the end of the counter. "Left half-eaten apple cores all over the place."

The man who'd attacked her at the Residence. He knew Ward? Had he found him? If she couldn't find Ward, maybe she could find this guy. She shivered at the prospect of meeting him again.

"When?"

"Sunday. Monday."

He'd attacked her Tuesday. "Has he been here since?"

"No, just those two nights."

"He was here twice?"

"Complaining at me the whole time, which is why I know your key-ring guy wasn't here."

"He mentioned the tattoo."

"He was blistering mad about something, going on and on about Romeo and Juliet."

The couple's name triggered a dim recollection in Lexi's head that had nothing to do with Shakespeare. "The play?"

"I doubt it. Said the warden tried to kill Romeo. 'Juliet's dead,' he mimicked, squinty again. 'Romeo was mine. If Romeo dies, the warden dies too.' I nearly flunked English, but I'm pretty sure they both died. And I don't remember a warden. Maybe that's your jailer guy, you think?"

She had nothing else to go on.

"The guy was a nut, in any case. Obsessed with death. The more he drank, the louder he got. I threw him out when he started chanting about some mortician."

A mortician?

Mort, at death's door last weekend. The dead cat Juliet. Romeo.

It was the only thin thread Lexi had to hold on to.

Molly had been gone from the school for two hours. From the Blue Devil, Lexi raced to the hospital, to the one connection she could see between her and Warden Pavo.

{ chapter 33 }

The presence of his mother-in-law was a great comfort to Grant during the time when he waited for Sheriff Dawson to cut the red tape.

He walked the three steps from one wall of the holding cell where he was cooped up, turned, and took another three steps, repeating this for long minutes while running his hand along the bars. *Thunk, thunk, thunk, thunk.* Alice sat on a bench outside the cell and listened without asking him to stop or seeming annoyed at his tigerlike restlessness.

When the clock on the wall clicked over to 2:17, Grant slammed the bars with the heel of his hand. What good was he doing in here when his daughter and wife were out there? This was the story of his sorry life.

At least Molly had one parent out there beating down doors for her.

Grant hit his cage again. He had to get out.

Alice muttered, "Small-town law!" under her breath. She left the area briefly, then returned with two cups of burned black coffee.

They sipped the bitter brew while another minute went by.

"Do you pray?" Grant asked her.

"I used to. Why?"

"I've been trying, lately. I don't really know how to do it. But I think we ought to. I think Molly needs us to."

"I'd do it if I thought my prayers mattered," Alice confided.

"Are you sure they don't?"

She shrugged. "If the evidence is any indication."

That was the first time Grant noticed that Alice had aged in the last seven years. The lines around her mouth were deeper. The roots of her hair were white. She didn't talk much about Tara, or her husband, Barrett or even what she'd been doing since his breakdown.

Grant said, "Richard keeps telling me it matters, even if we don't get the answers we want. I'm undecided, but it's probably time I make up my mind. I'd do anything for Molly and Lexi. I mean, what if?"

"What if? Now there's a question I ask a hundred times a day."

He lifted his coffee to his lips. Alice stared into the blackness of her open cup.

"What if we'd gotten out of Crag's Nest when the girls were little?"

"Why didn't you?"

"Barrett. He had a corner on the insurance market here."

The bitterness in her voice prevented Grant from saying anything.

"He ran a bucket shop on the side. Sold credit default swaps. That's where the real money was."

"I guess I don't know much about that."

"Well, most of what he did wasn't illegal at the time, but it should have been."

"Most?"

Alice looked at Grant. "You're not the only man in this world to have wanted more than he could have."

Grant nodded.

"Well, it's the sweat off good people's backs that's paying for his mental health now," she said. "What if he'd been caught?"

"He wasn't, though."

"And I'm not so sure that was the best thing." Alice returned to the bench and sat. "Lexi doesn't know that about her dad."

"I don't think she'd hold it against him."

"It's hard to say anymore."

Grant cleared his throat. "Lexi said she forgives me."

Alice grunted. "Well, at least you deserve it, Grant. You've done your time, paid the cost. You've tried to make amends."

"Do you think she meant it?"

"What? Meant it as in you two have a chance? I don't know."

"I thought this was something you wanted for her. For us."

"It was."

"Was?"

"If anything happens to Molly, I might wish my daughter had hurled herself off the edges of the earth."

"What's happened isn't Lexi's fault."

Alice's laugh was laced with misery. "We're all to blame for something."

"If anyone's to blame for bringing Ward into this family, it's me."

"Is it?" Her tone challenged Grant.

"Yes. All the more reason to cut each other some slack, don't you think?"

"No. I don't. I think some wrongs are worse than others."

"What has Lexi done that is so wrong? She's held down two jobs and kept a roof over her head. She's raised a beautiful little girl." A knot formed in the muscles of Grant's throat.

"Maybe she failed you first, Grant." She tipped her head back to rest against the cinder block wall.

"How?"

"She had an affair." She opened her eyes to watch how he took this news. "With Norman Von Ruden."

"That's what Ward said. Did he tell you that? It's the most ridiculous thing I've ever heard. I wouldn't trust him with the morning newspaper."

"Lexi told me. She was seeing him when Tara was killed. Tara was trying to stop them. For Molly. For you." Grant held onto the bars with both hands and bowed his head. This had been going on right under his nose? Of course, he was so wasted then he barely knew which house was his, let alone which woman.

But that didn't cool the burn.

How long had it gone on? Was it still going on? In secret? Had her feelings for Norman ever died?

Alice shook her head and sipped her coffee again. "What if? What if? Here's a thought: what if you'd married Tara instead of Lexi?"

Grant shot her a warning glance.

"Or what if Lexi had done what was right? My girl would still be here, wouldn't she?"

"Norman Von Ruden is a sick man. He might have done anything."

"She should have known. She should have seen how foolish—"

"She was young. We all were."

"Stop making excuses for her!" Alice was on her feet, waving her empty cup. "Aren't you mad about any of this? There is nothing happening right now that Lexi couldn't have prevented."

There was no way of knowing this, of course. Besides, the pain Grant felt for everything he thought *he* could have prevented smothered his mouth. The tangled mess of his sins and Lexi's had separated them from their daughter. Did it matter who was to blame, really? He was starting to think it didn't.

"I need you to call a friend of mine, please," he told Alice. "His name is Richard. He'll come. He'll pray for Molly."

Grant would ask him to pray for them too.

{ chapter 34 }

Alice called as Lexi entered the hospital parking lot.

"Are you with Grant?" Lexi asked.

"Yes. Still waiting. Sheriff Dawson says the car sighting was a dead end."

"So was the Blue Devil."

"The what?"

"Tell Grant it's just a nightclub. Nothing more. They don't know Ward."

Alice's voice moved away from her receiver. Judging by Grant's tone, his response was unbelieving.

"He wants to go there himself when we're done here," she said.

"How much longer 'til he's released?"

"Hard to say. The sheriff says not to lose heart."

"That would be easier if he'd let Grant go!"

"He meant a lot of tips are coming in from the Amber Alert. More than average."

"Well, what do you make of that?"

"What do you mean?"

"More than average? How many sightings can a small place like Crag's Nest and Riverbend have?"

"A certain amount are bogus, sure, but—"

"Mom, how much of what's going on seems to be like a magic show to you?"

"I have no idea what you're talking about."

"Magicians, they mess with your perceptions. They trick your eyes into seeing things that aren't . . . real. Like that letter from Grant to Molly. I read it twice. It was different both times."

"My granddaughter's vanishing act seems real enough to me!"

Of course it was. As real as Ward's phone call. As real as Lexi's racing heart and her skyrocketing blood pressure.

"I didn't mean that."

"Then what did you mean? What does this have to do with tips?"

Lexi thought of Angelo, rescuing her miraculously as she was attacked. She thought of the ugly assailant, disappearing on a breath of wind, leaving behind his empty clothes. How could she explain any of what had happened?

"Maybe nothing. I just feel like someone's messing with us—me, that's all."

"Well, figure that out later, okay? All we have time for now is what's absolutely true: we have to find Molly. Where are you headed now?"

"St. Luke's. There's a chance Mort Weatherby might know where Ward is. Or a friend of Ward's."

"Who's Mort?"

"A neighbor. He was driving Molly the night of the accident. It doesn't matter. Call me when Grant's out."

At the hospital reception desk, Lexi stopped and breathlessly asked for both Gina's and Mort's room numbers. Mort might know Ward's friend. Gina, the religious-studies student, might be able to tell Lexi what Ward meant when he wrote "unpardonable sin" in the school's checkout log.

Either—hopefully both—might point the way to Molly. Lexi was grasping at everything she could think of.

A pixie volunteer consulted her computer. "They're not in this building," she said.

"What? Where are they?"

"Division of Infectious Diseases." The girl grabbed a piece of scratch paper from her desk and started to draw a map. "We're here." She pointed to a box in the lower right corner of the paper. "DID is over here." In a box that appeared to be as far away from "here" as possible. "You'll want to drive past these three buildings, turn right, and look for the parking lot on your left. Then take the footpath through this archway . . ."

It took Lexi ten precious minutes to arrive.

The building was more lab than hospital at first glance. It occupied one floor of a larger facility and didn't seem to have many beds. Mort and Gina were in some kind of isolation room, separated from the rest of the world by glass and plastic and an intercom system. Gina's mother had set up camp in a cushioned vinyl chair outside and was knitting when Lexi showed up. A fishing magazine lay on the chair next to her. Maybe Mr. Harper's. Behind the window Mort slept, and Gina was reading a book.

"This is unexpected," Lexi observed of the two neighbors brought together in this strange circumstance.

"It's a bacterial infection, I'm told," Mrs. Harper explained, setting her knitting aside and standing to look with Lexi through the glass into their room. "The same thing showed up in their blood work, some new strain that no one recognized. They worried about a superbug, of course, and had a big debate over whether to bother with the usual antibiotics or go straight to the last resort."

"What's that?"

"Some kind of heavy-duty antibiotic. Not one they like to use very often. Can't remember what it's called. Anyway, they went the more traditional route, and Gina turned the corner yesterday, which means Mort might follow soon after, if he doesn't face complications from the accident."

"Is he talking?"

"Well sure. When he's awake. A sweetie, that one. It's no wonder Gina likes him."

"I need to wake him up."

"He just fell asl—"

"It's an emergency." Lexi fiddled with the intercom buttons. "Can we go in, since they're improving?"

Mrs. Harper shook her head. "Precautions."

Gina flinched at a high-pitched electronic screech, which Lexi took to mean she'd hit the right switch.

"Hey, blondie," Lexi said, trying to smile.

Gina lowered her book and beamed. "Hey yourself! You've come to bust me out?"

Lexi cast a knowing glance at Mort. "It doesn't look like you're suffering for good company."

"He doesn't talk much, but otherwise I can't complain. All those good looks in one room. If he needs a kidney, I'm here for him."

"I'm really glad you're okay."

"Not as glad as I am. You do *not* want this germ. Remember that the next time you're in a public restroom. Where's the munchkin? Mom says your mom's staying with you to help out—that must be interesting."

"Gina, I need to talk to Mort."

Her roommate's smile sagged into a concerned expression. "What's happening?"

"Molly's been kidnapped. I think Mort might be able to help me."

Gina sat straight up in bed. "Oh my gosh. And I didn't believe you when you tried to tell me about all the weirdness that was going on."

"It's okay. You were sick."

"What does Mort know about—"

"Maybe nothing. I don't know."

"Mort!" Gina picked up a Dixie cup on her bed table and crumpled it, then lobbed it at him. It landed on his chest. "Mort, wake up!" She heaved a small box of tissues next. The corner caught him on the nose, and Gina was rewarded with a groan. The box slid onto his pillow.

"What the—"

"Mort, someone's got Molly, and Lexi needs to—"

"Who?"

Lexi hoped Mort wasn't on any medications besides antibiotics.

She pressed the intercom button and said, "Mort, I need to ask you about the cat."

"Why is nobody making any sense?" He touched the bridge of his nose and examined his fingers as if they might be bloody.

"Mrs. Johnson's cat. Juliet. How did it die?"

He seized the box of tissues and hurled it back at Gina. She caught it midair.

"I have no idea, and I don't really care."

"Is it possible someone killed it?"

"Mrs. Johnson seems to think so."

"Who do you know who would want her to think you did it?"

Mort shook his head and closed his eyes. "And this is important because?"

"Because I think whoever killed that cat knows the man who took Molly. I've got to find her and I don't have much time."

"I wish I could help you, Lexi, but I don't have a clue. And the last time you asked me for help, things didn't go so well for me."

Gina said, "Enough with the martyr complex, Mort. There's a little girl missing who needs your help."

But what he'd said was true. Lexi's request that Mort look out for Gina and Molly was what put him in the car that was wrecked. Molly's description of Norman's driver as the evil dognapper of *A Hundred and One Dalmatians* and Lexi's encounter with the mental patient at the residence merged as one in her mind.

"What about the accident? Can you tell me about that?"

"Don't remember much."

"The driver of the other car—did you see him?" Maybe the police had taken a report. Lexi pulled Alice's phone out of the apron pocket—she realized she was still wearing her grocery-store uniform—and called up her mother's prepaid phone. Alice could ask Sheriff Dawson to look into it.

"I didn't see anything," Mort said.

Gina asked, "What if he was aiming for Molly and not Mort?"

The possibility hit Lexi under her ribs. "Aiming? Like it wasn't an accident?"

Gina didn't say anything.

If Ward and this other psycho were in cahoots, what was Norman's role in all this? She'd nearly forgotten that he was in that vehicle that struck Mort's car.

Alice wasn't answering her phone. Lexi disconnected the call and hoped she'd call back.

"Who took Molly?" Gina asked.

"Warden Pavo."

"The guy who wanted you to testify?"

Lexi nodded.

"Unbelievable. And Grant doesn't know where—"

"If he did, I wouldn't be here, Gina."

Lexi started to pace. Mrs. Harper, who'd been listening to all this with wide eyes and her hand at her throat, took up her knitting again.

"What's he asking for?" Gina wanted to know.

Lexi put both hands on top of her head. "Why does everyone think he wants something?" No one answered.

"Lexi, I can't hear you without the intercom."

She stomped back to the box and slammed her palm down on the red button. "He doesn't want anything. There is no ransom, only riddles. He's punishing Molly for my sins, he says. He's making me pay for some debt I didn't even know I had."

"That's what he said?"

"Of course that's what he said, Gina." She sighed. "I didn't mean to snap at you."

"No problem. But what *exactly* did he say? I'm good at riddles."

Lexi rubbed her eyes. Could she remember exactly? Did it matter? "Uh, he said, 'I punish the children for the sins of their mothers.' And something about a deadline for collecting the debt? He meant Molly. A year of jubilee? Something like that. What's jubilee?"

"It's an old Jewish tradition. Every fifty years everyone got a year off—a big sabbatical."

"I thought it was every seven years," Mort said.

"Seven cycles of seven years," Gina said.

"So that's forty-nine years," Mort said.

"Forty-nine, fifty, I don't know how they counted it. The point is, it was a year of fresh starts. Clean slates. Setting things back to the way they were. Land leases were canceled and property was returned to its original owner. No one planted anything, to give the fields a break. Slaves were set free to go back to their families."

"That doesn't sound like punishment," Lexi said.

"It wasn't. Over the years, jubilee came to refer to a time when sins were forgiven and debts were canceled, not collected. Whatever that guy was talking about, it's the opposite of what jubilee means traditionally."

"That's not helpful."

"Maybe it is. That bit about punishing the children for the sins of the mothers—that's off too."

"Off how?"

"The biblical version is that children are punished for the sins of the fathers."

"I don't see why the children have to be punished at all," Lexi said. "His riddles are getting muddier."

After a few seconds of silence, Gina said, "It seems like he's twisting truth."

"That's a leap."

"Not if you believe the Bible."

"Maybe it's a problem that I don't know the Bible better."

Gina shrugged. "There's always grace, Lexi."

"Is there grace for Molly?"

"Especially for Molly." Gina's smile was a glimmer of hope.

The clock in Lexi's mind was ticking down on Molly's terrible situation, but she had nowhere to go, no leads to follow. Her heart was breaking. Lexi grasped for something, anything that would tell her more about what Ward wanted and where he might be.

"If he *is* twisting the truth, why? What do you think it means?"

"It reminds me of when the devil tempted Jesus. Satan quoted Scriptures to do it."

"That's dumb. Wouldn't Jesus know the Scriptures better than he did?"

"That's right. And Jesus used that knowledge to beat Satan back."

"I'm not Jesus."

"No, but maybe this guy Warden is hedging his bets that you don't know the truth—that he can twist it up and sneak it past you, make you think he knows something that you don't."

"He knows plenty that I don't, starting with where my daughter is!"

"Listen, Lexi. I'm going to go out on a limb here, but listen for a minute. He says he wants to collect your debts—but your debts have already been forgiven. He says he's going to punish your daughter for your sins."

"But my sins have already been forgiven."

"Exactly."

"So what is he talking about?"

Gina sighed and bit her lip.

Then Lexi remembered her original reason for wanting to talk to Gina. "Ward wrote something on the sign-out sheet at Molly's school. He said the reason he took her was because of an unpardonable sin. What's that?"

"Rejecting Christ."

"But I'm a Christian. I haven't rejected Christ."

"Lexi, if Warden's messing with Scriptures, he probably didn't mean that literally."

"That's no help at all!" Lexi shoved her fisted hands into her pockets. She wanted to hit something! Instead she was poked in the knuckle by Angelo's note.

She pulled it out and read it to Gina.

"Don't listen to Warden Pavo. Listen to love, which keeps no record of wrongs. Choose love, and it will save you even now. Molly too."

"That's from 1 Corinthians."

"What is?"

"The part about love. It protects. It doesn't hold grudges. I'm having an idea about all this."

"Spill it, then, before I fall apart here."

"Jesus told this story about a guy who owed a king a boatload of money. The man couldn't pay it back, so the king ordered that his family and all his belongings be sold. The man begged the king to give him more time. Well, the king felt so sorry for this loser that he canceled the whole debt! Just let him go."

"Like jubilee."

"After that, the man went out and bumped into a friend who owed him just a little bit of money. When the friend wouldn't pay up, the man beat him and had him thrown into prison. Well, the king found out about this, and he was peeved. He said, 'I completely pardoned you when you asked me to—why couldn't you do that for someone in the same boat?' So he had the man thrown into prison and allowed the jailer to torture him until he could pay back his original debt, the whole whopping amount."

The jailer. The warden. "That's not fair. How can you pay back a debt if you're behind bars?"

"I know! And tortured! The man couldn't exactly get a paying job in jail, you can bet on it."

"I don't get how this relates," Lexi said, and yet understanding was beginning to take shape.

"Ward wants to collect a debt, but you're already forgiven. Angelo says love doesn't keep track of wrongs."

"That's right."

"Lexi, whose sins have *you* decided are unpardonable?"

{ chapter 35 }

Warden swore under his breath.

I *forgive* you?

I forgive *you*?

The shock waves of words Lexi should never have spoken to Grant hit Warden square behind the knees and dropped him onto the shiny floor of the Bedrock Mall. He recovered quickly and swore again, loud enough for Molly to hear.

She was balanced on her good leg, leaning into the upper-level railing that was a balcony overlooking the food court. She turned at his profanity, then averted her worried eyes and scanned the tables below. Likely looking for Daddy to rescue her from the big bad wolf.

How had this happened? Twisted perceptions were his area of expertise. Warden Pavo could spin a lie of any kind—lies of the mouth, of the ears, of the eyes. Especially lies of the eyes. And the heart. Few human emotions were more powerful than resentment, and by exploiting this fact he had been promoted from dealing with heathens to dealing with the self-righteous more than nine hundred years ago.

He among an elite few had succeeded, while his colleagues fell like wasted flies every three weeks. Why? Because he had no interest in spectacle. He had no need of heavy hammers and cataclysms, or of murdered pets and spectacular car crashes. Instead, he struck with understatement in the blind spots of the human soul. Not only did people never see it coming, but it never occurred to them when it happened that anything other than justice was at stake.

Deceive and divide. It *always* worked.

It had worked on Barrett and Alice Grüggen. Their name meant *grudge*, which was why he'd chosen them, and Barrett's parents before them. People lived up to their names because they didn't know how to create new identities for themselves. Lexi couldn't even marry out of it!

And yet, Lexi's three magic words had changed . . . not quite everything, but enough. Enough so that he wouldn't be able to linger here as he'd wanted, securing Molly's trust and loyalty.

Smothering her ability to trust the people who actually loved her would have to be enough.

Warden reduced his fury to irritation and joined Molly at the railing.

Above them, skylights filtered out UV rays and made the fast-food pit below look appealing. Down there, at the bottom of an escalator, a water feature designed to resemble a mountain range ran the length of the court and cut the dining area in half. Pumped water rushed down the peaks like river rapids, sprinkling the live plants on either side.

The scents of sweet funnel cakes and chlorinated fountain water mingled with the stench of starchy Chinese food and stale, recirculated oxygen.

"What'd I tell you? Pretty, huh?"

"It smells funny."

"Quit complaining."

Molly dropped her chin toward her chest.

"Pay attention, little lady. I've got a lot to tell you and not a lot of time to do it in. Look there. See?" Warden pointed to a bench built into the side of the fountain. The gray stone slab was bolted to the artificial rock and flanked by precisely arranged aspen trees.

Molly looked at Warden's finger.

"The bench."

The girl's face was a question mark.

He got behind her and placed his palms on either side of her face, forcing it in the direction of the seat.

"See that bench?"

When she nodded, he let go.

"That bench is the reason your mom never comes to this mall."

"Why?"

"That's where Tara died. Got a knife shoved right up under her ribs"—Warden made a thrusting motion with his right arm—"and bam, gone. No last supper, no dying words, just a slippery pool of blood and a few surprised Christmas shoppers who were a bit peeved to get their gifts dirty."

Molly was frowning at the bench.

"Who's Tara?"

"Who's Tar—ha-ha! Who's *Tara*? Oh, this is lovely." Grinning, Ward leaned his elbows on the railing and tilted his head into Molly's line of sight. She bit her lower lip. "Your aunt. Your mother's sister."

"Mom doesn't have a sister."

"Not anymore she doesn't."

Molly's eyebrows formed a worried peak. "I'd be sad if I had a sister and she died."

"Think about it, Molly. Why isn't your mom sad?"

"She is sometimes."

"There's a reason you didn't know you had an aunt."

Molly tilted her head and looked back at the empty bench.

"Your mom killed her."

The girl's eyes snapped back to Warden. "You're *lying*."

"Nope. The reason your mom never told you about her, and the reason why she's never sad about it, is because *she did it*."

"I don't believe you. My mom would never do anything like that."

"Doesn't change the truth."

Molly hugged herself and glared at Warden. She raised her voice. "You're a big fat liar."

"Ask her yourself."

Lexi's daughter huffed.

"Ask her yourself, little lady. You'll see. But think about it: if she could murder her sister and go home and wash off all that blood and never think about her again . . . what do you think she'll do to you when she finds out you know?"

Molly's eyes didn't waver from Warden's, but she started to flex the knee of her good leg—bend, straighten, bend, straighten—a quick and nervous fidget that caused the joint to bump the wall.

"What do you think that picture was all about? The one with the bull's-eye on it?"

"How did you know about that?"

"Did she explain it to you?"

"She said she didn't do it."

"Of course she'd say that! What did she say about why she won't let you see your dad? You want to know the *real* reason? It's because she's in love with another man."

Bend, straighten, bend, straighten.

"She's been in love with a lot of guys, actually," Warden went on, "which is kind of like having five best friends all at once. Well, sort of. You know what an affair is? No? It's a lot like murder, as far as the gross-factor goes."

Molly's expression was a portrait of confusion. Warden put an arm around the wobbling child and leaned in close to her ear, dropping his voice to a whisper as he explained the seedy truth of what it meant to be an unfaithful wife. Molly stilled as if her movements would prevent her from hearing every delicious word. Or perhaps shame froze her. Either way worked for him.

When Warden ended the story of Lexi's lurid choices, Molly was a statue, eyes locked on her shoes.

"Your aunt Tara tried to stop her, and she didn't want to," Warden said. He straightened but left his warm hand resting on her shoulder. Like a father would do. "That's why your mom killed her."

Molly didn't move. She said something to the floor.

"Speak up, girl."

"When will my dad get here?"

"Soon." Warden checked his watch. "He is running a little late, isn't he? I hope he didn't forget." He formed a pity pout for Molly but she still wasn't looking at him.

"He won't forget," she murmured, lacking conviction.

"He's a busy man. I mean, seven years' worth of busy can distract a guy. I'd understand if this little luncheon slipped his mind. Or maybe . . . maybe he was too embarrassed to come. Did you know he was in jail? Didn't mention that in his letter, did he?" Ward whistled. "I mean, go figure. You mom sleeps around and slashes up her sister and doesn't do a single day behind bars—can you imagine what your dad must have done?"

Molly was squeezing her own waist, glancing over her shoulder in search of the man who was simply not destined to arrive.

"Let's go eat. And talk some more. What do you say? We'll give him the time it takes to eat a double-dipped cone, and if he shows, we'll eat again."

"I want to go home."

"No can do. Your mom's not off work yet."

"Grandma will be there."

"What's your problem? I'm giving you a chance to eat dessert first, a shoulder to cry on, answers to all the questions you've ever asked, right here on a silver platter. What do you want to go home for?"

Molly's chin puckered. "I want my mom."

Warden felt his irritation morphing into something greater than it should've been. "Suck it up. You can't go home. She'd as soon kill you as feed you breakfast, the self-righteous b—"

"I don't care."

"Of course you do. Your dad doesn't want you and your mother never loved anyone but herself."

"She loves me."

"Does not."

"Does too." Molly lifted her face and begged. "I wanna go home."

"There *is* no home is what I'm trying to tell you."

"You're a liar."

Warden was so inclined to spit fire that the saliva in his mouth sizzled and evaporated. He barely held himself together, keeping in mind what happened when Craven lost his cool.

"It seems we keep repeating ourselves," he said. Warden placed his hands on his knees and lowered his nose to hers, stopping shy of her going cross-eyed. "Prove it. I dare you. Prove I'm a liar."

Her knee started flexing again.

He said, "I can show you all the truth you need to know, little lady. Letters, pictures. Eyewitness testimonies." Her brows came together, confused. "I can be very convincing."

After a brief pondering, Molly said, "Even if you're not lying, it's okay."

He swore and straightened. "I can see your mother has been a fine moral example to you."

"Huh?"

"You don't know a thing about right and wrong."

"Yes I do!"

Ward seized the child by the arm and shook her. "Until you know how to be offended, you don't know a thing."

"I love my mom."

"Why?"

"'Cause she's my mom."

"I have never heard a more flimsy excuse!" He shook her again and rattled the tears right out of her head.

"I love my mom."

"She doesn't deserve it! You should stop!"

"She loves me, too, she does, no matter what you say. And she'll say sorry if I ask her—"

"No she won't."

"And I'd tell her"—sobs chopped up Molly's words—"it's okay . . . and that I . . . love her anyway."

"Stop it!"

"You can't . . . make me!"

Warden had the stubborn girl by both arms. She was a mere doll, as weightless and worthless as a cheap toy. Only saints had patience and self-control enough for this, and he was no saint at all.

He heaved her over the rail.

{ chapter 36 }

Gina's insights sent Lexi stumbling outside the hospital into afternoon light that had no right to blaze so cheerfully. She staggered toward her rickety old car, knowing exactly where she needed to go and yet not wanting to.

For Molly, though, Lexi placed her keys in the Volvo's starter, turned over the engine, and weaved out of the parking lot.

She was as angry as she'd ever been since the night Ward showed up almost a week ago, demanding that she testify at Norm's hearing. Ward was some black angel, some executioner sent to cut off her hands and feet and then dig out her heart because she couldn't find it in her to ignore everyone who'd hurt her. It was hardly fair. Grant, Ward, Norman—nothing bad that had happened to her in the last few years would have happened if not for their contribution to her problems.

Lexi turned south onto the main boulevard and drove for several minutes without focusing on her surroundings. She was entering a major intersection when a blaring horn alerted her to the red light. Both of her feet hit the brakes of their own will, and she cried out.

A driver in the cross traffic swerved around her and made an obscene gesture.

Lexi's heart pounded. She sat, protruding into traffic, with no will to get out of the way. Her car was anchored in the same place where Mort's truck had been T-boned, where Molly had almost been killed by Norm's transport.

Human collisions wrecked lives every day, in cars and other encounters. Lexi was no one special.

And yet Gina's suggestion that Lexi ought to forgive rankled. Unearned forgiveness was so unfair. Wasn't it? Grant, now, she had believed he was contrite. And above all, Molly needed her to forgive him.

But as for the others, why should she?

Choose love.

Choose love. Love had chosen Lexi, in the most magnificent form of grace.

The answer seemed as glaring as her windshield. She must do it not because they deserved it, nor because it was justice, but because her own sanity demanded it. Her daughter's breath depended on it. Because love was the only choice that led to life instead of death.

Pain and grief broke through Lexi's indignation and she started to sob into the heels of her hands. More horns sounded behind her. Her light had turned green. Swiftly, without seeing everything she needed to, she jerked the car through first gear and across the street. She wiped her eyes on the sleeve of her white oxford shirt and tried to get enough control of herself to avoid another crash.

Within five blocks she was sniffing and puffy-eyed, but resolved. She turned off the road and followed a small rural highway five miles out to a solitary complex, a fortress of look-alike buildings isolated from the rest of town. There was no paved parking lot here, only a dusty clearing enclosed by chain link.

She left the car and followed the walkway to the visitor's entrance.

God, please spare my little girl.

Lexi opened the heavy door and wondered if that debtor in Gina's story had the guts to beg for mercy—again—and if he did, whether the king let him go or the man died in prison by slow torture.

She was about to find out.

At the security line, Lexi emptied her pockets of her keys, a roll of lip balm, and her mother's phone. She set them in a plastic bucket and reached for a pen on the adjacent counter to sign in.

"I need to see Norman Von Ruden," she said.

Nothing had gone as planned today. Not. One. Thing. Warden burst out of the mall in a fury of heat, shoving the glass doors open with such force that they snapped off their hinges and shattered. People standing outside the entrance screamed and dodged sharp shards and gave him space.

This was no time to be self-controlled. Warden muttered curses under his breath as he stormed out into the parking lot. Long strings of foul incantations and black vows of what he planned to do to Lexi Grüggen.

A teenager holding a skateboard in one hand and a cigarette in the other watched Warden make his exit. There was admiration in the boy's eyes as he exhaled smoke. Warden snarled at him. The cigarette ignited. The kid's admiration turned to fear. He swore and dropped the flaming cigarette, threw down the skateboard and took off.

Warden paused in a parking space and looked back at the Bedrock Mall. He allowed himself a moment—just a few seconds of indulgence—to close his eyes and envision a more fitting end than the one he'd left inside. The possibilities quickly took shape in his mind's eye. It would involve a small measure of theatrics, and though he preferred to avoid such gestures, there was a time for everything under heaven, after all.

Perhaps he shouldn't have left the brat behind. Warden had not watched Molly fall. He had turned away from the rail, furious to be forced into killing. That had never been his pleasure. What were people worth, dead in the ground? The only humans he had time for were the ones who were dead on their feet.

The child had plummeted without uttering a sound. The only screams he heard came from bystanders who saw her go over.

Warden wondered if he should he go back inside, devise a way to take the stupid rag-doll child with him.

He weighed his options, then decided.

Lexi had no idea what was coming to her.

{ chapter 37 }

It didn't seem possible that only twenty-four hours had passed since Lexi last sank into this same flimsy wooden chair at the foot of Norm's inclined hospital bed. The joints in the seat creaked and shifted under her weight.

"I wasn't expecting to see you until Friday," he said when their eyes met.

"I won't be testifying at your hearing," Lexi replied. "For you or against you."

Norm nodded. "I know." He sighed and reclined his head against the pillow, gazing at the ceiling.

She had been expecting the snarling, sinister Norm. "That's all? No biting comeback? No vow to squash me or hurt my little girl?"

He didn't say anything.

A crush of sorrow weighed down Lexi's shoulders. "Ward took Molly," she said.

"Can't say I didn't warn you."

"Do you know where they are?"

Norm turned his head in a tiny side-to-side motion on his pillow.

"Ward might have said something to you that—"

"Ward talks too much for anyone's good."

"You're the only one I know of who might have any idea what he had planned."

A recessed light in the ceiling of Norm's room flickered. Lexi's memory flashed back to the parking-lot light that blinked out over her Volvo a week ago.

"Ward's mind is set only on one thing," Norm said.

"What's that?"

"Using other people to do his dirty work."

Lexi wasn't sure what he meant.

"He took Molly without anyone's help," she said.

"If that's what you want to think."

She stood and took one step away from the chair. "Well, if you don't have any idea where he might have gone with—"

"I was remembering the first time I met Ward."

"I don't have time right now, Norm."

"You might want to make time." There was no threat in his words, only regret. Lexi remained standing but didn't move to go.

"It was at our house," she said. "You talked with me about Molly."

"That wasn't the first time."

"That you met Ward? I thought—"

"Yeah, well people always say that perception is reality, but it's not. It's just perception."

The light flickered again.

Norm said, "Grant set up the meeting, but Ward sought me out before that happened. Found me at work."

"What for?"

"He said antidepressants would be no problem for him, but he could hook me up with a spirit-lifter that worked better than any drug." Norm turned his face toward Lexi. "Said her name was Lexi Solomon."

Lexi's face grew hot. She didn't know what to say and felt confused over this story and the remark Ward had made to her days earlier. *You should have chosen me.*

Norm said, "He was right about that much at least."

"What does this have to do with Molly?"

"Ward found me again about a week ago, at the pen. Right before the accident. Told me he was getting ready to work over Grant and promised I could have my chance to get back at him for the blanks he sold me."

"Because I'd testify for you."

"I'm not sure why I believed him. It's not like my release is dependent on one person's word."

A soft thunking sound coming from the opposite side of the door caused Lexi to turn and look.

Norm said, "I guess we're apt to believe anything that promises to work in our favor. I didn't think about that until after you left yesterday. Everything was so clear. Did you know Ward promised me a chance to kill Grant when I got out?"

"What was clear? That you wanted Grant to be punished for what he did to you?"

"No. That everything Ward promised me had nothing to do with *me*." His eyebrows drew together, and Lexi thought he looked sad. "Ward was never interested in me. It was all about you and Grant, for reasons I'll never know."

Norman's breath shook as he inhaled. "I destroyed my entire life for a guy who bought me with empty promises, and for a couple I don't even care about."

Lexi felt her heart thawing toward this man. She felt pity.

"I'm sorry, Norm."

He grunted.

"Is that what you wanted—to kill Grant?"

He shrugged. "I don't know anymore. Mostly, I think I want someone to tell me that it wasn't my fault your sister died."

"It was my fault."

"And Grant's."

"Yes. It appears we're all mixed up in the blame together."

"What a handsome little love triangle we make." Bitterness rolled off his tongue.

The gentle banging on the door rose to a pounding. Lexi spoke above the noise, concerned that the meeting might end before she needed it to. "You suggested this had something to do with Molly."

"That's right. I'm thinking he won't kill her."

"What?"

"Ward doesn't kill, see? If he did, we'd all be dead now. He prefers suffering." He paused. "He kills our spirits."

Rather than feeling relieved, Lexi felt her mind being overtaken by terror. Ward might kill Molly if he wanted *Lexi* to suffer.

"That's quite a figure of speech."

Norm gripped the bedrail and pulled himself up into a sitting position. His expression was one of pain. "I'm being as literal as I know how."

The pounding on the door stopped.

Lexi took a step backward. "I need to get to Molly," she said.

"I hope you succeed."

Lexi turned to the exit and knocked to be let out. Her arms were shaking, and she didn't know where she'd go next.

Oh God, oh God! Please, don't let him kill Molly—or her gentle heart.

This room was filled with the oppression of a man whose spirit had indeed died. She felt the urgency to leave it and gratitude that she wasn't imprisoned here too. She paused and felt her heart quicken.

"I was serious about what I said." She looked at Norm over her shoulder. "It wasn't *only* your fault that my sister died," she said.

Irritation crossed Norm's features. "That's worth writing in a letter to my parole board."

"For my part in . . . in everything that shouldn't have happened, I'm sorry."

He sighed. "Easy words."

"And for your part in it, I forgive you."

"I don't need your forgiveness."

"I need to give it."

Norm's laugh broke her heart. "Whatever makes you feel better."

"Maybe you could accept it anyway. As something that is genuinely about you for once." She paused. "And for you."

He lowered himself back to the pillows.

"I don't deserve that anymore."

"No one does. But I'm going to let you go now."

Norm turned his head away.

The door opened.

It was the last thing in the crazy, nonsensical world that she expected, but when it happened, understanding rang clear and sharp through her brain: the light above Norm's bed blinked out, and Lexi found herself suddenly, unnaturally blind. Her whole body flinched, and she raised her hands.

Ward had come for her.

Strong fingers closed around her throat and pushed, and she was stumbling backward into Norm's cell. She felt hot breath on her face, and the smell of cigarette smoke and the stench of rotten eggs. Her shoulder blades hit the wall first and her head snapped back to meet the immovable cinder block. Thunder bounced off the backs of her eyeballs.

She crumpled and her knees hit the floor.

Ward kept hold of her throat and tossed her sideways. She reached out for balance. Her cheek smacked the adjoining wall and her body slumped like a wilting flower.

"Norman," she wheezed.

"He can't hear you." Warden's thumbs pressed down into the gentle curve of her neck at the top of her breastbone. "It was a stupid idea for you to come here. Norm hasn't been himself lately. He might snap and injure you."

Lexi groaned. "Where's Molly?"

"*Here.*"

"Molly!"

One of Ward's hands released her while the other kept her collared like a dog. Lexi heard a shuffling and heavy breathing, and then the warm, limp body of a child was thrust against her on the floor.

Lexi cried out. Struggling for air, she grasped for her daughter and pulled Molly tight against her chest. The weight of the ankle brace pulled awkwardly against Molly's length. Lexi raised her palm and spread her fingers across the back of Molly's head. She was dead weight, and Lexi thought she must be unconscious.

Ward released Lexi's throat and she drew in thick and humid air. He gripped her hair on both sides of her face and pulled her off the wall. Unwilling to relax her hold on Molly, Lexi let him do this. The child seemed so weak in her arms.

"She's dying," he said.

Lexi moaned and clutched Molly. She ran her hands up and down the child's curving spine, feeling for breath, for a pumping heart. She felt nothing.

"She's dying and there's nothing you can do. I asked so little of you, Sexy Lexi. In fact, what I wanted you to do would have been so much easier than what you have chosen. Frankly, I don't see the point."

Lexi shook her head vigorously, denying that her worst nightmares had found their way into reality. Sobs wracked her chest and bounced the little girl.

"You should have waited to come here until tomorrow," Ward said. "You should have kept the goal in sight."

"What g-goal? Hate? You . . . you want to kill us all."

"I'm not a murderer, Lexi. Not like the three of you are."

"Right, right." She drew a shaky breath. "Y-you kill love."

"Tell me. Is love worth the life of your daughter? Was it an even exchange?"

Lexi's arms tightened around her little girl and she found words between her cries. "I choose . . . love. I ch-choose it . . . because . . . because anything else . . . is a living hell."

"You don't know the half of it."

The dead light flashed twice, illuminating the room like a weak strobe. Ward's eyes were red. Molly's skin was ghostly white. Then blackness again.

"You'll regret this choice for the rest of your life. That brat's going to die in your arms and you'll die a thousand deaths and wish you'd never loved at all."

"I won't . . . I won't! You've never told . . . me the truth!"

The light flickered again, causing Lexi to squint and drop back into the corner of the wall. The roots of her hair screamed against Ward's grip. His cracked lips were parted.

Angelo stood behind him.

Lexi screamed.

The big man's arms crossed his broad chest, and his wild blond hair was windblown around his crown like an old straw hat. His eyes were on the back of Molly's head.

The light failed again.

At first she thought he was an illusion, but when the shock of seeing him passed, she felt no fear, only calm. Angelo was there, even though she couldn't see him.

Under the desperate squeeze of Lexi's hands, Molly's lungs filled with air and then exhaled. Once.

Lexi understood then that Angelo had come to Crag's Nest for Molly, and not for anyone else. Not directly anyway. Everything he had said to Lexi and done for Lexi had been for her child. The rescuing, the watching over, the protecting was all for Molly. Like an angel. Yes, very much like an angel sent from God.

Lexi took hold of the calm that Angelo had brought to her and willed it into new confidence.

As if he sensed a shift in Lexi's state of mind, and therefore, in the power struggle, Ward released her hair. Lexi found strength in his retreat.

"You're a liar, Warden Pavo."

The ceiling light found its energy again and returned to life, now steady.

Angelo stood tall behind him, and Lexi wondered if Ward knew he was there. How could he not?

The sneer of Ward's lips looked painful, stretched taut and exposing white teeth. "I'm the most powerful liar you've ever met."

An image of Angelo bent at the waist and spent, having defeated her attacker on the snowy slope of the Residence gardens, brought a response to her mind.

"You have no power here."

Ward opened his mouth wide, too shocked for words.

Lexi's hands grew hot against Molly's back. She did not understand what she was feeling. The girl was raging with fever, skyrocketing fever. Lexi didn't dare let her go.

Warden began to moan. A vapor began to rise off Molly's hair.

No, no, no. Lexi pressed her back against the wall and used the leverage to rise. She silently pleaded with Angelo for help. He only nodded at her.

Ward's moan turned into a scream. "You'll die! I'm going to kill you!"

"Then do it now!" Lexi shouted. "If you can do it at all, do it now!"

Ward doubled over and clapped his hands over his ears. He began an endless stream of swearing. Smoke poured out of his mouth along with vile, obscene words. Lexi turned Molly's body into the corner, shielding the girl.

"You have no more power here," Lexi repeated.

The child began to slide out of Lexi's embrace. Lexi squeezed tighter but couldn't hold on. Her arms and chest burned like they'd been doused in scalding water. She dropped to her knees as Molly went down, using her thighs to catch the girl.

The stench of something burning filled every passageway of Lexi's nose, throat, and lungs. A coughing fit overtook her.

Ward groaned and fell, tearing at his hair.

She rasped, "You leave us alone. You're not my jailer anymore."

Ward's moan grew to a shriek that pierced her ears. Lexi's breathing quickened as she saw smoke begin to rise from his hair, his hands, his shoes.

Lexi craned her neck toward Angelo, having no voice to beg for his help. Molly slipped off of Lexi's lap, escaped her mother's embrace as if she were water.

Ward exploded. That was the only way Lexi could think of it. His clothing rippled and flapped under the smoke. His hair was flaming. Then his screams ended as abruptly as if she'd hit a Mute button, and his cowering shape became a dying star, a bright ring of particles expanding from the center that had been him. Sharp pieces of Warden struck Lexi as they passed her, then hit the wall behind her and rained down onto the floor.

And then Molly disappeared—shriveled up, evaporated—in a steamy cloud of sulfur, and Lexi's blistering arms clutched nothing but a girl's jacket.

{ chapter 38 }

Sheriff Dawson's secretary was placing paper after paper in front of Grant, showing him where to sign, when the call came in.

There in the small Crag's Nest office, all the work spaces shared an open floor and everything that was said could be heard by everyone present. When the dispatcher picked up, Grant was signing a statement saying he'd received all his personal effects in as-was condition. Richard, who'd arrived a short time after Alice's call, was at his side.

Medics were reporting to emergency calls from the Bedrock Mall. Someone had destroyed the glass doors at the entrance. There were injuries. And a child had jumped from the upper level above the food court.

Alice and Grant looked at each other. His mind went to Tara. Alice placed her hand over her heart and glanced away.

The girl matched the description of a child featured in an Amber Alert earlier that day . . .

Alice started sobbing. "No, no, no . . ."

Grant knocked over his chair trying to get out from under that mountain of paperwork. He leaped toward the dispatcher, a petite woman who barely looked out of her teens. The secretary yelped. Richard jumped out of the way.

"Is she hurt? What happened to her?"

A sheriff grabbed Grant's arm. He wrenched it free but gave the dispatcher some space. She was scrambling away from him with wide eyes. "Please! What are they saying?"

"I—I don't have that information, sir."

Grant ran toward the door, then scrambled back to the desk when he realized he'd left the "personal effects," including his car keys and wallet.

"Dah! My car's back at Lexi's!"

Alice was light years ahead of him, already out the front door.

"I'll drive!" she shouted.

Sheriff Dawson was putting on his hat as fast as an astronaut puts on a space suit. "We'll meet you there," Grant said to him.

Richard hardly knew what to do.

Grant grabbed him by the hand. "C'mon!" At the front of the office, Grant turned around and said, "Wait! Dawson—talk to them for us. If Molly doesn't need to be transported, have them keep her there?"

The sheriff nodded.

"And ask your cruisers to give us an open road?"

Dawson chortled. "You're on your own with that, buddy."

For a woman in her late fifties, Alice Grüggen could move. Richard and Grant were no slowpokes, but Alice had the engine revved and her sedan in reverse by the time the men dropped into the seats.

Grant asked Richard to pray again—this time that they wouldn't get pulled over or, worse, end up in an accident. Richard relaxed into a full potbellied laugh and shouted, "Sweet Jesus, clear the way!"

Alice raced them down the mountain and through the rural outskirts of Riverbend and into the maze of streets.

"Alice, where's your phone?"

"It's in my hip pocket and I'm not about to pull over for you to use it."

"Richard, got a phone on you?"

From the backseat he passed it to Grant, who almost dropped it as Alice took a left-hand turn through a very pink light.

"What's your cell number?" Grant asked her.

"Why are you going to call me?"

"I'm talking about the phone Lexi has!"

Alice's mouth formed a small O, then she rattled off the number.

Grant called four times in a row and was dumped into voice mail on the sixth ring every time.

Where was she?

He left a message. They thought Molly was at the mall. They were on their way. She should get there as fast as she could. He'd call as soon as he knew anything for sure.

Alice reached the shopping center and drove up to the red curb at the food court entrance. She parked behind a fire engine.

Grant was out of the car before it had stopped moving, and his hands seized the handles of the double doors while the heels of Alice's shoes were still *clackety-clacking* down the concrete slab.

Molly was sitting in front of McDonald's with her bound ankle propped up on a chair. Someone had bought her a milkshake. Angelo was sitting on her other side, holding her hand. An EMT sat next to her while others packed up their gear.

The sight of his daughter out of harm's way took the breath out of Grant. He was in front of her in seconds, scooping her up as if she were still two years old and he'd come home at the end of a long day.

A very, very long day.

She clung to his neck while he gripped her around the waist. She was long and gangly in his embrace, all arms and legs.

"Hi, Molly-Wolly."

"Hi, Daddy." As if she'd never stopped knowing him.

"Oh no—I didn't—nothing's broken is it?" he released his powerhouse hug and held her gingerly.

"You're late," she whispered.

"I'm so sorry." His eyes burned.

The EMT stood. "She seems to be all in one piece, which is a miracle, considering."

"What happened?" Grant asked.

"Eyewitnesses said she climbed up and jumped." The man pointed to a spot above and behind Grant's head. Grant turned. The height sickened him. "Not sure how she did it wearing that contraption on her foot. No one seems to have seen that part. She landed there."

Next to the water fountain, a plush fern the size of a copy machine had been squashed.

"Quite a jump. We can't get her to talk about it, though, so we don't know much more than that." Molly hid her eyes against her dad's shoulder. "That brace didn't even get damaged."

"Doesn't seem possible, does it?" Grant said, looking at Angelo.

"Can't explain it, but I'm not going to complain. Heard she went missing this morning from school?"

Grant nodded. Angelo had stood silently, arms crossed. Richard had joined the big man at his side. Alice was patting Molly on the back.

"Her mom and I will get everything sorted out with the sheriff," Grant said. The medic nodded and raised his hand in a wave as he walked off. "Thank you."

"He caught me," Molly whispered into his cheek.

"What?"

"Angelo caught me. Angelo's my angel."

"I'll bet he is, honey." He thanked Angelo with his eyes. Whatever role the big man had played in Molly's life, once more it had proven miraculous. "You want to tell me how you got here?"

"He promised I could see you. Mr. Ward did. But . . ." She swallowed and started to cry quietly. "Mr. Ward is so mean. He said . . . he said . . ."

"That's okay, Molly-Wolly. You're okay now."

"Angelo made Ward go away."

"You don't have to see Ward anymore, okay?"

The little girl squeezed Grant's shoulders and kept crying. "Where's Mom?"

"Out looking for you. We haven't been able to—"

"What's he going to do to Mom?" Molly lifted her head and placed both her hands on Grant's cheeks. Worry lined her forehead. "What's Mr. Ward going to do to Mom?"

{ chapter 39 }

Lexi lay on the cold floor of Norm's cell, staring at the stained ceiling tiles and feeling nothing. She understood her numbness, in some detached way, as shock, the brain's worst-case-scenario survival mechanism. This was no victory.

This was the day Tara died, all over again.

And again and again and again. This was the day Grant walked out. The day Barrett's mind disappeared. The day Ward vanished, along with the truth of Molly's whereabouts.

This was the day her only child, her precious daughter, was lost to her forever.

"Angelo?" she whispered. Her desperate, last-ditch plea.

"What are you still doing here?" Not Angelo. She tried to grasp hold of the name. Norman.

Norm, norm, normal. The ridiculous simplicity of the word, the stupid, basic, mundane reality of it, awakened Lexi's nerves. She was holding something. The polyester shell of Molly's jacket. It was damp with the sweat of her own aching fingers, stiff in a frozen grip.

Lexi lifted the coat to her face and breathed it in. Her last breaths. She'd die of grief here on the floor in a prison of pain even though she was free to go. Ward would have found that amusing. He would have pointed out that she was freer in here, finally, than she ever had been out there, and wasn't the scenario a laugh?

The muscles of Lexi's face contorted into a silent cry under the jacket.

"Why haven't you gone yet?"

Because I have nowhere else to go.

But Norman Von Ruden's voice, filtered by the fabric, contained only concern. Lexi controlled her tears and slowly pushed herself off the floor. She wouldn't do her moaning here, with him, no matter how suitable that ending to this chapter of her life might have been.

Norm watched her rise. He lifted a hand and placed it on his bed rail, then pulled himself upright. She found it impossible to appreciate what must have been an excruciating effort.

"I was just leaving," she whispered.

He looked at her with the same unreadable expression he'd worn the day she first met him. Ruefulness mixed with yearning. And once again, he seemed to see the anguish in her that no one else had yet seen. Maybe because she and he were alike after all.

"He was here," Norm said.

Lexi nodded. Norm mirrored her.

"I sensed him. I know him."

Lexi's feet moved her to the door. Her knuckles rapped her request to be let out.

"But he's gone now," Norm said. "For good I mean."

She sighed. Was he? Could anyone really know? She raised her eyes to his and he looked away, an ashamed boy, but not before she saw their glassy clarity.

"Because of you. He's gone. You've done an"—his words cracked—"an amazing thing. Something I never had the strength to do."

"It wasn't strength." She couldn't name what it was, though. "It was . . .

need. Humiliation. I don't know. Desperation." And then the truth showed itself: "It wasn't me at all. It was mercy. For me."

But at what price?

The guard opened the door.

"You give me hope, Lexi."

Hope. For Norman Von Ruden. Someone in the world who needed it more than she did now, she supposed.

Her throat was knotty. "Hold onto it if you can," she said.

Lexi's long walk from Norm's cell into daylight was a surreal, sensory-stripped journey. Her legs knew where to go though her mind did not. She collected her keys, her mother's phone. She noted the message icon, thought vaguely that she couldn't access it without her mother's PIN. She thought she should call . . . someone. She signed something. She said something. She crossed a vast expanse of gray room and leaned into the gray-framed door and stepped outside onto a gray sidewalk.

The warm sun on her face was a kiss from God. Her father's understanding touch. *I'm so, so sorry.* Lexi closed her eyes and leaned into it slightly, not knowing where to go or what to do. Or whether comfort in this life could be had ever again.

Her mother's phone rang in her clenched fist. She stared at it. What could she possibly say?

"Yes?"

"Lexi? Thank God! Where have you been?" Grant.

I've been losing our daughter.

"She's okay!" he shouted, telling whoever he was with that he'd finally gotten through to his vanished wife. She imagined her mother. Lexi bowed her head.

"Lexi! Did you hear me?" *Hear what?* "She's okay. Molly's okay."

"Molly," she whispered. *Molly's okay?* God's warm kiss touched her again, sunshine on spirit. *I never let you go, child. Never.* The truth of it sank into Lexi's sudden and blindsiding joy. She was laughing and crying at the same time.

Grant said, "She's with me right now. She's—"

"Mom! Are you coming?" Molly's voice mingled with his over the phone, a harmony like colorful, cool water on Lexi's soul.

"Molly!" A happy shriek ran out of her heart, racing her to the car. *Oh yes, baby, I'm coming!* "I'm coming right now! Where are you?"

"I'm with Daddy!"

"Of course you are."

Exactly where she should be. Exactly.

{ chapter 40 }

Friday morning, which was the first day of spring, Lexi's family went to walk with Barrett at the Residence. Barrett pushed Molly in a wheelchair along the winding outdoor paths while Angelo stayed at his side. Grant and Lexi walked together a few yards behind the trio.

Alice had gone to Norm's hearing.

In the time since Ward's disappearance, Lexi's heart had done the work of sorting out her experiences. For the past two mornings she had awakened with the clarity of a vivid dream that stayed in sharp focus for half a second before the present moment blurred it all. During that brief time she understood everything. The strings between her physical and spiritual lives were pulled taut, and they vibrated with meaning. She expected the union of these experiences to reverberate through her heart for as long as possible—forever, she hoped, or at least until the day when she could finally explain the nuances.

To any reasonable witness, there might have been explanations for what happened that didn't have to rely on any miraculous reasoning. But Lexi knew better.

Molly called Angelo her angel, and of course, they all agreed he was. But

Molly still had the blessed innocence of a child who believed the world was a beautifully simple place. When she got that look in her eye and kept saying, "I mean *really*," Lexi understood this was a secret she and her daughter could share.

It wasn't so hard to believe. It was just so strange to say. Lexi worried that if she examined the truth of it too deeply, she might force it to become unbelievable. So she chose to tuck the bigness of it away in the most private corners of her heart until the day she could grow into Molly's childlike faith.

On the wooded grounds of her dad's home, she walked with the people she loved most without saying much, content with the sound of March wind in the pines. The snow had started to melt and created a steady stream that ran from the highest point of the property down to a gully at its perimeter. Barrett's "river," as he pointed out.

Grant took Lexi's hand and gently tugged her into a slower pace.

"Talk a minute?" he asked. They'd been surrounded by people since Molly's disappearance Wednesday morning.

"I guess it's about time," she said, wriggling her fingers out of his. She feared their moment of reckoning had come, and the conversation would be easier with her hands shoved into the pockets of her old high school jacket.

"I was thinking about Molly," he said, glancing at his empty hand.

"Oh. Right. What about her?"

"She seems to be bouncing back fast."

Lexi stopped on the trail. "Time will show us," she said.

He nodded. "We'll have to pay close attention to her, even if she seems fine."

"We?"

Grant cleared his throat. "I didn't mean to say . . . I meant . . . all of us will need to help her through the rough spots. Us. Your mom. Gina. You know."

"Of course."

They took a few steps without speaking.

Lexi said, "Did Molly tell you the whole story?"

"Yes. As far as I know."

"If she said she did, she did."

Grant nodded.

"The part about Norman—"

"I know."

Lexi looked up at the fresh pinecones forming at the top of the tall blue spruces. "Sometimes I look back at that time and try to figure out *why*. I can't believe the person who fell so fast and so hard was me."

"We've all done it. In different ways, but we've all done it."

"Grant, I wronged you." Lexi faced him. "I wronged you in the most awful way a wife can."

"You had every reason."

"Not one of them made it right."

"Okay. I'll agree with you. But we're different people now."

Lexi sighed. "I keep hoping it's true."

"It is for you, Lexi. It's obvious. Beautifully obvious."

"Does that mean you're letting me off the hook?"

Grant laughed, the first time Lexi had heard that baritone harmony since he'd returned to her. She smiled at the freedom of it. He said, "I'm not sure how it works for me to help you with that while I've got six bigger barbs snagged in the corner of my own mouth. But yes, Lexi, please do not waste any more time dangling from that hook."

"I won't if you won't."

He pursed his lips.

Lexi smiled at him. His nose was pink from the brisk wind.

"Gina's coming home tonight," she said. "Your daughter is cooking to celebrate. Join us?"

After their walk, Angelo turned in his employee badge at the nurse's station, where they seemed to be expecting it. Lexi and Molly went with him to the parking lot while Grant took Barrett back to his room.

Angelo had given notice two weeks ago, she learned. A whole week before she met him. There was a job he was supposed to start elsewhere Monday, but he didn't say what it was, and she didn't ask.

"How long have you been working here?" Lexi asked.

"Six years."

"That's how long my dad has . . ." And there, too, was another thought she chose not to chase too far. Instead, she tucked it into her heart's box. She felt mildly embarrassed that she'd ever looked at Angelo as a potential romantic.

She asked, "Who's going to look after Dad?"

"All the wonderful people who work here," Angelo said. "Get to know Julian."

He helped Molly into the Volvo and she gave him a kiss on the cheek. He put her wheelchair in the trunk.

Lexi nodded. "Thank you," she said, referring to so much more than his lifting the wheelchair.

"You're welcome." These words, too, seemed to acknowledge everything that went unsaid.

"Will I see you around?"

"If you ever have need of my cranberry Batmobile, you give me a call."

"I hope I never give you reason to have to come back here," she said. "But if I do, I'm going to handcuff you to Molly and make sure you never sleep."

"Keep feeding me those pies and your ice-cream coffee, and that will be fine with me."

Then he waved good-bye and that was all.

Lexi took the day off. It would short her seventy-five dollars for the week, and it didn't matter to her one bit. She took her daughter out of school and they spent the afternoon preparing to celebrate Gina's homecoming with a massive pan of lasagna, with extra oregano and three kinds of cheese.

Lexi asked her mother not to elaborate on what happened at Norm's hearing. Alice seemed happy to avoid the subject entirely and announced plans to dine with Barrett. She hadn't been inclined to say much at all to Lexi since Molly's safe return. Without Lexi's permission she did, however, buy Molly one of those kiddie cell phones with prepaid minutes and parental controls and all that, so she and Molly could talk plenty.

At six o'clock Lexi and Molly stood next to each other in the kitchen, mincing garlic for bread, and Lexi wondered if Molly was thinking about Angelo too.

Or Grant.

The doorbell rang and the two looked at each other. Molly grinned and hobbled out of the kitchen, thumping her new cast like a peg-leg pirate.

"Knife!" Lexi reminded.

Molly hustled back in, laid the blade next to the garlic cloves, and rushed back out again.

Lexi waited at the place where the hallway met the kitchen entrance and watched Molly throw the door open for her daddy. She was suddenly self-conscious of her unmanicured hands and plain face. She'd forgotten makeup and meant to put some on before he came.

Oh well.

Grant picked up Molly in a hug while holding onto a small brown paper bag.

"You smell like garlic."

"Gotta kiss me anyway," she said.

He planted a big wet one on her forehead before putting her down. She kept her arms around his neck and he stooped patiently.

"What's the chef got on the menu tonight?" he asked.

"Lasagna!"

"My favorite!"

"Did you bring dessert?"

"As requested."

"What is it?" She let go of his neck, grabbed his hand, and started dragging him toward the kitchen.

"Liver tofu."

"Eeewww! Dad!" She swiped at the bag. He held it over her head, out of reach, and handed it off to Lexi while the girl tried to intercept it. Lexi grinned and joined in the game.

"Hey!" Molly announced. "There's no such thing as liver tofu!"

"You'll be surprised."

"No I won't! Tofu doesn't have—"

"You'll be surprised because I'll tell you when dinner's over."

Lexi put the bag on top of the fridge.

"Can I guess?" Molly asked.

"You'll never."

"Lemon sorbet!"

"Strike one! Let me say hi to your mother."

Lexi was smiling when Grant looked at her, and the corners of his eyes wrinkled when he smiled back. He hadn't looked at her like that—sunshine happiness busting out of the human face—since the day Molly was born. She forgot what she had planned to say.

"Snickerdoodles!"

Finally she managed, "I'm glad you could come, Grant."

He seemed unprepared for that kind of warmth, because he stared at her for two seconds and then said, "Strike two."

Lexi pretended to be offended. He laughed. "It's good to be ho—" He stopped himself, shook his head. "Sorry."

"Carrot cake?" Molly asked.

"Don't be," Lexi said. "I'm glad you're here."

Molly said, "I'm glad you're here too. When are you going to move in with us?"

Lexi covered her mouth with the back of her hand and must have blushed, because Molly said, "What? It's not like you guys have to get married again, is it?"

That much was true, so Lexi wondered why it felt like she was on an exciting first date.

Grant opened his mouth to say something, or perhaps it was surprise that parted his lips. He looked at Lexi, turned back to Molly, and said, "Chips Ahoy."

Lexi said, "Molly, why don't you go get your report on the Pawnee to show to your dad?"

Molly grinned and put her hands on her hips. "All you have to do is ask for privacy," she said.

"Go get your report, goofball."

"Did you know that the Pawnee Indians wrapped their babies in bobcat furs?" she asked Grant. "They thought the spots looked like stars in the sky and said the heavens protected their children. Isn't that cool?"

"Very!"

"Angelo showed me that in a book I borrowed from the school library. I didn't have time to read the whole thing."

Lexi gave her a gentle shove in the direction of their room.

"I got a B plus!" she announced as she did a little hobble dance down the hall.

"Lower the volume, hon. Gina's resting," Lexi said.

Molly turned around and whispered loudly, "And I *love* Chips Ahoy!"

Lexi caught Grant's eye and gestured toward a kitchen chair, then began to pile Molly's garlic into a bowl of softened butter. Grant remained standing. "She's amazing," he said. "You've done such a great job with her, Lexi."

"Thank you." She mashed the mixture together with a fork.

"She looks like you."

"She's got your sense of humor. Which I've missed."

"She's so mature for her age."

"Wait 'til you get to know her!"

They laughed together, then fell into an easy silence. Grant came and leaned back against the counter, crossing his ankles.

"I'm sorry I missed so many years."

"You don't need to keep apologizing, Grant."

"I can't help it."

"It's done. It's okay. We'll work it out." As soon as she said it aloud, she believed it. Her hope was as real as his presence in the kitchen.

He sighed, a deep and heavy relief. "I'll do whatever it takes."

"Right now it will take you slicing open this loaf of Italian bread with an extremely dull knife." She handed both to him.

"I'm at your service." When the blade began to tear the loaf into a crumbling mess, he set down the knife and began to pry the thing open with his thumbs. "How pretty does this have to be?"

"Pretty is Molly's department. I'm good with edible."

"With standards like those, this might be easier than I thought." But the bread continued to disintegrate. Lexi debated whether to stop him before it was reduced to duck food. "On the other hand," he said, "instead of toast, how about we melt the garlic butter and dip the chunks?"

In that moment, nothing was as beautiful to Lexi as that mangled loaf of bread in Grant's hands—nothing as promising or tasty or reparable. She was so hungry. She'd been hungry for years.

"I love you, Grant."

He set the bread down in the crumbs.

Lexi started to weep. "I'm so glad you came back. I really needed you to come back."

He reached for her hand and pulled her toward him, then wrapped his arms around her. She rested her head on his shoulder, the tension of years falling away.

Grant whispered into her hair, "You're proof of God's grace in the world, Lexi Solomon."

Then the master called the servant in. "You wicked servant,"
he said, "I canceled all that debt of yours because you begged me to.
Shouldn't you have had mercy on your fellow servant just as I
had on you?" In anger his master turned him over to the jailers
to be tortured, until he should pay back all he owed.

MATTHEW 18:32–34

{ reading group guide}

1. In what ways is Lexi's love for Molly a compelling force in Lexi's life? How far does that love go in protecting Molly from Ward? What opposing forces in Lexi's heart limit the power of her love? Why?

2. What is the nature of the demands Ward makes of Lexi? Why does he choose those particular demands? How does his confrontation with Lexi play into his larger aim of destroying the Grüggen family?

3. Why is Grant compelled to return to his family? Why doesn't he give up when he runs into opposition?

4. Why was it easier for Alice to support Grant's efforts than for her to be with Barrett during his crisis?

5. How does each character acknowledge his or her sins and then seek to redeem them? Which attitudes and actions lead to the most desirable results? Why?

6. How does Lexi perceive her own sins in comparison to the way she perceives the sins of others? Why might there be a disparity between her viewpoints?

7. What are the obstacles that stand in the way of Lexi's forgiveness of Grant? Of Norm? Of her mother? What does she have to do to push these obstacles out of the way?

8. How does Lexi's relationship with her mother hamper Lexi's life? In what ways is their relationship nurturing? Their "issues" remain unresolved at the end of the story. What might each woman need to do to bring more peace to their relationship?

9. Angelo tells Lexi on more than one occasion to "listen to love." What does this advice mean to her at the beginning of her journey? How does it compare to her understanding of the wisdom at the end? How does Molly listen to love as a child compared to how Lexi must listen to it as an adult?

10. Why doesn't Angelo prevent Ward from entering Lexi's life? What is Angelo's goal? How does he accomplish it?

11. Ward has the ability to make people see what he wants them to see. How much of this ability is supernatural? How much of it is dependent upon his target's state of mind and heart? What might make them less susceptible to deception? Why couldn't Ward deceive Molly as much as he wanted to?

12. Which character in this story has the most accurate perception of what is true? What makes such perception possible?

{ with heartfelt thanks }

TO TIM, AMBER, AND JAROD
for your above-and-beyond patience and your big, big love

TO TED
for the thrilling ride

AND ALSO TO
Dan Raines
Kathy Helmers
Kevin Kaiser
Ami McConnell
Traci DePree
Leah Apineru
Mike and Lynn McMahan
All the bright minds at Creative Trust
Allen Arnold and the amazing Thomas Nelson team

{ author to author }

The Thomas Nelson Fiction team recently invited our authors to interview any other Thomas Nelson Fiction author in an unplugged Q&A session. They could ask any questions about any topic they wanted to know more about. What we love most about these conversations is that they reveal just as much about the ones asking the questions as they do the authors who are responding. So sit back and enjoy the discussion. Perhaps you'll even be intrigued enough to pick up one of their novels and discover a new favorite writer in the process.

Erin Healy: I came to novel writing after years as a fiction editor. My background didn't save me from a steep learning curve, though. Your journey took you through print journalism territory, where you were nominated for two Pulitzers. (I feel only Christian envy.) Did you have to learn any writing skills from scratch?

Sibella Giorello: Congrats on making the leap from editing to writing, Erin. Although I've never edited, I hear what you're saying about the steep learning curve. Sometimes it seems like every book presents a new one. It helps to turn that around and give thanks for how each book teaches us something new about character and plot—and boy, does this gig keep you humble!

But journalism was a fantastic boot camp. It taught me to produce words under any circumstances—including when some editor's barking (sorry), the phone's ringing, and the deadline looms seconds away. No time to waste; you just write! That experience helps on the inevitable mornings when I don't want to write. I write anyway.

That's how books get done—through discipline—not inspiration.

EH: Your novels have a strong sense of place, rooted in your protagonist Raleigh's profession as a forensic geologist. What is it about rocks that speaks to the human heart? What do they say to Raleigh?

SG: Probably from growing up in Alaska, place feels important to me. Alaska exerts itself. It's a landscape that refuses to be ignored. I spent hours staring at its snow, sky, and mountains wondering how it all came into existence. The big geology questions. But rocks, as you say, speak to us. For me, they seem like tangible pieces of poetry. One rock glimpses into the larger story, but also exists simply for its own beauty.

For Raleigh Harmon, rocks speak of justice and mercy. A forensic geologist, she uses mineralogy to solve crimes, examining everything from sand inside tire treads, to soil left at the scene, to zinc in a woman's lipstick.

But she's a scientist who recognizes her creator. Rocks also speak of God.

EH: Raleigh deals with pretty universal personal issues—professional, relational, spiritual—in each of her stories. How would you describe what's at the center of her larger life journey?

SG: For a young woman, Raleigh's dealing with serious pain. Her birth father left, her mother suffers from chronic mental illness, and her adopted father, the person she was closest to, was murdered. Her work for the FBI places her face-to-face with some of the worst human beings on the planet.

Some people would crack under those circumstances. Raleigh just gets stronger, holding fast to the knowledge that not only does God exist, but He also loves us. Even the most depraved among us.

EH: You and I share the uncommon connection of having lived in wild and rugged Alaska. Will Raleigh ever go there "to figure out Alaska's landscape," as you once dreamed of doing?

SG: So you know what I'm talking about! Everybody should see it, but especially a geologist, which is why Raleigh winds up there *The Mountains Bow Down*. It'll be out in 2011.

EH: Pardon my gushing, but you have a name worthy of a heroine. In my mind, it can only mean "so beautiful"! Is there a story behind how you came to have it (and what it actually means)?

SG: Full disclosure: I'm not Italian. My husband's Italian and he blessed me with a phonetically arranged marriage.

My first name comes from my mom's side, where all the women have some version of "Belle." My grandmother was Belle, my mother was AnnaBelle, and a cousin was Isabelle. "Sibella" combines my grandmothers' first names.

Looking back, I sometimes wonder if my mom knew I'd marry a hunk of Italy.